King of Hearts

Eileen Putman

King of Hearts

This book grew out of a story published in 1999 as *Never Trust a Rake*.

Formatting Rik Hall – Wild Seas Formatting
http://WildSeasFormatting.com

Cover Design – The Killion Group
http://thekilliongroupinc.com

First edition, 2017

Prologue

Spring 1815

London

He wasn't about to traipse all over London looking for virgins.

Not as long as Our Lady of Mercy convent lay cheek by jowl with the Market Street dock, where his newly acquired boat bobbed in waters swollen by high tide. With any luck, he could be on his way before the tide went out.

Like most of the ladies Gabriel Sinclair met, luck danced to his tune. This very night, luck had dealt him a perfect *vingt-et-un*, while the Earl of Sedbury had gone bust trying to improve on his puny pair of sevens — thereby gifting Gabriel with the earl's trim little yacht. Luck had not given him the courage to sneak into a convent full of sleeping nuns, but Gabriel had found that in the earl's wine.

The gnarled gypsy who had emerged from the midnight shadows as a glum Sedbury was showing him around the boat would have given any man pause. An ageless wisdom inhabited her wrinkled face, and her eyes gleamed with fury.

"Death," she intoned, pointing her bony finger at them. "Death seeks to bring you into his bosom. Bring me a lock of hair from a virgin's head, taken without harm, given without regret. Only then will death loose his grip on your soul."

Sedbury had shooed the woman away. "They haunt the docks," he grumbled. "It's that new prison hulk. Too close by half. Draws the riff-raff." He eyed the yacht wistfully. "Always meant to move her upriver."

They had shared a laugh at the old woman's attempt to scare them. Then a strange light had come into Sedbury's eyes, and the wine had flowed anew, and the gypsy's words became a reckless new bet that sent each man reeling drunkenly into the night in search of a lock of hair from a virgin, one of the scarcest commodities in all London.

The gypsy's curse hadn't bothered Gabriel. He was not afraid of death. In the years since leaving England for Jamaica, he had beaten that black angel more times than he could count. Boredom alone unsettled him, for it left him face to face with a man he did not care to visit long.

Besides, the gypsy had it wrong. Luck, not death, embraced him tonight. Luck had caused him to wander past this convent, thereby showing him the means of winning the new wager and depriving the earl of his London townhouse, the stakes Sedbury had put up in his desperate bid to regain his boat. But desperate men made unwise bets. The earl would never find a virgin at this hour, when chaste women slept peacefully in their own beds.

Gabriel suppressed a yawn. What did he need with Sedbury's house, anyway? He didn't intend to remain in England, though it might be diverting to sample the life he could have had if he'd been dealt a different hand years ago. A boat was all he needed. With it, he could bid the past farewell as sweetly as these sleeping maidens had said their evening prayers.

In the darkened convent bedchamber, he surveyed them. They were young — novitiates, perhaps. A veritable bevy of virgins. And none of them had thought to latch the front door. A trusting group, indeed.

Which would he choose? Gabriel studied their sleeping forms, forever removed from the world of men. He imagined them in the secular world, dressed in fine gowns and jewels, their hair piled high atop their heads and secured with combs of finest ivory. They would fan themselves coyly, each daring him to choose her. Would he select the blonde, the chestnut-haired, or the chit with the riot of auburn curls?

He usually had his pick, for women adored him. They were all alike: vain and prideful and needy. Even nuns, he suspected, had their vanity.

Gabriel slipped his knife from the slim leather holder he always wore under his waistcoat. He moved quickly past the bed of one young woman whose breathing was shallow and uneven — much too light a sleeper. He passed two others whose nightcaps obscured their hair. At last, he came to a young woman whose single blonde braid lay invitingly on the pillow. She snored so loudly that nothing short of cannon fire would wake her.

He stared at the knife and briefly wondered whether he'd lost his mind. *A lock of hair from a virgin's head, taken without harm, given without regret.* He didn't believe in the gypsy's words, but he did believe in fate that masqueraded as luck. For the moment, he would be its pawn.

Gingerly, he lifted the braid, feeling its weight, judging its substance. He could certainly take it without harm; he wasn't sure about the regret part. Then again, the girl could hardly regret what she didn't know. He shifted the knife to his right hand and bent over her.

"What are you doing?"

Gabriel froze. Carefully, he turned toward the voice. The girl he had pegged as a light sleeper sat upright, staring at him. "What are you doing to Mary?"

She looked just groggy enough that sleep still had a few tentacles in her. He pitched his voice low, so as not to wake the others. "Blessing her, of course." He was surprised that his words sounded slurred. Perhaps he should have left the cork in that second bottle.

"But —"

"Keep your voice down." He tried for a note of

command, but a whisper had its limitations. "It is forbidden to speak," he improvised.

The girl hesitated. "Who are you?"

"Gabriel." Here, of all places, that name should carry weight.

Apparently, it did. She stared. "The...angel?"

"Archangel," he recklessly volunteered.

"You do not look like an angel."

Insolent chit. "Appearances can be deceiving." He still held the sleeping girl's braid. If his annoyingly persistent questioner would just look the other way...

"What is that thing in your hand?" Her gaze was riveted on the knife, though the room was dark enough he doubted she could make it out distinctly.

"It's a, er, wand." Did angels carry wands? No, that was fairies. Hell.

The girl stared at him in stunned silence. Suddenly, her eyes widened.

"A knife! You've got a knife!"

"Quiet, brat," he growled. That did not sound very angelic. Well, he might as well have something to show for this night's labors. In one swift movement, he sliced off the sleeping Mary's braid. She never stopped snoring.

"Murderer!" the other girl shrieked.

Even as he dashed down the stairs, Gabriel heard footsteps on the landing.

"Mother Dolores! Help! Come quickly!" The answering screams of the others as they awoke rose in a jarring harmony that would have waked the dead.

When he gained the street, Gabriel looked wildly around. He had not planned for this. Sedbury's carriage was long gone, the traitor. Gabriel had no means of escape except his own two feet, and they were looking strangely blurred at the moment.

Suddenly, his gaze lit on a dray cart and horse standing placidly across the way. No sign of a driver. Once again, luck had intervened. He sprinted across the street, took a moment to tuck the braid safely into his pocket, and grabbed the reins.

But as he flicked them smartly on the horse's rump, a flock of nightgown-clad young women and one fire-breathing dragon of a Mother Superior in a hideous red nightcap streamed into the street. They threw themselves in front of the horse.

"Stop!" shrieked the dragon lady — the worthy Mother Dolores, no doubt. She clutched a chamber pot and waved it wildly at the horse. Like baby chicks following the mother hen, the novitiates raised their arms, too. And just like that, the street was filled with a mob of flailing, screaming females in high-necked night-rails.

Gabriel had a sinking feeling his luck had turned.

The horse did a nervous sideways dance and tried to rear, something no self-respecting dray nag would do. The women ran toward him — didn't they have better sense than to race into the path of a thrashing horse?

He jerked on the reins, forcing the horse to still. The horse shuffled backward, trying to ease the pressure of the bit. Gabriel bent forward just as the nag's tail whipped up and caught the corner of his eye. The searing pain brought tears to his eyes.

"My hair! He cut off my hair!" cried a young woman he took to be Mary, awake at last.

"Quiet, child!" cried Mother Dolores, whose nightcap dipped perilously low over one eye. She turned to Gabriel. "You shall die for this, you scoundrel. They will hang you forthwith, and I shall be among the spectators."

"Now, now," Gabriel warned. His eye hurt like hell, and he was in no mood for vengeful nuns. "You must set a proper example, Mother. Charity and forgiveness and all that."

Mother Dolores stared at him. "What sort of monster are you?"

"He claimed he was an angel," said the girl who had first discovered him.

"I see." Her face was grim. "Matilde, fetch the Watch."

"That is not necessary," Gabriel assured her. "I was on the point of leaving." Shielding his injured eye, he jumped down, squinting as he searched for a path through the sea of women. But their flailing forms pressed against him, forming a human wall.

Imprisoned by virgins. Was there anything more lowering?

"Ladies, step aside," he thundered, trying his best to sound archangelic. "My work here is done. The, er, heavens demand my return." He saw the indecision in their eyes. Almost, he had them. Then the dragon lady intervened.

"Sit on him, girls!" she commanded.

As one, the young women wrestled him to the cobblestones and planted themselves on him.

"Now, angel," she scoffed, waving the chamber pot at him. "Let's see you fly away."

"Alas, 'tis the molting season," Gabriel managed, forcing air through his badly compressed lungs. "My wings have been clipped."

"More than clipped, you heartless villain. Your goose, sir, is cooked!" With that, Mother Dolores brought the chamber pot down on his head.

Yes, virgins were nothing but trouble. He would never go near one again.

Chapter One

"The hanging is at noon," said a gruff masculine voice.

"I do hope Miss Wentworth will be brave." Louisa Peabody tied a black scarf over her hair, obscuring flaxen gold so gleaming it could be seen from a distance. She shrugged into a man's dark jacket several sizes too large. Then she placed a cap over the scarf and checked her appearance in the dingy tack room mirror. "I am afraid this is the best I can do."

The man at her side inspected her dark breeches, boots, and coat. When his gaze reached her head covering, he frowned uncertainly.

"Do not worry, David," she said. "I have tied the scarf tight. Not a strand of my hair is visible. Besides, I will be inside the carriage."

David Ferguson was a man of considerable size but few words. Although he did not reply, the tension in his jaw was answer enough. Louisa made one last effort to assuage his doubts. "Alice Wentworth has no one, David. All she did was steal a loaf of bread to feed her child. We must help her."

Their gazes met in pain shared and remembered. Then, without a word, David walked out to the carriage.

"Be careful," warned the only other occupant of the stable, a boy of about twelve. Holding the halter of a big black stallion, he regarded Louisa with a mixture of determination and doubt. The weight of nascent masculinity sat uncertainly upon his slender shoulders. "I still say you ought to let me go. Midnight and I could cut through a crowd like a knife through butter."

Louisa shook her head. "Midnight is too high-strung, and he is not yet ready to be ridden again. Besides," she added gently, "you are too young, Sam."

"If you got caught..." His voice, straddling the cusp of manhood, wavered.

"We will not."

"The last time —"

"Was unfortunate. But we learn from our mistakes. Do not worry. David will take care of me." She gave him a quick smile, then followed David out to the carriage.

***

His head was in the noose. Any moment, now, the executioner would release the lever on the scaffold and send him on a permanent trip to the Great Beyond. He supposed he should be filled with despair, but he felt nothing. Only a vast emptiness, far more desolate than the possibility of death.

The crowd was enormous, no doubt due to that nun's embellishments at his brief trial, which had been reported in all the newspapers. "Fallen Angel," the headlines had called him. It wouldn't surprise him if she was out there somewhere, waiting for him to die.

Through his suffocating hood, he could hear the impatient shouts, the jeers. A great clamoring mass of humanity had gathered outside Newgate to watch the life jerked out of him in the gruesome satisfaction of justice.

If there was any real justice in the world, those nuns would pay for their lies. They had made him out to be a rapist and attempted murderer. No wonder his trial had taken less than an hour.

Ah, well. The life of a scoundrel was mercifully short. And the life of a clumsy drunk with the stupidity to invade a convent armed with a knife even shorter.

In truth, many of the details of that night eluded him. He remembered the chamber pot being brought down on his head, then darkness. Still, a blow like that would not account for the gaps in his memory. He'd awoken in pain, chained to a wall in a dark cell crawling with vermin. He must have been beaten, for the darkness and pain entwined in him, leaving shadowy images of a thick beam brought down across his shoulders and many fists and implements applied to his person.

One day they had cleaned him up and brought him to the Old Bailey, where he could not summon enough brainpower even to speak his name or account for the circumstances that brought him there. Only after he saw the head nun — Mother Dolores, she styled herself — and listened to her vivid testimony had shreds of memories returned. Pieces were still missing, for a well-dressed Lord Something-or-other testified about events for which he similarly had no recollection; apparently he tried to steal his lordship's yacht.

Surely, the witnesses had exaggerated. Whatever his crimes, they could not be so heinous as attempted murder, rape, fraudulent taking of his lordship's yacht, and the theft of a cart and horse. He might be a scoundrel, but he was fairly certain he had no taste for crimes such as those.

Justice being what it was, his protestations of innocence mattered not. With no recollection of his actions, he could not supply a convincing alibi; nor could he summon character witnesses, having no memory even of his own name.

So he was here on the scaffold, a mere two days after his trial, wishing he could recall whatever it was he should know to prevent his imminent journey into Hell.

"Save yerself, angel!" jeered a voice.

"Fly away, angel," ridiculed another. "Fly on to heaven."

A chorus of laughter rose from the crowd. He felt the executioner check the ropes that bound his hands. Snug and tight. No way out there. He heard the man speak to the magistrate. He couldn't make out the words, but his imagination easily supplied them:

I'll let him swing long enough to please the crowds, then hand him over to that surgeon who's been after me to give him something for that anatomy class of his. Did you want him to suffer a bit first, my lord? Those nuns seemed awfully upset.

By all means, Executioner, let the bugger suffer. I've seen the way you snap that platform down, and if you do it just right, their necks don't break right away and they hang there reaching with their toes, trying to gain a purchase as the air sucks out of them. The crowd loves that.

Well, he was always one to please the crowds. And this was better than that new treadmill invention he had been threatened with, the cylinder of steps that had to be walked until one dropped. Better to die from hanging than boredom.

He supposed he should say a few words to his Maker, but he doubted anyone up there would hear him. Still, it was worth a shot.

I was looking forward to taking up residence at Sedbury's townhouse. Might have turned respectable, made something of my life, taken a seat in Parliament

Sedbury's townhouse? Parliament? Where had those thoughts come from?

Could've turned all those lords against slavery, told them about Jamaica and the plantations.

Jamaica. Another memory teased his brain.

What's that? Yes, I know it's late to make promises. No, I don't mean a word of them. Hell, the last thing I want is a home.

He knew in his bones that last was true. No home, no family. Never again.

More memories seeped from the recesses of his mind. Perhaps his own name would join them. Surely, he was someone. Surely, he knew people who could vouch for him.

Abruptly, the floor beneath him shuddered. No time,

then. Apparently there was no one Up There to hear the ramblings of a doomed man. He tried to swallow, but the noose cinched him, closing his throat. *I wouldn't have minded one last chance…*

A cheer went up from the crowd. Bloodthirsty buggers. He had barely formed the thought when his feet left the ground.

Excited shrieks came from somewhere, probably the vicinity of Mother Dolores. The rope cut into his neck, shooting dizzying pain through him. He could not breathe. His hands wanted to claw at the thing that was choking the life out of him. But they were bound, and it was only in his dreams that he grabbed the rope and flung it off, restoring blessed air to his lungs.

Soon he would slip the knot of his human misery.

The cheers of the crowd faded into oblivion. He heard a strange slashing noise. Felt a jerk. The noose released its hold, and he floated heavenward to his final reward.

Heaven was deuced uncomfortable, though. Heaven felt like a man's strong arms pulling him through the air, depositing him unceremoniously on his head on the floor of a carriage. Heaven sounded like a man's confused curse and a woman's urgent admonition as a blanket was flung over him and the vehicle lurched forward with angry shouts in pursuit.

He should have known he would go straight to Hell. How else to describe the sensation of being slammed about, blind to his surroundings save for the pain? His neck felt as if it had been seared by flames. His air-deprived lungs struggled for breath.

Every time he tried to right his bruised body, a booted foot pushed firmly on his posterior and a woman's sharp voice cut through his misery. "Stay down!"

He stayed down. He would not risk the ire of this Mistress of Hell. But he longed to remove the oppressive hood, to take in enough air to banish the dizziness that threatened his mind's thin hold on the events around him. The jostling of the carriage and the burning in his lungs and neck were his only reality.

Was this Heaven or Hell? Maybe there was no difference, after all.

At last, the carriage rolled to a stop, and someone lifted the blanket that covered him. He heard the woman gasp as her hands removed his hood.

"You are not Miss Wentworth!" She turned to the Goliath who suddenly appeared outside the carriage door. "It is a man, David, a *man*!"

She removed the cap from her head and a black scarf that had hidden hair the color of spun gold. But that was not what rendered him speechless. It was her eyes, which regarded him with a mixture of fury and confusion and which were as deep and bottomless and blue as the sea on a cloudless day. And the tiny birthmark that sat between her upper lip and the tip of her nose.

Hair kissed by the sun. Eyes bluer than blue. A small, tantalizing mark above her lip. If Heaven had angels like this, he had come to the right place.

"Madam," he rasped, his voice all but destroyed by the hangman's noose, "will you marry me?" He gave a wild, mirthless laugh as the world around him faded to black.

***

Louisa stared at the limp form at her feet. "What in the name of all that is holy am I to do?"

David shrugged. "Take him home, I suppose." He climbed back up to his perch and with a flick of the reins sent the team of horses barreling down the road.

Louisa crossed her arms and stared out the window, trying to look anywhere except at the motionless man on the floor. But outside held only trees and grass and the occasional cow. At her feet was the scourge of her sex.

A man. And from the look and sound of him, an

insolent, puffed-up, arrogant, shameless example of the breed. *Madam, will you marry me?* Mad hubris, indeed. Facing death had not humbled him. Doubtless he had deserved his death sentence.

And she, of all people, had saved him.

He lay on his side, filling the floor space between the seats and then some. Louisa curled her legs under her to avoid touching him and then decided that in his current state he would scarcely know if she rested her feet on his back.

His hands were still bound, and his body jostled roughly as the carriage raced over the road. Senseless, he was hardly a danger to her, so she reached down and tried to loosen his stiff bindings. At last she freed his hands, and they flopped limply at his sides. There was nothing harmless about their size, however. They were of a piece with that broad back; his shirt fabric strained across the wide expanse of muscle and bone.

The man they had saved was strong and dangerous. A criminal, likely a killer. Yet even if he had been none of those things, Louisa would have hated him on sight.

* * *

Gabriel awoke to find the giant towering over him. The man was six and a half feet, if he was an inch. His face bore deep, irregular scars, as if unskilled hands had chipped his features out of stubborn granite. His hair was dark, his chin bearded, and he resembled a savage ogre who feasted on naughty children and wayward princesses in fearsome fables. The man studied him from his impossible height, his face as expressive as stone.

His angel sat in a chair beside a hearth with a blazing fire. Her hands were crossed primly in her lap. She held herself stiffly and regarded him with an icy gaze. That long, golden hair flowed around her like a halo.

"Who are you?" Her voice was as dry and brittle as dead leaves.

He was lying on the floor. Not the way to meet an angel. It put him at a distinct disadvantage, for though he was not as tall as the giant, he could certainly stand as straight. And a man on his feet thought better than a man on his posterior.

Gabriel tried to rise. He struggled to his knees, pushed off from his hands, and tried to heave himself up. But he was weaker than he thought. Like a babe whose reach exceeds his grasp, he fell backward onto the floor.

He ached all over. His neck felt as if it was belted in edged steel. His lungs could not take in enough air. His stomach lurched queasily.

An encroaching blackness clawed at him, narrowing his sight to a pinpoint of light, pulling him into the blessedness of oblivion. And though he fought it, his brain felt fuzzy, as if it was packed in cotton wool.

"Name," he murmured, fighting off the blackness. He had to know her name.

"I am Louisa Peabody," she said crisply.

"Lu-we-sa Pe-body." He tried to say it, but his tongue seemed twisted. He must be hallucinating.

"Who are you?" she demanded.

"King," he managed.

"King?" He heard the note of puzzlement in her tone. "Mr. King?"

"Not mister," he said thickly. "King — Majesty."

He grinned. It was a little joke — bitter as sin, and too much work to explain, even if he could recall the details. Perhaps his joke would drive that chill from her voice.

"You are a king?"

He nodded, pleased that she understood. Too bad her features kept blurring around the edges. His eyes must be crossed, for her nose kept moving around on her face. It would be difficult to rivet her with one of his meaningful stares. Mistresses of Hell were probably impervious to masculine charm anyway.

Frowning, he tried to conjure the elusive memory at the edge of his awareness. He vaguely remembered talking to someone — or something — about mending his ways.

Where was he now? Among the living or the dead?

"The only king we have is old George," she said. "You do not look anything like him."

Mad George in Hell, too? He hadn't heard that the king had cocked up his toes, but then Newgate prisoners led a sheltered existence.

"Not George." His voice slurred. "Gabriel." That much had come back to him. Perhaps, there would be more.

"King Gabriel." She rolled the words around on her tongue. "Pray, what are you king of?"

He heard the derision in her tone. Gabriel looked up at her from his lowly position on the floor. She was studying him, her head tilted to one side, waiting. The firelight caught the lights in her hair and sent their shimmering warmth straight to his gut, a spear of heat that threatened a mortal wound. He tried to say the words that burned in his befogged brain.

"Take you there," he vowed.

A large booted toe nudged him in the ribs. He had forgotten about the giant. Gabriel ignored the man and smiled at her.

Her eyes filled with uncertainty. Good. He had her interest — much better than her contempt. Conquest would be his. Unless she really was an angel.

She turned toward the giant. "You had best fetch the doctor."

No doctor, Gabriel wanted to say. He was better now. He might even be alive. He raised his head, tried to speak. "Island. King of island," he said weakly.

Lu-we-sa Pe-body eyed him in disgust, then rose and left the room. The monster lifted him off the floor as if he were a sack of feathers, carted him up some stairs, and tossed him onto a soft feather bed. As Gabriel sank gratefully into it, letting the darkness take him, the man bent down close to his ear.

"And I," the giant snarled contemptuously, "am Queen Charlotte."

***

"What happened to Alice Wentworth?" Louisa eyed David worriedly.

"'Pears they thought this one" — he jerked his thumb skyward, indicating the upstairs where the stranger slept — "needed killing first."

"But...didn't they publish the list of executions?"

"Aye, and she was on it." He shrugged. "Wasn't until I'd driven us into the thick of things that I got a good look at the prisoner. By then, I'd cut the rope and the mongrel was falling into my arms. Nothing for it but to grab him and get out before the crowd closed in."

David had had all he could do to control the team and speed them away from the angry mob. Louisa hadn't wanted to take the cumbersome carriage, but after the debacle with Midnight at Violet's rescue, David had not wanted her to risk exposure. And so she'd sat helpless and protected inside while the mission went terribly awry. Never again, she vowed, would she abdicate her responsibility.

"Do you think they will proceed with her hanging?"

David shook his head. "Not for a while. Too much confusion after today."

Louisa paced the parlor in frustration. "Let us hope she is safe for now. In the meantime, what is to be done with him?"

David said nothing. There was no need. They both knew that no man had occupied a bed at Peabody Manor since her father moved away to the Continent. And Richard had not lived to do so. The fact that a heinous criminal now slept the sleep of the blameless upstairs was almost incomprehensible.

"I can't have a man here, David," she said in a wobbly voice. "You know that."

"Aye," he said softly. His hand came up, hovered over her trembling shoulders for a moment, then fell to his side without touching her. "We could put him in the dower house, but we couldn't watch him there. Besides, he is ill and can nae do ye harm."

David understood her fears, accepted them. "I will keep ye safe, lass," he added.

Louisa knew he would, as far as it was in his power to do so. But long ago she had learned that the only help for a woman alone in the world was her own two hands — and that was rarely enough. Women could not control their own money, much less their fate. They were married off to benefit the family's coffers, sold like chattel to the highest bidder.

Her father had traded her to a man with a charming smile and a soul as dark as the devil's. She had despised them both for making her an object to be bartered, no better than a whore. But she had survived, and adversity had made her strong. She had put the past behind her and devoted herself to helping women who couldn't help themselves.

There were no men in her life, save David. She was pleased with her carefully constructed world — as long as there was no reminder that it might topple in an instant if some clever male decided to apply himself to the task.

The man upstairs had to go. Besides being a criminal, he had the look of trouble — too charming by half, even fresh from the hangman's noose. A rakish brow bespoke devilish intentions under that tousled red hair. Green eyes glittered with daring and dash and promises never to be fulfilled. A self-mocking mouth hinted of devilish secrets.

Take her to his island, indeed. Nonsense uttered in the heady exultation of escaping a fate he had undoubtedly deserved.

A king, was he?

Aye, king of a thousand hearts he had doubtless broken. Louisa's gaze narrowed. She knew the breed well.

Chapter Two

The hand on his brow was cool, soothing. The low murmuring was warm, comforting. Had his angel relented, then, and deigned to favor him with her healing presence?

Sleep still caught at the edges of his awareness, but Gabriel moved swiftly, instinctively, to capture her hand. Bringing it to his lips, he nibbled lightly on her fingertips. They tasted vaguely of smoke. He frowned.

"My, ye are a bold one."

His eyes flew open. The movement pained him. Every part of him felt as if he had dashed down the road toward perdition and been caught in its fire. Gabriel forced himself to bring the images into focus. Above him a lacy white canopy spanned the bed like a thousand dancing snowflakes. Bright yellow and amber danced at the perimeter of his vision — the room was awash with colors of sunshine and cheer. He tried to move, but breathing was an effort. His throat was parched, his neck sore, as if he had been paraded about on a too-tight leash.

Slowly, he began to remember: The scaffold. The executioner. And miracle of miracles, being plucked from death's jaws by a heavenly vision.

He turned to the woman whose smoky fingers he had nibbled. Streaks of gray shot through her dark hair, and her ruddy cheeks sagged into jowls. Her gray eyes glinted like steel. A woman undoubtedly to be reckoned with — but most assuredly not his angel.

Instantly, Gabriel released her hand.

The hint of a twinkle appeared in her eyes, then

vanished. Gabriel tried to sit up, but his body rebelled. His head was still groggy from the deep, unnatural sleep of a man who has narrowly escaped death but tasted its pain.

"Where is —" He broke off, trying to remember. *Lu-we-sa*. "Louisa," he rasped. "Louisa Peabody."

The woman crossed her arms and regarded him with something akin to a smirk. A movement at the end of the bed caught Gabriel's eye. A boy, his eyes filled with hostility, stepped toward him.

"Who are you?" the lad demanded. "What have you done with Elizabeth's mother?"

"Sam." The voice, soft in its reproof, came from another woman, who suddenly appeared in his line of vision. She had straight brown hair and soft brown eyes that regarded him assessingly.

Gabriel rubbed his aching head. Who the devil was Elizabeth? Where was Louisa Peabody?

"I am Violet," the soft-spoken woman said. "This is Rose." She gestured toward the older woman whose fingers he had nibbled. "A woman named Alice Wentworth was supposed to hang at Newgate yesterday. You went in her stead. By the time David realized his mistake, the crowd was on him. He threw you into the carriage and fled."

"Men." Rose shook her head in disgust.

Violet's steady gaze did not waver. "We have Miss Wentworth's baby, Elizabeth." Her hands curved protectively over the front of her loose-fitting frock. Something registered in Gabriel's brain, but he couldn't complete the thought.

"We will raise the babe as our own if Miss Wentworth cannot be saved. But we hope you can tell us where the guards have taken her."

Babe. Now he had it. The brown-haired woman was increasing.

"We think they have moved her out of Newgate," Violet said. "Apparently, the disruption of your execution threw things into disarray."

Now that was a damned shame, Gabriel thought.

"Miss Wentworth's only crime was to steal food for her baby." Her expression was sorrowful. "Louisa would have saved her, had you not taken her place. We are very distressed about that."

Her frequent use of the plural was vaguely disquieting. Gabriel struggled to prop himself up on his elbow and looked around the room. "Where am I?" His voice sounded like a piece of rusty metal. "Who are you?"

"There are nine of us — five women and four children," Violet replied. "We live in Louisa's home. She has saved most of us from poverty, abuse, and other ills at the hands of men. Ours is a community of women."

A community of women. Gabriel tried to imagine five women like these two staring at him with somber, accusing eyes. Those damned nuns must have prayed mightily for revenge, for he had obviously skipped Purgatory and tumbled straight into Hell. Gabriel stared grimly at the yellow and amber walls — not the colors of sunshine and cheer, but of fire and brimstone.

Another figure stepped from the shadows, although how the shadows had contained him was anybody's guess. The giant wore a look of wrathful menace abetted by the deep scars on his face. One large, slashing scar extended downward, disappearing into the folds of his shirt just below his neck. A nearly fatal wound, that.

Now that he thought on it, the giant's presence did not make sense. "If you are a community of women, what the devil is he — a eunuch?"

The giant froze. Violet gasped. Rose arched one thick eyebrow. In that moment, another figure condensed from the shadows.

Louisa Peabody. Her brilliant blue gaze, filled with all the righteous anger of the ages, bore down on Gabriel. "Please leave us."

Since he was not in any condition to go anywhere, Gabriel assumed she meant the others. And they did leave, with soft rustlings and padded footsteps. All but the giant. He remained, frozen in place.

"David," she said softly.

He turned, and in the look that passed between them, Gabriel read the chilling truth.

Sweet Jesus. Five women, four brats, and one enormous eunuch. This was where fate had led him. To Hell, where women ruled and men were castrated.

Where he was apparently meant to pay for his crimes — and they were many, in the unforgiving eyes of women scorned.

Pay not with his neck, but with his manhood.

With a wild cry of denial, Gabriel bolted from the bed.

***

"Help me, David!" Louisa clutched the man's arms, trying to stop his fierce flight. Even in his weakened state, the criminal possessed an amazing strength. David quickly pulled him away from her. But with a deft move, the man dug his heel into David's ankle, throwing him off balance. Then the criminal reached for her. One hand went around her ribcage, the other her neck. She couldn't move. He held her hostage.

David found his footing but stilled when he saw the man's hands on her.

"If you value her life, stay where you are," the man growled.

Louisa shot David a look filled with apology. This was her doing. She had known the man was evil, yet had allowed him to stay the night in her house. Now he had turned on them, displayed his true stripes. Did he mean to murder them?

No wonder the authorities had pushed his execution ahead of poor Miss Wentworth's. All she had done was steal a loaf of bread. He had assaulted helpless nuns. David had learned the nature of Gabriel Sinclair's crimes just this morning, when he had ridden to town to determine Miss Wentworth's whereabouts.

Why, oh why, had they not left him on that scaffold?

His arm locked around Louisa, he edged them toward the door. Panic filled her. She feared the others would try to intervene and be killed.

"Please do not harm the children," she pleaded. "Do what you will with me, but let the children go."

"What the devil do you mean?"

Louisa knew she shouldn't have spoken. He hadn't even been thinking about the children, and now she'd given him the idea of using them for his own twisted ends. But it was too late to call back the words. "I beg you, do not hurt them. They haven't done anything and —"

"I have never harmed a child in my life."

Something in his injured tone told Louisa he spoke the truth. No matter, his crimes against the rest of them would more than offset his mercy to the children. "And what of the others?" she bit out. "What of those nuns? Can you say you never harmed them?"

"Look, Louisa Peabody, or Mistress of Hell or whoever you are," he snarled, "I'm no saint, but I've no intention of harming anyone. I just want to get out of this house of Bedlam before you turn me into one of those."

"Those?"

For an answer, he pointed at David. "You butchered him, didn't you?"

She stared at him without comprehension.

"Don't play the innocent," he growled. "I'm onto you and your little 'society.' You think to take revenge on every man who has served a female ill. As long as I draw breath, you won't get me."

It took her a moment to understand. A moment to get past the insult and indignation, to understand the import of his words. And then, oh wondrous poetic justice, it was clear as a bell.

"You thought we meant to..." She could not bring herself to say the words.

"Come now, Miss Peabody, don't be squeamish. Do you deny that you meant to relieve me of my manhood in punishment for whatever you imagine are my crimes against your sex?"

"Whatever manhood you possess," she said disdainfully, "is safe here."

The large hand around her middle tightened. "If this is a trick. I swear I will haunt you from the grave."

"It is no trick." His unyielding grip on her made Louisa queasy. "We mean you no harm."

His body shifted slightly, and she felt the tension in the pumping of his heart and the hard, corded muscles that supported her. "Then he is...whole?"

"As whole as ye, mongrel," David snarled.

The man's unnatural stillness told her he was weighing their words, trying to decide the truth. "The scars," he said. "How did you come by them?"

Only the merest twitch of David's jaw hinted at any emotion. "The Peninsular War. I was taken prisoner. Happens a Scot would rather die than lose his freedom. I did nae show the proper respect, so they carved me up. Even so, I was one of the lucky ones."

The man's arm grew slack. Louisa wanted to go to David, but the haunted look in his eyes kept her away. It was not the first time she had seen in his gaze a painful, deeply hidden secret. He might be physically whole, but prison had stolen his spirit, his vitality, his sense of worth. For all his strength and courage, he was a broken man.

"Mr. Ferguson's sister Molly lived here for a time, but she fell sick and died," Louisa said. "Sam — the lad you met — is her son."

She remembered the sadness in David's eyes when he

had shown up at her door in search of the sister he had not seen in years. Louisa had known instinctively that David wasn't a threat to them. His quiet, lonely sorrow had touched her heart. He'd spoken little about his time in prison, and she hated that the criminal had forced him to relive his torture.

Behind her, she felt her captor falter. She turned, and saw the color had drained from his face. It seemed to take all the strength he possessed to remain standing.

"I want —" The words came out a croak. He tried again. "Bed. Back to...bed." He swayed.

"But you cannot manage it, can you?" Louisa taunted, giving rein to her fury at last. He had ruined her plans, intruded on her world, drawn that awkward revelation from David. "Terror of the convent, king of all you possess — and you cannot walk ten steps to the bed."

His gaze darkened, and Louisa could not suppress a little shudder at the flecks of fire in those green depths. But he was spent. Somehow he had mustered the strength to flee the knives he imagined were after him, but that had vanished once panic left him.

Whoever this man was, whatever his crimes, at the moment he was as weak as a lamb.

David moved forward, but Louisa shook her head. She put her arm out to support the scoundrel. For now, he was helpless.

"Lean on me," she ordered.

His weight was more than she had bargained for, but she refused David's help. She wanted this man to feel her strength. He was her enemy, but the battle would be joined another time. She vowed it would be a battle between equals.

***

Once again, he had made a fool of himself before that woman, who was anything but angelic. Gabriel sank into the mattress, hoping sleep would ease him from the horrors of the last two days. It was difficult to separate truth from the dreams that had raged as that noose sucked the life out of him. Yet one truth shone clear enough: Louisa Peabody was no dream. She was a nightmare, and mad as a midsummer moon.

As best he could figure, she went about rescuing women from dire circumstances with the help of that fellow David, who would have been more than a match for his Biblical namesake.

The brush with death had befogged Gabriel's brain. How else to explain why he had seen her as a heavenly vision, the imperfection of that tiny birthmark a harbinger of hope for the truly imperfect like himself? He supposed even fools wanted to believe in something.

He wondered what Louisa Peabody, with her golden hair and fierce azure eyes, believed in. Probably not visions. For all her beauty, she was too grim by half. She was the serious sort of female he most detested. For that matter, everyone here was solemn as a judge. Even that lad, who couldn't be more than twelve, had worried eyes.

What a den of misfits he had stumbled into. And she was the worst — for letting him think, for one horrifying moment, that she was a vengeful Judith out for blood on account of his misdeeds against her sex.

And for making him realize that she would never, ever let him nibble on her fingers.

Chapter Three

"**A** prison ship?" Louisa was horrified. "Not one of those horrid river hulks!"

David nodded grimly. "They moved her there yesterday."

Neither of them voiced the thought uppermost in their minds: Hanging was the least of Alice Wentworth's worries now. The prison hulks, temporary holding pens for felons awaiting transportation to Botany Bay, were run by corrupt guards who were a law unto themselves. Reformers had complained about the hulks for years, but they remained bastions of misery.

A woman in such a place would be at the mercy of her guards. There was no need to speculate about her fate.

Terrible images filled Louisa's mind, and she shuddered. "We must get Miss Wentworth out of there. There is no time to lose."

"Aye."

At his somber tone, Louisa's heart sank. "It will be difficult, won't it?"

"I know nothing of boats, but I do nae think we can simply walk onto the deck, bold as ye please."

"There has to be another way in," she persisted.

"Even so, we've no notion where they are holding her."

"Gun deck, most likely," said a deep male voice. "Fore, if she's lucky. Aft, if she's not."

Louisa turned. Gabriel Sinclair stood at the threshold, evidently restored by his night's rest. He wore the same torn breeches and coarse shirt in which he had prepared to face his Maker, but the similarity between that man and this ended there.

This was no desperate fugitive, fearful of losing his manhood to her vengeance. This was not the man who had lain nearly senseless on the floor of her carriage as they fled the gallows, so dazed that he blurted out that silly marriage proposal.

This man appeared to be in full possession of his senses and, more to the point, fully confident in his masculinity. He stood with his legs slightly apart, taking his weight evenly on both feet in the self-assured manner of a man prepared for anything. His broad shoulders spanned the door frame; his loosely fisted hands rested lightly on his hips.

Masculine ease radiated from every angular plane and contoured muscle, from the high cheekbones and firm jaw that gave his features a noble arrogance to the expanse of chest exposed by his torn shirt. A cool alertness resided in his penetrating green eyes. The unruly red hair framed his face in fire.

A veritable paragon of male beauty, Louisa thought bitterly. A flame-haired god driving his chariot across the sky, dictating the span of a mere mortal's days and nights with typical male arrogance. But he was no god. Sinclair was a liar, a rapist, and any number of other despicable things besides. Beauty was not the measure of his soul.

He glanced only briefly at David, then fixed her with a slow, assessing gaze.

Lifting her chin, Louisa endured his inspection. So what if he was handsome? She was immune to masculine appeal in the way that a child who has weathered smallpox need never fear its ravages again.

As he was evidently immune to her, for she knew the moment he dismissed her as a woman. His brows arched, and his expression shifted from wary interest to careless indifference as he blinked her image away.

"What do you know of the matter?" she challenged, stung by his tacit rejection — though it should not have mattered what he thought of her.

"Of Miss Wentworth, nothing. Of ships, a thing or two." Sardonic amusement filled his gaze. "It's the best way to get to an island."

Louisa flushed. "I am not stupid, Mr. Sinclair —"

"Delighted to hear it. You have discovered my full name, I see."

"Yes, and your crimes as well."

"Heinous, are they not?"

"You make light of them?"

"It does not matter what I make of them. Do you have a change of clothes? I fear these have outlived their usefulness." He fingered his tattered shirt.

Taken aback by his abrupt change of subject, Louisa glanced helplessly at David, who leveled a gaze at him. "I do nae think my shirts will fit ye."

Sinclair shrugged. "Then I will be on my way. Fugitive from justice and all that." His tone was careless, but the green velvet of his eyes had transformed to hard jade. Louisa saw that he did not intend to stay another minute under her roof.

"Wait," she said.

His lazy gaze returned to her.

"My father was not as tall as you, but his clothes may serve," Louisa said. "They will be less noticeable than what you are wearing. We're little more than an hour from London. The authorities will be looking for you and —"

"You are loath to have me risk capture," he finished with a mirthless smile. "How touching."

Louisa frowned.

"Come, Miss Peabody. You have no interest in seeing my miserable life spared. No doubt you have been reproaching yourself for saving me from the execution I so richly deserved."

She stiffened, though he was close to the mark. "Do not put words into my mouth."

"I wouldn't dream of it. Point me in the direction of your father's clothes, and I shall not trouble you further."

"Please." Her voice wobbled. Mortified, she took a deep breath to regain her poise. "I must know why you think Miss Wentworth is being held in the...gun deck, was it?"

"Simple deduction. They would not leave her in the bowels of the ship, where the rest of the felons can have at her. The guards would want her more...accessible."

Louisa looked away. "Go on."

"In that case, they'd likely put her in the carpenter's or boatswain's quarters in the bow. The guards probably occupy the aft cabins."

"So she is separate from the other convicts as well as the guards?"

"If she's lucky. But if the guards wanted her more at hand, shall we say, they would put her aft with them. And if she was fortunate enough to attract the eye of the guard captain, she might find herself in an upper cabin."

"With them," Louisa echoed dully. "So that she would be accessible."

"Night and day. Not a moment's rest, I imagine. I will take those clothes now, if I may."

Her mouth fell open. "How can you be so indifferent to another person's suffering?"

"If you take the world's pain on your shoulders, Miss Peabody, you will have a miserable life. It is foolish to mourn what you cannot change. Since I can do nothing about Miss Wentworth's suffering, I choose to disregard it."

Louisa stared at him in disbelief. She walked over to him and fixed him with a hard stare. "You cannot disregard it. I will not allow you to do so."

He merely arched a brow.

His eyes, she noticed, were more intricate than they appeared from a distance. Amber flecks radiated from the green depths, pinpoints of topaz amid the jade. But there was a coldness in them now. Sinclair would never trouble himself over another person's misery.

"It is because of you that Miss Wentworth was moved," she said.

"No, it was your doing. You caused all that commotion by interrupting my execution."

"I deeply regret it, you may be sure. But the fact remains that Miss Wentworth would have been on that scaffold had it not been for you."

He shrugged. "A twist of fate."

"We would have rescued her," Louisa insisted, "and she would be sitting here now with her babe at her breast. You have an obligation, Mr. Sinclair, and I mean to see that you discharge it."

"I am obliged to no one."

"You are obliged to me, sir, for I saved your life."

"A mistake, as you have acknowledged."

"Mistake or no, you are beholden to us for your miserable existence. And though I am sure you have never done anything of worth in your entire life, you will now. You will help us save Alice Wentworth."

Louisa fairly quivered with rage as they stood toe to toe, but he seemed not the least moved. He studied her with wry amusement.

"You appeal to the conscience of a criminal? My dear Miss Peabody, you must know that a man who has committed the crimes of which I have been convicted would not let conscience get in the way of self-interest."

He was right, of course. Clearly, Gabriel Sinclair possessed not a shred of altruism, no sense of obligation. Louisa turned away, hiding her despair over Alice Wentworth's fate. They *would* free her. They had pulled off daring acts in the past, and they could again. Just because neither she nor David knew fore from aft didn't mean hope was lost.

Louisa looked at David for confirmation. He nodded slightly, and she knew he would be with her all the way. But she saw uncertainty in his gaze, too. And something else she could not label. He regarded Sinclair, then her, with a curious expression. She turned to Sinclair and found he was studying her.

"I mistook you for an angel, you know," he said. Unexpectedly he extended his finger and lightly touched the birthmark above her lip.

Stung, Louisa took a step backward. "Is that a joke?"

"Of course not. A man in my situation has no time for jokes." His gaze roved over her in frank scrutiny. "Now, about those clothes..."

She stared at him with loathing. David stepped forward before she could speak. "I will fetch the trunks."

Sinclair shot Louisa a beatific smile.

***

The moths must have loved Miss Peabody's father, for they had positively devoured his clothes. Gabriel found one pair of tan pantaloons they had let go with only a nibble, and a linen shirt and waistcoat that were relatively unscathed. The shirt was too small and the style a decade out of fashion, but all in all, the clothes were an improvement over his filthy prison togs.

Miss Peabody was daft as a loon. Neither she nor that giant knew the first thing about sneaking onto a ship. He would never fit through even a big ship's hawsehole, and Miss Peabody had never shinnied up an anchor cable in her life. The Wentworth woman hadn't a prayer.

Let the devil take the lot of them. The quicker he was away, the better. He was bound for home. What passed for home, anyway. A godforsaken chunk of rock jutting out of the sea east of Sheerness, perfectly positioned as friend or foe to the ships that skirted the sandbars of the Downs for a more direct route into the heart of England. It was a lonely, forgotten place, and he hated it. But his father had elected to spend eternity there, looking out over the whitecaps in an endless vigil for the desperate and doomed.

Unfortunately, Gabriel's memory was now fully intact. With it came the full weight of his ill-advised trip to Sinclair Isle.

Once, long ago, he had called another place home — a manor house near an ancient gray castle, with servants, tutors, and a stable of prized cattle. He vaguely recalled St. Thomas's Day, when the family would go wassailing. And Christmas, when he would help his father and brother drag in the yule log. Then would come a feast of roasted boar's head.

All had been right with the world back then — before his mother died of a fever and his brother perished in the attack on the French in the Battle of the Nile. Before Gabriel learned that all of Aloysius's hopes and dreams had rested on Robert.

He searched the trunks for boots, and found some leather top boots that were only a little tight. With any luck, they would stretch.

His brother had been nearly a decade older. Robert was to have had an illustrious naval career, married a genteel young lady, and provided Aloysius with grandchildren to entertain him in his old age while he tinkered with his inventions. Instead, his father lost his wife and firstborn son, and with them his tolerance for children, including him.

"Gabriel — a silly name," his father had groused. "Don't know why I let your mother talk me into it. People will expect you to strum a harp."

Not long after his brother's death, his father plucked Gabriel from Eton, packed a few belongings, and tossed them into a sailboat moored in the cove near the house. They sailed out to a spit of land his father called Sinclair Isle. And, like a true lord of the land, his father crowned himself king.

Gabriel had known then that his childhood was irrevocably lost. His father grew as wild and remote as the island, dedicating himself to avenging the son he had lost, ignoring the one who remained. And so the years passed. Through it all, his father tinkered madly with the thing in the cave, stopping only to lavish attention on the French emigres whose boats washed up on Sinclair Isle as they fled Napoleon's tyranny. Gabriel forgot about the wassailing that had brought families together in joyous celebration. He never saw that house or castle again.

When his father died, Gabriel buried him on the island's highest hill, facing east so he would always look out over the churning sea separating England and France. Then he sailed off in a craft he made himself and discovered something better than wassailing: carnal pleasures.

Forced to spend his adolescence on an island, Gabriel had no exposure in his youth to brothels or eager village maids. He had been an innocent of eighteen — a late bloomer, by the standards of the day — when he left Sinclair Isle, a man of seasoned sensuality when he returned to England these ten years later. A world had opened to him in those years, and if he had not quite recaptured the joy of his youth, it was something very like.

The ladies liked him, and he was happy to oblige. Such distractions made time pass pleasantly. Perhaps they even made life worth living. Because if they did not, what did?

Gabriel surveyed his image in the reflecting glass. His father's eyes, his mother's hair, and neither of them alive to see the man he had become. What would they think of him now?

Doubtless they, like Miss Peabody, would be unimpressed. Not that he cared what she thought. She was another mad fool like his father, risking her neck for every desperate cause. Perhaps, in return for the accident of his rescue, he would give her a few pointers for her foolish attempt on the prison hulk. But he was not about to do something as foolish as helping her rescue the poor soul she thought a candidate for sainthood.

He certainly wanted nothing to do with a woman whose view of life was bleaker than his.

To be sure, she was beautiful. And fierce, a Queen Boadicea win-or-perish sort of female with a glorious yellow mane that doubtless blinded her hapless masculine prey. A mantis, devouring any man fool enough to be drawn by her charms.

Her beauty did not disguise the fact that she had lost the joy of her own youth some time ago. He wondered what man had taken it and whether she had enjoyed the experience.

Probably not.

A small kernel of anger welled inside him for the loss of that which could not be replaced. He straightened his waistcoat and shrugged into her father's long jacket with the cutaway front.

A man learned to put away childish things. And to find joy where he could.

Chapter Four

"**D**aisy and Lily, this is Mr. Sinclair." Louisa turned to him. "You've already met Rose and Violet."

He bowed politely, then joined them at the table.

"As you have no doubt become aware," she told them, "Mr. Sinclair arrived two days ago when we mistakenly rescued him instead of Alice Wentworth."

Rose rolled her eyes. "Hare-brained scheme from the outset."

Louisa ignored her. "We have every reason to believe that Miss Wentworth still lives, though I shall not go into the particulars, for the usual reasons."

"The usual reasons?" Sinclair arched an inquiring brow.

"If David and I were caught, it is best for everyone else to know as little as possible about our actions," she said. "Fortunately, we haven't been in danger of capture."

Violet cleared her throat. Louisa hesitated. "We did have a close call a few months ago, when Violet came to us."

"Oh?" Sinclair fixed her with an interested gaze.

"A man in Violet's village —"

"Will," Violet said quietly. "My husband."

"He struck Midnight with his whip," Louisa explained. "Midnight is most averse to the whip. He reared and almost threw me. My cap fell off. Everyone got a good look at the horse, and my hair. Both are rather distinctive, I'm afraid."

His gaze traveled to her hair, then moved lower, settling in the vicinity of her mouth. "Indeed."

"Since then," she continued, trying to ignore his rude

inspection, "I have always worn a head covering for our undertakings."

Sinclair regarded the others around the dining table. His mouth curved in a slow smile as he met each woman's gaze; each one, in turn, seemed to blush. "How does it happen that everyone here is in bloom, so to speak?"

Titters rippled around the room. Oh, he was clever, this knave, Louisa thought.

"It would not do to let our real names get about," Daisy volunteered. "Some of us are judged to have broken the law. Violet was accused of murder."

Sinclair eyed the soft-spoken Violet. She lowered her gaze.

"Lily stole money from her employer — a wicked man who seduced her," Daisy said.

"I do not think Mr. Sinclair needs as much detail as that," Lily grumbled.

"Rose is a skilled healer, but I'm afraid some people regard that as witchery," Daisy continued. "She was accused of killing three husbands."

"I see," he murmured.

"Deserved it, every one of them," Rose muttered.

Daisy patted Rose's fleshy hand. "She didn't really murder them. They took sick and died. Consumption or some such, wasn't it, Rose?"

Rose made a noncommittal response and lit a cheroot. Louisa sighed. She had asked Rose not to smoke inside the house, but the older woman always went her own way. Lily waved her hand at the smoke, but Rose ignored her.

"People took to calling her the Black Widow," Daisy said. "Her trial was in the newspapers. Perhaps you read of it?"

"Afraid not," Sinclair replied. "I've been living abroad."

Daisy gave him a dazzling smile. "Then you wouldn't have heard how Louisa spirited her away —"

"Mr. Sinclair cannot wish to hear of such things," Louisa said quickly.

"On the contrary." Sinclair met her gaze across the table. "I am riveted."

"Disguised herself as a prison matron and walked her right out of the Old Bailey after her sentencing, with no one the wiser," Daisy said.

"Rose had been convicted?" His expression grew wary.

Daisy waved a dismissive hand. "Most of us have been convicted of some crime or, at the least, of violating acceptable female conduct. That's the point, you know. The justice system is weighted toward men. It brings no justice to women."

"He is not interested in our ideology," Louisa said quickly.

Sinclair crossed his arms and bestowed a smile on Daisy. She took that as encouragement to continued. "Louisa has a lovely flower garden, so each of us became a flower."

"We took new names because we have new lives," Violet added.

"The old ones were quite worn out," Daisy agreed. "But do not worry, Mr. Sinclair. We do not expect you to remember our names. There are too many of us."

"You do me a disservice." Then, to their utter delight, he proceeded to call each woman's name as his gaze traveled around the table.

It was an extraordinary performance, Louisa thought glumly, watching him charm her household into admiring submission. He was a clever rogue, with the looks to match, even in her father's outdated clothes. He wore the double-breasted cutaway as if it were made for him. Just above his waist, where the front of the jacket stopped, no unwanted flesh stretched the buttons of his waistcoat. He certainly had no need for the creaky corsets some men required in order to wear such a revealing style, nor did the large lapels begin to eclipse the breadth of his chest, as on some men. His form was lean, with hard musculature beneath the fabric — as she had learned all too well when he briefly held her captive.

Clearly, Mr. Sinclair was no stranger to physical labor. His hands looked strong and capable, in contrast to the soft, coddled appendages typical of fashionable gentlemen. And yet, his eyes radiated the willful gleam of a man accustomed to getting his way.

Doubtless women swooned when he entered a room. Even the women at the table — none of them inclined to look favorably on the male gender — smiled at him with interest. The man could coax a smile from a fencepost.

How she wished they had left him swinging from the gallows, especially since he had no inclination to help rescue Alice. That was a pity, for he seemed to know much about boats.

Suddenly, it occurred to her that she could put the matter to him in business terms. No doubt he had a price, and she had ample funds. She would purchase his skill and all that cocky confidence. Men had used women since time began, so why should not the tables be turned? Surely the Fates did not intend for Miss Wentworth to die in a floating prison of degradation and abuse, her babe in the care of others. If the devil held the key to her salvation, so be it.

"Trying to ease your conscience?" His voice was low, meant for her alone.

Louisa looked up from her plate. "I beg your pardon?"

"Guilt, Miss Peabody. That and discomfort lie within your lovely blue eyes. I must be the cause of it."

"You flatter yourself, sir."

Sinclair merely popped one of Lily's biscuits into his mouth and briefly closed his eyes in an expression of contentment. "Exquisite," he murmured. "Heaven has not seen biscuits like these." Then his gaze fixed appreciatively on Lily. "My compliments, ma'am."

Lily flushed and passed him the platter, which held one remaining biscuit. Violet shyly poured him another glass of wine. Daisy filled his plate with another helping of her dandelion greens. All eyes were riveted on him. Even Rose followed his every move. With no apparent effort, Sinclair held them in thrall.

"Stop," Louisa said.

He eyed her blandly. "Is something amiss?"

"You know the answer." She tossed her napkin on the table.

Sinclair eyed the solitary biscuit he had just plucked from the platter. "Very well," he said with a heavy sigh, placing it gently on her napkin. "Take the last one, then. I shall console myself with the knowledge that sacrifice imbues the soul with nobility."

Giggles filled the room. A lazy smile flitted over his lips, though his eyes seemed curiously devoid of mirth.

"You are much enamored of your own cleverness," Louisa said.

"Alas, you are not. Enamored, that is."

"You may think yourself a veritable king of hearts, but we are not the sort to be taken in by rogues —"

"King of hearts?" His brows rose. "Not that it doesn't have a fine ring to it, but —"

"— or despicable criminals," she finished.

He eyed her thoughtfully. "Though you are one, of course. And by their accounts, everyone in this room as well."

Louisa stared at him.

"Snatching prisoners from the jaws of their punishment seems to be something of a habit with you, Miss Peabody. I do not believe the law looks charitably upon the practice."

Did he mean to blackmail her? Surely not, for as a condemned man, Sinclair had much to lose himself.

Louisa's gaze flew to David, who sat on a stool near the door, a guarded expression on his face. He did not often take his meals with them, but she had asked him to stay for dinner in the event Sinclair did something rash.

Their guest did not look foolhardy, however. Masculine arrogance sat firmly upon his shoulders. He exuded the confidence of a man certain he could seduce any woman in the room.

In that, Louisa thought darkly, he was quite wrong.

"So, it seems that you and I have something in common — we are both criminals," he continued. "Indeed, you seem without remorse for your crimes. If you do not want that biscuit, by the way, I will take it back."

"I am not a criminal," she snapped.

He reached over and retrieved the biscuit from the folds of her napkin. As he took a bite, his eyelids slid down — almost, but not quite, veiling his intense pleasure. Louisa studied him uneasily. There was something about Sinclair that hinted at rare, unbridled appetites.

"But you are," he said at last, picking up their conversation. "If the authorities knew of your activities you'd be sitting in Newgate yourself this very minute. Or perhaps languishing in a rotted prison hulk, playing skittles with the guards, listening to the debauchery below deck, and hoping someone would have the foolishness to come up with a suicidal plan to rescue you."

The room had grown still. The women shifted awkwardly.

"We have broken the law," Louisa conceded. "Perhaps, in the eyes of some, we are criminals. But in truth we are victims —"

"Ah. That makes it all right, then." He turned, as if the subject were forgotten. "Miss Lily, I don't suppose you have any more of those biscuits hidden somewhere?"

Wordlessly, Lily rose and went into the kitchen, appearing moments later with a fresh pan.

Louisa looked around, wondering if anyone else felt her outrage. But the others were looking at her in confusion, as if they did not understand why she was engaged in a bitter battle of wits with such an extraordinary specimen of masculinity.

"Listen to me." Louisa's gaze moved from one woman to another. "This man is a despicable, irredeemable cad. A rapist. His victims were nuns."

Ignoring their shocked gasps, Louisa pressed on: "He is a brute, who takes what he wants without a care. Do not look at him as if he were some sort of hero."

Sinclair shrugged. "The very opposite of a hero, I would imagine."

Then he smiled at her, exposing straight white teeth. None appeared marred or chipped, testimony to the charmed life he had led. Truly, it was a sin for one man to possess so many natural gifts, especially a horrid man like Sinclair.

Louisa closed her eyes to block out the gold-flecked lashes that narrowed his eyes to amused slits. That she had been the instrument of saving this man who possessed such careless greed was cruelly ironic. She, who had vowed to live the rest of her life apart from men, had preserved the existence of a snake without conscience or caring.

"Beast," she declared.

The room was silent. And then: "Bravo, Miss Peabody. Bravo."

Her eyes flew open.

"That is as good a performance as I have seen," Sinclair said. "Next, you will tell me your own heart-wrenching tale of woe. Were you once a nun yourself, perhaps? Did a monster come and snatch you from your self-righteous cocoon and impale you on the staff of his desire? You have only to speak, and I will see that he hangs. But you'd best be sure, because I would hate to hang an innocent man. That is too depressing a thought. Truly, it shakes the very foundations of the universe — or at least of your highly developed sense of justice. It's all black and white for you, isn't it? Not a shade of gray anywhere."

He turned to the others. "Ladies, forgive me for casting a pall on your gathering. Let us change the subject. Shall I tell you about the West Indies? I have traveled there and many other places besides. It will be my pleasure to regale you with exotic tales, and I assure you there is not a nun in them."

***

Miss Peabody was one of those thoroughly rigid spinsters who had made it her life's work to protect womankind from the evils of men. Gabriel had seen a few of those in his time, though none so embittered as she. Some man had brought her to this pass, he was certain. Under other circumstances, he might have been tempted to take up the considerable challenge of bringing a charitable light to her lovely blue eyes. He rarely minded a challenge when it came to women, but Miss Peabody would require more time than he had. Centuries, perhaps.

Anyway, he had to figure out how to get to Sinclair Isle. His jailers had removed what little money he'd had on his person. Handbills offering a reward for his capture had probably gone up all over London. Had he come to his senses while at Newgate, he might have sent word of his plight to his father's solicitors, but he hadn't even recalled his name until he awoke in Miss Peabody's house.

It would be quite useless to contact them now. They knew better than most how impoverished was the state of his family's affairs; it had been a decade since they received even a shilling from him. Nor would he have funds until the sale of Sinclair Isle was finalized — though he didn't understand why anyone would want it.

Perhaps one day he would try to clear his name, but all he wanted now was to leave Miss Peabody's bastion of bleakness, the sooner the better. The Flowers were nice enough, though the notion of outcast females being reborn as garden specimens was a bit bizarre, even for his tastes.

"Mr. Sinclair?"

Gabriel looked over the rim of his glass as Miss Peabody sailed into the parlor, the giant trailing in her wake. She took a seat at a writing table near the chair in which he had been enjoying her father's port — one of the few things about this house he could commend. Certainly not the cuisine, for supper sat in his stomach like lead.

Though Lily had produced those excellent biscuits, Daisy had been responsible for the rest of the meal. She seemed proud of her dandelion greens and boiled turnips, but Gabriel had found the dish as appealing as seaweed.

No wonder the giant took his meals elsewhere. He probably had a secret supply of lamb or venison stashed in his cottage. Gabriel regarded the man with undisguised envy.

"I have a business proposition." Miss Peabody sat stiffly in her chair, eyeing him as if he were a spoonful of bitter medicine to be endured. "I am prepared to pay you to help us free Miss Wentworth."

Did she think him an idiot?

"I am a wanted man," he said dismissively. "I would be a fool to do such a thing." He drank deeply from his glass, then regarded her. "How much?"

"One hundred pounds."

"That would not begin to cover my services." But it would help toward the cost of a small boat, and some provisions besides. And it was a hundred pounds more than he had at the moment. Still, he would not risk his life for such a sum.

"One thousand, then."

Gabriel blinked, certain he had not heard aright.

At his silence, she frowned. "Two thousand? Three?"

He stared at her in amazement. For three thousand

pounds, he could buy the Royal Yacht, and more. "How is it that you possess such a sum?"

"My husband was very rich."

Husband? This man-hating female was somebody's wife? Gabriel stared at the giant, perched warily on a sofa much too small for him. He was the only other man Gabriel had seen here, but the giant did not look at her as a husband might. Wait — hadn't she used the past tense? "You were married?"

"For six hours. He died on our wedding trip." Her constricted features gave her the look of someone who had bitten into a sour apple. Gabriel tried to imagine Miss Peabody on a wedding trip and failed.

"Then...you are *Mrs*. Peabody?"

"No," she replied quickly. "I have chosen to act as if the marriage never existed. Accordingly, I have not taken my husband's name."

"Only his money."

She flushed. "The settlements had been duly prepared and signed. It was my due."

"I see." Married and widowed in six hours. A feat indeed, the mercenary little witch. Had she poisoned the man at their wedding feast?

"I doubt very much that you do, but that is neither here nor there. What say you to my proposition?"

Despite her firm tone, her lips trembled slightly and those blue eyes gleamed with unnatural brightness, perhaps evidence that the topic of her marriage distressed her. The notion of making her enticing person part of the bargain briefly entered his head, but he put it aside. That way lay disaster, on so many fronts.

Besides, money was what he needed, and Miss Peabody had the worst negotiating skills he'd ever seen. The Fates had handed him a gift, provided she had the funds.

"I would require half in advance," he said warily.

She put on a pair of spectacles and dipped her pen into the inkwell. She scribbled something on a piece of paper, then handed it to him.

He eyed the document skeptically. The promises of a woman who dashed about the country causing mayhem were worth little. Now if she were to drop a pile of bank notes in his lap, that would be something else entirely.

"I cannot give you half today, as my trustee will not release my quarterly allowance for a fortnight," she said. "He will balk at such a sum, but I have no doubt I can bring him around."

Did the woman think him a slow top? Gabriel was not about to risk his neck for a promise, no matter that it came from a mouth as lovely as any he'd seen recently. With a contemptuous smile, he looked up from the promissory note. "This is all well and good, but —"

"I can give you a third now, however. Will that be sufficient?" She thrust something at him.

Gabriel's gaze dropped to the large stack of notes emblazoned with the Bank of England crest. A thousand pounds. With this alone, he could purchase all he needed to sail to Sinclair Isle. Come to think of it, he wouldn't need to carry out Miss Wentworth's rescue at all. He could take this tidy little sum and —

"I am trusting you, Mr. Sinclair," she said sternly, proving herself an uncanny mind-reader, "though I know it is unwise. But if Miss Wentworth is to be freed, I have no other choice."

Gabriel plucked the notes from her hand. "Done." He took a bracing sip of port to celebrate his unexpected fortune.

Miss Peabody wore a look of distaste, as if she could scarcely bear to look at him. She settled herself at her desk again and dipped her pen into the inkwell once more. She eyed him expectantly, her hand poised over the blank paper.

"What is your plan?" she asked solemnly.

The spectacles gave her a studious air and obscured the full, startling beauty of those blue eyes. Most women did not wear spectacles in company. Miss Peabody seemed perfectly content to do so, though if she did not mend her judgmental ways, she would end up with wrinkles before her time. Gabriel wondered whether she ever smiled.

"Mr. Sinclair," she said impatiently. "I asked about your plan."

Gabriel found himself studying those pink lips, which at the moment were pursed in disapproval. "Plan?"

"To rescue Miss Wentworth, of course."

Gabriel took another sip of port. "Much depends on the type of ship on which Miss Wentworth is incarcerated. Can you tell me about the vessel?"

"No, but..." She looked uncertainly at the giant. "That is, David —"

"Cannot tell a warship from a barge, I imagine," Gabriel said. The giant glared at him but offered no denial.

"David has seen the ship, so he should be able to provide sufficient detail," she said.

Gabriel eyed the giant. "How many gun ports are there? Are they closed or open? How big are the hawseholes?"

No one spoke. Miss Peabody looked questioningly at the giant and then at him. "Gun ports — holes from which the guns would fire. Is that what you mean?" she asked.

Gabriel nodded.

"Well, now. That is simple enough." Hopefully, she turned to the man. "Did it have holes, David? You know, little round holes in the side where the guns —"

"Square," Gabriel corrected. "The holes are square."

"Square, then." She frowned. "But I am sure I have seen round holes on ships —"

"Portholes. A ship's windows, if you will. They are small. Smaller than gun ports and some hawseholes."

"Oh, dear." Miss Peabody looked confused. "Did the

ship have any holes, David? Big or little or round or square or...hawse-shaped?"

"Hell and damnation!" The giant stood up. "It looked like a blasted big boat, Louisa, and that is all I know."

Miss Peabody cleared her throat. "Does all of this really matter, Mr. Sinclair?"

Gabriel wondered about the relationship between Miss Peabody and Ferguson. They seemed to know each other well. Lovers, he might have said, if the frightfully earnest Miss Peabody hadn't been the last woman in the world to take a lover. But he'd have thought her the last woman to take a husband, too.

The brief marital union had probably not been enjoyably consummated. Women who had experienced carnal pleasure did not pucker up like a dried prune whenever a man looked at them with any sort of frank appreciation for their beauty.

"Mr. Sinclair?" she prodded testily. "I asked whether it mattered if the ship had all these holes. Would you not stare at me as if I'd just said the moon was made of green cheese?"

"How do you know it is not?" he offered. No doubt about it: Miss Peabody had the armor of a prickly pear. It was child's play to upset that carefully constructed universe of hers.

"I do nae think we are getting anywhere," the giant groused.

"Nor do I," she snapped. "Come, David. Mr. Sinclair undoubtedly needs time to devise a plan and —"

"Miss Peabody." Gabriel drained his port, set the glass upon the table, and rose. He let his shadow fall upon the paper on her desk. "If one intends to sneak onto a ship — or off it, for that matter — one has to find an alternative to the gangway."

She frowned, and he could see she was beginning to understand.

"One must be enterprising, or else walk right into the guards' arms. I should not like to see you behind bars. The experience is entirely too earthy."

"I am not afraid of capture," she declared.

"You should be. Do you have any idea what it is like in prison?"

She was silent.

"I thought not. Don't worry — I will not subject you to my litany of complaints. I'm no Reformer, but neither am I fool enough to try to breach a ship without having a notion as to what sort of craft it is. Gun ports would provide the easiest entry, for the guns have undoubtedly been removed. The gun ports on the large prisoner-of-war hulks at Portsmouth have been covered over, but I do not know whether that is true of the river hulks. Such details are useful if one is planning something like this."

"Mr. Sinclair —"

"I am not finished. The Thames hulks are anchored near the bank, not moored out in deeper waters as the Portsmouth hulks are. That's fortunate, for the Portsmouth hulks are accessible only by boat. One can walk onto a river hulk from the dock plank to the gangway — but guards will be there, so that way is closed to us."

She eyed him uncertainly.

"The only possible course is to sneak onto the ship from the water below, which requires climbing up the anchor chain, edging oneself along a very slender strip of wood, and slipping into one of those gun port openings the giant did not think to notice. Stealth is required. And agility, of course."

She absorbed that with a troubled air. "I'm afraid we will have to do the best we can. I have done some research on these ships, Mr. Sinclair. Sir Samuel Romilly has spoken in Parliament about the great depravity and wretchedness there. Many inmates die — even children have been discovered among them. There are no beds. Inmates are stacked atop each other in hammocks. Disease and illness is rampant —"

"It is a prison, madam, not Brighton Pavilion."

For a moment she appeared to struggle for composure. "The point, sir, is that every day Miss Wentworth endures on that awful ship is an abomination. We simply cannot wait. I would like to be more prepared, but…" She trailed off.

An ineffable sadness filled her gaze. Somehow, it crossed the space between them and settled unexpectedly in his gut.

Suddenly, Gabriel realized that he wanted to erase that sorrow from those lovely blue eyes. She was delusional, of course, and he should not care a whit about her obsessive quest for justice against the worst odds.

Still, as much as he wanted to take her money and take himself off, he found himself drawn to her cause. He, too, had been on the wrong end of that justice system. It might be gratifying to tip the scales just a bit. There wasn't a boat he didn't know from stem to stern, be it frigate or merchant clipper. Without his help, she'd end up in a prison cell, looking out with those sad blue eyes.

It might please him to confound her expectations and do something honorable.

Yes, he would take her money, but damned if he didn't want something else for his trouble, too. She was a strange woman with a prickly spine, not the sort of female he would usually waste his time on, but the knowledge that she could embrace such danger without a care for her own safety aroused him.

He lusted — if not for her, precisely, then for the possibility of shaping such passionate clay into raw sensuality. A woman who could face down death could certainly face sex. Something told him the earnest yet untutored Miss Peabody never did things by half-measures. He would ponder the sensual prospects.

But it was best not to let his imagination run amok. People didn't change, and Louisa Peabody would have to change dramatically before he would contemplate any sort of congress with her, even a fleeting one. Still, a man could be alert for the odd chance.

He felt the giant's eyes on him and looked over at the man. Ferguson stood with his arms folded across his sizable chest, as if daring Gabriel to touch one hair of Miss Peabody's deranged head. His eyes held a black warning, as if he could read Gabriel's very improper thoughts.

Gabriel shrugged. He would not apologize for the images that floated through his mind — Miss Peabody lying naked under him, enslaved to the pleasures he could give her. If the giant had never seen her thus, it was his loss. If he had, then every instinct Gabriel had about women was false — and that was quite impossible.

"Illicit acts are best undertaken under the cloak of darkness," he heard himself say. "A full moon would provide sufficient light so we need not carry torches that could give us away. We will need strong rope, a small skiff, a favorable tide, and someone with strong arms."

She began to scribble furiously on her paper.

He stared at her, aghast. "Never say you are taking notes."

"But of course." She looked puzzled. "How else am I to remember?"

"Notes are of no use in the darkness. And there will be no time for reading once the thing has begun."

She flushed. "Logic and planning do not come naturally to me. Writing things down makes them easier to remember."

"And easier for someone to find out what we are about. Didn't you say you wanted to keep the details from the Flowers?"

"Flowers?" she echoed, puzzled.

"Lily, Violet, Daisy —"

"Oh." She hesitated. "The notes are only for me. I am terrified of leaving out some crucial detail that could result in disaster. I write everything down and look at it from all possible angles just to make sure I have not forgotten something."

Gabriel sighed. "Then by all means take notes. Commit them to memory, then throw them into the fire. There is a full moon two days hence, I believe. That is when we undertake Miss Wentworth's freedom."

Abruptly, she rose to her feet. Her hands clenched in fists at her sides. Her blue eyes filled with fervor. She stood nearly toe to toe with him, her chin out, a soldier primed for battle.

"We shall!" she vowed. The feverish radiance in her gaze seemed to inhabit her entire person, for she positively trembled with excitement. "We shall indeed!"

Gabriel stared at her, astonished at the transformation. Before him stood a warrior, albeit one born into a decidedly female body. And, like many of the breed, this one was dosed with madness.

He glanced at the giant to see how the man was taking this uncommon display. Ferguson's features revealed no shock or surprise. Indeed, his eyes gleamed with respect for her. It was a look a man might give his captain.

Miss Peabody grabbed his hand and shook it violently. "We will pull this off, Mr. Sinclair. We will work together and prevail. Justice will be served, and Miss Wentworth will be saved."

Good God. Beneath that spinsterish exterior beat the heart of a bloody revolutionary. Boadicea — with spectacles.

Chapter Five

Louisa grabbed a fistful of grass and rubbed it in her hands, letting its smell seep into her skin. She'd lost ground with Midnight. She shouldn't have ridden him to rescue Violet three months ago. He hadn't been the same since Violet's husband attacked him with the whip.

Just before their marriage, Richard had bought the horse from her father. He'd been fascinated by Midnight's stature and power, never bothering to ascertain whether the stallion was suitable as a mount. Her father had been preoccupied with his debts and hadn't fully trained the horse. Soon after, he fled to the Continent to avoid his creditors. Richard tried all manner of ineffective methods to bend Midnight to his will and very nearly ruined him.

Richard wouldn't ride the horse without a metal bit, and even used a metal lead chain. Naturally, Midnight had been fearful, which made him unpredictable. But Louisa had worked around horses all her life and knew they were as predictable as day and night. Control and discipline didn't make a good horse; consistency did. That, and working with humans who weren't afraid. Confident riders made biddable horses.

After Richard's death Louisa had spent months working with the stallion. They'd made progress to the point that she could ride him, but only without a saddle. The incident with Violet's husband had been a setback, and Louisa was slowly retraining him.

Midnight eyed her nervously from his stall. The sun was setting and he was uneasy, for his eyes were still adjusting to the changing light. Louisa let the horse sniff her hands; as he inhaled the smell of grass, he snorted and bobbed his head. Some of the tension seemed to leave him.

Normally she put the horses to pasture at night, but she wanted Midnight in the stall for this exercise. She had already put some wet hay in with him. Now she placed a saddle at the far end of the stall.

Most women did not haunt the stables, but Louisa had never wished to be anywhere else, from the time her father began to teach her about his breeding stock. The rhythms of a horse's feeding, grooming, and other needs lent a soothing symmetry to her days. A horse did not care that she was female, did not expect her to dress in female frippery or execute a proper curtsey.

Louisa often wondered what would have happened if her mother had not died when she was young. Would she have abandoned the stable for more ladylike pursuits? Might she have gone to London, had a proper come-out, learned to simper helplessly at eligible bachelors? Would her father have been less reckless with his money, less eager to auction her off to the highest bidder to erase his debts?

None of that mattered now. Her life was rich with purpose. She was content.

Louisa placed some carrots on the saddle. Last night, she'd put the saddle in his stall without the carrots. He hadn't gone near it, but tonight the carrots had him interested.

She had always loved this big black horse. Where Richard had seen a wild, ungovernable animal only the manliest of gentlemen could tame by force, Louisa saw a mistreated creature with a valiant and noble spirit. It was not a violent nature that had made the stallion difficult to manage but his master's application of the whip.

Perhaps she and Midnight were kindred spirits — peaceful, for the most part, but driven to rebellion by tyrants.

The horse ambled over to the saddle and sniffed the

carrots. If he ate them, she would bring in two saddles tomorrow and put them at opposite ends of the stall, each with carrots. One day soon, she hoped, he would come to tolerate the saddle on his back.

David entered the stable with a bucket of fresh water. Silently, he filled the trough. Then he studied her.

"Do ye trust him?"

Louisa knew he wasn't referring to Midnight, but Sinclair. Unlike the stallion, Sinclair wasn't predictable, and certainly not biddable. But he recognized strength when he saw it, and Louisa had learned to be strong; a woman alone couldn't be weak.

Oh, Sinclair had his tricks; she didn't know the half of them, whereas Midnight had shown her his full repertoire. In that sense, she didn't know the man. But if she could manage a horse that weighed nearly eighty stone, she could manage a scoundrel. Couldn't she?

"We have no choice, David."

He watched the horse. "I do nae like it."

"You have had the dreams again." David was plagued by nightmares. Louisa suspected they stemmed from the atrocities he suffered in prison. Sometimes the dreams left him with a lingering sense of foreboding she had learned not to dismiss. On the day they had ridden to Aylesford to rescue Violet, David had had such a premonition.

The memory of Violet's rescue still rankled. Violet had been accused of seducing another woman's husband, then poisoning him to prevent the affair from becoming known. Louisa couldn't imagine anyone thinking the soft-spoken Violet capable of such acts. But Violet's husband had echoed the accusation, so her fate was sealed. She'd been made to stand in the village square for weekly floggings that Will administered himself. He made a show of hitting only her back so as to spare the babe, which was assumed to be the dead man's get.

The case attracted no small number of gawkers who

gathered to watch Violet's humiliation. Aylesford was not far from Peabody Manor; Louisa happened to be in the village on Market Day and was stunned to witness Violet's punishment.

The next week, Louisa and David had ridden into the crowded village square as Violet stood for her flogging. When they tried to free her, Violet's husband lashed out at them with his whip. As Louisa fought to control Midnight, David lifted Violet onto his horse, and they fled. It was the nearest they'd come to disaster on any mission.

"Aye, I dreamed last night," David said. "I suspect the mongrel means to leave us in the lurch."

"I am paying him well," Louisa said. Midnight, she saw, was munching on the carrots.

"Money can nae buy everything."

"Sinclair needs what I have."

"As to that, I'm thinking ye be right, lass. But there's more than one kind of need."

Louisa frowned. "I don't understand."

"What that man needs no one can give him. Do nae think otherwise. Mark my words, he'll be trouble."

The word had never sounded so ominous.

***

Gabriel strode along the path that ran a few hundred yards from Miss Peabody's house. All she'd revealed about their location was that it was about an hour from London. But he didn't need more. He knew this land as well as he knew his own name.

Smells of sawgrass and salt marsh catapulted him back to another time, when the delights of a boy's day had been sufficient, when life had no existence beyond the present. Where ancient woodlands gave way to farmland that ran to the sandy river flowing between bay and sea. A coastline like none other, meandering from flat meadows to chalky cliffs, from placid lighthouses to stone forts. Centuries of invaders had looked out from their ships and coveted this land across the water, and the land had rebuffed them. It would not be civilized, and its shifting sands would never be tamed into permanence.

Kent.

His home and his curse. It would always reside somewhere inside him, like a bullet lodged near the heart, too close to that frail muscle to be anything other than a mortal wound, waiting to lay him low. How ironic, then, that Louisa Peabody had brought him here. His old family home could not be more than a short ride away.

Inhaling the salt-tinged air, Gabriel walked along the path up a gently rolling hill. He wondered how the castle had fared, whether the woods had reclaimed it or the sea had breached its stone defenses. Had the turrets that had protected him and Robert from the dragons of their imaginations crumbled under the weight of time and broken dreams?

A few months ago, the letter from a solicitor whose name he didn't recognize had reached him in Jamaica. The offer to purchase Sinclair Isle had given him pause. After some consideration, he decided to journey home to see for himself how things stood.

But he had intended only to make a final pilgrimage to the island, avoiding the ancient coastal homestead that had fired his boyhood imagination with dreams that turned out to be as illusory as ghosts and as bitter as weeds. Never would he have willingly come to this land or stood at the top of a hill and looked out over the ancient wood at the speck of blue that was the river estuary he knew so well. Never would he have sought out this chilling moment of recognition, when the past rushed up and ambushed him with the inexorable force of memory and loss.

He expelled a great, useless sigh. Damn Louisa Peabody for plucking him from his fate and bringing him to this place that ran through his blood like a poison.

***

"That's right, Sam," Louisa said encouragingly. "Put the bowl in the same spot as yesterday. Away from the fence."

He set a bowl of grain in the middle of the round pen in which they were training Midnight. Sam showed promise, but she would not let him work the stallion until she was certain the horse trusted him. She had devised exercises toward that aim.

Sam was getting taller by the week. Soon he'd clear the highest fence rail, and although his face still had the rounded features of a boy, his cheekbones were showing the sharper angles of adolescence. He had a direct gaze, brown eyes like his mother's, and light brown hair. Sam was eager to learn, but he was also prone to worry. Perhaps that was to be expected from one who'd lost his mother so young. If he could gain confidence around such a fearsome specimen as Midnight, he might be able to shed those other burdens. That was Louisa's hope, anyway.

"Why not near the fence?" Sam asked.

"He'd feel cornered against the rail," Louisa replied. "The middle is open territory, more what he'd be accustomed to in the wild. Set the bowl down, but don't walk away."

Sam stood there as Midnight loped around the pen, seemingly ignoring him. Then the horse slowed, and moved toward the bowl.

"See how he's eyeing you? He's thinking about it, weighing his choices."

"His ears are back," Sam said. "Mayhap he's angry."

"It's because he hasn't made his mind up about you," Louisa said. "He's trying to figure out if you are lower or higher than him in the hierarchy of his world."

Sam eyed the stallion uneasily. "Not much doubt about that. He's *much* bigger than me."

"Size is not the measure of mastery, but it does make

it easier for him to intimidate you."

The lad took a step backward.

"Stand your ground," she urged. "He wants you to move away. If you do, he becomes the master. Ever after, he knows he can have his way with you. If you stay, he sees you're in charge."

Midnight wasn't a horse easily stared down, but to Sam's credit, he stood there and tried.

"Now walk toward him," Louisa said. "Put your hands up in the air, so you appear bigger."

Cautiously, Sam followed her instructions. Midnight blew out of his nostrils, and Sam froze. "He's snorting at me."

"He's releasing tension," she said. "If he pawed the ground and squared at you, it would be time to worry. But he's not. He's merely trying to get you to back down."

Sam looked dubious. Horse and boy faced one another for a long moment, a few feet apart.

Then Louisa saw what she'd been waiting for. "Tell me what's different, Sam."

The boy regarded the horse. "His ears aren't back anymore!"

"Right. He wanted you to leave, but you did the opposite. You forced him to back down. Now you can turn and walk away. He understands you are his master. For today, at least, you've made your point." She smiled. "There will be other opportunities. Training is a long game."

Sam beamed. Both horse and boy were coming along fine, Louisa thought as Midnight approached the grain bowl and begin to eat.

"Nicely done," said a masculine voice.

She turned to see Sinclair leaning on the fence in a pose that managed to seem both relaxed and alert. The man had a disconcerting way of looking her up and down without appearing to move his eyes. But she could feel his gaze on her, and his mouth curved upward, as if he was enjoying some private amusement.

Louisa found her own gaze wandering from his tousled red hair down to the broad shoulders and long arms. His hands rested on the fence in an easy pose that suggested they'd be instantly available should she wish his assistance in any task that involved applying them to her person.

Dear Lord. Where had that thought come from?

"Sam's instincts weren't wrong." Her voice, at least, sounded calm. "Midnight would intimidate anyone."

"Except you, apparently. What's his history?"

She glanced at the horse. "He was mistreated. I'd made some progress with him, but he had a setback when we rescued Violet. He'll be all right if we don't rush him."

"Where do you come by your horse sense?"

"My father was a breeder. I learned early."

"And well, it seems."

She shrugged. "I had no use for the usual female things. All of my time went into horses."

"Hmm. One wonders at the loss."

Louisa frowned. "What loss?"

"Ballrooms throughout England must have mourned the absence of Louisa Peabody in her debutante pastels. Why, think of the dance cards waiting to be filled. The suitors waiting to fawn over her gloved hand —"

"I dislike pastels."

He arched a brow.

"Dancing, too," she added. "Fawning, most of all."

Sinclair favored her with a curious look, then turned to Midnight. "What makes you think this one's biddable?"

"He's biddable enough in the right circumstances."

"You'll have to convince me, I'm afraid. What circumstances?"

Louisa moved toward the horse, now regarding her benignly. "Oh, he's a horse for the ages," she said softly.

And it was true. Midnight never failed to draw all eyes. He was ink black, save for three white stockinged feet, and large for a Hanoverian — well over seventeen hands. Her grandfather had been fascinated by the workhorse breed, equally fascinated by the Arabian a friend brought back from Syria. He bred them, got horses with lightning speed as well as strength. To that, her father had added Prussian warmblood.

Midnight possessed the best traits from those breeds. He was exceedingly athletic, with the spring of a jumper but blazing speed, powerful haunches, and a twenty-foot stride. At full gallop he looked to be floating on air.

Perhaps he could have used more of the warmblood's gentle temperament. Still, the stallion did wish to please, which made him trainable in the right hands.

Louisa ran her hand over the horse's muzzle. It was soft like fine suede, but she didn't linger there, as he'd been known to take a friendly nip or two. His eyes were a liquid, soulful brown, but anyone who didn't see the warning there lacked horse sense.

Her fingers tangled in the coarse hairs of Midnight's mane, and she rubbed the spot underneath the long hairs that made him tremble in delight. She slid her hands down the large muscle of his neck and brought her face closer, inhaling his scent, earthy as dirt and grass. The heat from his exercise with Sam was still burning off, and Louisa smoothed her hands over his taut coat, savoring the warm, twitching muscles under her touch.

Quivering with life, Midnight was so much more than consolation for the debutante world Louisa never wanted to be part of. She turned to Sinclair, only to find him regarding her with an expectant air. Belatedly, she realized he was awaiting her response as to how she intended to train the stallion.

"We won't show him fear," she said. "We'll make him move when he doesn't want to, school him to the harness, make him take the saddle. What we won't do is force a metal bit on him or use a whip. We aren't out to break his spirit or cause him pain."

"No bit, no whip." Sinclair's gaze was assessing. "Why are you are so eager to take on the impossible?"

"It's not impossible. You need only look at the situation through the horse's eyes. Big as he is, he sees us as predators and himself as prey. That fearsome exterior notwithstanding, he only wants one thing: to be led. We need only show him a leader he will wish to follow. That's me, for now. And Sam, in time."

"Fascinating. But I wasn't referring to the horse."

She frowned. "What then?"

"Have you a suit of armor hidden somewhere, Miss Peabody? Something that protects you against the dangers that would fell mere mortals? Say, those on a prison ship filled with guards and their carbines?"

Was that amusement in those green eyes? Louisa reminded herself not to be taken in by a scoundrel's charm. "I collect you refer to the rescue. I have no armor, sir, only passion."

"Ah."

"It's the same passion that will demand your head on a platter if you fail us with Miss Wentworth," she added sternly.

His features formed into an expression of shock. "I cannot describe what your blood-lusty talk is doing to my sensibilities."

For a long moment they stared at one another, much as Sam and Midnight had faced off earlier. Sinclair's eyes held amber flecks that beckoned her into their depths, although Louisa knew it was only another of his tricks. That knowledge didn't prevent the little shiver that rippled through her, as if he'd touched some secret pleasure spot like the one on Midnight's neck.

"I have placed my faith in you," she said. "I trust you will not betray it."

Sinclair gave an exaggerated sigh. "Your optimism is

such a burden. Inspiring, to be sure, but wildly unrealistic for the task ahead. Your blind confidence may appeal to the horse, but it's a bit off-putting to this human. Makes me want to square off, paw the ground, and take you on."

Louisa did not want to think about the possible meanings of that sentence. Her chin rose. "I would stand my ground, Sinclair. You may be sure of that."

"I don't doubt it. Do you never laugh, Miss Peabody?"

That took her aback. "When something is amusing."

"This does not strike you as such?" He made a sweeping gesture.

"This?"

"This bit of jousting between us. I say something, you bristle at it, then insist on your own viewpoint with an earnestness that in any other female would be ludicrous."

Louisa drew herself up. "Ludicrous? Why, I —"

"And then you get angry. It seems to be a pattern, does it not?"

"I do not understand you, Mr. Sinclair. Nor do I care to. All I care is that you live up to your part of our bargain."

All amusement vanished from his features. "You do realize the thing may end in disaster?"

"I am prepared to accept failure," she said. "But if we fail, it must not be on account of you."

"If we are to be partners, there should be trust between us."

Louisa eyed him coldly. "I have no choice but to trust you for now. Do not fail me."

"Since you have appealed to my better nature, I could not possibly." He paused. "Though I expect I will have to look for it."

"It?"

"My better nature. I am sure it is around somewhere. I have only to recall where I last saw it."

With that, he ambled off, leaving her to stare at the back of those broad shoulders and take note of the easy and confident way he carried himself, as if he could charm the world into doing his bidding — and had, more times than it was possible to count. Yes, his amorous conquests must be beyond number. The man appeared to think that all he need do was drop a few clever *bon mots* and the world would fall at his feet. He was all style and no substance.

This was the man she was counting on to lead them?

She must be thoroughly mad.

Louisa did not see Sinclair again until a few hours later in the parlor, where they were to meet to discuss the final details of the plan to free Miss Wentworth. He was alone and staring out the window when she entered the room. He did not turn to acknowledge her.

She told herself not to take offense at his lack of manners. She had purchased only his skills, not his good will.

"David has found a fisherman who will provide us with a rowboat," she said. "Sam will wait with the carriage along the river just east of the hulk. Once we have Miss Wentworth, we need only row downriver to him, hide the boat, and be off. I believe that is everything on the list."

Now he turned. "You rely on a boy to hold a coach and four?"

"Sam is capable of managing a team. He practically lives in the stable."

"Forgive me," he said, with elaborate politeness. "For a moment I thought you were relying on an untrained lad to do a man's job." His mouth thinned into a mirthless smirk. "Ah, but he is not untrained, is he? You must have used him previously in your schemes. Did he have any choice in the matter?"

Louisa sensed a resentment in him that went beyond the simple fact of Sam's involvement. "They are not 'schemes.' They are missions to help those who cannot defend themselves against the men who run our legal system."

"The boy feels as you do, of course."

She hesitated. Sam repeatedly begged to be allowed to help, but his enthusiasm derived more from the pull of adventure than principle. She had taken care to use him only in support roles well away from their most daring activities, but perhaps even that put him at risk.

"Come, now, madam," Sinclair prodded, "you must know what the lad thinks about risking his neck to flout the king's laws. Surely you are aware that his age will offer scant protection should he be caught."

In that, he had a point, Louisa realized. A soldier or guard likely would not take the time to discern whether he was but a lad. "Sam is fully capable of the responsibilities we give him, but perhaps we should examine whether his presence is necessary in the future."

"And whether he is entitled to a childhood."

That startled her. She wondered at the tension in his voice, but he quickly belied that, idly brushing a piece of lint from the lapel of his coat and stifling a yawn. "With all due regard to your late father, I do not believe I will wear this jacket tonight. It is rather tight about the shoulders and would hamper —"

"Sam will be out of harm's way," Louisa insisted. "All he need do is watch the horses."

"My dear Miss Peabody," he replied in apparent surprise, "I never suggested otherwise."

It was as if she had entered a hall of mirrors in which every reflection was distorted. Each conversation with Sinclair bent her sense of him into a different image. Try as she might, Louisa could not get a fix on the man.

She would not believe that he cared two figs about Sam or, indeed, about anything. He seemed too hollow, too empty, too devoid of real warmth. Indeed, his flippant remarks and sardonic humor bespoke nothing so much as contempt. He would not have helped them tonight without her princely payment; Sinclair cared for no one but himself.

Of compassion and empathy he had none. That practiced smile, that easy wit — they did not fool her. He was a despicable human being, a rake, a scoundrel, a snake, a —

"Finished?" he asked.

Louisa nearly jumped. "I-I beg your pardon?"

"I merely wondered whether you had finished cataloguing my sins and were ready to go over the plans for tonight."

She felt her face flush. "Yes, of course."

"Shouldn't you summon the giant? I assume he still means to accompany us. I shouldn't like to think of you rowing me and Miss Wentworth all that distance alone."

"David will join us shortly." Louisa sat in the chair at her writing table, trying to recover her poise. She pretended to study her notes, anything to avoid meeting the man's gaze. He saw too much — and worse, kept her off balance.

To her dismay, Sinclair crossed the room and stood over her in that intimidating fashion.

"What is it?" she demanded, looking up at him.

He made a great show of studying her table. "Ah. Here they are." He retrieved her spectacles, half-hidden by her papers, and held them out to her. "I doubt you can see anything on those papers you are pushing about so violently without these."

She snatched the spectacles from him and put them on. "I know what you are about, sir."

"Oh?" Sinclair wore an expression of wounded innocence. "Which of my nefarious tricks are you onto?"

"All of them," she retorted. "You mean to lull us into false complacency, to present yourself as the most innocuous of men, when everyone knows you are the proverbial wolf in sheep's clothing."

"Alas, I am undone," he said mournfully. "Thank the heavens for your perspicacity, else all of the women under your roof would surely become my victims."

Louisa glared at him.

"As you have so correctly observed," he continued, "a scoundrel is not bound by the principles of common decency. Indeed, I am not fit to move in your very righteous universe. Why, the very notion that a handbill might have your face on it is unthinkable." He stroked his chin. "'Louisa Peabody, Feloness.' Not that it doesn't have an intriguing ring to it."

Louisa rose. The top of her head came no higher than his chin. He was standing far too close for comfort, but she was determined not to be cowed. "You have the understanding of a flea, Mr. Sinclair, but that does not matter as long as you are fit to guide us tonight. Afterward, you may fall off the face of the earth with my blessing. Is that clear?"

"Quite." His gaze roved lazily from her face down to her toes, pausing rather insolently at the parts of her that no true gentleman would linger on, before settling on her face again.

Louisa tried to banish the very peculiar warmth that extended to places where warmth was not in the least desired. She would not give him the satisfaction of seeing the effect his inspection had on her. Instead, she leveled a gaze at him. "Will you do as you promised — help us free Miss Wentworth to the best of your ability?"

"Insofar as I have any ability for breaking into prison hulks and spiriting away its female denizens, I shall dedicate it to your mission, madam."

"There!" she said accusingly. "You are doing it again. You do not say what you mean, and everything you say is meaningless."

"Surely not everything."

"Will you be serious, sir, or will you persist in these ridiculous jokes?" To her dismay, her voice broke. "If you plan to leave us in the lurch, I ask that you not wait until tonight to do so. It is not my fate that concerns me but that of Miss Wentworth. You would not be so cruel as to let us think you mean to help her and then —" She broke off in mortification as a tear spilled over onto her cheek.

To her dismay, he reached out and brushed the tear away with his thumb. "Do not despair, madam," he said lightly. "Your money has purchased my loyalty — for the night, anyway."

The intimacy of his touch shocked her. But that was nothing compared to the alarm that filled her when his hand slid insolently around the nape of her neck before falling away from her.

Louisa recoiled. "I did not give you leave to fondle me."

An arrested expression crossed his features. For a moment he looked startled, and she had the distinct impression she was seeing the man himself beneath that cavalier mask. But too quickly, the mask slid into place again.

"Miss Peabody," he said solemnly, "if you believe that to be fondling, someone has given you a rather inferior lesson on the subject."

Embarrassment swept her. Louisa was acutely aware of the scant space between them and the knowing gleam in his eyes. Quickly, she took a step backward.

"What I believe is not your concern," she said. "You need only know that I have no wish to be touched by you or any man, that I find such contact abhorrent, and — *what* are you doing?"

As she stared at him in horror, Sinclair lowered his face to hers and kissed her full on the mouth. It was not a crude kiss, in the way one might expect of such a raffish man. Rather, his mouth was feathery-soft, so disarming that Louisa stood rooted to the spot while his lips touched hers as if it were the most natural thing in the world to do so.

Then he withdrew.

So fleetingly had their lips met, Louisa might have imagined it. She gaped at him in stunned amazement.

"I beg your pardon —" he began.

"I should hope so, you wretched man," she said. "I did not give you leave to —"

"—because that was a vastly inferior kiss," he finished.

Before Louisa could absorb that statement, Sinclair kissed her again, this time his mouth settling over hers with gentle but insistent pressure. His hands slid around her waist, pulling her toward him.

As she registered the feel of that tautly muscled chest, a flood of unwelcome sensations swept her. She tried to steady herself, her fingers curling around the fabric of his shirt. Louisa fought to calm her breathing but instead inhaled intoxicating scents of sandalwood and something earthy and masculine that made her insides tremble.

Instantly, she pushed him away.

Sinclair looked faintly puzzled.

Louisa held herself rigid while he studied her as if she were some foreign species. No man had kissed her in such a cajoling fashion. Richard had been cruel and crude, without a care for her sensibilities. Sinclair might not be cut from that cloth, but he was a practiced seducer with skill to match his insolence.

She almost had her reeling senses under control when he reached out and carefully removed her spectacles. He set them on the desk atop the papers she had pretended to read.

Before Louisa could protest, his hands slid down her arms, lightly imprisoning them at her sides as he drew their bodies together. His mouth descended to hers once more, this time with greater heat. His lips coaxed hers apart, and his tongue flirted shamelessly with hers. She stood there in shock as her defenses retreated, even as something noxious bubbled up within.

Sinclair backed her against the writing table. His thighs pressed against hers, as did the whole long length of him, firm and taut and overwhelming. On and on he kissed her, his mouth crushing hers, and Louisa wanted none of it, but her brain had frozen and all the weapons she might have brought to bear were nowhere to be found.

Dizziness swamped her.

Sinclair didn't know, of course. His hands roamed upward over her arms, his thumbs lingering over the inner curve of her elbows, stroking lightly over the pulse points there. Was it her imagination, or did his fingers lightly graze the outside of her breasts?

Terror settled in the pit of Louisa's stomach. She could not breathe.

He must have sensed something, for suddenly he released her.

They stood there in a silence thick with something horrid and strange.

Louisa tried to swallow, but her throat constricted. "I-I feel..."

"Overwhelmed?" he suggested. "Swept away beyond your wildest imaginings?"

Sheer masculine confidence radiated from those green eyes. Louisa could not begin to right herself. Her stomach lurched.

"No," she said weakly. "I feel —"

"Breathless? Driven by desire?" He bent to nibble at her earlobe.

"*Sick.*" Her innards pitched wildly. "You arrogant man, I am going to be sick!" She pushed him away and put her hands over her face, swaying unsteadily.

Suddenly, Sinclair was pulling her to the window and raising the sash. Louisa inhaled long, deep gulps of fresh air as she fought to calm the tumult. She had no idea how long she stood with her head at the window and his steadying hands at her waist.

At last the sickening sensation retreated. The floor no longer seemed to pitch or spin. Louisa leaned against the window frame, drawing in deep, calming breaths. Finally, she opened her eyes and found the courage to look at Sinclair.

He was staring at her as if she had sprouted two heads. "Jesus. You truly are a Bedlamite."

"And you," she said hoarsely, "are a rapist and scoundrel."

"I have never raped anyone in my life."

Louisa's brain felt thick. She could not make sense of his words. "Those nuns —"

"Are as crazed as you. In fact, I'm beginning to believe that every female in England is short a sheet." He shook his head in bewilderment, then strode from the room.

Louisa clutched the windowsill and took in another great gulp of air.

Chapter Six

The prison hulk rode high in the water. Its guns had been removed, likely salvaged for another ship of the line. Gabriel couldn't yet see whether the gun ports were covered. Even if they were, it wouldn't be difficult to pry the cover loose. But perhaps luck was merely toying with him, seducing him into thinking they might actually carry off this mad scheme.

They'd found the skiff at a dock west of the Woolwich parish church, as Ferguson had arranged. The tide was manageable — just past the high mark and headed low, favorable for a downriver escape. The wind was light, so the usual chaotic Thames chop was absent. The full moon was both a blessing and a curse. It afforded them sufficient light to see, but its reflection on the water could betray them to guards making rounds on the ship. Having done his share of watch duty, however, Gabriel suspected that by this time of night whatever alertness the guards possessed was dulled from boredom.

As the giant rowed them silently toward the hulk, Gabriel wondered whether he had lost his mind. Just days from the hangman's noose, he was flirting with death as if it were a cherished lover. All because of a woman as mad as the blazing moon that bathed the river in its light.

Gabriel eyed the thin wafting clouds, willing them toward that shining silver orb. With luck, they'd obscure the moon for a moment or two so he could scale the anchor cable. But with a woman's coyness, they drifted aimlessly, taking their time.

Watching those insubstantial wisps float airily toward

the moon, Gabriel reminded himself how much he needed the funds Miss Peabody was paying him. He would never have played the hero otherwise. Heroes were fools who paid homage to antiquated notions of glory to mask the madness inside them. His father had been such a man, and if there was one lesson Gabriel had learned from observing the man, it was the folly of self-delusion.

Gabriel prided himself on seeing the world as it was, not as some poor fool thought it ought to be. As long as a man possessed a heightened sense of the ridiculous, he could float quite well amid the flotsam and jetsam of life. He was sure Miss Peabody would disapprove of his artful dodging, but she heartily disapproved of him anyway. Still, he couldn't resist studying her, wishing she was not as crazy as a loon.

She sat motionless in the boat, her glorious hair covered with a dark scarf, her face blackened with coal dust. She wore boys' breeches and looked as much at home in a rough woolen jacket as any seaman. Staring out over the water, her gaze fixed intently on the hulking shadow ahead, she betrayed no hint of nervousness. Determination was etched in every line of her still, quiet silhouette.

What gave her the courage to sail into the teeth of danger, grimly challenging the forces of man and nature with her wild, ridiculous schemes? Doubtless it was the same delusional daring that had sent his father into treacherous seas in a metal coffin to challenge Napoleon's fleet.

She did not even know how to kiss, for God's sake.

Never had his kisses made a woman ill, but it was not wounded pride that made Gabriel rue that scene in her parlor. Her reaction troubled him less than his own: He wanted to kiss her again, to coax that still, stubborn mouth beyond the resistance he suspected was as deep and resilient as that mad spirit of hers.

Hell, that wasn't the half of it. He wanted to do all

manner of outlandish things to her person to erase that solemn contempt in her eyes and make that strange illness of hers vanish. His mind's eye gave him a vision of them making love in this rowboat as the moonlit river rocked them to a different sort of madness.

As Gabriel considered that intriguing image, he looked up and found the giant staring at him. Suspicion darkened the man's eyes. The bastard *knew*. Knew that she had infected him like a plague, that he'd count himself happy if she ever touched him with half the enthusiasm she'd shown caressing that horse.

The clouds picked that moment to cast their flimsy veils over the moon, smothering the treacherous moonlight. Perhaps their luck would hold long enough for him to slip onto the ship. In an hour it would be over. Miss Peabody would have another wronged woman for her flock, and he would have enough money to sail away in a boat a damned sight better than this one.

Unless, of course, they were all at the bottom of the river, riddled with bullet holes. Or clapped in chains and tossed to the fish, or tortured into confessions that would gain them speedy executions.

"Dear Lord," she whispered. "It is enormous."

Gabriel tore his mind from its gloomy contemplation of their fate. He blinked as the ship came into focus. Good God. It was the *Defiance* — among the fastest of warships in its day. The ship had a long and distinguished record, even saw action at Trafalgar.

Her masts and rigging had been removed — all she could do now was play host to depraved humanity, her innards reconfigured into cells. She was a gaping skeleton, far removed from her former magnificence.

The hulk loomed not two dozen yards away. And though it was the dead of night and they had blackened their faces and the river had been smooth enough to allow them to slip through the waters with silent ease, Gabriel saw immediately that they were doomed.

For like a jealous lover, the moon suddenly slipped the flirtatious clouds and unleashed its full, glorious light on their little craft just as two guards rounded the upper deck of the rotting warship. Unless the men were drunk and blind, they would notice them just below.

Instantly, Ferguson stilled the oars, but the current was in play, and the river's steady lapping against the hulk produced little ripples that sucked the rowboat inexorably toward the ship.

In another moment they would crash into the hulk, Gabriel saw. The noise would alert the guards. He reached for the anchor cable and braced his body to absorb the force of the collision. He muffled a grunt of pain as the impact shot down his arms and through his shoulders.

Rebounding, the skiff lurched sideways. Gabriel held onto the anchor cable and slowly rose, straddling the little boat as he tried to stabilize it. Then, with more effort than he would have guessed, he used the cable to slowly pull them back toward the hulk.

They waited, silent and still, to learn whether they were discovered. But the guards' bored tones never wavered, and the two men ambled away.

Gabriel gauged the distance up to the gun deck. In his youth, he would've shinnied up the cable with ease. Tonight, he felt positively ancient. Perhaps that was due to the absurdity of risking his life for a cause he did not regard.

His iron scraper was securely tied to his waist along with the knife he was never without. He had also purloined an assortment of sewing needles and hooks from the Flowers — hoping they wouldn't be unnecessary, since he'd never actually picked a lock but only witnessed a drunken cutpurse demonstrate the skill one night in a Jamaican tavern.

"Keep it steady, but not too close to the ship," he told Ferguson in a low voice. "You want to be able to row like hell once I've handed over the woman. The tide will help, but you'll need to be ready."

"I am coming with you," Miss Peabody said in an urgent whisper.

"We've been over that," Gabriel said. "You'd only slow me down."

"But poor Miss Wentworth will be frightened if you simply present yourself and demand that she come with you. The presence of another woman would —"

"Ruin everything. If I find the sainted Miss Wentworth, I'm going to have my hands full getting her out without alerting the guards. I can't worry about you."

"He's right, Louisa," Ferguson said.

Satisfied that the giant had the willful Miss Peabody well in hand, Gabriel took a deep breath and began to climb.

It had been a long time since his legs had mastered a cable as big around as a man's thigh or edged over a spit of rake without a breast-band to keep him from slipping. Far too long, perhaps He loved ships. As a youth, he'd once stowed away on a trade ship that put in at Sinclair Isle. The irate captain had given him a tongue-lashing before returning him to his father. But the man had also taken pity on him and taught him more than he'd thought possible about boats.

Since then, Gabriel had sailed everything from an Irish curragh to a four-masted barque with ease — although once, in the Royal Navy, his ship was hit broadside by enemy fire and sank. That was no fault of his, however. Ships were a work of art. It was the fools who captained them one had to watch out for.

Climbing up the cable was still child's play, Gabriel discovered. His legs were still nimble, his feet sure, his arms strong.

The rake was trickier. His feet edged carefully along the slender spit of wood. Once he slipped and barely avoided falling into the river. By the time he reached the first gun port, he was breathing hard. Once more, his luck held: The port cover was closed but not nailed shut. Gabriel wedged it open with his scraper and slipped inside.

He could almost imagine Durham, the *Defiance's* distinguished commander, lying in a cot strung amid the cannons, making battle plans to the lapping of the waves. Alas, the ship's glory would not come again. The gun ports were barren, the planking dented and rotting. The odor of gunpowder had given way to the stench of bilge water and human waste; rats scurried in the darkness.

As Gabriel stood motionless in the shadows, letting his eyes adjust to the solitary lantern that hung from one of the beams, he heard within the ship the unmistakable sounds of human degradation. Rage, debauchery, wild laughter. The hulk had been given over to human misery.

Above it all, came a loud, distinctly feminine shriek.

***

He had been gone half an hour. Louisa felt utterly useless. Minute after minute passed without any sign of Sinclair. She sat motionless on the little boat's hard, damp bench, her eyes searching the hulk's dark shadows for any sign of activity.

Only the two guards, their discourse laced with slurred obscenities, jarred the silence as they came around again. But they were either too drunk or too bored to think of looking down to see whether a tiny skiff waited in the shadows to spirit one of their charges away.

Watching Sinclair climb that cable, Louisa realized she never could have done so. The little spit of wood on which he had balanced while prying that port cover loose would not have held her nervous feet. For the good of the mission, it had to be him, alone.

How she resented that.

She didn't trust him. Oh, he wouldn't betray them, for he needed the money. But he did not share her sense of injustice, her burning need to right wrongs. Unlike David, Sinclair had no well of pain and suffering that allowed him to empathize with those less fortunate. He was an empty, hollow man who cared for no one, who set no principle above self-interest. A man like that couldn't be trusted to steer by the same moral compass that guided her.

"He is clever, lass," David said. "If she can be saved, he will do it."

Yes, Sinclair was clever enough to slip through the nooks and crannies of that awful ship, find Miss Wentworth, and free her. Clever enough to kiss a woman who loathed a man's touch and make her sick from confusion and revulsion and a strange kind of longing.

"There!" came David's sharp whisper.

Louisa's gaze followed his upward. Two figures stood silhouetted against the gun port, one of them unmistakably Sinclair, the other a woman.

Wonder and exultation filled her. He had done it! He had saved Alice Wentworth.

Sinclair balanced on the tiny ledge that jutted only a few inches out from the port. Louisa saw him speak to Miss Wentworth, who looked to be paralyzed with fear. Then, to Louisa's amazement, the woman started to laugh.

Her wild cackling echoed over the water. Fear had obviously made the woman hysterical. Didn't she realize the sound would bring the guards?

Sinclair clapped a hand over the woman's mouth. David stood carefully and strained upward, but even with his great height, Miss Wentworth and Sinclair were an impossible distance above them. Worse, David's movement made their boat rock. All Louisa could do was hold onto the sides of the craft and watch disaster unfold above their heads.

When Sinclair removed his hand from Miss Wentworth's mouth, the wild laughter started anew. Louisa heard a muttered oath and caught her breath as Sinclair positioned Miss Wentworth's arms around his neck and leaped for the anchor cable. He caught it, jolting them both. They hung there precariously as the woman's wild screeching turned to shrieks.

"I'm going to die!" she wailed, clawing at Sinclair's head.

"Silence!" came his rough command. Louisa suppressed a shriek of her own as Sinclair's grip on the cable slipped. As he fought to hold on, Miss Wentworth gave a bloodcurdling cry.

"Who goes there?" came a sharp voice from above.

"Sinclair!" Louisa said. "Hurry!"

A grunt was the only reply, and she watched in breathless horror as he inched down the cable, Miss Wentworth clinging to his neck and kicking her legs for all she was worth.

A shot rang out. Miss Wentworth shrieked once more and flailed wildly. Sinclair lost all purchase, and both of them plummeted into the black, swirling waters of the Thames.

David began to row toward the spot where they entered the water. The report of a pistol sounded overhead.

"Halt!" came the sharp order.

For one long agonizing moment, Louisa and David could see nothing of Sinclair and the woman. Then two heads bobbed up not three feet from them. A pair of hands caught at the side of the skiff, and Sinclair heaved Miss Wentworth up and over into the craft. As David worked to prevent the boat from being swamped, Louisa pulled the woman in. But Miss Wentworth's clawing hands were wet and slippery. As Louisa tried to grasp them, another shot boomed across the water.

Louisa lost her balance and tumbled overboard.

The shock of the frigid water immobilized her. Louisa sank like a stone as the river closed over her. Even had she had known what to do, she could not command her limbs.

There was nothing to stop her descent to a watery grave.

And then something did.

Sinclair caught her arms and pulled her up and up, until at last her face broke the surface. As Louisa coughed and drew air in great sputtering gasps, he barked an order to David. To her horror, the little boat containing David and Miss Wentworth began to glide away in the shadows.

Sinclair held her lightly under her arms. "Don't worry. We'll swim for it. The carriage isn't far downriver and the current is in our favor. If those clouds hold and we keep to the shadows, the guards won't pick us out."

Louisa stared up at the thin clouds that had drifted over the moon. Above them loomed the hulk and shouting guards. Her eyes tried and failed to penetrate the unrelenting blackness where river and sky met in an invisible horizon.

"We'll swim just below the surface until we're out of range," he said. "I'll be right beside you. Ready?" He treaded water easily, his legs generating slow, circular movements that seemed to require no effort at all.

"No!" Cold terror filled her.

More gunshots sounded, and bullets rippled the water precariously close to them. "No time to be hen-hearted," Sinclair growled. "If they launch a dinghy, we're done for."

"I-I can't."

"Can't? What do you mean?" he demanded.

"Swim." The word came out a sob.

Incredulous, Sinclair stared at her. "You can't swim?"

Louisa shook her head. Something entered the water at the level of her shoulder. A bullet, she thought, wondering why she had not heard the report.

And then she heard the booming sound. It echoed in her ear and merged with the curse on Sinclair's lips.

Chapter Seven

It wanted only this.

Bad enough that the Wentworth woman had sunk her teeth into his hand and then nearly strangled him by grabbing his neck so tightly he could scarcely breathe. Bad enough that the water around him rippled with the plinking of bullets as the skiff glided away with the object of their misguided adventure shrieking the heavens down. Bad enough that the river's stench filled his nostrils, that his limbs were numb, his head ached, and he was tired as hell. On top of all that, he was going to have to tow Miss Peabody downriver.

Her eyes were wide with horror, her lips trembling, doubtless blue with cold. Even on a spring night, the river had a bite to it. Then there was the undertow.

"Lean back, against me," he told her. "Let the water hold you up."

Her hands flailed wildly, then closed over his eyes and nose.

"God's blood!" Gabriel pried her fingers from his face. But her arms went around his neck, cutting off his air, and then they were both sinking

A strange lightheadedness assailed him, fraying the edges of his awareness. Images of the past rushed in.

"The lad doesn't know how to swim? Where's his father?"

"Riptide's bad. Fetch Aloysius!"

"No time!"

A stranger, a French émigré who'd found his way to Aloysius's island, had braved the swells to rescue a boy foolish enough to think he could build a leaky raft and sail away. Before the man left Sinclair Isle, he taught Gabriel to swim, taught him not to fight a deadly current but wait until it freed him.

Thus Gabriel was long acquainted with treacherous waters. And he was not about to drown in the putrid Thames with Louisa Peabody's hands around his throat.

Lungs burning, he wrenched her body sideways, and put one arm firmly around her. He gave a powerful kick and prayed it would be enough to take them up.

It was.

As they broke the surface, the blessed wind whipped against his face. Gabriel took slow, deep breaths and hoped she had the sense to do the same. She sputtered and gagged, but at last grew still. Likely she was exhausted, but since she'd nearly drowned them both Gabriel spared her little sympathy. If she was too tired to fight, it was the best thing that had happened to him all night. Gabriel locked his arms around her and let the current take them.

They floated away from the hulk, away from the bullets, away from the chaos.

But the moon was playing them false; at times he couldn't see where they were headed. He wanted to shake his fist at the capriciousness of the heavens, but that would take more effort than he had. The carriage was a quarter mile downriver; he hoped they would find it before they passed Woolwich.

At last he saw the skiff. It rested on a sliver of mud, pulled up out of harm's way. The carriage was nearby. Three silhouettes stood on the shore. There was no mistaking Ferguson's great hulking form or that of the woman, whose shrill voice rent the night. He wondered why Ferguson had not shut her up. Surely the man understood the danger.

"It's them!" It was the boy, excited and thrilled, as if he had just won a game of ninepins. Which was how he should be spending his time, Gabriel thought darkly. The lad was too young to risk his neck like this.

Ferguson waded out to them. Gabriel's free arm cut smoothly through the water as he propelled them toward the giant's waiting arms. He shoved Miss Peabody at Ferguson, but his own legs were wobbly, and he had to crawl out of the river on his hands and knees.

She was coughing and sputtering when she finally sat up. Dazed, she looked over at Gabriel.

"We must go," he growled. "The guards will be upon us."

Ferguson pulled Miss Peabody to her feet, and the boy ran to open the carriage door. She stood there for a moment, getting her bearings. Gabriel advanced on her, ready to toss her into the carriage himself.

Then he froze.

Her wet hair clung to her head in matted tangles. The coal dust had washed away, and her face looked unnaturally pale in the glow of the contrary moon. Her wet breeches clung to her legs, outlining them quite clearly. But the worst of it was that the river had stolen her thick woolen jacket. Her wet muslin shirt clung to her, revealing a pair of truly spectacular breasts.

Gabriel swallowed hard.

"That's right," wailed a shrill voice, "forget about Alice. Forget ye ruined my evening. Why, that ruffian over there" — she eyed Gabriel in disdain — "beaned old Tom afore I could give him what the poor man paid for. Now I'll be known as a cheat. Lord save a working girl from the horses' asses in this world!"

Ferguson and Gabriel locked gazes over the top of Miss Peabody's head. Without a word, the giant threw Alice over his shoulder, walked to the carriage, and stuffed her inside.

Yes, it wanted only this.

✳✳✳

Miss Wentworth cursed all the way to Kent. Louisa had never heard such language, and she did not understand much of it. Cold and shivering, the two women shared a blanket on one side of the carriage. Sinclair sat on the opposite seat, arms crossed over his chest, eyes closed. He might have been asleep, but Louisa suspected he had merely adopted the pose to shut them out.

She had to admit that he had done everything expected of him and then some. She owed him her life, as did Miss Wentworth. It was clear that he neither expected nor wished for their gratitude, however. Indeed, he looked as if he would rather be anywhere else.

"Sinclair?" Louisa began, when Miss Wentworth finally lapsed into silence.

His eyelids opened halfway. He regarded her without interest.

Louisa cleared her throat. "I wish to thank you for rising to the occasion tonight. We are both" — she glanced at the other woman — "grateful for your perseverance and courage."

"Yes, I can see that Miss Wentworth is bubbling over with gratitude."

"Horses' asses," Alice muttered.

Louisa flushed. "She has had a great shock. I am sure she will be herself after a bit."

Sinclair's lip curled. "We will all eagerly await that moment."

Alice yanked the blanket up to her neck, uttered another oath, and closed her eyes. In the next minute, she was snoring loudly as the carriage rumbled over the road.

Louisa felt keenly the absence of the blanket. She was wet through and could not stop shivering. What's more, a burning sensation had begun to spread outward from her shoulder. When she touched the source of the warmth, her hand encountered a sticky substance. She stared at the dark blotch growing across her shirt.

"I think," she said slowly, "that I may have been shot."

Sinclair frowned. Then he crossed the space between their seats. Before she could object, he loosened the top laces of her shirt.

Gingerly, he lifted the edge of the fabric to expose her bare shoulder. Louisa saw a dark wound at the base of her collarbone, and the darkness was spreading. Part of the material stuck to the blood and she cried out in pain when he touched it.

Sinclair didn't appear alarmed. "Doesn't look too deep, but it needs proper cleaning, and the bleeding must be stopped."

He tore a strip from the bottom of his shirt and pressed it firmly against her wound. With his other hand, he reached for the blanket to cover her, but Alice gave a great snore and pulled it around herself more tightly.

"Something to be said for letting sleeping dogs lie," Sinclair observed darkly. He slid an arm under Louisa and lifted her onto the opposite seat with him.

The movement jostled her shoulder and she flinched at the pain — and at the intimacy when he reapplied pressure to her wound. He did not bother to hide his irritation as she tried to brush his hand away.

"Pressure is required to stop the bleeding. If you can't abide my touch, you will have to do it yourself."

Louisa tried to hold the makeshift bandage, but her hands trembled. Feeling as helpless as a new kitten, she shook her head, acknowledging defeat.

And so, they drove to Peabody Manor with Sinclair's hand pressed firmly on the front of her shoulder. Louisa felt every rut in the road, every jostling move of the carriage. By the time they arrived home, she was weak with pain.

***

The Flowers lined up to greet them. No matter that it was nearly dawn, they were a veritable bouquet of cheer as the groggy Alice stepped from the carriage.

"You will wish to see your baby right away, I expect," Violet gave her a warm smile.

"She is the cutest thing," Daisy said. "The precious little angel looks just like you."

"This is your home for as long as you wish it," Lily assured her. "Should you like to be Petunia? We do not have a Petunia."

Rose studied Alice. "You could be Petunia, I suppose. Though you look more like —"

"Deadly Nightshade," Gabriel muttered.

Alice stared at them and frowned. Then she opened her mouth and shrieked for rum. The women looked at one another in confusion.

"Miss Wentworth has had a difficult night," Miss Peabody said, brushing away Gabriel's proffered hand as she tried to descend the carriage steps. But she swayed slightly, and he quickly lifted her into his arms.

Lily rushed to her side. "You are hurt!"

"It's but a small injury," she replied faintly as Gabriel carried her up the front steps.

"I'll send Sam for the doctor," Ferguson said.

"No doctor," Rose said. "Too many questions. I'll see to the wound."

"That's right. Make a big to-do over *her*," Alice complained. "What about me? I'm the one what was ripped from a profitable night's work!"

"Nightshade it is," Gabriel said darkly.

Miss Peabody stared up at him, uncomprehending.

"Her new Flower name," he explained. "Although I suppose a case could be made for Stinging Nettle."

"Stop."

"Certainly. It would not do to offend Miss Wentworth's delicate sensibilities." Gabriel shifted the soggy burden in his arms as Daisy held the door open. Would this night ever end?

"I can walk on my own," she said.

He looked down at her. "Yes, you can do everything. You need no help, least of all mine. But if you reopen that wound, I shall be obliged to put pressure to it once more. Not the worst of fates, from my standpoint, but I imagine my touch will once again cause you to retch or go crazy or whatever it is you do. A bit lowering for me, but I shall try to rise above it."

She looked away, but Gabriel had accomplished his goal, which was to prevent her from doing further damage to her wound. He decided to reward himself by contemplating the feminine attributes that had been inadvertently revealed to him tonight.

Doubtless Miss Peabody would sooner slice a man to ribbons than subject herself to masculine admiration. Nevertheless, he had discerned well enough that the revelation of her wet shirt was no mirage. She had perfect breasts, alabaster smooth, with nipples that pointed heavenward through the scant protection of her wet muslin shirt, taunting him the entire time that his fingers had pressed the bandage only inches away. Amazing how much information could be had from a bit of wet fabric.

Yes, her life's blood had been oozing out of her, and he'd been salivating over her breasts. Well, it had been a long night, what with ripping Alice away from the diligent work she was performing on an ecstatic guard, who'd been happily and conveniently bound ankle and wrist to a cot. Not to mention that Gabriel had swallowed half the Thames to get himself and the mastermind of this scheme to safety. He refused to feel guilty at indulging in a bit of lechery.

Besides, he did not think her wound was life-threatening, although she could still contract a fever. That would bear watching, but the Flowers would be vigilant.

Gabriel carried her upstairs and laid her carefully on the canopied bed in her chamber. Several of the Flowers came into the room and busied themselves lighting candles and fluffing her pillow.

Rose put a half-smoked cheroot on a table near the bed. Gently she removed the bandage Gabriel had made from his shirttail and nodded approvingly. "Bleeding's stopped. Good."

"At least some good has come of this night," he muttered.

"*Much* good has come of it," Miss Peabody corrected from the bed, though her voice lacked its usual vigor. "Miss Wentworth has been restored to her child. A grave injustice has been rectified."

"Ah," Gabriel said. "Now you have only to persuade her of that fact."

"I believe she is merely overwrought," she responded, "and so are we all tonight."

"Only those of us you dragged to the river bottom," he corrected. "What possessed you to step into that boat when you didn't know how to swim?"

She leaned back against a pillow. "I didn't know it would be necessary. I did not mean to be a burden."

"So you did not intend to put both of our lives at risk?"

"You have a clever tongue, Sinclair," she said faintly. "You leave a person very nearly defenseless against it."

Gabriel bent over her and was gratified to see her shrink from whatever she saw in his eyes. "*You* defenseless, madam? I think not. Moreover, even you must own that the woman is not what you thought."

She looked away. "Perhaps Miss Wentworth is surprising, but —" Her words trailed off.

"Mr. Sinclair," Rose warned. "Louisa must rest."

But Gabriel was not done. "I am not opposed to surprises, Miss Peabody. But I prefer them without the scent of a harlot."

She lifted her chin. "Miss Wentworth is —"

"A whore. Not to put too fine a point on it."

She flushed. "It is obvious that she has not had the

benefit of education, and I'll grant you that her speech is somewhat coarse, but beneath that rough exterior beats the heart of —"

"A whore, plain and simple," Gabriel said. "I am not judging by that foul mouth of hers, by the way, but by the activity in which she was engaged when I found her. If I remember aright — and a man does not easily forget such a scene — the sainted Miss Wentworth was diligently applying a whip to the back of a guard. Did I mention that he was naked and in the throes of pleasure at the time? Needless to say, the man was in no condition to deter her hasty departure."

She colored. "You have given me a headache. Perhaps you would be good enough to allow me to rest."

Rose eyed Gabriel sternly. "He is just leaving."

He was more than glad to go. Thank God this night's work was done, he thought as he moved toward the door. He could not wait to put distance between him and this garden of madwomen.

At the door, he hesitated. "It looks to be a clean wound, Rose, with no shrapnel. But what's in that river can kill. With an open wound she'll be at risk of infection."

The other woman nodded. "We'll get rid of those foul clothes and treat the wound with basilicum. But she's got a constitution like a horse. My money's on her, bullet wound or no."

"Sinclair?" Miss Peabody said softly.

Gabriel turned.

"Thank you for saving my life."

Hell. She had to ruin his exit by being grateful. "You may add a few more guineas to my fee, if that makes you feel better," he said gruffly. "Good night, madam. Or perhaps I should say good day. That is the sun through the window, if I am not mistaken."

"Your fee," she echoed dully. "Of course. I had nearly forgotten."

"Forgotten? Come, now, Miss Peabody, you cannot believe I would have gone through this night for nothing."

Mutely, she shook her head.

"That would be a fatal mistake indeed." He sauntered out of the room, leaving her to make of that what she would.

Chapter Eight

"**P**uny little mite, ain't she?"

Violet smiled down at the sleeping babe in her arms. "She has missed her mother, Miss Wentworth. We knew you would like to see her as soon as you awoke."

In truth, the women had been surprised that Alice showed no interest in seeing Baby Elizabeth upon her arrival. They told one another that she had simply been overcome by the rigors of the ordeal she had endured.

"Would you like to hold her?" Violet asked.

Alice ignored her. Her gaze traveled around the nursery, where Lily's twins and Daisy's daughter were playing happily. "These yours?"

"No," Violet said. "The little girl is Mary. She is three. The twins, Joshua and Jeremy, are two. We take turns watching them, and there is a woman from the village, Mrs. Hanford, who comes to help sometimes. As you can see, we are quite accustomed to children here. We have tried to take good care of your baby, but there is no substitute for her own mother."

"Yer about ready to pop one yerself, if I don't miss my guess."

Violet colored. "My babe is due in a few weeks."

"No husband in sight, I'll wager."

Taken aback by the woman's blunt speaking, Violet could only shake her head.

Alice gave Violet a knowing wink. "Wish I'd known about those things that stop a man from planting his seed. Sponges and the like." For the first time, her gaze lingered on the babe in Violet's arms. "How did she come to be here?"

"Louisa was shopping in Piccadilly when the commotion began. You had taken a loaf of bread from the bakery window."

"No harm in that," Alice grumbled. "A gel's got to live."

Violet brightened. "Oh, we quite agree. The baker should not have summoned the Watch for such a petty thing. Louisa was outraged. She'd seen you hide your babe under the bakery steps to protect her while you found food."

"Protect her?" Alice scoffed. "Not bloody likely."

Violet eyed Alice uncertainly. "When the Watch took you, Louisa rescued the babe from her hiding place and brought her here. We call her Elizabeth. It seems to suit her, but we are most eager to learn her real name." She waited expectantly.

Alice shrugged. "Elizabeth is as good as any, I suppose."

Violet stared at her. "You...have not named her?"

"Wasn't necessary." Alice pushed an untidy shock of black hair off her face and yawned. "Is there food? I'm a fair way to starving."

Violet's eyes widened in disbelief. "Why did you not name the child?"

"Ye think I'm not much of a mother, don't ye?"

"I-I would never presume…"

Alice gave a bitter laugh. "Some women are cut out for it, some aren't. Ever try to walk the streets with a babe at yer breast? Not good for business, dearie."

Violet stared at the woman, the truth beginning to dawn. "Do you mean to say that you left Elizabeth under those steps intentionally? You abandoned her?"

Alice gave her a crafty smile. "No harm's been done, has it now? She looks well enough."

"But —"

"I'm too hungry for sermons, dearie." Alice brushed

passed her into the hall, where she collided with David as he was about to enter the nursery.

"Forgive me, ma'am," he said quickly. "Are ye all right?"

Alice looked him up and down appreciatively. "Right as rain." Then, with a broad wink at Violet, she added, "Pair of grand shoulders on this one, dearie. Shouldn't wonder if he'd make ye a good man. Big in the shoulders, big elsewhere, I always say." With a shrill cackle, she moved on.

Violet and David stood there, both too mortified to speak. At last he cleared his throat. "Miss Wentworth is nae what we expected."

"No." Violet regarded the sleeping baby in her arms. "Perhaps she will come to feel more charitably toward the babe over time."

David stared at the child nestled between Violet's ample breasts and the place where her own child was growing. "'Tis a shame."

"I-I think I understand some of what Miss Wentworth must have felt," Violet confessed.

"I can nae believe that. Ye and that woman are as different as night and day."

Her clear brown eyes met his. "I did not want the child I am carrying. This babe was not conceived in love."

David looked down at his shoes. Violet suspected he wanted to be anywhere else but here, listening to such a confession. She touched his sleeve, trying to make him understand. "Since coming here, though, I've come to see that the future can be different from the past. Regardless of how it was conceived, I've come to want this child more than life itself." Her voice broke, and she gave him a watery smile. "A babe is the promise that life starts anew each day, don't you think?"

He eyed her hand on his arm and took a step backward, away from her. "I came to take the children outside."

Violet knew she had said too much. David had no wish to engage in confidences; he kept to himself more than anyone she'd known. He took most of his meals in that solitary cottage near the woods and came to the house only to confer with Louisa or take the children on outings.

"They would like that." She hesitated. "So would I."

"Ye should rest," he said quickly. "Getting around can nae be easy when ye are so —" He broke off, reddening.

"Large?" She shot him a rueful smile. "It is all right, David. I know I look like a cow."

His face was scarlet. "I did nae mean that."

"Elephant, then," Violet amended, determined to push past the awkwardness between them. She turned to the children. "Uncle David is here to take you outside."

She thrust the baby into his arms and began to wrestle little Joshua into his shoes.

David stared down at the baby. Her eyes were open now, and she regarded him solemnly. Her mouth pursed in a round "O" shape, as if she was surprised to find him looking down at her from such a height. Suddenly, she smiled. Her tiny, delighted grin spread from ear to ear and, despite her size, seemed to him to encompass the world.

All the world that mattered, anyway.

***

Louisa regarded her reflection in the mirror. The woman who stared back appeared pale, fragile. She looked incapable of rescuing anyone, least of all herself.

The rescues had started with Molly. Two years ago she had come to Louisa's door with Sam, seeking work. What Molly hadn't known was that Louisa herself needed rescuing. Richard had been dead a full month, and she had not gathered strength or resolve even to leave the house. The disaster of her wedding night was seared into her brain. Each day, she awoke to the fresh, full horror of it.

But when Louisa had looked into Sam's big brown

eyes and Molly's solemn ones, she knew, somehow, that her life was about to change.

Molly's husband had been killed on the Peninsula fighting Napoleon's forces. Without his pay, she couldn't keep their small cottage. Finding work was difficult — war widows and families competed for jobs with the wounded men returning home. Molly was in desperate straits, but there'd been no pleading in her tone that day. Louisa instantly took them in.

Gradually, the house came to be filled with joy. Sam was an eager, winsome child. Molly's steady nature grounded them all. Her example taught Louisa it was possible to survive, even thrive, amid adversity. Or, as Molly would say, her brown eyes twinkling, "Be happy while ye live, for ye are a long time dead."

One day, Molly returned from the village market feeling sick. She had stopped to comfort a crying toddler, not realizing the child was severely ill. Molly developed a fever, then rashes and pustules — hallmarks of the pox.

Having worked with animals all her life, Louisa had been exposed to cow pox and wasn't afraid of getting the human form. She tended Molly throughout her illness, to no avail. Molly's death left Sam an orphan and stole the joy Louisa had begun to find in her own life.

For a while she was at sea. She did not know how to raise a child, how to chase the sorrow in her or in Sam. So she turned to what she did know — horses.

Louisa took Sam to the stable and began to teach him as she'd been taught by her father. She showed him how to load the grain buckets, tie a quick-release knot, pick a horse's hooves. She taught him to groom the animal by first brushing against the hair to lift the dirt, then with the hair to remove it. He took to the work quickly.

David arrived six months after Molly's death, invalided home after a grievous time in a French prison, with scars to show for it. He arrived at Louisa's door with a letter from Molly giving him her direction. When Louisa told him of his sister's death, he showed little reaction, though she knew him well enough now to realize he'd been riven with grief. David felt deeply, but kept his feelings to himself.

Sam needed his uncle, and David needed him. Louisa offered David work and the caretaker's cottage near the stable; after a minute's hesitation, he accepted both. He took Sam to live with him, and the boy had thrived under David's steady, strong guidance.

But David was a man of few words, and it was months before he and Louisa were easy in one another's company. Now, of course, they were comrades in arms.

They hadn't started out to rescue mistreated women. One day when Louisa was shopping in Newton, she'd seen a woman — Lily — turned out in the street with her two babies. Louisa could see no course but to bring them to Peabody Manor. As with Sam, Lily's twins brought joy to the house. Lily herself was even-tempered and kind. Louisa could not fathom why anyone would have treated her so cruelly.

Helping Lily had felt right. Gradually, Louisa began to wonder whether there might be a higher purpose for her life — an obligation to help others with the money Richard had left her, a chance to forge good from evil.

As word spread that Louisa offered sanctuary for those in need, other women came, often with their children. Most did not stay long, but some, like Daisy, did. It was Daisy, married to a farmer, who tended the lush flower garden near the house.

Some of the women had committed crimes. But it seemed to Louisa that women who ran afoul of the law were treated more harshly than men, punished not only for breaking the law but also for violating the rules of female behavior. Moreover, many of their "crimes" arose from trying to maintain a meager existence and feed their children.

Louisa began to research the subject and found herself much moved by Samuel Romilly's treatises on the plight of women prisoners. Just three years ago, a leading Quaker Reformer visited the women's section of Newgate and found 300 women crowded into three rooms. Many were ill, but received no medical care.

Rose's rescue resulted from Louisa's research; she had read florid newspaper accounts of the "Black Widow" and wondered if they'd been embellished, perhaps to sell papers. Since Rose had lived in a village not far from Newton, Louisa drove there one day to learn more. The village rector's wife had been talkative; Rose's first husband had been drunken and abusive, she said, and the village magistrate had seen no reason to think his death unusual.

But widowhood left Rose without resources, so she remarried quickly — too quickly for the village wags. Her second husband was more philanderer than abuser; they got on well enough, until he turned up dead in his bed one morning. An official inquiry was begun at the quarter session but no conclusions drawn.

By the time Rose married for a third time, bets were taken at the village pub as to how long the third husband, a blacksmith, would survive — especially since his temper was known to rise with drink. When the man drew his last breath after consuming Rose's porridge, the magistrate forwarded the case for the Assizes. There were rumblings of witchcraft, though the vicar's wife assured Louisa that no one truly believed such a thing.

Louisa studied the records of Rose's trial. The local quack had testified to a peculiar odor about the deceased man's breath; with no more evidence than that it was decided he'd been poisoned. Under questioning, Rose made no pretense of mourning. She agreed she disliked her husbands, save one, whose name she could not immediately recall. In the end, she drew a death sentence.

Masquerading as a prison matron was simplicity itself, Louisa discovered. Matrons were largely invisible; they existed only so judges could claim, as they sent a female defendant to her fate, that proprieties had been maintained. Instead of escorting Rose to prison after sentencing, Louisa had simply walked them through the prison gates to the carriage where David awaited.

In retrospect, however, Louisa realized her elation at that success had given her false confidence. Violet's rescue nearly ended in disaster; Alice's would have, if Sinclair had not been there.

Sinclair's admonition about Sam had stung, but he was right: Louisa had put Sam in harm's way by involving him in even a minor role. For all that he was growing into a strapping lad, he was not an adult. From now on, he would stay behind.

Louisa sighed. She had thought to go downstairs today for the first time since Sinclair had deposited her in bed three days ago; looking at her reflection, she wasn't sure. Her hair, tied by a ribbon at the nape of her neck, was flat and lifeless. Her birthmark stood out against the unnatural pallor of her skin. Her haunted expression gave her a fearful air, as if something dark and dangerous stalked her.

Something did.

Doubt.

What, really, was she doing with her life? Miss Wentworth did not seem to welcome her rescue. Louisa's plan had been wildly ambitious; although she had done her best to research prison hulks and all that had been written about them, she was woefully ignorant of ships.

Louisa had thought this path her rightful calling, but uncertainty filled her now. It gave her a haunted look, the same one she'd worn two years ago gazing into this very mirror, distraught over her father's words.

"Time to earn your keep," he'd snarled, deep into his

third bottle.

She had kept his books, managed his household, supervised his stable, tried to keep him from gambling away every penny they had. It wasn't enough.

"Time you made yourself useful, girl. Milbrook's chit snagged herself an earl, and she's not even a beauty like you. If you'd shown the slightest interest in a Season, I might have given you time to choose a husband. But I'm into Richard Dunworth for five thousand pounds. He won't forgive such a debt unless you marry him."

Richard was a reputed libertine, but her father had brushed aside her objections. "A debt's a debt, and you're the only currency I possess. If it's the marriage bed that worries you, take comfort in the fact that after you give the man his heir, he'll leave you alone."

Louisa had listened in shock, wondering why her father cared so little for her that he would consign her to life with a barbarian. In the end, she had stood at the altar, all the while eyeing Richard's large, cruel hands and wondering what would happen on their wedding night. Soon enough, she found out.

Afterward, she vowed no other man would touch her. And none had. Even David kept his distance, knowing the distress even accidental physical contact caused her.

Yet she'd put her life and her person in Sinclair's hands, and he had not failed her. Louisa couldn't forget how his strong arms secured her as they floated downriver, how his fingers staunched the blood from her wound. She owed her life to a scoundrel who had touched her body more intimately than any man, save Richard. But Richard's kisses had revolted her. Sinclair's unsettled her in an entirely different way.

He was a clever rogue for whom seduction surely was as easy as breathing. Even as Louisa had fought that dizzying nausea when he kissed her, a part of her had been mesmerized by the mischievous promise in his eyes.

She did not want to know the secrets lurking in those green depths. Her world was the way she wanted it. Widowhood had freed her from masculine cruelty. Richard's death had been a rough sort of justice.

The women she and David rescued had become her family, the only one she wanted or needed. She certainly had no wish to engage in any meaningful way with a rogue who ran roughshod over hearts. Above all, she would not turn him into a hero.

And yet. *And yet.*

Sinclair could have saved his own skin and let her sink to the bottom of the river. He could have abandoned her with impunity, with no one the wiser.

He had not.

Doubtless it was the money. Even now, he would be downstairs, waiting for his due.

It was past time to face him.

Moving her shoulder was difficult — she'd never manage a frock with buttons, and she wasn't about to call one of the women to help her dress. She threw on the pair of Sam's breeches she used for riding, and one of her father's old, ill-fitting shirts.

But Sinclair wasn't downstairs. Louisa walked to the stables without encountering anyone but Sam, who brightened when he saw her. If she looked like death, he did not remark on it.

"I put the two saddles in with Midnight last night, like you told me," he said. "And carrots."

"Did he eat them?"

"Right off the saddles, like you said. Does that mean he's ready to be ridden?"

"Not yet," Louisa said. "Leastways not with a saddle." She eyed the stallion, looking remarkably sanguine out in the paddock as he nosed at some hay. "He may allow a bareback rider."

Sam's eyes widened. "Can I try?"

Even as Louisa shook her head, another thought formed. She had neglected the estate books, which would annoy Frederick should he decide to personally deliver the funds she'd requested for Sinclair. The sum was large, but perhaps he would send his man of business to deliver it. Still, she ought to be prepared in the event her trustee wished to personally inspect the ledgers.

She would get that chore out of the way, and then judge for herself just how successful Midnight's training had been.

***

If he had to endure one more meal with that woman shrieking in wild laughter, Gabriel knew he would go insane. As he strode away from the house, he had half a mind to seek out Ferguson and discover once and for all whether the man had a secret source of food. Daisy's eggs and onions sat in his stomach like lead.

But he did not head to Ferguson's cottage. His feet took him to the stable instead. Three days of waiting for Miss Peabody to recover — and her trustee to send funds — had made him restless.

Four horses were in the stable, along with a gig and two large carriages, one of them an antiquated landau. But he wouldn't need a carriage for this errand, so he focused on the horses.

The black stallion was out in the paddock, prancing and frisky in the sun. He was a rare prize, all sleek muscle and peerless bone.

"Easy to see which of you is the early riser," Gabriel chided the mares. He wondered whether anyone would object if he appropriated one of them for a time.

He found Sam in the tack room, hunched over a long open box, concentration etched on his features. Gabriel endured a moment of stark recognition as the boy carefully wound a string around a small wooden top as if it were the most important task in the world. He placed the top inside the box, yanked the string, and watched as the top twirled madly, only to collapse on its side after a few seconds. The lad's shoulders slumped in defeat.

"It helps to wind the string from top to bottom," Gabriel offered.

"Mr. Sinclair!" Sam beamed. "You've played skittles?"

"A time or two." Enough for two lifetimes, Gabriel thought. "I carved a set for myself when I was about your age. It helped the days pass." But not fast enough.

"This was my father's," Sam said proudly.

Gabriel studied the smoothly polished wood, the intricately carved opening from one section of the box to another, the deftly turned scoring pins. Time had removed the set's sheen, but obviously not its luster for Sam. "Did he make it himself?"

"I don't know," Sam confessed. "I don't remember him much. He died on the Peninsula. My mother said he was a hero."

Gabriel decided not to notice the boy's faltering tone. "Wrapping the string from the bottom up makes for an unstable spin."

He knelt and, as though it had not been over a decade since he'd played the game, wound the string around the top, careful to keep his index finger over the coils to prevent tangling. Gabriel threaded the string through the box's launch slot and gave it a firm, steady tug.

The top spun through the narrow opening, knocking over one pin after the other.

"A hundred points!" Sam exclaimed. "Two hundred!" When the top finally went down, Sam eyed Gabriel with unconcealed admiration.

Gabriel looked into the lad's face, alight with excitement, and knew his errand would be delayed. "Here," he said. "I'll teach you."

They worked on Sam's technique for the better part of an hour, and Gabriel could not help but feel he was staring his own youth in the face. He hoped Ferguson had the sense to stop allowing the boy to participate in Miss Peabody's adventures. The responsibility was too heavy for his thin shoulders, the danger too real. He was entitled to a childhood, for God's sake.

"Look!" Sam exclaimed as the top knocked down pin after pin. "Care to go another round?"

Careful, Gabriel told himself. It wouldn't do to let himself get drawn in. "I'm afraid I have an errand. I thought to take one of the horses. It's not far."

Sam sprang to his feet. "Take Mainstay. She hasn't had her exercise this morning. You'll find her the eager sort."

"Must be only female around here who is," Gabriel muttered.

"What did you say, sir?" Sam lugged a saddle toward the horse.

"Nothing." Gabriel appraised the roan. A frisky mount, no doubt about it. But she took the saddle without complaint. He swung himself up and was on the point of leaving when he chanced to look back at Sam. The lad was regarding him with a hopeful look.

"What is it, boy?" he asked.

"I didn't know if you needed any help, sir. Finding your way about and all. I could go with you if you did." The boy flushed.

"I do not need help."

"Oh." Sam looked crestfallen. "Well, if you change your mind, sir —"

Gabriel's gaze narrowed. "When did I become 'sir'? If I recall aright, you've been anything but thrilled with my presence here."

Sam grinned shyly. "That was before."

"Before?" Gabriel had a sense of foreboding.

"Before you rescued Louisa. And Miss Wentworth, of

course. David told me how you sneaked onto that ship right under the noses of those guards."

So that was the way of things. But he wasn't looking to earn a halo. "They were drunk as skunks," Gabriel said. "Wouldn't have noticed if I'd lit a keg of gunpowder under them."

"He said you dodged those bullets." Awe filled Sam's eyes.

Gabriel shook his head. "Those guards wouldn't have been able to hit the *Victory* broadside if she pulled to within an inch of their guns."

"But —"

"There are no heroes in this world, Sam — only fools with dumb luck," Gabriel said, more harshly than he intended. "Keep a knife at your side and your wits about you, and you'll fare better than most. And never make the mistake of relying on anyone other than yourself."

Gabriel flicked Mainstay's reins. He did not look back, for he did not want to see the disappointment on the boy's face. The quicker the lad lost his illusions, the better.

Sam knew his horseflesh, though. Mainstay made short work of the countryside as they headed east. Too quickly, Gabriel found himself following the winding banks of the Medway. Suddenly, the old village lay before him, its thatched roofs and stone cottages seemingly unchanged since he'd last seen them. Beyond, on the cliffs above the sandy bay, its crumbling turrets silhouetted against the blazing sun, lay the ruins of Sinclair Castle.

To the east of everything. Reaching for the light, but not quite finding it.

Gabriel rode past the village toward the pile of stones that had once contained his own illusions. Dismounting, he looped the reins around the branch of a gnarled tree.

Here was where his dreams were born and where, but for fate and his father's madness, they would have been nurtured for many more years before evaporating in the inevitable dust of disillusionment. As he looked around, Gabriel realized that time had done what his memory could not: erased all trace of his boyhood.

The years had not been kind to the castle. The towers, remnants of a past when invaders were as plentiful as the terns that likely now nested in the rafters, teetered precariously over the walled courtyard. A small boy would not be able to climb to the top now or stare out to sea imagining himself as a victorious Sir Francis Drake sailing home with treasure for his queen. The walls on which Gabriel had balanced as a lad, pretending to swing the lead line around his head and heave it into the sea, were crumbling remnants of their past glory.

The outbuildings, constructed by later generations of Sinclairs who sought more comfort than a drafty castle provided, had fared better. His grandfather had built the manor house between the village and the castle gates. Gabriel had grown up in this warm and spacious home, where sunshine chased the sea-damp chill.

Some of its windows were broken, he saw. Still, the house looked mostly intact, perhaps because it had been rented out for a time after he and his father moved to the island.

Now that he looked closer, however, he saw that the porch where his mother had sat on a summer's night, straining to see her needlework in the waning light, was little more than rotted boards and broken railing. The field where they gathered to celebrate St. Thomas's Day had gone to weeds.

No, there was nothing left of his childhood. And he had known it would be this way, known from the first time he walked out of Miss Peabody's house and smelled the sawgrass and salt marshes on the wind, that he must come to this place he never expected or wanted to see again.

When he was a boy — too small to know boyhood dreams could lurk in a forgotten corner of a man's brain —

Gabriel dreamed of restoring the castle of his forebears. Dreamed of setting legions of craftsmen to work on that magnificent pile of stones and giving it back the glory of the time when it had stood against lawless invaders bound for London and the head of a king.

Back then, he'd climbed on the castle walls and seen his destiny in the ships bringing riches from afar, spreading the news of exotic new worlds. Adventure, daring deeds, spectacular feats — all would be his. And when he grew past the age of daring, he would return to his ancestral home and fill it with children of his own. A family that would bring the past full circle, create new memories to cherish with the old.

But the castle was as useless and broken as his youth. Gabriel turned away, wishing he had not felt the ill wind that had called him to this most desolate of places in the shadow of dreams.

And then he saw her.

Pale and swaying on the enormous black stallion — bareback, in breeches and a man's shirt, her golden hair held back with a careless ribbon. Her attention was riveted on the Grecian marble edifice a half-demented Sinclair had built near the castle long ago, hedging his bets against the whims of fate. Her gaze drifted to the ground and the fallen statue that lay there.

Gabriel strode toward her, resenting the intrusion. She had no right to follow him to his abandoned, wretched castle.

"I see you have discovered the temple." His voice was hard.

She frowned. "Temple?"

"To Apollo. God of light, healing, justice, and all that nonsense. That would be the god himself there on the ground, in pieces." He pointed to it, thinking of how this must appear to her like so much madness.

What was wrong with him that he'd sought meaning in

this pile of useless stones? It was merely the past; it held only as much truth and meaning as he granted.

So why did it hold so much more than he wished?

When she stared at him blankly, it occurred to him that he might seem incoherent. Perhaps he was as mad as his father.

And then she smiled, a tentative upward curve of her lips that shot to an unfamiliar place in him that held a bevy of broken dreams. A place he never visited voluntarily.

"Apollo," she repeated slowly. "Of course."

She slid off the horse and landed on the ground in a formless heap.

Chapter Nine

Louisa awoke to find herself lying next to the statue, looking up at a face ringed by a fiery mane that evoked the sun god himself. Not Apollo — Sinclair. His words soon brought her awake with a cold dash of reality.

"God's blood, woman. If you are bent on killing yourself, must you always involve me?"

Groggily, Louisa sat up — or tried to. Something heavy rested on her shoulder: Sinclair's firm, restraining hand. "Be still," he ordered. "You've reopened that wound."

His fingers pressed against her bandage, and she saw that he had untied the laces of her father's shirt. Never mind that he was right — a small blot of blood had seeped through the bandage — Louisa was mortified at how much of her was revealed for his inspection.

"You are not my guardian angel," she retorted. "I can take care of myself."

"About as well as you can swim, I imagine."

Louisa flushed. "I am perfectly capable of riding —"

"You've done nothing more strenuous than keep to your room for three days, but today you decide to ride over hill and dale without even a saddle to cling to. No wonder you fainted."

She lifted her chin. "My pace was quite sedate. We are but a few miles from Peabody Manor."

Sinclair eyed Midnight, nibbling on clover a few yards from the tree where he'd tied Mainstay. "That's more than you ought to have ridden on that stallion. He's anything but sedate."

Louisa brushed his hands away and fumbled to retie the laces. Her fingers had never felt so clumsy as now, with Sinclair watching. Finally she finished and struggled to her feet. He made no move to help her up, for which she was grateful. She wanted no further opportunities to be indebted to the man or to give herself over to his ministrations. When she shot him a triumphant look, he merely regarded her with a brooding gaze.

"You followed me," he said. "Why?"

How to explain the sudden urge that had seized her? She had planned only a brief turn on Midnight to see whether the horse would take a bareback rider. But as she looked up from her tedious ledger work, she spied Sinclair through the window on Mainstay, heading east. Something in her had panicked, thinking he was leaving them, despite the fact he had not been fully paid. Why his departure should send her into such a state she did not know.

Louisa cleared her throat. "As you say, I have kept to my room for several days. It was a fine morning, and when I saw you riding, I decided the exercise would do me good."

Turning away from his scrutiny, she regarded her surroundings more closely. The temple and fallen statue seemed wholly incongruous, although perhaps they fit with the overall air of decay. A few dozen yards away was a large manor house with cracked windows and a front door that sat crookedly on its hinges. The ruins of a large castle sat atop a chalky cliff overlooking a picturesque cove.

"What is this place?"

His gaze was hard. "It is what you perceive it to be: ruins of lives past."

"That explains nothing," Louisa said. "I don't understand you, Sinclair. You confound my expectations."

"I did not know you had expectations of me, Miss Peabody. I am flattered."

Her face grew warm. "One comes to expect that a

person will act in a certain way based on his reputation and, er, past actions —"

"Speak plainly, woman," he growled. "What in heaven's name have I done now?"

She hesitated. "It is what you have *not* done."

"Ah." His brow cleared. "I am a known criminal, yet I have not murdered you in your bed or robbed you of all you possess. The lad thinks I hung the moon, and the Flowers are ever-solicitous. It confounds me also. What do you suppose is the reason I have not run amok?"

"You are making sport of me."

He shrugged. The man was as impenetrable as the statue at her feet.

"I had every reason to expect the worst from you," she conceded, "and yet you rescued Miss Wentworth and saved my life —"

"Only because you are paying me. When might I expect to see the balance of the funds?"

Louisa tried not to show her disappointment. Heroism notwithstanding, the man had not a shred of altruism. "My trustee has not replied to my urgent request, but I promise you shall have it soon."

"And you never break promises."

Sinclair's tone was mocking, but she sensed that his barbs were aimed more at himself than her. She studied him more closely. "You were being truthful when you said you didn't assault those nuns."

His mouth thinned. "Careful, madam. You cannot replace these devil's horns with a halo."

"I thought you were joking when you said you'd never raped anyone," she said.

"Your estimation of my sense of humor is gratifying."

Louisa frowned. "You didn't commit any of the crimes of which you were convicted, did you?"

His gaze raked over her. "No."

"Then why —" She halted. Perhaps she was not as fit

as she thought, for a peculiar light-headedness suddenly swept her. "I-I think I will just sit for a moment."

Instantly Sinclair's hand was under her elbow, easing her down to the step beside him. "Bend your head down," he commanded.

Why was she always at her worst with this man? "I am not usually so weak," she protested.

"You have been wounded. Anyone would have difficulty." He patted her back lightly, in a consoling gesture.

"There! That is just what I mean. Now you are being solicitous. It is not what I expect."

Sinclair did not reply. For a moment his gaze fixed on the castle ruins silhouetted on the hill. His hand moved absently in idle circles over her back.

Louisa felt herself relax into his touch. An odd contentment crept over her as she inhaled the salty air and regarded the horseshoe-shaped cove where the river widened to the sea. On a clear day, the view from the castle turrets would have been magnificent. Perhaps one could even see the Continent in the far distance.

She stole a look at Sinclair. His attention still seemed elsewhere. Gingerly, she edged away.

"Don't." He turned to her, his eyes now focused on her. He reached out and tucked a strand of her hair behind her ear.

She froze.

"You do not like to be touched."

"No."

"Did that husband of yours manage to alienate your affections in those few short hours you were wed?"

Louisa stared at her feet. "There was nothing short about them."

Sinclair touched her chin, tilting her face upward. "I should hate to be the man who tries to use Louisa Peabody ill. The very thought strikes terror into my heart."

"I'll thank you not to make jokes at my expense."

"It was no joke. Fierce women make my knees grow weak. I can do aught but tremble in their presence."

Louisa glared at him.

He sighed. "There seems to be little room for mirth in that brainbox of yours."

"Perhaps I do not possess your careless disregard for injustice or your easy tolerance of evil."

"You wound me, madam. To suggest that I sit cheek and jowl with evil, no less." His gaze narrowed. "I believe I must demand satisfaction."

"Must everything be a source of amusement for you, Sinclair?" Louisa demanded. "Is there nothing that provokes you?"

"Why, yes, Miss Peabody." His voice softened, wrapped around her name like a caress. "*You* provoke me." There was a pause. "Alas, I fear I must kiss you."

In the next moment, his mouth brushed hers. Though it was only a fleeting touch, it should have repulsed her. Strangely, it didn't. When his lips lingered, she allowed herself to feel their softness, their warmth. The sensation was surprisingly pleasant, even when the pressure of his mouth increased.

Sinclair's hand slid to her waist, drew her against his chest. She felt his solid strength, his power against her softness. An unfamiliar warmth engulfed her.

Panic came at her in a sudden, overwhelming rush.

Louisa pushed at him. Instantly he released her.

"Take a deep breath," he said quietly.

She couldn't. Her breathing was too fast, too shallow. Her airway constricted. Her hands went to her throat.

Sinclair caught them, gently raised her hands above her head. "Breathe slowly." His voice was soothing, calm.

Louisa drew in a tiny, shaky breath.

"More slowly. To my count. One, two, three…"

She managed a longer, deeper breath. He nodded

encouragingly. "Now exhale slowly. Lower your arms. To my count. One, two…"

Concentrating on his cadence helped. Gradually, the terror began to recede. Her breathing grew less labored.

"So it is true," he said. "You cannot abide a man's touch."

Tears sprang to her eyes. She felt foolish, defective. Richard's legacy. Even from the grave, he had marked her.

Sinclair did not look as if he thought her defective. Instead, his mouth curved into a wry smile. "Most women are usually captivated by the first kiss, enslaved by the second. I've rarely had to resort to a third, but perhaps with you it might be necessary."

Louisa's eyes widened in alarm. Surely he did not intend —

"That was a joke." He sighed. "It's quite all right to make a joke now and then, Miss Peabody. Sometimes that is the only alternative to despair. Give me your hand."

"What?"

"Your hand."

A new, disarming light flared in his eyes, but Louisa extended her hand anyway.

He placed her palm flat against his chest. The curvature of his chest muscles molded to her hand, the masculine curves so very different from her own. Louisa felt the rapid pounding of his heart through his shirt.

"See? My heart is racing, just like yours," he said. "That is the way of things between men and women. 'Tis as natural as breathing."

Louisa flushed. "I am not a child. I know what it is like." She tried to reclaim her hand, but he covered it with his own and held it there, against his chest.

"Do you?" His eyes were grave.

"Yes. Messy and painful and ugly and degrading."

"No room for argument there, I see," he said solemnly. "Alas, for it would have been pleasant to make love to you at Apollo's feet and refute those prejudices of yours."

She wrenched her hand away. "Arrogant man."

"Ah. You are far too smart to be taken in by an unprincipled scapegrace."

Louisa frowned. "You said you didn't commit those crimes."

"But I never claimed to be other than a scoundrel."

Her head was beginning to ache. "Who are you, Sinclair?" she demanded. "Why do I find you in this moldy place, waiting to torment me with jests and barbs? You are as slippery as an eel. I am certain I shall dance with glee on the day you are gone from my life."

Suddenly, it was as if a curtain descended, banishing the warmth and charm from his gaze. When he spoke, his voice sounded distant.

"I am the twentieth Baron Sinclair, the last of my line. This castle is mine and the temple and all of these ruins and the manor house and the land for as far as you can see. And no one is alive to know it, Miss Peabody, or rejoice in the fact that the prodigal has returned at last."

His raw, bitter grin tore a gaping hole in her heart.

***

"The men in my family have a tendency to madness. It skips generations here and there, but the odds are greatly against any Sinclair escaping this life with his sanity intact."

Gabriel did not look at her. He did not wish to see whatever revulsion lay in her eyes. "Legend has it," he continued in a self-mocking tone, "that the first Sinclair anyone knows about — Peregrine — devised a way to magnify the light from the stars to aid nighttime navigation. It involved parabolic mirrors and very precise mathematical calculations. King Richard II was only twelve at the time, so naturally he was captivated."

When she did not speak, he plunged ahead. "The king expressed his pleasure by ordering that very castle you see on the cliff built for Peregrine. It came with a vast parcel of land, and the king issued a writ acknowledging Peregrine's special talents. A favorite bedtime story for later generations of Sinclairs was Peregrine's invention of a unique adhesive to hold the stars in place. Perhaps it will not surprise you to know that particular claim was never substantiated."

She regarded him curiously — and who could blame her? He had doubtless rendered her insensible with his barrage of babble. Recklessly, Gabriel pressed on: "We are a family of inventors, you see, albeit misguided ones. Perhaps you will see the irony, since it all began with Peregrine's effort to guide sailors at night."

A slight furrow creased her brow.

"You are puzzled," he said. "Perhaps you are still mulling the meaning of 'parabolic.' Think of it as a U-shaped sphere that collects and focuses waves of light. Unless that description confuses; in that event, feel free to disregard it entirely."

He was tossing a great incoherent jumble of words at her, with no purpose other than to watch that tiny furrow in her brow deepen and the concentration in her lovely blue eyes intensify. Gabriel yearned to know what was transpiring in the brain under that lovely golden hair.

"Inventors?" she said at last.

"Ah. You found your voice. Clearly, you are not put off by a bit of madness. That is fortunate, since you will find plenty of it here. All around, in fact." He made a sweeping gesture that did not entirely exclude himself.

Her gaze focused intently on him. Gabriel found himself wondering how her features might look when perceived from a different angle, say, with her in a prone position looking up at him with fire in those sapphire eyes.

But no. This was the woman who could not abide a man's touch. He cleared his throat. "It was not Peregrine but his descendant Harold who started all the trouble. Adored everything Greek. He constructed this shrine to Apollo, thinking it would gift him with insights into the future, rather like the ancient oracle at Delphi."

She smiled suddenly. "And did it?"

Gabriel found himself rendered nearly senseless by the fact that Louisa Peabody could smile such a smile. Indeed, he thought he might die of shock at the sight of those dusky lips turning upward in such a beguiling fashion.

"Er, no," he managed. "Harold was thus forced to conclude that Apollo's skill at prophecy was not transferrable. But the god's passion for justice struck a chord in him. In an effort to capture a bit of immortality for himself, Harold became a meddler."

"A meddler." Now her smile began to turn in a different direction — down, as if she saw where he was going with this.

Just as well, he thought. It wouldn't do to get too lost in that smile of hers. "Meddled in people's lives. Conceived the strange notion that he could right all the wrongs in the world." At the obvious parallel to her own circumstances, he had the grace to look apologetic. "Unfortunately, he unwisely tried to tell Henry VIII he had no right to ruin the lives of all those wives. Got beheaded for his trouble."

Her eyes widened.

Well, at least she was not casting up her accounts at the thought of him touching her.

"It was the merest stroke of luck that Henry did not seize the Sinclair lands and banish the family," he added. "Perhaps he was caught up in the task of disposing of yet another wife. For whatever reason, Sinclairs lived quietly for almost two hundred years. And despite a flirtation with peerage — the Stuarts were intent on packing the House of Lords — we've always been more feudal than princely. Except with our obsessions. Those, I'm afraid, are writ large."

Gabriel was heartened to see a spark of renewed

interest supplant indignation in that gaze. "Eventually, trouble surfaced anew in the person of Aloysius Sinclair, my father. He, too, had a passion for inventing things."

Now she appeared keenly interested — a hundred times better than nausea.

"Once, he rigged an elaborate device for feeding chickens," Gabriel said. "It required the birds to peck at levers, which would send a quantity of corn down a chute and into a trough. The idea was that when they weren't hungry, the corn would remain stowed in a large bag at the top of the chute. His intention was that the corn not be wasted but rationed to the birds' needs."

She clapped her hands in delight. "He rigged it so the chickens fed themselves!"

Hell. He might have to become her slave, merely for grasping the concept of his father's chicken feeder so quickly.

Gabriel took a deep breath. "What a quick mind you have, Miss Peabody. However, it was only a theory. And therein lies the downfall of many an inventor: Theories exist to be proven — or disproven, as in this instance."

"What happened?"

"He failed to take into account the nature of chickens. Turns out they are incessant peckers. Hungry or no, they have very little else to do."

"Too much feed ended up in the trough?"

Gabriel regarded her solemnly. "Worse. When my father came to check on his invention, he found the chickens buried under a mountain of corn. Not a single kernel remained in the bag or a trace of life in the chickens. Their pecking had caused a fatal avalanche — they pecked themselves to death, as it were."

Her smile blossomed anew. Truly, it was a thing of beauty. Gabriel wanted to kiss her again. In his mind's eye he saw himself working his way over the softness of her lips, along the graceful curve of her jawline, down the smooth column of her neck, past the edges of her shirt, over that unsightly bandage —

"I'm sure every inventor has his setbacks," she said, pulling him back to reality. "It makes for a good story, all the same."

Yes, the foibles of past Sinclairs — real and imagined — rolled off his tongue with ease. Gabriel had loved hearing the stories as a child. His mother had embraced the Sinclair legends with love and humor, and she alone had been able to calm his father when his inventions went awry. But she had died, Robert had perished in Egypt fighting the French, and Aloysius had quietly lost his mind. The eccentricities of Gabriel's ancestors were no longer something to laugh about around the hearth on a winter's eve.

Doubtless the signs of his father's madness had been there all along, even in that halcyon time of Gabriel's childhood. Grief had merely unleashed the lunacy.

"My father did not stop with the chickens," he said. "His greatest invention was to come. Unfortunately, it was also his most useless."

"What was it?"

"An underwater boat." His voice held no pride. Aloysius's obsession for the thing in the cave had stolen the last vestiges of his rationality. It had robbed Gabriel of his father when he needed him most.

"I have never heard of such." She eyed him in wonder. Since her blue gaze usually ran to ice when it was trained on him, Gabriel accepted her regard, even though it was caused by the invention he'd loathed.

"Oh, they've been around in one form or another for centuries, envisioned as a weapon for naval warfare," he said. "The idea is to slip under an enemy ship and deliver an explosive charge to the hull. But no one has figured a way to stay submerged long enough or to navigate effectively below the surface. After my mother and brother died, my father threw his effort into devising such a craft.

He wanted to avenge my brother's death by blowing up the French fleet."

Her lovely blue eyes transformed into limpid pools of empathy. He might have known she would have great quantities of that.

Gabriel took a deep breath. "My father bought an island east of Sheerness, which he believed would be in the path of any French strike at London. He moved the two of us there and began testing his craft."

"How intriguing." Her expression held no pity, thank God. Instead, she merely regarded him in that earnest fashion — as if his words *meant* something.

Didn't she see the truth — that his father had ruined everything?

Gabriel felt his moorings slip. He tried to reel himself back. "There were rumors that Boney was digging an underwater channel to England. The War Office was suddenly very interested by my father's work. Then Nelson broke the French fleet at Trafalgar, and —"

"The War Office lost interest."

Again, that quickness.

Empathy. Brilliance. Beauty. That these should exist in the woman who'd been such a trial was wholly unjust. And, quite possibly, irresistible.

"My father did not," Gabriel said. "He devoted the rest of his life — less than a year, as it happened — to the submersible. He would sail it out looking for French warships. I often went with him, since my arms were better at turning the crank that propelled the craft. Once he found an old French frigate and managed to attach a charge, but it failed to explode. He never stopped trying. Like Harold, he had pledged himself to seek justice."

"I see."

"You cannot possibly." Emotion gave his voice a rough edge. He willed her to understand, no longer caring why it was important to him that she did. "You cannot fathom the depth of my father's madness. He envisioned Sinclair Isle as a base for launching all manner of avenging missions on the French. He took to calling himself king, though the only subjects he had were me and the French refugees who occasionally landed there."

Gabriel could no longer look into those compassionate eyes. His gaze fixed on the horizon. "But they hadn't risked their lives escaping from France to end up in the sway of another mad tyrant. They took the food, shelter, and clothing he offered, and left us as quickly as they could."

There. He was done. No more words.

She was silent for a moment. Then: "How old were you when you moved to the island?"

"Eleven."

"How long did you live there?"

"Seven years. Felt like a century."

More silence. It seemed she'd lost interest. But when Gabriel finally ripped his gaze from the spot where the sea met the cloudless sky, it was to discover her watching him intently.

"King," she said softly. "That is what you meant when you claimed to be king of an island."

He shrugged. "A stupid joke. My father used to sit and stare out at the sea and talk about how the island would be mine one day. He took his royalty quite seriously."

"You have been away a long time."

"Since his death — ten years." His gaze slid over the castle ruins. "Almost twenty since I've seen this place." A lifetime.

"Why did you return?"

"This is as far as the story goes, Miss Peabody. There isn't any happy ending, like those rescues you are so fond of staging."

She ignored his churlish tone. "There must be a reason you came back after all this time."

"Word reached me in Jamaica that there is a buyer for

the island. I have returned to see to the sale and, I suppose, see his grave for the last time."

"He is buried on the island?"

"Yes." He gestured toward the castle. "But I never intended to come here, to this place."

"Why not?"

Gabriel sighed. "Because this is where it started."

"It?"

"The madness. The lunacy. The end of innocence." He knew he sounded bitter. "By the time my father moved us to the island, he walked around in a crown of bayberry leaves. *Bayberry leaves,* for God's sake."

A sense of loss filled him. He'd never told a soul about his father's madness. Dredging it up forced him to confront a raw truth: The harsh memories would always be there, never to be replaced by anything better. No matter how many years or miles passed, Sinclair Isle and that cursed bayberry crown would always reside within him.

"You have returned to face it, haven't you?" she persisted. "To embrace the past —"

"No." Anger roiled him. "I embrace nothing."

She regarded him. "You are afraid of growing mad like your father."

Gabriel scowled. "I live in the real world, Miss Peabody, not the world I would prefer to imagine. Unlike you, I know that one human being cannot right all the wrongs, that meddling with fate is the choice of fools, that the only way to get through life without succumbing to lunacy is to keep away from people like you who think to save us all."

He saw her stiffen.

"The world does not want saving, madam," he added ruthlessly. "It wants to go on spinning as it has done for centuries, without the interference of mindless mortals like you and me. It wants to spin and spin until the past, present, and future are a senseless jumble that mocks our feeble attempts to make sense of it all. It does not need anyone to stick stars in the skies or build temples to false gods. It does not want your heroics or my father's inventions."

"To believe that is to give up," she said quietly.

"No. It's to stay sane, to stay alive. We cannot change the world. To think anything else is to go stark, raving mad from the enormity of the task."

Abruptly Gabriel rose. He strode over to Mainstay and untied the reins. His hands were shaking so much that he barely accomplished the job.

"Blasted female," he muttered into Mainstay's ear.

The horse gave him a soulful look.

Chapter Ten

*A*pollo. Watching Sinclair untie Mainstay, Louisa decided she must be a little mad herself. Her mind spun a fantasy in which Sinclair stood as that arrogant god. Perhaps that image wasn't too far off, for there was a fire in him he tried to deny. It was in the flaming red hair and enigmatic green eyes that conjured wild, undisciplined journeys to the unknown. It was unpredictable, even frightening. Perhaps that is why he would not acknowledge it.

Sinclair was at pains to show he cared for nothing. And yet, a man who burned as he did could not be as cold as ice. She'd glimpsed the war within him — the struggle between detachment and passion, folly and obsession.

No, he wasn't a rapist or murderer, but that fact only made him harder to understand. It would be easy to despise a man who committed such heinous crimes, easy to disregard his charm as the wiles of an immoral scoundrel. But Sinclair wasn't evil, in the sense Louisa had come to know evil in men. He was even capable of heroics — provided the price was right.

She could never esteem a man driven by such mercenary motives, and yet, she'd seen something else in him just now. That tale of his childhood tugged at her heart. She saw a boy, his world collapsing around him, forced to live out his youth on a remote island with a father lost in sorrow and madness. She imagined him watching helplessly as his father's brilliance curdled to bitterness over the deaths of his wife and son. She understood the loneliness, neglect, and sadness he must have felt, for she had known those things as well.

Louisa thought about David, whose imprisonment and torture had given him empathy and a need to help others. David had a well of compassion in him as deep as the sea.

But Sinclair had gone another way. Suffering had made him shun other sufferers. He batted away misery like a pesky fly, lacerated it with the barb of careless humor that masked a chilling truth: He was as isolated as any island.

And dangerous. A man who cut himself off from humanity was entirely capable of using others for his own ends. Perhaps that is why his kisses were calculated to seduce.

Amusement, whimsy, cleverness — these tools kept the world at bay. They allowed him only to skim the shallows, never plumb the depths.

It would be folly to drop her guard with him. And yet, he could disarm her by something as simple as letting her feel his heartbeat. He made her yearn to help him shed that armor he wore.

"Ready?"

Startled, Louisa looked up to find him regarding her with a dark expression. Mainstay's reins were coiled around his fist. The mare whinnied, and Midnight looked up from where he had been grazing near the temple. Louisa reached for his halter.

Sinclair eyed the stallion dubiously. "I don't think you should ride him."

"Nonsense. He carried me here."

His gaze swept from the top of her head down to her breeches and riding boots. "You'll have no control without a saddle."

"I have more control," she insisted. "He feels my touch more directly."

"In that case, you'll have no trouble mounting him on your own. Or have you trained him to kneel like a camel for your convenience?"

Louisa gave him a fulminating look. Usually she didn't

need a mounting block, but her strength was not what it had been before her injury. In the paddock, she'd had to use a fence rail. Doubtless Sinclair expected her to beg for a leg up, but she would not give him the satisfaction.

With a deep breath, she took a few steps backward, then dashed forward, grasping Midnight's mane as she tried to vault herself onto him. Her shoulder repaid her with a sharp, stabbing pain, and she lost all purchase on the horse. She slid toward the ground, only to feel a firm hand on her bottom and an equally firm push upward.

And suddenly she sat atop Midnight, her pride in shambles.

"That was excessively familiar." Her face was burning.

"Was it? I hadn't noticed. No, of course I did. But had I not intervened, you would have fallen on that lovely posterior. Is it bad manners to point out that obvious fact?"

"I have been able to mount my own horse since the age of six," she said frostily.

Sinclair swung himself up onto Mainstay without another word.

Louisa tried to relax her upper body and her lower legs, wanting none of her tension to add to Midnight's unease. When she felt he horse settle, she urged him forward at a sedate pace.

Sinclair watched them. After a minute or two he pulled Mainstay even with her.

"I am perfectly capable —" she began.

But just at that moment, a rabbit darted in front of Midnight, and the horse startled. Louisa might have controlled him had not her vision suddenly constricted to tiny pinpoints of light in the sun's glare. She felt herself sway.

Sensing her loss of control, Midnight lunged forward.

Instantly, Sinclair looped one arm around her and pulled her onto Mainstay with him. Pain shot through Louisa's injured shoulder as he brought her sideways against his chest.

"This is excessively —"

"Familiar? Yes. Would you rather walk?" He reached around her to flick Mainstay's reins.

"I cannot leave Midnight," Louisa protested.

"If your training methods are as good as you claim, he'll follow."

Rigid as a stone, Louisa sat across his thighs, a position that afforded far too much intimacy. It was also unstable. With every step Mainstay took, Louisa was jostled.

"Awkward as it may be," Sinclair said after a moment, "I am obliged to point out that you must hold on to me. I cannot direct the horse and see to your safety at the same time."

He held the reins loosely in his right hand, his right arm extended mere inches from her chest, his left curled protectively around her middle. Louisa had no wish to discover what additional intimacy could be achieved if he needed to secure her position further.

Gingerly, she slid her right arm around his torso. "Midnight would never hurt me."

As if to agree, the stallion loped toward them, the rabbit nowhere in sight.

But already, Louisa's body was rebelling at the closeness with Sinclair. Her stomach felt queasy.

Sinclair kept his eyes forward. "He is no lady's mount."

"More lady's than man's," she retorted. But the dread swirled in her like a gathering wave. Her thoughts splintered. "Midnight and I understand each other. I-I owe him a debt."

"Oh?" He looked down at her.

"He gave me my freedom."

"Never say he dashed some knave to pieces for you?"

Louisa smiled thinly. "In a manner of speaking, yes. He killed my husband."

***

Gabriel decided not to ask. He had no doubt that the huge beast ambling amiably beside them could kill, but he had no wish to hear the tale. The castle, the island, his father, the memories — all of it swirled chaotically inside his brain, sweeping every rational thought into a churning jumble of despair. He would not add Miss Peabody's departed husband to the mix.

He was acutely conscious of her softly rounded form against his, no matter that she held herself as stiffly as a board. Despite his resolve, thoughts of the man who'd known her in ways Gabriel had not — *carnal* ways — kept intruding.

How the devil did the man get himself killed within six hours of his wedding? Riding at breakneck speed over some hurdle or other to impress his bride? Had the stallion balked at a jump and catapulted him to his doom?

Gabriel glanced at Midnight, placid now that the distraction of the rabbit had disappeared. Bred to the bone, that one. Wouldn't balk at a jump if his life depended on it. Perhaps her fool of a husband had simply fallen off in a drunken stupor and landed wrong.

If he, Gabriel Sinclair, had just been handed a woman like Louisa Peabody, he would not spend his first six hours of connubial bliss anywhere near a horse.

No, he would sweep her away to his chamber — assuming he had one, which, given the state of his finances, was only a dubious possibility — and swiftly relieve her of those yards of fabric and furbelows brides tended to adorn themselves with. He'd go slowly, because otherwise she would likely cast up her accounts, but sooner or later he was bound to get round that.

Then he would make love to her until the only word on her lips was his name. She wouldn't say it in that chilly tone she used with him now, but in the breathless, uncontrolled cries of a woman enslaved by passion.

He wondered if her eyes would lose that guarded air and unlock for him the intriguing mystery that was Louisa Peabody.

That thought stopped him. He wasn't one to delve into a woman's secrets or seek deeper meaning in the carnal act. For him it was purely physical, nary an emotion at stake. A man had to preserve his freedom.

With Louisa Peabody, that wouldn't be possible.

Hell. Was he really imagining himself making love to her? Perhaps it was a measure of how seeing his childhood home again had unsettled him.

Gabriel knew better than to think that this woman who fit so nicely within the circle of his arms — even if she *did* flinch every time the horse's movements sent her hip sliding against his inner thigh — was different from countless others he'd known. Yet she was different, as mad as could be, what with her rescues and schemes and loathing of any man who got within arm's length.

Still: What kind of man chose to spend his wedding night straddling a horse instead of her?

"Damnation," he growled. "What happened?"

She frowned. "When?"

"When your husband was killed."

She was silent for a long moment. "After the ceremony we drove to an inn. Richard rode outside the carriage on Midnight."

Gabriel was incredulous. A man with any kindness or skill would have built a torrid fire in his new bride there in the carriage. But her husband had left her sitting alone watching the passing scenery. Even she must have wondered about his preference for the horse over her.

"Richard settled Midnight in the stable with the other horses. Then he came to our room." Her voice sounded distant, remote.

Gabriel stared at her rigid profile with a dire sense of foreboding.

"By then I had climbed out the window." She hesitated. "I hadn't wanted to marry, but my father lost everything gambling. He gave me to Richard to clear his debts and save the estate. But Richard had acquired a fortune in India. He did not need Peabody Manor or anything we had —"

"Except you." Gabriel could well imagine how the man had desired her, not just for her beauty, but for her foolish courage.

Yet Richard did not sound like the sort who liked courageous women; perhaps it was only her golden hair he admired, or her deep blue eyes, or those spectacular breasts, or the soft hips that taunted him intimately with Mainstay's every step. Or that tiny birthmark, so emblematic of her imperfect charm.

Her chin came up. "He didn't want me, not really. He saw me as a challenge, a conquest. A woman to break to the bit, as he had broken Midnight. In Richard's view, a woman and a horse were exactly the same. Only he hadn't truly broken Midnight. Or me."

Gabriel looked down at her. "You did not intend to keep your end of the bargain."

"On the contrary," she said stiffly. "If I did not grant him his husbandly rights, he would have the marriage annulled, and ruin my father. I intended to fulfill my marital duties."

"That's why you climbed out of the window before the opportunity to do so presented itself."

"I was afraid," she said simply.

Such an admission did not come easily to her, Gabriel knew. He wished he had not pressed her for this accounting. He no longer wished to hear the details. Most especially, he didn't want to feel this growing outrage on her behalf.

"I thought I could submit to him," she said. "I hadn't realized how impossible it would be to give myself to a man I neither loved nor respected."

"Even I could have told you that," he muttered. Louisa Peabody submit to a man she did not respect? Ridiculous notion.

Gabriel didn't want to hear the rest. He searched wildly for a change of subject — anything besides the confession that was causing his insides to curdle. "Apollo didn't really drive that chariot of fire across the sky, you know. It was Helios, a lesser god —"

"He caught me in the stable." Her voice was flat, remote.

She was determined to get through it, Gabriel realized. Her eyes had taken on a glassy look, and she wasn't seeing him, but the past. He'd be the first to sympathize with the fact that the past could be an unpleasant sight. But he didn't want to hear her bleak story. He'd had enough bleakness to last a lifetime.

"The reason Apollo wore a laurel wreath —"

"He tore my clothes."

"Daphne was a wood nymph who had the misfortune to infatuate him —"

"He laughed and rutted over me like a pig."

"Hell. Don't, Louisa."

But she wouldn't be silenced. "He forced himself on me — cruelly, brutally. His touch revolted me, made me ill. That's where the sickness began."

Something sickening stirred in Gabriel.

"I tried to crawl away. I made it to Midnight's stall and threw myself in. I didn't have time to close the stall door."

He could guess the rest. "The commotion upset the stallion."

She nodded. "Midnight reared. I wasn't frightened of him. In truth, I'd rather have died there than submit to Richard again. But Midnight rushed out and trampled him."

The stallion was now sniffing benignly at a juniper bush, but Gabriel had no difficulty imagining the horse's murderous side.

"I've rarely seen Midnight upset by anything since," she said. "Only the whip — Richard used it constantly — and a storm now and then."

Her sudden, fey smile took Gabriel's breath away. "And so you see, Sinclair, I know what men are up to. They're predators. Their codes of honor are empty. Their justice is rigged against us."

"Louisa —"

"Pray, do not pretend to be solicitous." She glared at him. "You are no different from any other man. Even now, your arm presses under the fullness of my bosom as if that were necessary, which, you must own, it is not."

Gabriel frowned. His right arm, the one that held the reins, did indeed appear to be guilty of the accused infraction. Gingerly, he tried to move it a few inches away from her person.

"Richard's death made me wealthy, so I suppose those six hours of married life were worth the investment."

He opened his mouth to speak, but she cut him off, her eyes cold shards. "So yes, I have no interest in being touched," she said. "I have triumphed over base male desire, and will continue to do so on behalf of myself and all other abused women as long as I draw breath."

Hell. She had to go and break his heart.

****

"Easy there, Violet," David said gruffly. "'Tis one thing for the children to scramble around those rocks, but another for a woman in your condition to —"

"Cavort like a baby elephant? Thank you, but I have had quite enough of your warnings," Violet grumbled. "I am aware of my condition. Indeed, I could not be more aware of it."

"I did nae mean —"

"I have not slept comfortably in weeks, so I am quite familiar with my limitations," she added crossly. For the last

three days, David had accompanied her and the children —
Daisy's daughter Mary and Lily's twins — on their morning
outings. One day they went to the village market; on
another, they took the children to play with the puppies Mrs.
Hanford's dog had birthed. Violet was grateful for David's
help, for she could scarcely carry anything these days and
was often tired. But pregnant or no, she was not an invalid
and wouldn't be treated as such.

"Ball," Joshua said, giggling as he heaved a small red
leather sphere at David, who caught it and rolled it back.

Immediately, Jeremy jumped into the game and
proceeded to fall on the ball. Joshua tried to wrench it away.
Blows were avoided only when David distracted them with
a large beetle that had crawled onto a rock. Lily's boys were
lively, and David genuinely seemed to enjoy playing with
the children. Even shy Mary, who could often be eclipsed
by the twins' boisterousness, seemed to blossom under his
attention.

Violet regretted her show of temper. Being with the
children was one of her pleasures. She loved the way the
twins babbled constantly to each other in a language no one
had managed to decipher. And Mary was a dear, always
crawling up to sleep in her lap when she was tired, her little
fingers curling tightly around Violet's. Lately she had
preferred David's lap, and who could blame her? Violet's
had disappeared weeks ago.

It was not only lack of sleep that made her so irritable,
but also the knowledge that the babe's arrival would bring
new problems. She and her child would be alone in the
world, for she did not want to live on Louisa's charity much
longer. One day, perhaps, she would find a man who valued
and respected her. Or perhaps not. Life was not like fairy
tales, as well she knew.

Stifling a yawn, Violet watched David as he let the
twins tug on his hands, and then slowly lifted his arms so
they dangled a little above the ground. He was a big man,

yet gentle and careful. She wondered how he got those awful scars. In prison, Louisa had said. A place where life was not gentle. It troubled Violet that such a good man had been forced to endure such treatment.

Her brain grew fuzzy, and Violet put her head down on a little pile of leaves the children had kicked up. As her eyelids closed, she was dimly aware of a large hand placing one of the children's blankets over her. David, she decided.

David would not beat his wife or conspire with another woman against her. He was good-hearted and unfailingly polite. He was close to Louisa, but there was nothing romantical in their relationship. Besides, Mr. Sinclair seemed intent on stirring the coals of that particular fire. Violet did not think he had committed those awful crimes; yet there was something unpredictable and mysterious about the man.

She snuggled deeper under the blanket. David was not unpredictable. He was kind to a fault. It was as if all of the deeper passions had been leached out of him. He kept to himself; only with Sam or the other children did he ever let down his guard. And yet, those scars on his face bore eloquent witness to the fact that life had not been kind to him.

Kindness in men was rare, but she sensed that David would take care of a woman with the same gentleness he displayed toward the children.

Violet did not wish to be treated like a child. She did not wish to be treated as if she were made of fine porcelain that might break at any moment. David was not for her — not that he would ever entertain such a foolish notion.

As she drifted off to sleep, sadness overwhelmed her. She was ungainly, clumsy, awkward. No man would ever feel passion for her. She had no right to expect it. And yet there was a wanting in her as deep as loss.

Chapter Eleven

Frederick Sandingham, Lord Upton, stared at the creature who opened the door in response to his knock. Her bodice dipped rather lower than he was accustomed to seeing among household servants, exposing an extraordinary amount of her ample breasts. She was missing a front tooth, and her beady black eyes narrowed in an almost predatory manner.

"What yer want?" she demanded. Her voice was not the respectful, deferential tone one usually heard from members of the lower orders. She reminded him of the sort of female one would encounter in a bawdy house.

This was Peabody Manor, however. The home of Louisa Peabody, as she preferred to style herself — his late brother's wife, a woman he fervently wanted to bed.

"Inform your mistress Lord Upton is here," he told the female coldly.

"Horse's ass."

Lord Upton frowned, whereupon the woman began to cackle like a jackdaw. "'Tell yer mistress Lord Uppity is here,'" she mimicked. "And what a grand gent he is, too. Well, Alice Wentworth has no mistress." With that she strolled off down the hall, without another look in his direction.

Frederick stood at the threshold for a long moment. Where, he wondered, was Louisa? And the other servants? If this was the sort of female she kept around the house, he would have to speak sternly to her.

The notion of giving Louisa a talking-to pleased him. He imagined her meek and trembling, accepting his rebuke like the gently bred young lady she was. Unfortunately, over the course of two years as her trustee, Frederick had come to realize that Louisa had not a meek bone in her body. Pity, for he had at one time contemplated making her his wife.

Such a marriage would normally have been prohibited, as she was his brother's widow. But Frederick had thought the legal difficulties could be got round. The marriage had lasted but a few hours; it could persuasively be argued that it was never consummated. Few people knew of the union. Moreover, Louisa had never styled herself a widow; she didn't use Richard's surname — something Frederick had considered shocking at the time, but had come to see as convenient.

Thus, Frederick had permitted himself to entertain hopes. He had gone so far as to imagine his own wedding night, sampling all the pleasures that had been denied his younger brother.

Over time, reality had intervened. The more he came to know Louisa, the more he realized that any man would be daft to want such an independent woman for a wife. She would, however, make a perfectly adequate mistress. Which is why, a few months after becoming her trustee, Frederick began planning her seduction.

Progress had not been swift. Louisa treated him politely enough, especially when he came to make his quarterly reports on the estate. He had dreamed of clandestine forays to her room, of nights spent in passionate splendor in her bed.

Alas, his hopes remained only that. She kept him at a distance, never granting him any exceptional familiarity. Despite the fact that he held the strings of the fat purse Richard had so unwisely left her, Louisa had always lodged him in one of the ancillary buildings, a paltry structure fit only for a dower house.

Peabody Manor had no room for guests, she insisted, since it was occupied by her female friends. Frederick could never remember their names, only that there were a great number of them. The coarse female who had opened the door just now evidently was one, though she had the air of the doxies who plied their trade in Covent Garden. That Louisa allowed such a person under her roof while she shunted her brother-in-law off to a dower house galled him.

As he stood in the empty foyer listening to sounds from elsewhere in the house — an infant's cry, children's shrieks, and above it all, that infernal woman's cackling — Frederick decided that two years was long enough to wait. Her request for funds had been unusually urgent. Frederick intended to make it clear there was only one way to win his cooperation.

He showed himself into Louisa's parlor, poured out a glass of her sherry, and sat down to wait.

***

Louisa ignored Sinclair's proffered hand. "I don't need your assistance to dismount. And I am quite capable of seeing to Midnight's rubdown myself."

"That's my job, Louisa." Sam looked downcast at the prospect of being deprived of the job.

Louisa suppressed a sigh. "Yes, of course. Thank you, Sam. Where is David?"

"He took the children and Violet on a picnic," Sam replied. "But the gig is here, so they must have returned. Did you wish me to fetch him?"

"No," Sinclair said, answering for her. Without further debate, he simply lifted her off Mainstay. Then, rather than releasing her, he shifted her in his arms and carried her toward the house.

"Put me down." Louisa pushed at his arm. "I'm not ill. It was only the one time that I —"

"Slid off your horse? Once is enough. I'll not release you until Rose sees you."

Louisa felt spent and out of sorts. Following Sinclair

today had been ill-advised. Telling him about her wedding night was a mistake as well. He could not know what that had cost her. What had she been thinking to confide in him something she'd never told anyone in such detail?

He looked down at her, and something in his gaze made her still. "I am not Richard," he said quietly. "I would not harm you."

Somehow she knew that was so. Nevertheless, he had unsettled her today with all of his touching — kissing her, placing her hand on his chest, holding her across his body on Mainstay. And now, he carried her as if she was his personal possession, in full view of anyone in the house.

Raising a ruckus would only make things worse, so Louisa forced herself to endure his misplaced chivalry.

To her dismay, however, there on the drive was Frederick's carriage — emblazoned with his coat of arms, attended by six liveried servants, and accompanied by a baggage coach.

"Put me down!" she said urgently.

"Not until Rose sees you."

"You do not understand. My trustee is here. He must have the funds you are due. He cannot see us like this or think — dear Lord, he must not think that we, that I —"

"Are lovers?" Sinclair's lip curled. "If he knows you at all, madam, he will not think that."

Louisa tried to make him understand. "I have worked hard to discourage his interest in me. This will change his view of my character. Now he will think me a...a loose woman."

"I doubt he's that stupid."

They were at the front door, but Sinclair still did not set her on her feet. Instead, he stuck out his foot and pushed the door open. It rebounded against the wall, announcing their presence with a loud thud.

"Please, Sinclair," she whispered. "Put me down."

"Please?" he repeated loudly. "Of course, my dear —

since you insist. I do like to hear you beg."

That outlandish declaration was uttered in a voice that must have carried to the parlor, where Frederick was probably waiting. Louisa closed her eyes in mortification.

When Sinclair finally set her down, her limbs had turned to rubber. She reached for his arm to steady herself, looked up, and saw her incredulous brother-in-law standing there.

"Louisa! What the devil are you about?"

She lifted her chin. "My lord."

***

Gabriel had never heard Louisa address anyone as "my lord," and he did not much like the sound of it. To be sure, it had been wicked of him to call attention to them while he held her in his arms, guessing that her toplofty trustee would come running.

Lord Upton did not look as if he could run anywhere, however. His elegant clothing barely contained his ample form, which was compressed by stays so that he resembled a turnip banded at the middle. His florid features, balding pate, and labored breathing gave him an unhealthy air.

Upton's gaze shot from Louisa to Gabriel, who gave him a cursory nod. "I see you've got sherry there, Upton. Don't mind a spot myself." He strode past the appalled trustee, poured himself a glass, and settled himself into a chair as Louisa sank onto a nearby settee.

"Who is this person?" Lord Upton demanded.

Gabriel smiled encouragingly at Louisa as his brain supplied the dialogue: *Just a man I rescued from the gallows.* He took a sip of sherry.

She glared at him.

A man who has wanted to make love to me since he laid eyes on me. That was very near the mark, now that he thought on it. Gabriel frowned at the amber liquid.

"Frederick," she began.

He has touched me rather intimately, my lord, though not as intimately as he desires. And if I can just get over the wretched illness I feel whenever he touches me, we might have a grand night of passion.

One night, to erase the horror of her husband's brutality and replace it with something infinitely more pleasurable. An intriguing thought, that. But he might as well ask for the moon and the stars. Louisa found him eminently resistible, and for that he should count himself fortunate. No man in his right mind would involve himself with her, even if she could overcome that bone-deep loathing of being touched.

Gabriel schooled his expression to blandness, hoping she did not discern his desire. It wasn't the detached desire he usually felt when beholding a beautiful female. No, it was focused most particularly on this charmingly bewildered widow struggling to formulate a response.

Ah, well. It was an inconvenience, nothing more. He'd soon be on his way. Wherever he went next would have normal women, which is to say those who appreciated the delights of the flesh and did not grow ill contemplating them.

Gabriel pasted a careless smile on his face and prepared to be entertained as Louisa attempted to explain to her corpulent trustee.

"This is Mr. Sinclair" — she told Upton, mustering a polite, frozen smile in Gabriel's direction — "my fiancé."

Gabriel nearly choked on his sherry.

It took Upton a moment to find his tongue. "What is this nonsense, Louisa? I have not heard a word about your remarrying. I should have been notified at once." He lowered himself unsteadily into an overstuffed wing chair.

"I did not notify you, my lord, for the simple reason that my betrothal has only just occurred. Mr. Sinclair proposed this very day." She fluttered her lashes at Gabriel.

Lash-fluttering was not a skill she possessed, however.

It looked as if there was a foreign object in her eye.

"Actually, it is *Lord* Sinclair," she added. "His family is one of the oldest in Kent."

In for a penny, in for a pound, Gabriel thought grimly.

Upton regarded him. "I know of no Lord Sinclair."

Gabriel shot a black look at Louisa, but she merely returned him a dazzling smile. "I daresay you are not well-acquainted with Kent, my lord. The family has been here for hundreds of years. Indeed, they own the largest estate for miles."

Lord Upton tilted his head consideringly. Gabriel could almost see the rusted mechanism of the man's brain try to shake off its cobwebs.

"Your timing is perfect, my lord, as we were just celebrating our betrothal," Louisa said. She paused for a heartbeat. "I trust you brought the funds I requested?"

Upton frowned. The man might be a slow-top, but he was no idiot.

"You have taken me by surprise," Upton said at last. "I had planned to stay for several days so that we may discuss your extraordinary request. Perhaps you will be good enough to explain what you intend to do with such a large sum."

"Why, of course," Louisa said. "Lord Sinclair and I are planning our wedding. Significant expense is involved."

Upton eyed him suspiciously. "Sinclair is unable to cover it?"

Gabriel dismissed the question with a vague wave of his hand. "Tied up in investments."

Louisa beamed. Gabriel wanted to strangle her. Did she know what she had started? Upton would have him investigated when he returned to London. Moreover, as soon as her thick trustee recollected that she had requested the funds well *before* the betrothal, he'd see through her lie. Lying was another skill she should not delude herself into thinking she possessed.

Upton pursed his lips. "I should like to discuss the matter of the settlements with Lord Sinclair and his solicitors —"

"Broughton, Wilshire, and Stevens." Gabriel said in resignation. "St. James's." Perhaps his father's old solicitors would vouch for him, perhaps not. It hardly mattered. By the time Upton contacted them, he would be long gone.

Upton cleared his throat. "If all proves to be in order, I will advance you the sum. I see no need for haste, however."

As she hesitated, Gabriel saw uncertainty dawn. By inventing a betrothal, she had hoped both to explain Gabriel's presence and send Upton on his way two thousand pounds lighter, reassured about her future.

But she had miscalculated. Upton was neither stupid nor devoted to her welfare. Moreover, the lust Gabriel had detected in his froglike gaze hadn't vanished upon word of her "betrothal."

Louisa turned to him. Gabriel read the plea in her lovely blue eyes, the very eyes that had brimmed with such empathy upon hearing his childhood saga. She understood, finally, that she had trapped herself in a tangled web of lies.

Far better to leave the lying to a master spinner, such as himself.

Well, he was always one to help a lady in distress. Gabriel rose, strolled over to Louisa, took her hand, and brought it to his lips. His mouth lingered on her skin long enough for the gesture to be judged most improper. Then he turned to Lord Upton.

"We are both men of the world, Upton, so you will understand our predicament." Gabriel tucked her hand under his arm and patted it possessively. "It's like this: We've anticipated the wedding vows."

His lordship blinked.

"At this very moment," Gabriel continued, regarding Louisa affectionately, "there may be a little Lord Sinclair bouncing around in my betrothed's lovely, er, person. In short, the die has been cast, so you might as well come across with the blunt."

It took Upton a moment to recover. "You, sir, are unbearably crude. I cannot believe that Louisa would —"

"Tell him, my dear." Gabriel eyed her fondly.

Louisa's gaze was murderous, but she had little choice. "My fiancé is more direct than one might wish. But I will not disagree with his account."

Gabriel grinned. "Sherry, Upton?" He poured the trustee another glass and held it out magnanimously.

The man instantly drained it.

***

What he needed was one of Lily's biscuits. Gabriel could think of no other readily available consolation for the unexpected disaster of finding himself betrothed, however transitory that state might turn out to be. The reckless perpetrator of the aforementioned disaster had fled to the sanctuary of her room, a cowardly act he intended to point out to her at the first opportunity.

As soon as he regained his powers of speech, that is. And reason. And every other function Louisa Peabody had obliterated with the heartbreaking story of her wedding night, topped off with the horrendous lie about their betrothal. It was enough to make a man incoherent.

To be sure, he'd been the one to come up with the scandalous pregnancy possibility, but what had she expected when her blue eyes sent that desperate plea to him? Perhaps his wasn't the most elegant of solutions, but it had knocked Upton on his heel, which was all that mattered. The man was likely still consoling himself with spirits in the parlor.

Gabriel yearned to console himself with something, as long as it was nowhere near Louisa's trustee — or Louisa. He could retreat to the stables, but he had no wish to ponder such cataclysmic events surrounded by the scent of horse manure. So the kitchen it was. There was sure to be a comforting fire in the hearth in preparation for dinner.

Lily's biscuits and a fire — now that was enough to raise a man's spirits.

But when he walked into the kitchen, instead of Lily's lighter-than-air confections, Gabriel found himself confronted with a brick-like loaf of bread, one of several such specimens Daisy had removed from the oven. She was eyeing it glumly.

"I fear it is inedible," she said.

Of that there could be little doubt. But Daisy looked so stricken that guilt seized him. "What sort of bread is it?" he asked politely.

She brightened at his interest. "It's made from eringus root. I boil the root until it is tender, then dry it and remove the pith. Then I grind it for bread. Or braid the pieces and boil them in sugar and rosewater, like candy."

Gabriel tried to imagine such a dreadful thing in his stomach.

"Eringus is but a fancy name for common sea holly, which is plentiful here. It is well to live off the land, do you not think, Mr. Sinclair? My Henry thought it a sin not to use the land for its proper purpose."

Gabriel wondered who Henry was, and why Daisy's voice rose at the mention of his name.

"The earth has so many gifts," she continued with a forced smile. "It is our obligation to appreciate them. That is what Henry says."

Gabriel tried to figure how he might gracefully make his exit so that he could ponder the disasters of the day. But Daisy fixed him with an earnest gaze; apparently the eringus root discussion was not yet at an end.

"When eringus root is mixed with ginger, it is said to be an effective aphrodisiac," she said.

He could think of no fitting response to that.

Daisy colored. "I did not mean — that is, I do not suggest that you and Louisa would need such. And Rose is more familiar with potions and the like, so if you do need such assistance during your marriage or, indeed, at any time, which you almost certainly would not — she would be able to provide it." She halted. "I am making this much worse, am I not?"

"I fear so."

With that, she burst into tears.

Gabriel eyed her in alarm. "Do not distress yourself. Miss Peabody and I are not actually betroth —"

"We're all quite broken, you know," she sobbed.

He frowned. "Broken?"

Daisy's watery brown eyes held his. "You once made that joke about us all being in bloom, but we are not in bloom, Mr. Sinclair. We are not!"

Gabriel eyed her in bewilderment. He had thought Daisy among the more even-tempered of the Flowers. Indeed, hers had always seemed a cheerful disposition. Her dark hair and sun-burnished skin gave her a wholesome appearance, and her eyes usually sparkled with life.

Not now, though. He hadn't meant anything by that joke, but something was amiss. What?

He had little experience with women who turned into watering pots or were overset by some dreadful, consuming emotion. Yet it seemed to be his fate to run into them today. He supposed it was required to console or comfort them, or at the very least listen — radical notions, all.

But perhaps not so radical at that, he thought, as tears streamed down Daisy's face.

There was a stool next to the work table. Gabriel took a deep breath and sat. He forced his mind not to think longingly of Lily's biscuits, not to ponder the debacles of the day. Instead, he sat silent and still as if he had nothing else to do, nowhere else to be.

And waited.

Daisy dabbed at her eyes with the edges of a towel. Her dark hair had escaped its pins and she tucked it behind her ears. "You see, we are between our old lives and the ones we will make anew. Sometimes it seems impossible to envision those new lives."

Yes, Gabriel could imagine the difficulty. He had been Between. Perhaps he was even now.

"I do not know what comes next," she continued. "I only know I cannot go back to what was, and it overwhelms me at times. And then" — her voice wobbled — "and then I cannot even make a decent loaf of bread."

So it was — and was not — about the bread.

Gabriel did not know much about Daisy, apart from the fact she persisted in thinking she could cook when it was abundantly clear she had no talent for it. He guessed she was about twenty-five. He wondered how she had come to Peabody Manor. Surely, this mild young woman was not a husband-killer like Rose. Then again, he would not have thought her the sort to fall apart over a loaf of bread.

Daisy stared at it morosely. Gabriel did not know what to do.

And yet, perhaps he could do something.

He spied a knife on the table and reached for the loaf. He carved off a slice, though it was like sawing wood. A man could break a tooth on the thing, but he had something else in mind.

"Have you a long fork?" he asked.

Daisy eyed him curiously. She fished through a crock of implements and pulled out a big fork. "I don't know what you are about, Mr. Sinclair, but I daresay this monstrosity is not salvageable."

"We shall see." Gabriel stuck the slice on the fork and walked over to the fire. He extended the bread above the flames. It grew brown on one side, and he turned it over so the other side browned. At last, he withdrew it from the fire and placed the slice on the table. It was burnished to a crisp, golden brown.

Daisy stared at it. "I wonder…perhaps some butter or marmalade?"

"Just the thing," Gabriel said encouragingly.

She spread butter on the slice, then took a bite. "Why, it is delicious! The fire made it crunchy on the inside." She shot him a tremulous smile. "You scorched it in the fires of Perdition, but rescued it before hope was lost."

He wasn't sure about that last. "I am glad it is more palatable."

"Yes, and sweeter, too."

Gabriel felt ridiculously pleased at having accomplished such a small thing. "If you like, I can rig a device that will allow you to toast more than one slice at a time."

"That would be wonderful. You are a genius, Mr. Sinclair!"

"Not at all. Toasting is simplicity itself." He thought for a moment. "With some pliant metal, I can construct a hinged holder."

"Hinged?"

"So you can swing it in and out of the flame. I'll attach it to the side of the fireplace."

Daisy surprised him by coming around the table and embracing him. Then she took a step back and wiped her eyes. "Thank you for salvaging my afternoon's labors."

"I will work on the device tomorrow," he promised.

"You cannot imagine how rewarding it is to feel that my cooking is contributing to the wellbeing of our little community," Daisy said with a watery smile.

Gabriel vowed to be more charitable toward her cooking in the future.

"When Louisa took us in, we had nowhere else to go. We were outcasts, Mary and I. Henry did not want us." She hesitated. "I suppose that is harsh. He *did* want us, just not in the way we wanted him."

"I see." Though he didn't.

"There was another woman." Daisy's voice quavered. "I did not want my marriage to end, but there was no choice."

"I am sorry fate dealt you an unfaithful husband."

"No, Mr. Sinclair. Fate dealt Henry an unfaithful wife."

Gabriel tried to absorb that.

"Sarah was my dearest friend. And then one day she became more than a friend." Daisy hesitated. "I suppose you will think that unnatural."

The Flowers were certainly full of surprises. "I do not suppose it matters what I think," he said. "It is between the two — er, three — of you."

"It's only me now. Sarah regretted our time together. Perhaps I do as well. The cost has been dearer than I imagined. Henry was devoted to us. I-I do miss him." She tried to smile. "He is a farmer. He works so very hard, and he deserves so much more than what I have given him."

"Does he not wish to see the child?" Gabriel asked.

"I expect Henry is beside himself to see her," Daisy said. "I have been afraid to send him my direction. I fear he will try to take Mary away from me."

Gabriel considered that. "He would take a child from her mother?"

"I do not know. In truth, he is a reasonable man — a *good* man. He tried to be a good husband, but he did not know — that is, *I* did not know — and then Sarah…" She trailed off, leaving Gabriel mystified.

"Henry didn't understand how I could be drawn to someone of my own sex," she finished. "By the way you are staring at me, I do not think you do either."

Though he wouldn't have thought that anything could make him blush at this stage of his life, Gabriel felt his face burn.

"Part of me wishes I could explain it to him," Daisy

said. "Yet it is complicated, and Henry is not one for complexity. Besides, I do not think men wish to hear such frankness from women."

Gabriel yearned mightily to change the subject. "I, er, suppose that depends on whether there is affection yet between you."

Daisy pondered that. "We had known one another for years when we married, and there was certainly affection between us then. He is very handsome and so very honest. I was glad to marry him. Henry is not given to sentiment. I do not know what he thinks of me now."

"Do you wish to find out?" Gabriel asked.

"I have thought about that. We did not part on good terms. I have tried not to remember those last moments between us, for then I see only my failures." She sighed. "As much as I like being here with the others, at times I feel isolated, like an island in the sea, waiting for something but not knowing what."

An island. Yes, he understood that.

"How did you find Louisa?" Gabriel asked.

"After Henry and I quarreled, Mary and I went to Sarah's. But she hadn't bargained on a child. She didn't want Mary."

Gabriel thought of Daisy's shy little girl and couldn't imagine anyone refusing her. "I'm sorry."

"I hired a man from our village to take me as far as my money would allow. He left us off in Newton. We stayed for a time with a farmer and his wife who needed help with the planting." She brightened. "That is one thing I know how to do. Henry was always glad of my help in the field. The farmer's wife told me about Louisa and the women who lived with her. Her husband brought us here. I didn't know whether they would accept me."

"We are lucky to have you both."

They turned. Louisa stood in the doorway, regarding Daisy with a smile.

The sight of his faux betrothed caused Gabriel's pulse to abandon its usual steady pace. Instead, it leapt up and began to race as if the hounds of Hell were on his heels.

There was no reason for such a reaction. No matter that she was an intriguing combination of intelligence, beauty, compassion, and grit — just the sort of woman to fire his spirits, carnal and otherwise — she might as well have a sign over her head forbidding any man to touch her.

Nevertheless, Gabriel allowed himself to study her. She'd changed out of those breeches, perhaps to conform to her trustee's idea of proper attire. Instead, she wore a shapeless, mud-colored frock, emphatically designed not to turn heads. There was an extra bit of thickness at the shoulder, where the fabric shielded her bandage.

He wondered whether she had recovered from her earlier weakness and whether he might cajole her into a private discussion about that betrothal she had stabbed him with. Truly, a man needed no enemies with Louisa Peabody around.

Her gaze shifted to the slice of toast on the table. "What is this?"

"Mr. Sinclair toasted it in the fire," Daisy said. "He says he can construct a device that will hold more than one slice at a time."

Louisa regarded him in surprise. "I have never seen such a thing."

"It's nothing out of the ordinary," Gabriel said. "With a piece of tin I can fashion slots for several slices. I'll make an arm that attaches to the side of the hearth and swings into the fire for toasting and out when it's done."

Shapeless frock notwithstanding, Louisa's slow smile nearly robbed him of breath. "Why, Mr. Sinclair, I believe you are an inventor at heart."

Gabriel stiffened. After the saga he'd given her about his family's misguided inventions, she had to know that such an observation would strike terror into his soul.

Perhaps that was intended as repayment for the lascivious embellishment he had added to her betrothal tale.

He bowed politely. "Please excuse me, ladies. I find I have pressing duties elsewhere."

The stable was suddenly appealing, manure and all.

***

"Delicious biscuits. And the seaweed stew is...most unusual." Frederick had recovered himself sufficiently to partake of dinner.

"Not seaweed — dandelion," Daisy said, as Frederick looked at her blankly. "I picked them myself. People think of them as weeds, but they are quite delicious and useful in many dishes."

"Weeds," Frederick repeated. The fork slid out of his hand, and his pasty complexion paled further. Fortunately, Daisy did not appear to notice.

Word of Louisa's "betrothal" had spread through the house. Louisa planned to tell the women it was a sham as soon as Frederick departed. But he declared his intention of staying for the night, perhaps longer. For now, she endured their felicitations — although Rose, for one, eyed her with open skepticism.

Sinclair accepted their excited good wishes with easy aplomb. The man was shameless. It was her own fault that he had manipulated her into that embarrassing proclamation of a possible pregnancy. Now she was stuck with the lie until Frederick left.

That the betrothal falsehood had come so easily to her was shocking. She, who trusted no man, had seized on the most conventional of excuses for why she needed funds: marriage. Why should she have had to invent a fiancé to pry her own money from her trustee? She ought to have insisted on her right to the funds. Instead, she had chosen expedience, and in so doing betrayed her own sovereignty.

Perhaps she had simply been too weary to fight.

Sometimes she despaired of the Sisyphean tasks she set for herself. Injustice was everywhere. How much good had she really accomplished? To be sure, she had created a sanctuary for women in distress. But they weren't truly safe, because in the eyes of the law they had transgressed. The law would never take into account the abuse Rose and Violet suffered at the hands of their husbands; nor would it excuse Lily's theft to provide for her children.

No, her work would never be finished. And if she were caught, no one would save her from the law's heavy hand. Not Frederick, certainly. David might try, but he had no leverage with the courts.

Louisa could not meet David's gaze tonight. Though she had never revealed to him the full, sordid story of her wedding night, he knew enough to believe she never intended to wed again. He, too, was doubtless filled with suspicion about the betrothal.

Alice had her own ideas. "I saw from the first he had a hankering for ye," she said, pointing to Sinclair. "Don't surprise me that ye let him have his way. I'd do the same, if I had the chance." Her peal of laughter rang loud and hollow across the dinner table.

Violet gave Louisa a shy, encouraging smile. On Louisa's right sat Sinclair, his expression unreadable. But under the tablecloth, out of view of prying eyes, his hand moved to cover hers.

Startled, Louisa met his gaze. Alice's laughter faded. David's searching stare drifted away. Even Violet's smile was lost in the swirling current that arced between them.

In that moment, Louisa saw someone else — not the condemned prisoner who had landed at her feet in the carriage, not the practiced seducer who'd boldly kissed her at will, not the clever rogue who had insinuated himself into her household as easily as breathing. Instead, his eyes held a reassuring strength that slipped past her fears and connected with something wholly unfamiliar in her. It was as if he saw the wounds on her soul, and the sight did not repulse him.

Sinclair understood what it was to be outside the law, outside the framework society had constructed for its own survival. He had his own code. When she invented that outlandish betrothal, she'd known that he would not betray her.

Instinctively, her fingers curled around his. She felt his answering pressure. And suddenly, Louisa felt something she had never felt in her life.

Safe.

Chapter Twelve

"They look like angels, do they not?" Lily tucked blankets over the twins.

Daisy watched Mary sleeping, her hands folded under her chin. "I wish Henry could see her now. It makes me sad that he will not be able to watch her grow up." She sighed. "Sometimes I wonder how it would have been if I had told him…things."

"No use thinking about the past," Lily said quietly.

"No, I suppose not," Daisy said.

Violet loved the nursery this time of night. Quiet and still, it seemed a world removed from the noisy, rambunctious place it was during the day. Asleep, the children looked content, as if trusting that the night would bring no evils that couldn't be banished by a stuffed animal or a comforting thumb.

Violet draped a blanket over Baby Elizabeth, who slept on her stomach with her feet curled under her. "It doesn't matter about the circumstances, does it? How they came to be, I mean."

Lily's gaze met hers in understanding. "No."

Tears sprang to Violet's eyes, as they did so often these days.

Lily patted her shoulder. "My boys' father wasn't a good man. Worked us in his shop from dawn to night. Children, too. But when I look at the twins, I see their innocence and joy. They're not tarnished by his wickedness. Your babe won't be either."

Violet nodded. Lily rarely talked about the knitting shop owner who had seduced her.

"I was foolish," Lily said. "He made me feel wanted, relieved the dreariness in my life. When his wife discovered I was increasing, she threatened to send me packing. But they were short of workers, and needed me." Her mouth thinned. "After I stole from the till, she did turn me out. I shouldn't have taken the money, but I needed it for my babes."

"You did what you had to," Violet reassured her. "You weren't to blame."

"No more than you are to blame for that husband of yours," Lily said. "You weren't wrong to stay with him as long as you did. It's not wrong to hope for a bit of magic in a life."

A shadow crossed Daisy's features. "Surely not," she said.

"I suppose some things are meant to be," Lily said. "Louisa was standing outside the shop with a pair of stockings she'd just purchased, when the babes and I were put on the street. I had nowhere to go, but she took us in. I've come about — we all have."

Violet sighed. "I know. I am sorry to have been so unsettled lately."

"It is because your time is near," Lily said. "You cannot go back, but you cannot yet go ahead. Have faith, Violet. Life with no man is better than life with a bad one."

"Henry was — is — a good man," Daisy said.

Lily regarded her. "You wouldn't have come here if all was well."

"No," Daisy conceded. "All was not well."

"You have freedom now," Lily said. "Your life is your own."

"Yes," Daisy said.

Lily turned to give Violet a hug. "Have faith, Violet."

Faith. Yes, she would try to find some. But at times she felt so frightened and worried.

"Good night," Violet murmured as the other women

left. The nursery was her favorite place. She often remained long into the night, watching the children sleep, absorbing the quiet peace.

The knowledge that her babe would soon join them filled her with anticipation and dread. She tried to imagine her child's face, the eyes that would look to her for every need, the smile that would offer perfect trust.

She did not know whether she could earn that trust, or whether she could keep her babe safe. She had no home, no husband, no money. All she had was Louisa's generosity, and while that had saved her life, Violet needed something more: a future.

Clouds drifted across the moon as she moved to the window and stared out into the night. The world seemed far too big to accommodate one frightened woman and a tiny babe. And yet her hopes had once been as big as that round ball in the sky — before Will, before her world shrank to the size of his fists. Long ago, she had been a girl on the cusp of womanhood, with dreams and hopes as grand as the night.

She had thought them gone forever, but as she gazed upon the moon, feeling her babe stir in its impatience to join her, Violet wondered whether it was possible to get hope back. She was about to bring a child into the world; surely there could be no greater hope than that.

Closing the nursery door softly, she made her way down the hall. She wanted to bask in the glow of that moon while she could still keep her babe safe under her heart. A moment later, she opened the front door and stepped out into the night.

A quilt of starlight covered the heavens. Its soft radiance bathed her face in glowing gossamer. It was impossible to stare up at that sky and not feel hope. Easing herself down to one of the steps, Violet leaned back against a column and watched the stars.

***

Sam sat in the shadow of the stable, idly scratching figures in the dirt with a stick. He looked up as David approached.

"'Tis late, boy."

"I couldn't sleep," Sam confessed. "I...I keep wondering what's going to happen now that Louisa is to marry Mr. Sinclair."

David's eyes narrowed. "I would nae put too much stock in that."

"You mean they might not wed?"

"We'll find out soon enough."

Sam studied his feet. "If they do marry, will we still live here?"

David put a reassuring hand on his shoulder. "Whatever happens, we'll be together, lad. Do nae worry about that."

Sam looked up at the man who had become mother and father to him and everything in between. David's steady brown eyes were the very image of his mother's, as best as Sam remembered her eyes. "Nothing stays the same, does it?" To his mortification, his voice broke on the last.

"Change is part of life, lad."

"But not always for good." Sam's gaze drifted toward the porch. "Look at Miss Violet over there. She seems sad, even though she's going to have a baby. Why would she be sad?"

David looked startled. "How long has she been there?"

"A while." Sam hesitated. "Do you think she's worried about having a baby?"

"'Tis a big event for a woman."

"Maybe she misses her husband."

"Nay."

Sam eyed him curiously. "You know him?"

"The day we rode into Aylesford, he was there. Beat her in front of the whole village. It was obvious she was increasing, but he made her bare her back for the whip."

Sam was horrified. "Poor Miss Violet!"

"A real man does nae treat his woman like that, boy. Remember that."

Sam nodded, unable to imagine anyone wanting to hit Miss Violet. She was so gentle and pretty, with soft brown eyes that sparkled with kindness.

"Yer father was a fine man. Treated your ma like the pearl she was." David's voice was thick with emotion. "If Molly had lived you would have learned much from her. As it is, I'm supposed to show you what's what. But I'm nae kind of teacher."

That was nonsense, Sam thought. There wasn't a thing his uncle didn't know about hunting — he'd come home with an enormous buck just yesterday — or anything else Sam wished to learn. But his ready denial died in his throat when he saw his uncle's forlorn expression.

"I'm nae good with women," David said. "Can never think what to say to them, so I can nae teach you that. You need someone who knows the breed."

"Like Mr. Sinclair?" Sam ventured.

David frowned. "Did nae mean him, exactly." He cleared his throat.

"Who's there?" called a feminine voice.

Sam jumped. "It's Miss Violet," he whispered. "I hope she doesn't think we are spying on her."

David muttered something under his breath, then stepped from the shadows into the moonlight. "Sam and I were taking care of some late chores," he said gruffly.

Violet rose awkwardly, her body heavy and stiff. "Good night, then," she said brightly. She waved at them, turned, and slipped into the house.

"I guess I was wrong about Miss Violet's being sad," Sam said. "Her voice sounded happy."

"Nay, you had the right of it. She is sad."

Sam eyed him in confusion. "I thought you said you didn't know about women."

David ruffled Sam's hair. "Come on, boy, 'tis late."

***

Lord Upton could not sleep. The meal had not agreed with him. The biscuits were adequate, but the rest of the food made his stomach feel devilish queer. He walked the length of his room several times, glad he had insisted on staying under Louisa's roof tonight. She did not dare to put him in the dower house — not with that Sinclair fellow having the run of the place.

It galled him that she had chosen Sinclair, an obviously penniless cad with a worthless title, over him, an earl of fine lineage and some wealth. To be sure, most of his funds came from what he could siphon off from Louisa's inheritance. How Richard had let Louisa's father bamboozle him into drafting a will that left her so much money he could not imagine.

But it was useless to cry over spilt milk. Frederick didn't want to marry Louisa; he simply wanted to bed her. That seemed less likely now, with her betrothed. But there were plenty of other women in this house. Nearly half a dozen, if he had counted right.

One of them would be sure to appreciate his worth.

He stepped into the long hallway. He knew which room was Louisa's, but Sinclair was probably there, sampling the delights of unwedded bliss. Although he'd had too much wine — to wash away the taste of those weeds — Frederick had paid special attention to the direction the women had taken as they'd bade one another good night.

Teetering down the hall, Frederick stopped to listen at the various rooms. In one he heard women talking, so he passed that one by. He wasn't up to more than one woman tonight. Finally, he came to a closed door at the end of the hall. He heard no feminine chattering inside, only someone humming tunelessly.

Humming was usually a solitary event. Frederick

figured he had found his bed partner. He pushed the door open.

A woman stood at the window. Her silhouette bespoke a well-proportioned and ample figure. Frederick beamed. His pulse quickened.

She turned and stepped out of the shadows. He paled.

"Hello, ducks," she said with a grin.

***

Gabriel had not slept. There was too much activity out in the hall. First one door opened, then another. The footsteps sounded heavy and plodding, as if they belonged to a corpulent lord. He grabbed Louisa's father's dressing gown and slipped out of his room.

There had been no mistaking the speculative gleam in Upton's gaze as it roved over the women at dinner. Upton's chamber was next to his, and, as Gabriel feared, it was empty. The trustee had indeed gone wandering. Gabriel made a quick, efficient search of the man's room, and headed toward Louisa's chamber.

At her door, he stilled, listening for any sound that something was amiss. The quiet within did not reassure him. Upton could have found any number of ways to silence her. Ready to do battle, Gabriel opened the door.

To be sure, his motives were not entirely pure. Making sure she was safe was his aim, but the scoundrel in him — or was it the dreamer? — had others. His fertile imagination formed an image of him dashing in to rescue Louisa from her lecherous trustee. Filled with appreciation of his heroics, she would open her arms to him with the zeal she gave her treasured causes.

Almost immediately, he discerned that the real Louisa Peabody, the one who existed apart from his rampant imagination, slept alone. Her thick golden hair fanned out over her pillow like a shimmering veil. Her breathing was slow, peaceful. She had no need of saving tonight.

Disappointment rose in his throat. It was an unpleasant taste, rather like Daisy's dinners. He knew he ought to leave it at that. A gentleman would slip away, closing the door behind him.

Gabriel closed the door.

Stayed.

Curiosity drew him to the bed to see whether sleep had borne away that guarded expression she always wore. It had. She lay on her back, her features relaxed and untroubled, her lips parted slightly to emit a tiny snore. He wondered whether she knew she snored. Probably not. It was the sort of thing that only a lover would point out.

The little birthmark that so fascinated him was barely visible in the darkness. Her spectacles rested on a side table near the bed, along with a large book open to the spot where sleep had overwhelmed her. He glanced at the title. *The Ingenious Gentleman Don Quixote of La Mancha.*

Madmen tilting at windmills. He should have guessed.

One of her arms was flung sideways over the empty space a lover should have occupied, had she been inclined to take one, which was about as likely as Hell freezing over. Her husband's assault had left deep and lasting scars. She was steeped in bitterness and fear, barriers no man could easily overcome. Only a fool would try.

And yet, the dreamer in him yearned to show her how it could be. Except that she wouldn't want the only gift he could give her, the gift of pleasure between a man and a woman. No, Louisa would want something else entirely. She would want a man's soul.

Commitment.

Even as a woman alone, she had formed a family of sorts with the Flowers. Gabriel had no interest in family. You could never be done with family, even if the people in it were madmen.

No, Louisa would expect a man to share her vigilante justice and her wild-eyed schemes. She would want a helpmeet riding alongside that homicidal stallion, sweeping into towns and villages all over England to right the wrongs against women since the beginning of civilization. She would want a man to believe in her cause and to be ready to die for it — and the poor devil *would* die, because her plans were hopelessly ill-conceived. She would not care about her own safety, or whether she could swim in the perilous waters of self-righteousness without dragging herself and everyone else down to disaster with her.

Well, he was not Ferguson. He would not follow her blindly, nor risk his neck again. No cause was worth dying for. Alice's rescue had been a close call, and a man didn't get many of those. Gabriel knew he should turn around and walk out of her room without a backward look.

Instead, he lowered himself into the chair beside her bed.

All he wanted was to watch her sleep for a moment. A harmless stolen pleasure. She would never know. After Upton departed, Gabriel would be on his way, never to see her again. He'd leave without a care or regret. Caring destroyed a man. *Bayberry leaves*, for God's sake. And regret was simply nostalgia, which he could not abide.

A sly moonbeam slipped between the curtains to fall across her face, highlighting that tiny imperfection above her lip. He liked that she had that mark, that she wore spectacles for reading, that she dressed in breeches and rode astride. She was unlike any woman he'd ever met.

Her hair was a rare splendor. She seemed unaware of its beauty and was forever tying it back off her face or stuffing it into one of those caps borrowed from Sam.

Gabriel yearned to touch it.

But he wasn't the sort to touch a woman without her knowledge. The women he touched were willing. The ones who weren't — well, he couldn't recall any of those.

Except her. Slumbering like the dead, parting her lips in a way she never would if she were awake. It would be wrong to touch her now. Utterly wrong.

Perhaps just her hair.

Gabriel reached out and smoothed the tendril that fanned over the pillowcase. It felt like spun silk, gossamer, and gold — a king's ransom. He wound it around the tip of his finger and marveled at how eagerly it clung to him. Like a woman embracing her lover.

He felt a surge of satisfaction. Even her husband, the dreadful Richard, had been denied the privilege of watching her sleep, of seeing that golden hair on her pillow. Had the man even kissed her? Louisa did not kiss like a woman who had received many kisses. She kept her lips clamped shut.

So he was the first, then. The first to kiss her properly, the first to touch her in slumber. Awe filled him — and just as quickly brought him up short. A wise man would not go anywhere near this woman.

Louisa Peabody would not be trifled with, whereas he lived to trifle.

What had she called him? *King of Hearts.* But he wasn't king of anything except a tiny island, and that was his father's mad conceit. As for hearts, he hoped he hadn't broken any, but he didn't know for certain.

He did know when a woman was not for trifling with. Hanging was too good for a man stupid enough to think Louisa Peabody would change.

There was no harm, though, in sitting here and watching her sleep. In sleep, her lips parted naturally, without coaxing. He thought of that fleeting kiss they had shared on the temple steps. Almost, they'd been on to something. For a moment she had dropped her guard, let the longing guide her.

He should count himself fortunate that she'd felt ill and stopped it. For if Louisa Peabody ever unleashed her longing — all the pent-up, deep-and-buried, forever-denied force of it — it would likely kill him. He'd lose his head, which was the only thing that kept him sane.

If he was sane. What sane man stole into a woman's bedchamber, just to watch her sleep?

Gabriel wondered what she wore. She had the covers pulled up high, so he couldn't see. Was it a silky confection, made for conjuring pleasure? Or a thick flannel night-rail that hid every inch of her? He didn't need to peek to know that Louisa was all flannel.

But he *would* peek — else what was the reason for sitting here without a soul to know that he had invaded the vestal's sanctum? It was either that or go back to his room. No contest, really. Gingerly, Gabriel lifted a corner of the coverlet.

Flannel, with a floral design. She was a Flower, after all.

He ought to leave. That was not what he wanted, however. He longed to invade her dreams, to coax her awake with languid kisses.

Ah, well. Some roads were best not taken. With a wistful glance at his sleeping beauty, Gabriel rose from the chair. Life was too short to live in a fantasy world. He had nothing to give her, save the desire that she'd never accept.

He hesitated.

One kiss wouldn't hurt. One tiny kiss, stolen when those lips were unaware and parted so invitingly. One kiss, without risk of making her sick.

Gingerly, Gabriel perched on the edge of the bed. A sea of differences stood between them, though she lay but inches away. Those would never be reconciled.

Still, it was just one kiss.

He bent down and brushed his lips over hers. Her mouth was soft as silk. She didn't stir.

Now he would leave.

Now.

It hadn't really been a proper kiss. He could do better. *Much* better.

This time, when he touched her mouth, there was fire.

***

Louisa struggled to separate dream from reality, for it seemed she had dreamed of a kiss like this. But she couldn't have, for this kiss stirred a yearning she'd never known.

As she came awake, Louisa realized it was no dream. Sinclair was here, on her bed. His kiss had caught her unawares, which must be why she was kissing him back. One of his hands was entwined in her hair. Perhaps she should have been frightened. But he'd caught her in the space between sleep and waking, and it seemed her dreams lingered still.

A strange, gathering warmth coiled around her. The only time she'd felt its like was when he had kissed her at Apollo's temple. That thought brought Louisa fully awake at last. "Dear God, Sinclair. What are you doing?"

"Kissing you," he murmured. "Only that. But I expect you'll want an apology."

Louisa sat upright and edged backward, against the headboard. She eyed him warily.

Moonlight highlighted the slope of his forehead and the undisciplined shock of hair that tumbled artlessly across it. Shadows hid much of his face, but Louisa had no difficulty detecting that unsettling gleam in his eyes.

Though her nightgown was far less revealing than the clothes most women wore during the day, Louisa yanked the coverlet up to her chin. "Go away. I feel —"

"Overwhelmed?" The ragged voice belied his self-mocking smile. "Swept away beyond your wildest imagining?"

She ignored that. "Why are you here?"

"Sleepwalked."

In spite of herself, Louisa smiled.

"You want to be careful," he warned. "I might take that for an invitation."

His sardonic tone did not surprise her — Sinclair never said anything without a twist to it. Yet there was no mockery in his eyes.

"I demand to know why you are in my room," Louisa said.

"Now you are being fierce. I cannot think clearly when you are fierce."

At her mutinous expression, he sighed. "I heard noises and suspected your trusty trustee had gone wandering. I thought he might have come here to settle accounts."

"Frederick? He would never do such a thing."

"He would. Don't tell me you haven't seen that in his eyes. I came to discover whether you were safe. I've been sitting in that chair, watching you. Did you know that you snore?"

"That is an unforgiveable breach of privacy. You're insufferable, Sinclair."

"Gabriel," he said softly. "My name is Gabriel."

"Like the angel, which you emphatically are not. I prefer Sinclair. It is less…intimate."

"Alas, no surprise there."

Something in his expression made Louisa's pulse quicken. His gaze settled on her mouth. For a moment she thought he meant to kiss her again. But he merely arched a brow, as if he knew where her thoughts had wandered.

"To that point," he said, "perhaps you care to enlighten me as to how long you wish us to be betrothed."

Dear Lord. She'd almost forgotten!

"I-I…don't have a plan," Louisa confessed.

"That much is obvious. Indeed, I suspect you have no talent for it."

"It?"

"Planning. I imagine that every time your brain tries to point you in a logical direction, emotion dashes out to bring it to a halt."

He could not have known how close he was to the truth. Her emotions always *did* seem to take over, despite her best efforts. Even now, they were leading her astray, for

Louisa found herself studying the play of shadow and light across his features. She could not help but notice how her father's dressing gown, too small for Sinclair's muscled frame, strained across his shoulders. How it failed to fully cover his bare chest.

His strength should have frightened her — they were alone in her room, after all. Instead, Louisa found herself wondering how that masculine torso would look without the dressing gown. She was glad the darkness hid her blushes.

Sinclair cleared his throat. "About the betrothal."

"I thought that if Frederick supposed me to be betrothed, he would see no need to worry about my finances. I assumed he would give me the funds straightaway."

"I suspect Lord Upton is not one to relinquish the purse strings a moment too soon."

Louisa nodded. "I should have realized that there must be paperwork and solicitors and the like involved. He will wish to have you investigated and — " Her eyes widened. "He will discover the charges against you and inform the authorities. You will be recaptured!"

"Do I gather that it would distress you if I were hauled back to Newgate?"

"Yes, of course. I would be responsible for…for your death." Louisa was appalled. She had set something terrible in motion. "Oh, Sinclair, I am sorry!"

"Keep your voice down," he warned. "Unless you mean to summon the entire household, thereby causing a bit of awkwardness even I cannot imagine explaining away."

But she was beside herself. He had risked much to rescue Miss Wentworth, and had saved her own life as well. Whatever his character flaws, he did not deserve this betrayal. "What can I do?" she whispered.

"A subject that certainly bears exploring." He crossed his arms and regarded her. "For now, however, I will just take a moment to savor the sight of a beautiful woman groveling before me. It does not happen nearly often enough."

Louisa flung a pillow at him. But his reflexes were quick; he deflected it onto the floor. "Be serious for once," she pleaded. "What are we to do?"

"I will take another moment to savor the fact that you include yourself in the 'we' affected by this dreadful state of affairs."

"I am the cause of this. Why would I not be affected?"

"Indeed. Yet my question remains unanswered: Do you plan to cry off? Or was the 'betrothal' simply a public admission that you cannot live without me?"

The man was maddening. "Of course I shall cry off. Once Frederick returns to London, I will send him a note informing him that you and I have decided we do not suit."

"Such a relief."

Louisa stared at him. "You could not possibly think that I mean to trap you into marriage."

"No," he agreed. "Too conventional for your tastes."

"I shall never marry again. You know the reason."

"Ah, yes — the dreadful Richard. You mean to carry him to your grave. And you loathe men."

Louisa prayed for patience. "I think it is only you I loathe, Sinclair."

He appeared to consider that. "Perhaps. Let us try an experiment." He covered her hand with his. "Does this make you feel ill?"

She blinked. "I — no."

He turned her palm over and his forefinger began to sketch lazy circles over it. "And this?"

Sinclair's hand dwarfed hers, yet his finger moved over her palm with such exquisite delicacy that Louisa was mesmerized watching it.

"Well?" he asked softly.

"It doesn't...bother me."

"Yet there is that slight frown on your face."

"I feel an odd sensation," she acknowledged. "A fluttering."

Now it was Sinclair's turn to frown.

"Undulation," she amended.

"Ah." His frown vanished.

"It starts in my palm and spreads to other…places."

Sinclair lifted her hand and lightly kissed the inside of her wrist.

Louisa shivered.

"Too much undulation?" he offered.

"I did not realize that one's hand was so sensitive," she said. "Surely I should have discovered that before now."

"Perhaps," he murmured. "And perhaps not."

Louisa stared at him. "You are trying to put me under some sort of spell."

His low, rumbling laugh caught her by surprise. The corners of his eyes crinkled in amusement, and his lips curved upward in a disarming smile. Louisa gave herself a mental shake. It would not do to succumb to Sinclair's charm.

"You wound me, madam." Now his finger returned to tracing those idle circles over her palm. "I merely wished to know whether this sort of touching makes you feel ill."

"To what end?"

"Oh, the very best." His fingertip trailed up her arm, over the sleeve of her night-rail. Through the fabric, his thumb stroked the pulse point at her inner elbow. "Do you find this tolerable?"

Tolerable? No, that was not the word. Riveting, perhaps. By the time his thumb moved higher still and grazed her cheek, Louisa's brain felt as thick as cotton.

She took a deep breath. "I wish you to stop this…touching. I did not give you leave."

Instantly, his hand fell away from her. For a moment she felt a twinge of disappointment. Then he captured her hand and placed it flat against his chest, as he'd done at

Apollo's temple.

Now, as then, Louisa's palm curved over the contours of his chest. This time, however, the barrier between them was only the thin silk of his dressing gown — no shield at all from the warmth of his skin and the solid muscles under her palm.

Then Sinclair slipped her hand under the silk to touch his bare chest.

The sudden, shocking intimacy should have repelled her. Instead, Louisa's rebellious palm curved over his firm musculature. Her fingers curled around the short, wiry hairs. She felt his heart pounding rapidly — too rapidly, perhaps, for a man who appeared so calm and self-possessed. Her gaze was questioning as it met his.

"Animal urges, acting up." Sinclair gave her a pained smile. "Disregard them. I am a master of control. Haven't you ever wanted to touch a man like this, Louisa?"

"No. Men are —"

"Coarse," he said, "like those little hairs of mine you have wrapped around your fingers."

"Not that, exactly —"

"Smooth, then. Like those muscles you are caressing so delightfully."

Louisa snatched her hand away. "I was not caressing them."

Sinclair easily recaptured it; he guided her fingers to his nipple. "See how it perks up when you address it? When you touch me, I feel the same reeling inside as you. But what I feel is the other side."

"I don't understand." Seemingly of its own accord, Louisa's hand drifted lower, to his rib cage, hard ridges with taut valleys between. There was strength here, so unlike her own. Strangely, it did not revolt her.

"The other side of fear is desire." His voice was lower, rougher. "Polar opposites, but the sensation is similar. Your innards constrict, then waves come shooting up inside. Let them take you, Louisa. I promise it will be all right."

"Waves? Like the dizziness?"

"Better."

Curious, Louisa slid her fingers to Sinclair's other nipple. It, too, puckered up.

Instantly, he removed her hand.

"Did I do something wrong?"

"Merely stirred up the waves too much." A muscle moved in his jaw.

"Do you feel sick, then?" she asked.

"I shall recover. You may continue. I am loath to disappoint you."

He was making sport of her. Yet that wasn't mirth in his eyes. Amber sparks lurked in those green depths; they drew her into their shimmering heat. Hesitantly, she slid both of her hands under the silk, savoring the warmth of his flesh.

Sinclair whispered her name in a way no one had ever said it before, violent and gentle at the same time: "*Louisa.*"

She knew she shouldn't allow herself to be moved by a man as aimless as the wind, as empty as a sigh. But even as she formed that thought, her fingers caressed him and she felt his answering shudder. A tiny thrill shot through her at the knowledge that she affected him thus.

She did not feel ill. Somehow, he knew.

"It's fear that makes you sick," he said quietly. "You were badly treated. That won't easily fade."

"I don't fear you." She'd meant to sound defiant, but her words came out a whisper.

"Then dare, Louisa. Dare to take a chance." His mouth curved into a half-smile. "First you dare; then you soar."

She eyed him blankly.

"You really don't know, do you? That man did everything he could to ruin it." Sinclair's gaze darkened. "I want to touch you."

His arms slid lightly around her. Something terrifying

shot through her.

"Stay with it," he murmured. "Face the fear."

For a moment, she mastered the reeling. Then his lips brushed hers, and turmoil erupted anew. "It's *you*, Sinclair. You're the cause. You make it worse."

"It gets worse," he whispered against her mouth, "and then it gets better."

For his arrogant daring, for his easy assumption that he could kiss her whenever he wished — here in her bedroom, with her in night clothes — Louisa wanted to be outraged. Instead, she sat there motionless and pliant as Sinclair kissed her deeper into the dizziness.

His lips brushed her cheek. Her eyelids. Her forehead. The tip of her ear. Feather-light, his kisses warmed each place they touched.

It was frightening.

Thrilling.

Closing her eyes, Louisa allowed her senses to experience the full measure of Sinclair's artistry. Just for this moment, she would permit herself to be kissed as no one had ever kissed her. Caressed, as if she were some rare treasure.

She leaned into him and felt a wave of something heady and magical rise in her. She gave a little sigh of pleasure.

With a low growl, Sinclair crushed her against his chest.

The dizziness returned in a great, roaring rush. Louisa's throat constricted; fear seized her. Her body stiffened, as if something deadly had its tentacles in her.

But in that moment — her fearful worst — Sinclair pulled back to look at her. His eyes held no veil, no pretense. Those green depths opened to her without guile. Desire, need, passion — all of that was visible there.

But not greed, not evil, not cruelty.

Not Richard.

Something else inhabited his gaze, something wild and mysterious. It called to her.

"Breathe slowly," he said. "Count, if you need to. As you did at the temple."

She held his gaze, counted silently.

"That's it." He stroked her hair, calming her as if she were a child.

Gradually, her breathing eased. Her pulse quieted.

That is when her brain finally roused itself. It agreed that Sinclair represented all that she feared — the masculine power her father and Richard had wielded so brutally, causing her such pain. It agreed Sinclair was a knave and seducer with no interest in her causes. It agreed she was right to be wary of that mysterious fire in him.

But perhaps, her brain added, you might find the courage to face the tantalizing unknown, if only for a moment.

Just to see.

Sinclair sat back, giving her space. And though he was as still as that fallen statue of Apollo, Louisa saw how full of life he was. The shadows did not obscure the lean line of his jaw, the slope of his nose, the sensual curve of his lips, the fire that even now burned in his eyes.

Slowly, she leaned forward and kissed the corner of his mouth. Because he was Sinclair. Because he was all the wild wonder she was afraid of.

And wildness was in the bruising kiss Sinclair returned to her. His mouth seared hers, claiming her in no uncertain terms. Louisa had never been kissed like this — soft and fierce all at once, with a primitive heat that demanded to own her.

Raw pleasure filled her as Sinclair's mouth coaxed her lips apart and his tongue explored hers. Instinctively, Louisa answered in kind, not understanding how she knew such a wanton thing. His arms wrapped around her, and she felt every silken fiber of the dressing gown that pooled around his torso, so incongruous against the strong arms that held her. Inhaling, she caught the intoxicating scents of sandalwood and oak and something purely masculine.

Deeper and deeper he drew her into his blistering fire, until her world spun. Louisa could only hold onto Sinclair and let him take her where he willed, into the wild unknown.

When his hand slid under her — easing her down in the bed, fitting her form to his — it seemed as natural as breathing to allow him that mastery over her. He called forth something raw and feminine within her, and she arched upward, meeting his strength with her own.

Sinclair shifted his weight over her, asserting his power, daring her to object.

Surely, she meant to. Surely, she had no wish to discover the many ways in which Sinclair could make her lose herself. She'd only meant to dip her toe into the waters, to dare for a moment.

Yet already, she could not find her center. That was what happened when daring took hold. There could be no halfway measure, no simple darting in and pulling back.

She heard skittering sounds on the floor — the buttons from her night-rail. Then Sinclair's mouth was on her bare breast, white-hot heat against her softness. She had never known such delicious sensation. His knee wedged between hers, against the most intimate part of her. His palm settled over her abdomen, summoning a need deep inside for all he offered.

Dear Lord. It wasn't just physical need he conjured. Sinclair kindled a desperate, treacherous hope in her that a kindred spirit had found her, would never let her go. It grew and grew, that deadly need, that traitorous hope.

Now Louisa understood: Sinclair was more dangerous than Richard, because he made her feel as if beneath that wry facade he cared just a little, as if he could give her something precious and rare. He caused even the most shocking intimacies to seem natural and even so independent a woman as herself to cooperate in her own seduction.

Because he was the King of Hearts. Why could she not remember that? Sinclair was no kindred soul, only a seducer of the first order.

"Sinclair." Her voice sounded raw, broken.

Their gazes locked. Held.

He gave a great, shuddering breath. Disentangled their legs. Eased himself away from her.

"My fault," he said.

"Your fault? That I did not wish you to maul me?" Louisa covered her dismay by retreating into anger. "Arrogant man!"

But Sinclair would not let her escape into false fury. Instead, he propped himself on one elbow, and studied her. "My fault for not guessing the humbling lesson fate had in store for me. You want baby steps. I want all."

Louisa pulled the coverlet up over the parts of her he had so easily uncovered. "I don't want baby steps. I don't want any of this."

"You do."

"You know nothing of me."

"I know you'd sooner swim the putrid waters of the Thames than allow me to touch you." His gaze was thoughtful. "There may be grounds for cautious optimism, however."

She stared at him.

"You are beautiful, Louisa."

"That's absurd. I know nothing of the feminine arts. I grew up in the stable."

Sinclair frowned. "No mother?"

"She died when I was six."

"Ah. The exact age you learned to mount a horse yourself. Father left you to the horses, did he?"

"It was what I wanted." Why was he confusing her with such odd questions and at such a time? "I didn't wish to learn useless skills like flirting or —"

"Your ignorance is dangerous."

Louisa lifted her chin. "I have no wish to learn such arts. They are manipulative and false."

"Without them, you have no idea how to protect yourself. Nor do you realize what passions you provoke in the masculine breast." His gaze darkened. "Who will protect men like me from your ignorance, I wonder?"

"The day *you* need protection from a woman —"

Sinclair leaned toward her and silenced her with a kiss so unexpected and gentle that Louisa's words evaporated amid its exquisite kindness. His lips brush hers lightly, then again, as delicately as fine silk. He made no effort to embrace her. His mouth simply met hers with such beguiling sweetness that it stole her breath away.

Then he withdrew.

Instinctively, Louisa reached for him. Her hand touched his shoulder. What she wanted, she wasn't sure. Perhaps another of those harmless kisses. But he held himself apart from her, and she let her hand fall away.

What had happened? Louisa wondered. Was he repulsed by her disdain of the feminine arts? His reserve confused her; worse, it made her wish to shatter it.

She could read nothing in his expression; his gaze had grown hooded, exposing only a sliver of green.

"Sinclair?"

He sighed. Slowly, almost reluctantly, he closed the distance between them once more. His mouth settled over hers in a kiss so soft and benign that Louisa felt something in her flow effortlessly out to him.

It was a flawless kiss.

Or nearly so. Something was missing. Having tasted that earlier heat, Louisa found herself wishing for more...passion. Perhaps he held himself back out of consideration for her illness.

She pressed her mouth more firmly against his. When

he did not respond in kind, Louisa put her arms around his neck and kissed him more forcefully.

Instantly, he pulled away.

Her small protest brought a flicker of masculine satisfaction to his eyes.

"Now that, you see, is entirely the purpose," he said.

Louisa blinked. "What?"

"A kiss should create a desire — indeed, a *need* — for more intense kissing. You would do well to remember that in the event you need to protect yourself from any dishonorable intentions you might provoke."

"I see. That was a demonstration. How kind."

Sinclair was a portrait in studied innocence. "I have only your welfare at heart. You must have your wits about you in the presence of rakes and such."

"Pray continue," Louisa said evenly. "How might I unwittingly provoke passions in the masculine breast? So that I know what to watch out for."

He frowned. "Er, you would do the things that women do."

"What things? I do not know how to flutter a fan, or my eyelashes, or —"

"God, no. You treated Upton to lash-fluttering. Looked as if you had something in your eye. Or were winking. Either way, not passion-provoking. Don't think of trying that again."

"Thank you," Louisa said. "It is not often one receives advice from the King of Hearts."

His gaze narrowed.

"What else ought I to avoid? Having male guests who invade one's bedchamber and watch as one lies sleeping? Surely no gentleman would do such a thing." Louisa ignored his deepening scowl. "Pray, is there further wise counsel you wish to offer? If not, then I must plead fatigue and ask you to —"

"There is one thing."

"Yes?"

"If you do find a man in your chamber, you must throw the bounder out straightaway. Otherwise…" He trailed off.

"Otherwise?" she prodded.

"He might not leave." He eyed her darkly. "You need no lessons in provoking passion. You are quite provoking as it is."

Louisa frowned. "I have done nothing to incite any excess of feeling."

"No, you have merely been yourself. Alas, I fear that is sufficient."

"On the subject of passion," she said.

His mouth curved upward. "You wish for more lessons?"

"No. I wish you to leave me be."

Sinclair was silent for a moment.

"'No,'" he repeated in a musing tone. "Such a simple word, yet perhaps you care to clarify. No, you do not think the time is right? No, you do not wish me to caress your lovely person in ways that will forever banish your loathing of the masculine touch?"

"That," she said.

"Ah."

And in that moment, Louisa saw something in his eyes that was not mockery or disdain or even whimsy. It drew her more than any artifice.

"Sinclair, I —"

A loud, terrifying shriek pierced the night. It appeared to come from out in the hall.

Louisa gasped. "Dear Lord — what has happened?"

His gaze slid to the chamber door. "Perhaps Lord Upton has finally met his match," he said lightly. "It happens to the best of us."

Chapter Thirteen

Gabriel studied the interesting pattern Lord Upton's blood made on the carpet in the man's chamber.

"My God, Alice!" Louisa cried. "Have you killed him?"

Alice shrugged. "Not likely, though he deserved it. A gel don't give herself to just anyone."

Louisa eyed her in horror. "Never say Lord Upton forced himself on you!"

"Tricked me," Alice grumbled. "Lured me to his chamber and turned on me like a snake."

"And you had to defend yourself with those candlesticks." Louisa looked stricken. "Oh, Alice. I am so sorry. In my own house, too! I had no idea Frederick was capable of this." She turned to Rose, who was gingerly wiping blood from Upton's forehead. "Is his wound bad?"

"I cannot tell yet," she said. "Head injuries bleed more than others, even when the wound is not grave."

As Rose worked over Lord Upton's balding pate, Gabriel decided the charade had gone far enough. Louisa wore blinders when it came to the sainted Alice.

"Not a shilling to be found, eh, Miss Wentworth?"

Alice shook her head. "Him with his grand clothes and airs — promised me twenty pounds!"

"He couldn't lay his hands on the money?" Gabriel prodded.

"Not a bit of it." Alice scowled at the man lying senseless on the floor. "I should have known better. A gel doesn't come across with the goods until she has the blunt.

But he looked good for it, so I let him have his way. Then he brought me to his room and made a great show of searching for the money. But he had nothing!"

Alice bent closer. "Do you know how much he claimed to have in this very room?"

"About two thousand pounds?"

Louisa slanted a suspicious gaze at him. "What are you about, Sinclair?"

He shrugged. "I tried to imagine what sum might command Miss Wentworth's undivided attention, and the number simply came to me."

"That's it, exactly!" Alice beamed. "Would that every gent had your understanding of a gel's needs. I don't suppose you're interested in —"

"Unfortunately," he put in quickly, "I have duties elsewhere. Packing and the like." He beat a hasty retreat from Lord Upton's room.

He hadn't gone two steps toward his chamber before he heard Louisa behind him.

"A moment, Sinclair."

Gabriel turned and regarded her politely, as if they were not both wearing dressing gowns, as if he did not know that beneath hers was a flannel night-rail adorned with flowers.

"Yes, Miss Peabody?"

Their gazes met. Hers, suspicious and knowing, his, undisciplined and restless as it roved over her, recalling in minute detail the nascent desire she had shown him. If he had another lifetime, he might have done something more with that desire — no, more like *two* lifetimes, he thought glumly.

"So Frederick did bring the money after all?" she asked.

A mere four feet separated them. Not beyond his reach, certainly, but the frosty look in her eyes put her miles away. "So it seems."

"You stole it from his room."

"A man cannot steal what is rightfully his," he responded. "Besides, when I entered Upton's room to check on his nocturnal pursuits, the purse was in plain view on his bedside table."

"Why couldn't you wait until he gave it to me?" she asked. "I would have paid you."

Gabriel gave her a pitying look. "He never intended to hand over the money. On the contrary, our betrothal gave him the excuse to withhold it until he could have me investigated."

That seemed to take her aback. "Will he still? Have you investigated, that is?"

Gabriel rather enjoyed the flush that guilt brought to her lovely features.

"Assuming Alice's blow did not kill him, he will likely take himself off at first light. He has the name of my father's solicitors. They will not have heard that they are supposed to be negotiating a marriage settlement. That will confuse him for a time. If he learns of my crimes, it's possible he will try to force you to grant him an exorbitant sum in exchange for his silence."

"But if I inform him that the betrothal is ended, he will perceive that I have no reason to shield you from the authorities," she said. "He might turn you in."

"By then I will be gone, away from the law's reach. Upton will undoubtedly console himself with the fact that he still handles your funds. I doubt you'll have difficulty with him, especially if Alice joins the Flowers."

She looked troubled. "Alice has shown no sign of taking to Baby Elizabeth. In truth, she doesn't seem to fit in here. Still, Elizabeth needs her mother."

"She needs *a* mother. I seriously doubt she needs that one," Gabriel said grimly. "You would do well to be wary around her."

Louisa frowned. "What do you mean?"

"Surely you have guessed that she did not receive her death sentence merely for stealing a loaf of bread," he said. "The Reformers have made some inroads, after all. She would have been imprisoned for only a short while, if at all."

"Stealing bread was her only crime," Louisa protested. "I saw her myself that day in Piccadilly."

"You saw what you wanted to see, Louisa." Gabriel discovered he liked the intimacy of using her given name, even if she wouldn't use his. "What you saw was a woman who had probably been wanted for many crimes. Alice is a thief and a whore and many more things besides. She will never care for that babe, and she will stay here only until she finds something better. Tonight she had the chance to pluck a fine pigeon. The fact it went wrong merely whetted her appetite. She knows her future is not here, but in town, where wealthy pigeons are plentiful."

"Aye, listen to him, dearie." A piercing cackle reverberated in the hall. "He's a clever one, and not bad to look at, neither."

"Alice!" Louisa turned. "I am sorry. We did not mean to insult you."

"No offense taken, ducks. What he says is no more than the truth." Alice regarded Gabriel expectantly. "A gel likes to be paid for her labors."

He returned her a level gaze. "You want to watch out for that greed, Miss Wentworth. Do not take offense, but I have difficulty imagining your going rate is anywhere near twenty pounds."

"How would ye know?" Alice tossed her head. "Probably get yer gels for free."

Gabriel reached into his dressing gown and pulled out some bank notes. Upton's bank notes, to be precise — or Louisa's, the chain of ownership now being a bit murky.

Alice's gaze was riveted on the bills. "Must be about a hundred pounds there, eh, ducks?"

"Yours, madam — if you catch my drift." Gabriel's gaze bored into hers until he was satisfied she understood.

With a loud cackle, Alice pranced off to her own room. "Come and see me, ducks," she called. "It won't cost you a penny more."

Louisa's expression tightened. "I'll leave you to your pleasures, then."

Pleasures. As she strode off, the word echoed in his brain, along with some foolish others. *First you dare, then you soar.* Gabriel gave a rueful sigh. *And then you fall on your ass.*

***

"Alice! Where are you going?" Louisa stared at Alice, who was carrying a bandbox and wearing a pretty bonnet.

Frederick — still unwell, but desperate to flee — had left at dawn, just as Sinclair had predicted, and now Alice stood in the foyer of Peabody Manor, looking as if she were about to embark on a grand adventure.

"Don't think I'm ungrateful, dearie," Alice said. "Country life's not for me. I'm a city gel, always have been."

Violet eyed her in bewilderment. "What about Elizabeth?"

"No place for a babe where I'm going," Alice said. "Shouldn't wonder if ye think that's wrong, me being her natural mother and all. Fact is, she's better off here."

Violet and Louisa exchanged glances. Baby Elizabeth *was* better off here — and if it seemed harsh to separate mother and child, it was perhaps harsher still to keep these two together.

"We will take good care of her," Louisa promised. "You need never worry for her welfare."

Alice chuckled. "Worry is something I never do. Even when they threw me onto that prison ship, I did just fine. The guards were happy to have a willing woman instead of those screaming ninnies who fight them. With me it was an even trade. I let them do what they wanted, and got a nice cabin and blunt besides. The other gels hadn't a clue how to better themselves."

Louisa stared at her. "There are other women on the prison ship?"

Alice straightened her bonnet. "Where is that nice Mr. Sinclair? He promised to escort me as far as the village."

"How many?"

But Alice wasn't listening. "Said he'd be here at nine, and an ungodly hour it is, too. That's one thing about men, ducks. They don't do what they say unless you make it worth their while."

"How many other women are on that ship?" Louisa demanded.

"Don't get uppity, dearie. Let me think. About five. No, the young one died. A frail sort. Didn't get along with the guards, so they put her down with the male prisoners. Me, I had a nice bunk and a breeze at night. Oh, here's Mr. Sinclair now. I'll be leaving. Don't think I'm ungrateful, but a gel has to go with the main chance."

Sinclair sat atop Mainstay, his features expressionless as Alice flounced down the steps. David waited in the gig. Louisa couldn't imagine why it took two men to escort Alice to the mail coach. Then she realized that Sinclair must be leaving, too, now that he had his money.

"Sinclair," she said.

When he looked at her, his gaze was devoid of the fire she'd seen last night.

"You are going to London?" Where his name and likeness were probably on handbills all over town.

He nodded. "I must purchase a horse, a boat, supplies. I'll return Mainstay after that, then be on my way."

On his way. A chill shot through her. "But —"

"Enough talk, ducks." Alice eyed him expectantly. Bank notes passed from Sinclair to her nimble fingers. Then

Alice settled herself in the gig next to David.

It was then Louisa realized she had misunderstood that conversation in the hall last night. Sinclair had purchased Alice's departure, not her favors.

She had been awake much of the night imagining the two of them together, certain that Sinclair was comparing her unfavorably with Alice. After all, Alice was an expert in such matters, whereas Louisa only had that one degrading night with Richard.

But Sinclair had slept alone. Like her.

Louisa could only watch helplessly as he prepared to ride away. She'd misjudged him once again.

As he reached the road, Daisy ran out from the house, calling his name. He stopped and waited for her. As they exchanged goodbyes, she handed him a piece of paper and he smiled. Louisa found herself envying Daisy. She must have written him a note of thanks for her new toaster.

"It was clever of Mr. Sinclair to arrange for Alice's departure." Violet's soft voice broke into Louisa's tumultuous thoughts.

Yes, Sinclair was clever. Almost, he'd made her believe in his magic. He certainly knew how to make a woman fall under his spell.

"How nice it must be to have a choice," Violet said. Her voice quavered slightly.

Louisa turned to her. "Now is not the time to think about choices," she said gently. "Your babe will need all of your strength. There will be time later to think about the future."

"The future is all I can think about," Violet said. "You have been very generous, Louisa, but I cannot live on your generosity forever."

"Your child will have playmates here. We are your friends and family. It is not a bad life."

Violet sighed. "I feel ashamed for wanting more. But somehow I must make a home for myself."

"Is it your husband? Do you miss him?"

Violet's laugh was bitter. "No."

"Did you love him once?" It was a foolish question, Louisa knew. Love was a poetic notion foisted on women while their fathers negotiated settlements binding them to some man for life. It was a mercenary arrangement — perhaps with more flattery and pretense than her marriage to Richard, but mercenary nevertheless.

Violet stared at the horizon. "It is hard to know now. The drink turned him into a monster. I tried to tell myself that my Will was still inside that monster, but finally I stopped believing it. That was the worst — that I had to stop believing."

"I'm sorry," Louisa said.

"My heart is so full of wonder that I will soon see my babe." Violet's eyes held unshed tears. "But there's sadness, too. Surely it's not too much to hope for a man to share this joy."

Louisa enveloped her in her arms. Violet hoped for too much — no woman should pin her happiness on something as ephemeral and illusory as love. And yet, there seemed to be within the female breast, perhaps even in her own, a tiny hope that the poets were right.

Face the fear. The other side of fear is desire.

But she needed the fear. Fear kept her whole. Fear prevented her from falling prey to the fire in those green eyes. Fear stepped in when desire tried to topple her defenses, when Sinclair's touch summoned a treacherous need deep inside her.

Fear had saved her. But only just.

Thank goodness Gabriel Sinclair was gone from her life.

***

A smart man would count himself lucky if he never set eyes on Louisa Peabody again.

"They be fast goers, mister. Can't do better than these bays. Perfectly matched, too."

Resolutely, Gabriel forced his attention to the horses being paraded under the covered alley. He hadn't been to Tattersall's in years, but little had changed. Amid the chaos of bartering horseflesh, all was neat and orderly — the arched passage from Grosvenor Square, the counting house door, and the crack of a whip that signaled each new lot. The dome still stood in the crowded courtyard, the bust of the prince, forever in his eighteenth year, presiding.

A man in a hurry could do no better than Tattersall's yard for excellent horseflesh, and Gabriel didn't have the luxury of time. Although he hadn't seen any handbills with his likeness, the quicker he left London, the better. He wouldn't spare the time now to seek out the solicitor who'd sent him the offer to buy Sinclair Isle. That could wait until after he'd gone to the island and made his peace with it. Then he'd return to finalize the sale and leave England for good.

"Good bottom, that gray," the auctioneer said. "I usually go for geldings myself, but the mare is special. Look at those haunches. You can drive her hard. She'll take you to the brink and back, milor'."

Gabriel regarded the big gray, then shifted his attention to the next horse.

"The chestnut's an excellent leader," the man said, following his gaze. "Won't pull or shy off the bit. Good for more than a dozen years of strong driving."

Besides the chestnut, there was a stately black that caught his eye. But the gray drew him.

To the brink and back. Hard-driving. Like Louisa.

Ah, the agonies of unrequited desire. It turned men — even gods — into fools. Hadn't Apollo chased Daphne until she had herself turned into a laurel tree? Gabriel had always thought that if the god was so foolish as to desire the one woman who despised him, he deserved such a fate. Now, however, he was inclined to look more charitably on the poor devil.

He wanted Louisa. He wished he knew why, since there were any number of other women — say, the entire female population of England — who'd be easier to cajole into his bed. It wasn't about the challenge; he was not one to pursue impossible possibilities. It wasn't because he cared; it was not in him to feel tender emotions. Nor was he interested in the do-or-die commitment Louisa lived and breathed. He was relentlessly unfettered, and meant to remain so.

What he could not get to the bottom of was why Louisa unleashed in him something beyond the sensual appetites he relied on to keep boredom at bay. Why she intrigued him beyond all reason. Thank God she found him resistible, because this sort of thing was dangerous. Something odd had come over him in her room; whatever it was, he had to run far and fast from it.

And if the Fates decreed that he was to be filled with eternal longing for a woman as aloof as a laurel tree, so be it. Gabriel could manage longing. He'd had a lifetime of it.

He wasn't sure what it was he had always longed for. Perhaps a connection that transcended life's twists and turns, one that endured. Faith, maybe, but more solid. Not trust, because a man couldn't rely on anyone but himself. Not love, because love didn't last. Surely not a soul, because he probably had one already — though it was doubtless an empty and rootless specimen.

Whatever it was he yearned for, he'd be a fool to think Louisa could provide it. As it was, Gabriel sensed he'd been hovering on the brink of something dangerous. It wasn't the danger he minded so much as the possibility he might not return from wherever she took him.

Yes, perhaps he had a few fears himself, and maybe Louisa Peabody ought to be at the top of the list. Thank God he was well away from her.

Studying the horses, Gabriel tried to think of anything but her lips, her hair, her curves, her intriguing little birthmark. He would not think about wanting her, or the fact she had wanted him, at least for a moment. He'd seen the need come upon her, and it was a riveting sight indeed.

But she had stopped things — again. She wouldn't allow herself to be truly touched, not in the way lovers claim one another. She'd ever hold herself back, always beyond reach.

He, too, excelled at withholding, especially in the matter of emotions. He would never give anyone that power over him. But when it came to physical pleasure, he gave in full measure. Louisa wouldn't have regretted taking that from him.

Gabriel had never let a woman drive him to madness. And he'd go mad with longing if he spent another moment with Louisa. Yes, he was well away from her.

He regarded the horses once more. The chestnut had speed and beauty. The black possessed steadiness. The third, that dappled gray mare, had bottom. To the brink and back, indeed.

How could a man resist?

Perhaps it was fitting that Louisa should inspire his choice of horseflesh. Gabriel moved to the gray. "I'm afraid I must have you," he murmured. "Shall we charge to the brink together?"

The horse whinnied, in perfect accord.

Suddenly, a shadow moved between the horse and the sun, blighting the mare's features. Frowning, Gabriel turned.

"Hello, Gabe."

Gabriel had not thought to encounter that cool, calculating gaze again in his lifetime — and no wish to.

"Go to hell," he said.

***

"How were we to know the Spanish frigates in the Caribbean had but thirty-four guns?" Andrew Maitland — his eyes dark as the devil's, but amiable for all that — poured out a generous quantity of brandy. "One blasted warship looked like another to me in those days."

"And to Wetherall, more's the pity." Gabriel's hand closed around the crystal glass.

No one had ever accused Drew Maitland of stocking inferior spirits. Gabriel inhaled the assertive aroma. Fruity, with notes of vanilla, oak, and a subversive hint of apple. Indisputably French. He surveyed the study's claret leather upholstery, brass oil lamps, and mahogany shelves filled with books tooled in dark leather and edged in gold leaf.

Maitland occupied a prime residence in Mayfair, just off Grosvenor Square. It was but one of his family's many properties. His father, Lord Lindsay, rarely came to town, much preferring to stride the countryside with his dogs than to dodge carriages on Bond Street. His lordship had also preferred that Drew devote himself to the family's vast estates rather than taking himself off to sea at a young age and, these few years later, applying himself to the murky business of safeguarding the Crown.

Gabriel knew the outlines of Drew's family history; they had overlapped at Eton and again in the Royal Navy. There the similarities ended, however.

Drew was, to all appearances, the well-appointed gentleman; his boots were Weston's, his tailcoat indisputably Cork Street. Yet he did not embellish; his attire was appropriate for one who moved in the highest circles but wished to attract no special sartorial notice.

Gabriel had no use for Weston or Cork Street, or for the many ways in which a neck cloth could be sculpted. Nor did he wish for a townhouse in Grosvenor Square, which was so far beyond his means as to be laughable.

They did share one additional commonality: the avid shunning of sentiment. That required no effort on Drew's part, since the man undoubtedly had never experienced an ounce of real feeling, whereas Gabriel had been so tormented by the knot of emotions that formed his childhood that he'd locked them in a mental box and flung the key to the Seven Seas.

Was it better to have buried one's untidy lot of misery, or never to have had misery in the first place? Gabriel had no answer. All he knew at the moment was that the room in which they shared this fine brandy had seen its share of intrigue.

And, that no good would come of this night.

"Damnation, Gabe," Drew protested mildly. "I was a lowly seaman."

"Your memory is slipping," Gabriel said, though Drew had a tenuous relationship with truth in the best of circumstances. "You stood for the lieutenant exam, same as me, although why you didn't just have your father put in a good word in Smith's ear is beyond me. You could have shaved a year or two off the wait."

Drew merely inclined his head. "The fact remains that it was not my fault Wetherall mistook the French ship for a Spanish ally —"

"The French ship had forty guns. No self-respecting naval officer would mistake it."

"Wetherall was green," Drew parried. "He'd had the command for all of thirteen days."

"Pity he didn't think twice when he cleared the *Junon* to pull alongside the French just before they hit us broadside. By the time we were in flames, you and Wetherall were well away."

"It would have been hopeless for us to rush to your defense. There was no reason to hand two British ships to the French."

That statement perfectly sum up Drew Maitland's logic. Dispassionate and detached, he possessed an infinite capacity to find or invent new rationales when old ones failed.

This had taken him far. Drew had ascended to the top of an agency that existed in the shadows, with the goal of enhancing England's power in the world. Whether that meant the defeat of Napoleon and his eagles, or the removal of a politician enmeshed in an unsavory scandal that threatened the Crown, mattered not. Drew tackled everything with aplomb. He was neither ideologue nor zealot, Whig nor Tory. He did his job efficiently and without regret.

Which made him extremely dangerous.

Gabriel drained his glass. "As impeccable as your logic is, Drew, it's of no consolation to those killed or taken prisoner."

"Think of it this way: You learned all manner of things during the exceedingly short time you were captive on the *Clorinde*. For which we remain grateful."

For a long moment, Gabriel regarded the other man over the rim of his glass. "You knew I was at Newgate, didn't you?"

Drew did not reply.

"Was the gallows part of your plan as well?" Gabriel asked softly. "Were you in the crowd that day, ready to watch me swing?"

"That was not supposed to happen," Drew said. "The plan was to arrange for your freedom so you would be sufficiently grateful to help us with a project. I thought we had more time, but they moved up the execution. It was not on the published list for that day."

"Ah. My hanging was a mistake, then, much like that French ship. Cold comfort that would have been in the Great Hereafter." Gabriel's gaze narrowed. "Do you have any notion what a rope necklace is like, Drew? I still have a bit of a burn. Not that it signifies."

"But luck follows you, Gabe." Drew's smile did not reach his eyes. "How else to explain that very odd escape of yours?"

That singular, chilling smile told Gabriel more than words. Slowly, truth dawned: His escape at Louisa's hands had brought her activities to Drew's attention. She would be no match for him, should Drew decide that her goals did not align with the Crown's.

Gabriel set his glass down. "What do you want?"

The other man regarded him with a bland expression. "As it happens, I am in need of a man with special talents."

"Which are?"

"My requirements are rather precise: I need a man with the sea in his blood, a talent for survival, and the skill to put things together in creative ways that can only be learned when passed down from one generation to the next." Drew drained his glass and set it on the table next to Gabriel's. "I don't suppose you know anyone like that?"

Gabriel eyed him coldly. "My father died chasing a dream. What he attempted could not be done."

"Perhaps it can, with the proper craftsman."

"I am done risking my life for England."

"That won't be necessary." Drew shot him an easy smile. "All you need do is finish the work your father started."

Gabriel shook his head. "Even if the thing could be made to work, it would serve no purpose. He was never able to sail it far enough or descend more than a few feet. There's too little air to support a lengthy trip, and insufficient light to steer by when submerged."

Drew refilled Gabriel's glass, then his own. "My predecessor visited your father just before Trafalgar. He was treated to a demonstration that impressed him. He has not forgotten. He wants your assistance. Requests it, rather."

"Castlereagh." Gabriel could not keep the bitterness from his voice. "He ought not to have encouraged my father. It became his obsession."

Drew shrugged. "Lord Castlereagh remains determined."

"Frigates and big guns defeat the French," Gabriel said. "Not a tiny metal container that hasn't a prayer of becoming what my father envisioned."

The other man sighed. "You've always been such a lively wit, Gabe. Quick with a joke, light on your feet. The very last person to dash cold water on a brilliant idea."

"Brilliant is not the word for my father's boat. And I am not him."

"No, you are a practical man. You know what needs to be done, and you've got an uncanny knack for seeing how to do it." Drew paused. "And you have heart. You were willing to come all this way to bid adieu to your father's final resting place."

Now it made sense. That letter from solicitors he'd never heard of, offering such generous terms. Gabriel eyed the other man contemptuously. "I wonder, Drew: Will I find your name on the contract to purchase Sinclair Isle?"

Drew's brow furrowed. "No, I believe it is Lord Beresford — you would not know him —"

"Nor does anyone, I'll wager."

"— who wishes to possess a little island directly in line with any path the French fleet would take should it wish to invade us."

"The French have no thought of invasion," Gabriel insisted. "They cannot even maintain a cordon defense around their own country."

"Still, one must be alert to the odd chance."

"The answer is no."

The other man sighed. "What can I do to persuade you, my old friend, to come to England's aid in her time of need?"

"*Friend* was not the word that came to my mind as you sailed away from the burning ship on which I was trapped."

"I was not in command of that ship," Drew said

patiently. "You cannot blame me for that."

"I find I am impervious to logic these days."

The other man was silent. Then: "Does that fact have anything to do with Miss Louisa Peabody and her flock of avenging females?"

Dread knifed through him, but Gabriel maintained an outward calm. "What do you know of her?"

Drew shrugged. "Only that she is responsible for an assortment of episodes that seem to have as their goal the rescue of abused females."

"How tiresome," Gabriel said in a bored tone.

"Not that I hold that against her," Drew added. "Most of her actions would likely be seen by a jury as well-intentioned measures intended to right certain injustices."

Now we've come to it, Gabriel thought. He waited for Drew to tighten the noose.

"Juries — and magistrates, too, for that matter — are mostly men, however. Rather, I should say they are *all* men." Drew took another sip of brandy. "Now that I think on it, I am not entirely sure they would agree with her cause."

Gabriel merely regarded him silently.

"Recently, there was an interesting incident involving a prison ship," Drew continued. "And here, Gabe, I must be frank: There are those around me who view helping convicted felons escape as a grave offense. They wonder at the abilities of a mere woman to execute such a daring operation without the assistance of someone who knows a thing or two about ships."

Gabriel set his glass down with a thump. "Oddly, I have never been one to respond to threats. Indeed, they have the opposite effect. Rather than encouraging my cooperation, they tend to send me out into the night in search of more pleasant company."

He moved toward the study door. "You are welcome to the submersible, Drew. By all means, put your best minds on it. Perhaps in a few dozen years they will figure out how to make it work. But you'll not have my help. Not when all you can offer are threats and promises you won't keep."

"Sinclair."

"Excellent brandy," Gabriel added as he pushed the door open. "My compliments to the smugglers."

He heard a curse. Drew must be slipping, to be so easily drawn into a display of temper.

"Name your price, damn you," Drew growled.

Gabriel turned. "I'd be a fool to enter into any bargain with you."

"God's blood, Gabe. England is at stake."

"It is not," Gabriel said. "The French are not sailors. That French ship was lucky — it found the only British ship of the line escorted by a man who didn't know a forty-gun frigate from a thirty-four-gun Spanish beauty. Boney isn't going to come sailing up the Thames, and you know it."

"War is about hedging bets," Drew said coolly. "There's hope that Wellington can win it all but with Napoleon returned to power, it would be foolish to bet on one horse. It makes impeccable sense to try all options."

Gabriel was not fooled by his appeal to logic. The man would stop at nothing to compel his cooperation, which meant that Louisa's situation had just become exceedingly perilous.

Drew knew he had won. And, since Gabriel saw no readily available sabre or pistol he could use to erase that smug look from the man's features, the solution was painfully obvious.

"Pay close attention, Drew." Gabriel's voice was hard as stone. "This is how it will be."

Chapter Fourteen

"**G**et the tail. Hurry, lad! Mind the hooves — ye don't want to get trampled."

Violet, who had come to summon Sam to dinner, stood at the entrance to the breeding shed and watched as Sam and David facilitated the mating between Midnight and the mare. David stood at Starfire's head, holding her halter and lead rope, as she whinnied loudly. Sam had the simple but tricky job of pulling the mare's tail aside at the right moment. It made her uneasy, but she knew David wouldn't have given him the task unless he thought Sam up to it.

Nostrils flaring, the stallion kicked out wildly as he tried to get at the other horse. The mare switched her tail and stepped nervously from side to side. Dodging the stallion's flailing hooves, Sam pulled Starfire's tail out of the way just as Midnight mounted her. The act was completed in less time than it took the boy to breathe a huge sigh of relief.

Afterward, Midnight condescended to take a carrot from Sam and to be led away. Violet knew it wasn't her imagination that Sam squared his shoulders, proud of a job well done.

Lingering in the shadows, Violet stared at the stallion as he pranced away without sparing the mare so much as a glance. Typical male, she thought.

David moved his hands over the mare, checking for injuries, then offered Starfire a carrot.

"How complacent she looks," Violet said. "You'd think that after such a violent joining she would be out of sorts, at the very least."

Startled, David turned. "Starfire's accustomed to the stallion," he said after a moment. "He has given her three foals."

Violet drew near the horse, who munched placidly on the carrot. "Am I to assume that she considers herself lucky?"

David flushed. "I'm sorry you witnessed the joining. 'Tis nae for a gently bred female."

"I am not gently bred," she said softly. "I have seen it all before, and then some."

Only Starfire's chewing disrupted the prolonged, awkward silence that followed her words. David checked the mare's halter, then checked it again. When Sam dashed back into the shed, David's relief was evident.

"That was something!" Sam said excitedly. "Did you see the way Midnight came at her? Thought I was going to get poked myself." The boy laughed. "Being buggered by a horse — now that would be a bit of odd fish!"

"Sam." David cleared his throat.

The boy looked around, saw Violet, and turned crimson. "Sorry, Miss Violet. I didn't know you were here."

"It is all right, Sam. I am quite familiar with the process of procreation."

The boy's glance went to her protruding abdomen before he recalled himself, then looked as if he wanted to sink into a hole. Violet took pity on him. "Lily sent me to call you for dinner. She's made biscuits."

The lad brightened. "I'll go along, then." He looked a plea at David, who nodded his assent. Sam raced off. He was at that awkward age when sexual matters were a source of fascination, bewilderment, and embarrassment. Violet hoped he would not grow into a man who treated women as Midnight treated his mares. And yet, Starfire did not look displeased.

"Perhaps animals have the right of it," Violet said, half to herself. "They do not take offense or persist in foolish expectations."

"'Tis no wonder you've taken men in dislike," David said. "Like Louisa, you've been treated badly."

Violet looked at him in surprise. He was inspecting Starfire's halter as if he found it intensely interesting. "It's only one man I detest. Many would fault me for that. They believe it is a husband's right to do as he wishes with his wife."

"Nay." David's normally placid brown eyes filled with anger. "I've seen death and more besides, Violet, but I've never seen a woman treated as you were that day at the hands of that mongrel ye married."

Hot tears sprang to her eyes. Violet quickly lowered her lashes, but David had already seen. He looked stricken. "I should nae have spoken. Forgive me."

"I cannot get it out of my mind," she said.

He hesitated. "The floggings?"

"The stallion. He didn't care who she was. Or if he hurt her."

The mare nuzzled David's pockets, looking for another treat. He took out a second carrot and gave it to her. Then he glanced at Violet. "Do ye pine for him?"

"Will? How could I?"

"Ye must have cared for him some. Ye are having his babe. Otherwise, ye wouldn't have —" David broke off, his face scarlet.

He had not asked out of prurient interest, Violet knew. David was a man of few words, but she had always sensed an inner torment within that broad chest.

What was the cause of it? she wondered. Why was there no woman in his life? He was kind and loyal and caring, a man who would never use his considerable strength against a woman, as Will had.

"I welcome this babe," Violet said. "I will hold it to my breast and love it as much as any woman has ever loved her child. But I did not consent to its conception."

"Violet." His eyes were filled with anguish. "There is no need to —"

"I had learned that Will was unfaithful. When I confronted him, he lost his temper."

"He beat you?"

Violet nodded. "Then he mounted me like an animal, like Midnight covering that mare."

She heard David's sharp intake of breath, but she could not stop her words. Somehow it seemed right to tell this big, taciturn man who had helped her to freedom.

"That was how he liked it — the beatings and the takings together. It was his right as my husband." Violet leveled a gaze at him. "I fear him, David, and God help me, I suppose I hate him. But hate and fear — no, those are not part of love."

"He deserves to die." David's voice was ragged.

Violet shook her head. "It is in the past. He cannot hurt me now."

"No one is beyond reach of the past." David's jaw clenched as he looked down at her from his great height. Whatever the source of his pain, it was etched in him like those jagged scars. She wondered if his soul was as battered as that rugged exterior.

"David," she said softly.

"I know what fear is, Violet. It was nae until that French prison that I realized how much I could endure." He looked away. "I swore that if I survived, I'd use my strength for good. Louisa gave me that chance. I'd kill any man who tried to hurt her."

Violet could not help wishing she had such a man as her champion. "Louisa is fortunate."

"Nay, I'm the lucky one. She gave me a purpose when I had none. Without her and Sam, I'd have been lost. Now I've a family." He hesitated. "Ye are part of it, too. And the others. I will do my best to protect ye, lass, if it should come to that."

Violet was much touched by his words. A family. Yes, that was it. She wanted someone to love, someone to lie with her at night and share the wonder of the babe's kicks. Simple pleasures. Solid and good.

David turned away, and from the set of his broad shoulders she knew there would be no more words from him. Already, he'd said more to her than he had in a month. The silence lengthened. He caught Starfire's rope, ready to move the horse to the paddock.

"I had best go in for dinner," Violet said.

He did not reply. Violet wondered how she had ever thought him uninteresting. There were secrets in him. How she wished he would share them. She walked to the house as quickly as she could, given the fact that she possessed the girth of a cow.

It was only later that she began to mull their conversation. What Will had done was despicable, and it had marked her for life. But for all that, she could not wish him dead. More violence was not the answer. Only one thing could vanquish the terrors of the past.

Love. And she hadn't a prayer of finding it.

***

Louisa couldn't forget Alice's words. Four other women were imprisoned on that ship — forced to submit to the guards' depravity or be tossed into the bowels of the ship with the male inmates and almost certain death. Though Alice had bartered her way to more comfortable conditions, the other women might not have.

"Don't you think so, Louisa?"

Louisa looked up. It was Lily who had spoken, but the others eyed her expectantly. "I'm afraid I was not attending."

"We are determined to help Mr. Sinclair," Lily said.

The others nodded, except for Violet, who seemed lost in a world of her own. Sam had finished his dinner quickly and had gone to help David with evening chores. It was the time of night when the women lingered at the table to exchange confidences or gossip.

"Help Sinclair?" Louisa stared at her. "Whatever do you mean?"

"The poor man is quite adrift," Daisy said. "Surely you noticed."

Louisa frowned. "Sinclair goes his own way. He is not our concern."

"Yes, he is," Daisy insisted. "He has done so much for us. We know that he pretended to be your fiancé just to get rid of that nasty Lord Upton. Forgive me, dear. I know he is your trustee, but I could not like the man."

"Alice taught him proper, didn't she?" Rose said. The others laughed.

"It was Mr. Sinclair who deserves the credit," Daisy reminded them. "He rescued her, after all. The fact that she chose not to stay here — and we must thank the saints for that — does not detract from his bravery."

Even absent, Sinclair worked his strange magic on women, Louisa realized. "Sinclair played the hero because he was paid to do so."

Lily glanced at the others. "With respect, Louisa, we think you are biased in the matter."

"We hold you in the highest esteem," Daisy said. "But you took Mr. Sinclair in dislike from the first." She shot Louisa a mischievous look. "Lately, we have been gratified to see progress."

Around the table, gazes met meaningfully. Louisa was baffled.

Rose reached for her cheroot and rolled it between her fingers. "Lily and Daisy saw him enter your chamber the night Alice settled her, er, accounts with Lord Upton."

Louisa flushed.

"We know that husband of yours made you suffer," Rose said. "A bad husband can ruin a woman's outlook. It did mine."

"Otherwise, Louisa, you would not have embarked on this quest," Daisy said.

"What quest?" Louisa said stiffly.

"To avenge yourself on men," Lily said gently.

Rose smirked. "Cut their hearts out and stake 'em on the nearest fencepost, more like. Take it from someone who's been there, Louisa: You're out for vengeance."

"I never —"

"Perhaps you did not set out to do so," Daisy said. "Your courage is commendable. So little is done to help the plight of cast-out females these days. But it's possible, dear, that you have taken that too much to heart. Not that we don't appreciate what you've done."

Lily nodded. "The twins and I would have starved had you not been there to buy those stockings that day."

"I would've been hanged." Rose blew a smoke ring over the table.

Lily batted it away. "But while it is true that our woes were caused by men, not all men are cut from the same cloth."

"We think Mr. Sinclair is cut from a different bolt altogether," Daisy said.

Stunned, Louisa stared them. "Sinclair and I are not lovers."

There was a long silence, followed by a collective sigh of disappointment.

"We were hoping you had finally found a man you could like," Lily said.

"He came to my chamber to make sure I was safe from Lord Upton," Louisa said.

Daisy tittered. "It certainly took him a long time to do so."

"If you haven't taken him as your lover, you should," Rose declared. "He is clever and handsome, and from the way he fills out those breeches, nicely proportioned —"

"Please, Rose," Daisy admonished. "Kindly remember that some of us are maiden ladies."

Rose's gaze narrowed. "Just who would that be?"

The Flowers looked at each other.

"No one to make the claim outright, I see," Rose observed. "As I was saying, ladies, you have only to look at Sinclair and the mind fills in the rest. He has the look."

"The look?" Louisa frowned.

Rose nodded. "You can tell by the eyes. Some men could care less about a woman — one's as good as another, then they're on to the next."

"That's a perfect description of Sinclair," Louisa insisted.

"No, those men are takers," Rose said. "Sinclair's not. You can see in his eyes that he'll give as good as he gets."

When Louisa regarded her blankly, Rose rolled her eyes. "*Pleasure,* Louisa. He'll see to a woman's pleasure. Won't be no chore for him either."

More titters around the table.

Daisy looked thoughtful. "How can you tell if someone has the look?"

"His eyes won't be open wide-like," Rose said.

"A squint, then?" Daisy asked.

"Nothing so obvious. Eyelids down part way, enough so he can study a woman sly-like. There'll be a gleam, too. He won't hide that. He wants you to see that he's thinking about it."

Louisa eyed her in confusion. "It?"

Rose sighed. "*Fornication,* Louisa. When the man takes his prick and —"

"I wonder," Daisy said quickly, "if it is necessary to paint quite such a vivid image."

Lily giggled. Even Violet, woolgathering through most of the conversation, looked startled, as if she had suddenly become aware of their conversation.

"If a man looked at me like that, eyes half open and

gleaming, I'd think he was deranged," Louisa said.

"And you'd miss the promise," Rose said.

"Promise?"

Rose nodded. "There's a thickness in the air, an awareness. Maybe his gaze wanders to your mouth, maybe elsewhere. That gleam tells you that it will be his pleasure to see to yours."

Richard's image burned in Louisa's brain. "I've seen that gleam. It's full of greed and lust."

"I'm not saying there's no lust," Rose said. "But there's more to it than that. You have only to look at Sinclair to see he has it, and then some."

"What of your husbands, Rose?" Daisy asked. "Did they have the look?"

"Only Billy, the second one," Rose said.

Daisy hesitated. "So you, er, didn't kill him?"

The older woman's gaze softened. "I adored that man. He drank himself to death." Her gaze shifted to Louisa. "Billy knew how to please a woman. So does Sinclair. Take him as a lover, dear. You won't regret it."

Louisa flushed. They had turned against her, and it was Sinclair's fault. The man could charm a snake.

"I wonder why he is so lonely," Lily said.

That took her aback. Louisa had not thought of Sinclair as lonely. To be sure, his jokes often held more bite than mirth. His wit was his armor against the world. Why was he so determined to keep people at a distance? she wondered. Was it because of the pain of his childhood?

"That man needs the right woman." Rose blew another smoke ring. "Mayhap that's you."

Only a fool would try to breach that fortress around Sinclair's heart. Even so, that night in her room he'd almost made her wish to try. Louisa closed her eyes, seeing Sinclair as he placed her hand on his chest, let her feel his rampaging heartbeat.

She remembered the magic he stirred within her. That

treacherous hope. Thank goodness he was gone.

"Good evening, ladies. I see I am in time for dinner. May I join you?"

Louisa's eyes shot open. Sinclair's velvet gaze slammed into hers.

Like a fool, she smiled.

Chapter Fifteen

Was there a hint of warmth in those blue eyes? Gabriel couldn't be sure. She wore a loose-fitting blue frock, not breeches, and he tried to wrench his brain away from the image of those buttons that begged to be dispensed with.

He plucked one of Lily's biscuits from the platter. A quick meal, a brief farewell to the Flowers — that was all he had intended when he'd stopped to return Mainstay and allowed himself to be lured into the house by the aroma of fresh biscuits.

Perhaps he wanted to see her, too.

Gabriel had braced himself for her brittle, disapproving gaze. But Louisa had aimed that smile at him, stabbed him with it. Then she looked quickly away.

"We have all missed you, Mr. Sinclair," said Lily, with a meaningful glance at Louisa.

"Louisa has not been herself since you left." Daisy set a glass of water on the table for him, followed by a plate of food.

Gabriel studied them warily. Something was not right.

"Too subtle, dears." Rose admonished. She shot him a knowing look as he bit into a biscuit. "The fact of the matter is that Louisa hasn't slept a wink since you left her bed."

He nearly choked on his biscuit.

"Hush, Rose!" Lily glared at her. "You may know a thing or two about men, but you are positively cow-handed at stirring the caldron of romance."

The caldron of romance. How poetic, Gabriel thought darkly.

Daisy smiled. In fact, all of the Flowers wore

mysterious smiles. A vague sense of alarm filled him. Rose soon enlightened him. "We have been discussing your visit to Louisa's chamber the night Alice thrashed Lord Upton."

Gabriel's gaze shot to Louisa. Did they mean to suggest he had compromised her? Did they wish to push him into marriage?

"Don't worry, Sinclair." Her eyes held steel. "I wouldn't have you."

"We don't mean to embarrass you," Lily assured him. "But you must see that you and Louisa are well-suited."

Everyone eyed him expectantly. Gabriel cleared his throat. "I —"

"What Sinclair means to say is that he's not the marrying sort," Louisa said. "Neither am I. You know I invented that betrothal to mislead Lord Upton."

Thank the gods that charade was done, Gabriel thought. Marriage to Louisa would be a living hell. Besides, the position he now found himself in as a result of his trip to London would keep him well away from her, which was decidedly for the best.

Lily eyed him mournfully. "Is that true, Mr. Sinclair? You are not the marrying sort?"

"Afraid not." Gabriel tried to sound suitably apologetic.

The dining room fell silent.

"Perhaps," Daisy said tactfully, "we should speak of something else. Pray, what are your plans, Mr. Sinclair?"

Plans. Yes, one must have them. Otherwise, life was bound to be chaotic — unlike his life now, which was coming apart at the seams.

"I've purchased a small rig that I'll sail to the island where my father is buried. The island is being sold, so it's a farewell journey. A pilgrimage of sorts."

That was the scenario Andrew Maitland had set into motion those months ago, by arranging for the island's "sale." There was just enough truth in Gabriel's tale that it sounded convincing. They nodded encouragingly, as if sailing to his father's island grave made perfect sense.

"Where is the boat now?" Louisa's gaze was thoughtful.

Gabriel noted that look with a sense of foreboding. "I hired a crew to sail her to the cove at Sinclair Castle."

Daisy's eyes widened. "You own a castle?"

"Not much of one," he replied. "It has long since crumbled, along with most of the other buildings on the property. There's a manor house in better condition because it was leased to tenants, but it has not been lived in for several years."

Lily's eyes bore a dreamy look. "You have returned from your travels to reclaim your past. The restless wanderer at last returns to restore his ancestral home. Only then can he take a bride and start a family of his own."

Gabriel eyed her in alarm.

"Lily," Rose warned. "I fear we are making Mr. Sinclair uncomfortable."

Lily shot him a misty smile. "Forgive me. Of course you are not ready to marry. You must make your peace with the past. Only then can you put down roots —"

"You have been reading too many of those Minerva novels," Louisa groused.

"I have no plans to restore the property," Gabriel said firmly. "It may tumble into the sea with my blessing."

"Oh, but you must!" Daisy protested. "You cannot let a perfectly good castle go to waste."

"I am in England only to finalize the island's sale," he said. "That's where I was bound weeks ago, before I had the bad judgment to undertake the drunken bet that landed me on the gallows."

Gabriel didn't doubt that Sedbury had been part of that night's charade, judging by the man's false testimony at the trial. Drew probably had more than a little compromising information on the man to compel his cooperation.

"So you see, ladies, the sooner I leave England the better," he finished.

"A drunken bet." Louisa studied him. "Was that how you ended up in that convent?"

He nodded. "That night I'd won Lord Sedbury's yacht in a card game. But he wanted another go. Sympathetic fellow that I am, I gave him a chance to recoup the loss: his townhouse against the boat. Whoever could first secure a lock of hair from a virgin's head would carry the day." Not for the first time, Gabriel cursed his stupidity.

Lily clapped her hands. "How clever!"

Louisa frowned. "I fail to see —"

"*Virgins*, Louisa," Rose said. "Quite a lot of them in a convent, I should imagine." She turned to him. "Did you get what you wanted?"

"It's fair to say that the experience brought rather more than I anticipated," Gabriel replied.

Rose and the others dissolved in laughter. Louisa looked away, as if to say she wanted no part of a man who'd risk his neck on an absurd, drunken bet.

"The yacht is gone, I suppose," Rose said.

"Quite," Gabriel replied. "But the rig I purchased is enough for my needs. A little Bermuda sloop, easy for one man to handle."

"With your estate in disrepair and the island sold, you have nothing permanent." Lily's eyes filled with concern.

"Such are the fortunes of a felon," he said lightly.

"Perhaps," said Daisy, "we can help you restore your home."

Gabriel prayed he had not heard aright.

Rose nodded. "I know a bit about such things. My late husband — the first one, may he burn in Hell — was a carpenter. I might be able to draw up plans. We'll hire workers to do the job."

"After that," Lily put in happily, "you and Louisa will be free to plan a future together."

Gabriel rose. This discussion had gone on long enough. "I do not wish to seem ungrateful, ladies, but restoring that old pile of stones is the furthest thing from my mind. About as far away as marriage. Please excuse me. I must be on my way."

"Stay the night, at least," Rose declared. "It is too late to dash off now." As Gabriel's expression darkened, she added: "Isn't that right, Louisa?"

Louisa did not even glance in his direction.

***

When the others had waxed eloquent about a match between her and Sinclair, Louisa realized an alarming truth: She and Sinclair had become symbols of their dreams.

Lily had hopes. And Violet. Daisy, perhaps even Rose. None had given up on the dream of finding love. For all the abuse they had suffered at the hands of men, for all that they were infinitely better off now and thrived in one another's company — they still yearned for romance. Perhaps they figured that if such an unlikely pair as she and Sinclair could find happiness together, there was hope for them.

Louisa did not want to carry the burden of their hopes and dreams. She and Sinclair were nothing alike. A union between them was unthinkable. Besides, he was not a man who put down roots. Any interest he had in her was simply lust.

For tonight, that was quite perfect.

She strode purposefully toward the stable. He had not been in the house since dinner. Likely he was avoiding them, and who could blame him? Lily's head was filled with nonsense, and the usually practical Rose had taken leave of her senses. Why did women lose their bearings around him? But it was useless to dwell on that question. She had more pressing concerns.

The plan had come to her when Sinclair spoke of his boat. He was sure to be difficult, but she thought his cooperation could be had. If money failed to sway him, she had something else to barter. Louisa swallowed hard as she walked across the stable yard.

Night had settled in, illuminating a curtain of stars above. The animals had quieted, and the familiar smells of hay and horses wafted from the stable. Louisa hesitated, and then slipped inside.

Sinclair was there, tending a big gray. Midnight pawed nervously in his stall as he eyed the mare. Sam had placed two saddles in with the stallion, each with carrots, although Midnight was ignoring those for the gray.

Only a single lantern burned, but Louisa saw well enough that the gray was a prize. Her eyes were clear, her coat gleaming, and there was no tension about the ears. Despite Midnight's unrest, the mare didn't seem nervous. She greeted Louisa with a soft nickering sound.

"She's beautiful," she said. "No wonder Midnight is agitated."

Sinclair did not look at her. He continued to work a comb over the mare's flanks.

"We could move him out to the paddock for the night," Louisa offered, "though I expect he will settle down once he gets accustomed to the fact she's not here for his own personal use."

"Wouldn't want him to think that, would we?"

Louisa wondered at the rigid set of his shoulders. Perhaps the women's words at dinner had unsettled him. Surely he didn't believe she would try to force him into marriage.

The silence lengthened. Sinclair's shirt strained over his shoulders as he groomed the gray. The shirt was new, she realized, as was that superfine coat that lay on the straw.

"Your new clothes are lovely — er, handsome." She cringed. Lily might have carried off such a flirtatious remark, but Louisa knew she didn't have the skill for it.

Sinclair glanced at her, his gaze cool and impersonal.

"I had your father's clothes laundered in town. You will find them on a table in the foyer." He returned his attention to the gray.

Louisa wondered how to broach the subject uppermost in her mind. But she had no talent for subtlety, so she decided to plunge ahead: "Alice said there were four other women on the prison ship. I wish to engage you and your boat to rescue them."

Sinclair ran his hands over one of the gray's forelegs, feeling for burrs.

When he did not respond, she rushed on: "There would be too many people for a rowboat. And after last time, the guards might be on the lookout for one."

Silence.

"They wouldn't be looking for a sailboat, though. We could sail yours up the river to the hulk, big as you please, and —"

"No." He did not look at her.

"I'd pay you twice what I paid you for rescuing Alice."

"I'd be twice the fool for taking it."

Louisa's heart sank. "Those women aren't strong like Alice, Sinclair. She says they wouldn't trade their bodies for better accommodations as she did. They'll be thrown into the hold with the male prisoners —"

"All the more impossible to reach them."

"They're being treated no better than slaves." Louisa willed him to face her.

Sinclair tied a feedbag on the gray. "It would be suicide. We got lucky with Alice — the tide was in our favor, the wind, the current, the moon. Had any of those gone the other way, we'd have failed. It's futile, Louisa. When will you realize that you can't save the world?"

"When are you going to realize you can't live your life apart from the world?" she challenged. "Every person has an obligation to humanity. We're all connected, Sinclair."

"No one is obliged to sail into the teeth of certain death

to rescue four hopeless felons."

Angry tears welled in her eyes. "Your life's not worth much now, Sinclair. How could death make much difference?"

The minute the words were out, Louisa regretted them.

Sinclair turned to her, his expression unreadable. "Good night." He hung the grooming tools on the wall next to the whip, picked up his coat, and walked toward the stable yard.

"Wait!" Louisa cried. "I'll pay you more. Three times as much."

He moved past her as if he hadn't heard.

"I'll...I'll let you make love to me." Her trump card.

He halted.

"Whenever you want, Sinclair. On my oath. I'll not object or take sick or complain. Tonight, if you wish. Come to my room. Or I'll come to yours. It doesn't matter."

Sinclair turned. His gaze raked over her, his contempt plain. "Yes, I can see that it doesn't. It is unwise to give the goods away beforehand, Louisa. Alice would never approve. It would be a bad bargain. Besides, I do not want your sacrifice on my conscience."

He made no move toward her. Her proposal didn't interest him. She was a fool to think he would risk his life for a night in her bed. Her proposition must seem laughable.

But he was not laughing. His expression was grim.

"Please, Sinclair. I can't save those women without you." Dear Lord, she thought in mortification. She was all but begging him to make love to her.

"As appealing as your offer is," he said with unbearable politeness, "I must decline."

"You cannot!"

He arched a brow. "I am doing you a favor. I'm a scoundrel — remember? You'd never know whether I would live up to my end of things."

"I am willing to take that chance." Louisa tried to keep

the desperation from her voice.

Sinclair's lips curled in a self-mocking smile. "Allow me to be noble once. I promise the opportunity will not come again."

He had declined her offer with a perfect mix of civility and indifference. Yet his mask was not seamless, for there was a dark glint in his eyes that gave her hope.

Louisa reached out and touched his arm.

He flinched as if she'd struck him.

"Go away, Louisa," he growled. "Take your lofty goals and your valiant sacrifice elsewhere. They are meaningless to me."

"Touch me, Sinclair."

"No."

She caught his hand and placed it over her heart. Held it there. The warmth of his palm burned through the fabric of her frock.

He stood rigid as stone. A muscle clenched in his jaw.

"Why won't you make love to me?" she asked. "Am I…loathsome?"

"God's teeth." Scowling, he reclaimed his hand. "I won't because I cannot promise you a thing. That's the whole of it. It has naught to do with your being loathsome. You aren't. Loathsome, that is."

Louisa stared at him in confusion.

He sighed. "My plans have…changed. I do not expect we will see one another again."

That startled her. She had known he would be on his way, but hadn't been prepared to hear such finality in his tone. "I cannot believe you are unmoved by the plight of those women. You are not a monster."

"I'm no hero, either." He gave a ragged laugh.

"You do not know what you can be. People don't have to be prisoners of their pasts. You can be more than you are —"

"I have no wish to be more than I am. People don't

change, Louisa. You won't, and I can't. No miracle would happen if I made love to you. I'd still be on my way in the morning, and you'd still be plotting to save womankind. Only you'd have one more man to hate."

"I don't hate you." It was true. Whatever she felt for him, it wasn't that.

He shot her a brooding look. "Save yourself for someone who deserves you."

With that, he strode out of the stable into the night.

***

The mantle of nobility sat comfortably on his shoulders, though it had been a near thing. Gabriel congratulated himself on resisting Louisa's awkward offer. That way lay danger, along with a host of murky emotions he had no desire to examine.

I'm no hero. Good line, that. He must remember to trot it out again sometime when confronted with a frighteningly earnest female.

Louisa never ceased to surprise him. Who would have guessed that she deemed a night in his arms such a sacrifice? That she would deign to touch him, providing he was prepared to risk his life for the privilege?

Anger stirred in him. She had no idea how fortunate she was that he hadn't taken her up on her offer. He would have taken his pleasure and left her lying there with only her lofty ideals for comfort. He certainly wouldn't have involved himself in her ridiculous scheme.

Besides, he didn't want her that way, cold and calculating, figuring the worth of each liberty she granted him. He wanted her beyond rational thought, helpless with longing, needing him, craving him, the cost be damned. He knew just how to make a woman melt with desire.

Just not, apparently, this particular woman.

Ah, well, it was just one failure, nothing to brood about. There would be other women. What did he need with this one? She was a menace. She looked like a man's notion of perfection, but she was as crazy as a loon.

When she placed his hand over her breast, let him feel that nipple harden under his touch, it felt like the answer to a prayer. But she wanted his life. He was not about to squander that again.

If only he could stop her from risking hers. The devil's pact he'd made with Maitland would spare her for now, but another rescue attempt would put her irretrievably in peril.

Her future was her own, he reminded himself. No man in his right mind would try to be Louisa Peabody's keeper.

To the brink and back, indeed. He had damned near lost his reason in London — all because he hadn't seen her for a few days. Gabriel still hadn't made sense of what had happened between them that night in her room. He couldn't forget the image of Louisa, shielded in flannel, asleep with her long golden hair fanned over her pillow, her mouth parted in unwitting invitation.

Reality had since set in. Like water and oil, they would never suit. He'd be gone at dawn, grateful for escape. Desire, caring — those things didn't last. They weren't worth dying for.

"Sinclair." Her voice came from behind him.

Gabriel turned.

Louisa stood in the stable yard — naked.

"Sinclair." She said his name low and fierce, with all the authority of a warrior queen — if Boadicea had fought naked, that is.

"God's blood!" he swore. "Where are your clothes?"

She lifted her chin defiantly. "In the stable."

"Go put them on. Someone might come out at any moment."

"I don't care."

"I do." With a curse, Gabriel ripped off his coat, marched over to her, and wrapped it around her shoulders. She shot him a mutinous gaze and didn't move. So he picked her up and carried her into the stable.

The gray nickered a greeting. Midnight snorted loudly,

"Turn your heads," Gabriel muttered. He dropped Louisa none too gently onto the straw where her clothes lay in a pile. "Get dressed."

He turned his back to give her privacy, though he'd seen every inch of her — the image now seared in his brain for all eternity.

She didn't speak. The horses quickly lost interest, and Midnight resumed his edgy contemplation of the gray. Gabriel almost envied the horses their narrow world, where a newcomer to the stable was as exciting as it got. He could use a little less excitement. The sight of Louisa naked in the stable yard was too rich for his blood. He wanted only to get a good night's sleep and leave this house full of Bedlamites at first light.

"Sinclair?" Her voice, soft and hesitant, drifted out of the shadows behind him.

"What?" he growled.

"I don't understand. Don't you want me? When you came to my room that night, it seemed that you wanted to..." Her voice trailed off.

Gabriel closed his eyes, prayed for strength. "Yes."

"Yes?" she echoed, her tone puzzled. "You did want me?"

"Did. Do. Get dressed, Louisa."

"Then why —"

Gabriel whirled to face her, and froze.

She had not gotten dressed. She sat there on the straw, huddled under his coat, which did not begin to cover the parts of her that should have been covered.

"Hell." His heart jumped to his throat and stayed there. "Hell and damnation."

Chapter Sixteen

He'd given the game away. As Louisa sat in the straw looking up at him, Gabriel couldn't hide the desire that swept him like a fever. His eyes feasted on her body, devouring that which he hungered to possess. She had the basic female parts — he had seen that well enough outside — but it was how they spoke to him that undid him. Her breasts were full and perfectly shaped, the dusky nipples begging to be touched. Her hips, slender and boyish, pleaded for his caress. Her lissome legs yearned to be wrapped around him.

Gabriel felt like an adolescent in the throes of first lust, fixated on the feminine form as if it were the beginning and end of all knowing. He stared at Louisa as if she were the first naked woman he'd ever seen.

Then she made it worse. She stood up and left his coat behind in the straw. "You want me, Sinclair. Here I am."

Everything he'd told her was true. He could promise her nothing. She shouldn't waste herself on a man who couldn't hold onto the treasure she offered.

Once, he might have enjoyed seducing her, for he'd always been one for the chase. But tonight she'd put things on a different footing, made herself advance payment for rescuing those women. Gabriel knew he should walk away and preserve whatever nobility was left to him.

But nobility was best left to honorable men. Looking at Louisa in all her naked glory, Gabriel knew he was not that.

She smiled the tantalizing smile women had owned since Eve and took a step toward him. "Sinclair."

Gabriel hated the way she said his name, her voice husky and low, curling around it as if it were more than just a name. The way she tried to make him so much more than just a man.

No, he wouldn't prostitute himself for her foolish ideals. Ideals couldn't protect her from her reckless schemes, or from Maitland, if he got wind of them.

Louisa stood on her toes and pressed her lips to his.

Reason tried to assert itself, but it grew weaker by the moment. He was caught like some hapless fish in a net. Desire stabbed him through and through, like a bitter hook that would not be dislodged.

Arms rigid at his sides, Gabriel made one last effort and stepped away from her. "I won't help you," he growled. "I'm leaving in the morning."

She tilted her head. "Enough talk, Sinclair. You want me. I won't make a fuss about it."

Right. He had a pretty good idea of how it would be. She would lie there and let him take his pleasure, enduring it as merely the currency in her latest scheme. She wouldn't end all breathless and flushed, embarrassed and surprised by her own desire. She'd withhold herself.

Not if he could help it.

Gabriel knew he could puncture that indifference and confound every twisted notion she had about sex. She didn't know the first thing about desire, about letting it take her to the heavens and back. He yearned to wipe that cajoling smile off her face and disprove her fears.

Yes, he was working his way around to the idea.

He would be disciplined and cool and masterful. He would make it so perfect that she would never again think of him and the dreadful Richard in the same thought. That is what he would do.

Then she reached for him. Her fingers fumbled with the laces of his shirt, slipped under the fabric to touch his bare flesh. Gabriel felt his moorings slip.

She slid the shirt back off his shoulders. Her fingers caressed his chest, flirted with his nipples, the way he'd shown her a century ago. She bent to kiss him there, her tongue drawing lazy circles around the tips.

He was undone — just like his new shirt, which she slid off his shoulders and dropped onto the straw with the remnants of his cocky male pride.

***

Louisa's hands shook as her fingers splayed over Sinclair's bare chest. Did he desire her? He'd said so, but he didn't move.

Perhaps she wasn't doing this right. Or, perhaps he truly was immovable — he had refused her terms, after all.

Whatever the cause of Sinclair's stony silence, Louisa wasn't ready to give up. Her arms skimmed slowly down his, then slipped around his torso. She pressed against his chest, relished the sensation of her flesh against his, her softness against his strength.

She felt his answering shudder. Emboldened, she slid her hands down his back, along the curve that disappeared into his trousers.

Sinclair inhaled sharply. Still, he made no move to touch her.

Panic filled her. If she couldn't reach him, those women on the hulk would be lost. If she could, well, Sinclair had to have a shred of honor in him somewhere. He'd have to help those women — wouldn't he?

But it was time to stop deluding herself: She had created her own false bargain. Sinclair had made her no promises. Moreover, he didn't want her, for he remained as unyielding as a stone.

Rejection.

Her ineptitude in the feminine arts was painfully obvious. Her nakedness had revealed to him all her faults: Her body was ugly, her hips boyish, her legs spindly.

Sinclair, who'd doubtless had his pick of women practically since birth, must be revolted.

Louisa's arms fell away from him. She did not want him to see her pain and humiliation, so she turned away, struggling to gather whatever dignity was left to her. Why did it matter so very much that he didn't want her?

Just as she reached for her clothes, she felt Sinclair's hand on her bare shoulder.

A sob rose in her throat. "Leave me be."

He simply turned her around, pulled her into his arms, nestled her against his chest. And there it was again — that treacherous hope of something deep and lasting.

Such a foolish, foolish hope. Sinclair was rootless and arrogant. He couldn't be otherwise. And yet, there was something in him that her spirit yearned for.

Louisa burst into tears.

He wrapped his arms around her, gathered her into his strength, murmured her name again and again. His thumb brushed away her tears, and his mouth trailed soft kisses along the trail of moisture. His tenderness made her want to believe in all the promises he'd never keep.

What, dear God, was she doing?

When Sinclair lifted his head to look at her, Louisa saw the answer. There, in his eyes, was the wild spirit she craved. And when his mouth finally claimed hers with the full force of that wild, reckless fire, Louisa knew deep in her bones that something in her belonged to him.

"Sinclair," she whispered against his mouth. "What are you doing to me?"

"Kissing you," he murmured. "Only that."

But it was so much more. His hands slid down her back, cupping her bottom, crushing her against his arousal. Dizziness flared briefly, but his kisses swept it into waves of escalating desire. Every place he touched filled with heat. The need in her built and built.

Even as her body thrummed with wicked delight, an

inner voice sounded a warning: She might lose herself in that fire, have nothing of herself left.

Louisa put her hands on his chest and pushed herself away from him. "I think —"

"Pray, do not. That would spoil it." His tone was light, but something unsettling lurked in his gaze.

Louisa tried to gather herself. "I-I may have overstepped."

"Yes," he agreed. "It's beyond you, isn't it?"

She shook her head. "It isn't. That's what scares me."

"Louisa Peabody, afraid? You will not persuade me. Don't you always stand your ground?"

"With Richard…it was an ordeal, painful and humiliating," she said haltingly. "But it was over and done quickly. I-I thought with you it would be —"

"Like that? No, Louisa. Nothing like."

How foolish she'd been. This was no bloodless bartering. She wouldn't walk away unscathed. Something in her would belong to him long after he'd gone. Could she give herself to a man who caused such shameless need to rise in her, who kindled such treacherous hope? Who would abandon her at first light?

"Perhaps we should stop," she said.

"I told you it was a bad bargain." His lips brushed her forehead. "Your choice, Louisa. But make it, and quickly."

Again, his tone was light. But his body tensed, as for battle. His breathing was uneven, ragged. The pulse point below his jawline throbbed visibly. And while his eyes radiated desire, they also looked troubled.

"Are you afraid?" she asked in wonder.

"Deathly so."

"You are making sport of me."

Sinclair exhaled slowly. "Decide, Louisa. There'll not be another chance."

For an instant Louisa thought she saw past the whimsy, into very heart of his darkness.

"You *are* afraid," she said softly. "That makes it all right, then."

She put her arms around his neck and kissed him for all she was worth.

***

To the brink and back. Hell. She meant to see it through. Pluck to the bone, as if he hadn't already known. The warrior queen, throwing down her gauntlet with expectation of a battle joined.

Her lips, soft satin, left him with no defense. A nagging question tried to badger him, something about who he was and whether making love to Louisa betrayed them both. But his brain shut down, and he could only watch, metaphorically speaking, as it sailed out into the night and left him with a naked woman who had suddenly gotten much better at overcoming her fear.

Gabriel closed his eyes as her mouth pressed against his, her arms wrapped around his neck, and her lithe form melded to his body. His own arms snaked around her, desperate to touch her, as if all touching up to now had been merely practice. Her skin was smooth as marble, soft as a cloud, and if he died this very moment he would still take the memory of it to his grave.

So this was to be the battlefield, here amid the pungent stable smells and the intrusive eyes of that killer stallion, which, like his mistress, saw everything in black and white, right and wrong. This was where he would give what little honor he had into the keeping of Louisa Peabody.

It was so wrong, and so right.

His hands curved around her hips, molding them to his, pressing her close — not yet close enough. Louisa's mouth moved to his jawline, then the tip of his ear, and the warmth of her lips there nearly undid him. She trailed kisses along his neck, down to his chest, taunting him anew as her tongue once more teased his nipples.

She was such a fast learner.

Something coiled within him, then violently unspooled like a tightly wound top launching itself at those pins in Sam's game. With a low growl, Gabriel put his hands under Louisa's thighs and lifted her off the ground, cradling her against him.

And even though he knew the Richard Fiend had taught her nothing, it did not surprise him when her legs wrapped around him, as if she'd known that part all along. She yoked them together, her naked feminine warmth nestled against the very part of him that most yearned for it.

Desire blinded him. All that existed was the woman in his arms and the craving for completion to the death. And if it was to the death, then death would surely be a blessing if it put a stop to this mad, feverish need she had caused to fester in him like a plague.

Ah, but his trousers. Gabriel wanted to tear them to shreds.

"Louisa," he rasped. "Stop. I need to —"

"I won't stop," she murmured against his lips. "Show me, Sinclair. Show me how it is done."

Her kiss, sweet and lusty, nearly made his knees buckle. He invaded her mouth with his tongue, a lush pantomime of what he desperately wished to do elsewhere.

Louisa's legs were still locked around him when he lurched forward, crashing them into the stable wall. A horse snorted in surprise. Gabriel swore, tried to focus his lust-crazed vision enough to see if he'd injured her.

Her eyes held a trace of mirth. "I did not expect bruises. Does it get worse from here on?"

"No," he managed, barely. "Better."

Slowly, she began to untangle herself from him, easing herself down his body, along his length, tormenting him *in extremis* until at last her feet touched the ground. "Tell me what to do, Sinclair," she said in a sultry voice. "Show me how to please you."

"Clothes." It was the only word he could speak.

"Since I am not wearing any, you must refer to yours."

Her hands went to the fall of his trousers and began to work the buttons. When at last her hand closed around him, a raw, primitive sound emerged from deep inside him, from a place his brain never ventured, as it was hostile to all thought.

Instantly, she released him. "I'm sorry. I did not mean to —"

With a fierce growl, he bore her down into the straw.

And then he was looming over her, taking his weight on his arms, knowing he would not be able to stop — ever, probably, and certainly not in time to do what he wished for her. Gabriel shuddered, and somehow found the breath to murmur an apology as he buried himself in her and lost himself in a way that he knew, deep down, was fatal.

***

The gray neighed softly. Midnight answered with a snort and kicked at the door of his stall. Gabriel regarded the stallion with a jaundiced eye.

"Don't let her get to you. You're better off on your own, believe me."

He lurched to his feet. It felt well past midnight. Louisa must have slipped away after sleep overwhelmed him. Unless she hadn't been here at all and he had dreamed the whole thing.

Gabriel knew he hadn't. His trousers were in disarray and his shirt lay in the straw where she had tossed it a lifetime ago. Groggily, he struggled into them.

Respectable once more. Everything back to normal. No one would guess what had happened in this pile of hay.

Well, almost no one.

A figure entered the stable. Ferguson. He paused, surveyed the horses with a critical eye, and turned his gaze on Gabriel.

Ferguson *knew*. The man's next words confirmed it.

"I don't know whether to consign ye to the devil or wish ye happy," the giant snarled.

Gabriel was in no mood to listen to the man's moralizing. ''Go away.''

Ferguson's eyes narrowed. "If ye hurt her —"

"Is this what you do at night — lurk around spying on furtive couplings?" Gabriel demanded. "Your life must be at a sorry pass indeed."

Ferguson stiffened. "I was nae spying. I do nae sleep well. Too many...dreams."

Gabriel regarded him more closely. The man looked wretched.

"Sometimes I hear voices." Ferguson averted his gaze. "In the dreams, I mean. Does that happen to ye?"

Gabriel had no wish to stand here exchanging confidences to figure out which of them was crazier. Then again, it was not as if Louisa was waiting inside the house, tenderly warming his bed. More likely she was regaling the Flowers with the story of her nocturnal conquest.

"Once in a while," he heard himself confess. Mostly, they were voices from the past — his mother's laughter, the bantering of his brother.

"I hear screams," Ferguson said. "Slow, agonizing screams."

Despite his size and bulging muscles, the man looked positively haunted. His face was covered in sweat, his eyes bloodshot.

"The war?" Gabriel asked.

Ferguson nodded. "Remember when ye first came here? Ye thought we were going to —"

"Cut off my balls. I'm not likely to forget."

"The guards in that French prison were an evil breed. Sometimes they'd butcher one of us for the fun of it. We'd lie awake at night and listen to the poor bugger's screams. I've heard those screams in my head every night since then."

Comprehension dawned. "You didn't — that is, they didn't...?"

"Nay. But they might as well have. I haven't had a woman in years, Sinclair. I can nae. It's the screams. I can't forget."

No, some things a man couldn't forget. The gallows, for instance. That, too, had left a voice in Gabriel's head.

Might have made something of my life.

Like what? Sitting in the parlor with Louisa, planning schemes to rescue womankind from tribulations meted out by a society that didn't give a damn? Making long-winded speeches before Parliament no one cared to hear? Siring a brood of revolutionaries, their little minds molded by their mother into thinking that they, too, could change the world?

Wouldn't have minded one last chance.

But dreams and second chances were for those who cared enough to try for them with their last breath. That wasn't him.

And if that meant he was wasting his life, he'd go on wasting it because the alternative was to hang himself out there like those poor devils in Ferguson's prison who had given their all and gotten their balls chopped off for their trouble.

Besides, he had nothing to give. A long time ago, the boy he'd been entrusted his heart to a father who chose revenge and a crown of bayberry leaves instead. That lesson was forever seared on Gabriel's soul.

"Don't hurt her, Sinclair."

Gabriel was incredulous. "Hurt her? If you had seen her standing there —"

"I saw."

"Hell." Gabriel shot him a murderous glare.

Ferguson shifted awkwardly. "I could nae sleep. I stepped out of my cottage for some fresh air. I saw ye carry her in here. I put my head down and took a long walk. I've been walking half the night."

"You wanted her for yourself, didn't you?" Gabriel said. "You thought she'd be the woman to cure you."

Ferguson shook his head. "I do nae think of Louisa that way. But I worry about her. I worry that someday she'll let down her guard long enough for some bastard to hurt her like that husband of hers did." He gave Gabriel a long, hard look. "I worry that man is ye."

Gabriel gave a bitter laugh. "She hasn't let down her guard. She wanted to persuade me to help free the other women on that ship."

Ferguson swore. "'Twould be suicide."

"Yes."

The man fell silent, which suited Gabriel fine. He was not about to discuss all that had transpired in that pile of straw tonight.

If only he'd had more control. He had never taken a woman so selfishly, never lost his mastery of the sexual act. She hadn't objected, of course, since it was part of her scheme to cajole him into the new rescues. He had spent himself inside her, but she had withheld herself. He hadn't had the woman, only her body.

Hell. He wanted both.

Gabriel didn't look up when Ferguson slipped away. He stared at the straw that had been the site of his undoing. It was the wanting that hit him the hardest. He'd wanted Louisa as he had never wanted anything in his life.

Except maybe love.

Chapter Seventeen

"**E**asy, boy." Louisa kept her voice low and soothing as she examined a scrape on Midnight's foreleg. He must have acquired it when he covered Starfire. She'd already checked the mare, which had come through the encounter unscathed.

How ironic that the stallion, rather than the mare, had been injured. It was the very opposite for humans. For her, anyway.

Deep within, in a place Louisa tried to ignore, she ached for Sinclair. The ache had nothing to do with their hasty, fevered joining. What troubled her was not physical.

I won't help you save those women. I won't be around to see the results of this night. Sinclair might be a scoundrel, but he'd been honest. Her sacrifice had been for naught. It wasn't even a sacrifice. When he joined their bodies, Louisa had not felt pain or revulsion, only hunger and a yearning that lingered still.

What did Sinclair feel? Was last night only another of his many meaningless conquests?

She had waited until mid-morning to inspect the horses, knowing he'd be gone. And he was. The gray's stall was empty. Midnight seemed oblivious. It was if the gray had never existed.

Louisa envied the horses their nonchalance, for Sinclair had haunted her dreams last night. The ache inside grew worse every time her mind played out that scene in the stable.

She had never wanted a man in this way. How ironic that her yearning was for a man whose only promise was that he would leave her.

Louisa led Midnight into the round pen. She had intended only to ride one of the mares this morning and clear her head. But after inspecting Midnight, she saw he needed exercise. She shouldn't have worn her riding skirt, though; it was too cumbersome, even for light work.

Soon, she would teach him to tolerate the whip. Every day she took the whip from the stable wall and let him examine it. She would never use it on him, but Midnight needed to be weaned from the fear of it. Fear made a horse unpredictable. All that any horse — even a fearsome stallion — wanted was to be safe from fear.

If only people could find such sanctuary. Louisa wished she could find relief from the forces Sinclair had unleashed within her. They threatened to upend her world.

Perhaps they already had. Something fundamental in her had altered — no matter that she'd never see him again. For the first time, her cause did not seem enough. Her house, her friends, her horses — not enough. She felt as unsettled as those dark, gray clouds gathering in the sky above.

"Can I help?" Sam stood on the rail, his expression hopeful.

Louisa forced a smile. "He has a slight injury and might not be in the mood for training."

Sam's face fell.

"Let's find out, though," she quickly added. "I can't do much with this riding skirt. You take the rope."

Instantly, he climbed over the rail.

"If he comes at you, swing the rope out in front," she said. "It'll make him think twice."

As Louisa suspected, Midnight was unsettled. He pawed at the ground. His nostrils flared. Sam eyed the stallion uneasily.

"It's all right, Sam," she said. "Walk toward him."

That seemed to make the horse more uneasy. He tossed his head.

"Will he rear?" Sam asked nervously.

"If he does, I'll talk you through it." Louisa edged closer to the stallion. With two of them moving toward him, Midnight's ears went back. Louisa took the lead rope from Sam and looped a knot in it so it wouldn't slip through his hands if the horse pulled him.

Sam looked dubious as she returned the rope to him.

"You have good hands, Sam. More importantly, the right feel. You're ready." Louisa didn't take her eyes off Midnight. "If he rises up, don't try to pull him down. He knows you can't, and it will only prove him the superior being. Remember: You're his master."

Sam eyed the horse uncertainly. Midnight pawed the ground again, and Sam edged closer. Just as he did, however, a clap of thunder sounded. The stallion reared. Sam looked terrified, but he held on to the lead rope.

"Pull the rope to the side." Louisa's voice was low, calm. "Move to his flank."

Sam did. Now he was out of range of the horse's flailing hooves.

"Good," she said. "Flick at his rear with the rope."

Midnight tried to spin away. But with Sam pulling him to the side, the horse skidded backward.

"See? He's backing away. He can't rear while he's backing. Pull him to the side."

Sam kept tugging the lead toward the horse's flank.

"He'll try to spin again," Louisa warned. "Stay with it."

The horse and the boy engaged in a battle of wills for some minutes. At last, Midnight grew still. He shook his head. Finally, his ears relaxed. He regarded Sam with a bored look.

"Well done, Sam," Louisa said. "Now you can release the rope."

Sam dropped the lead and turned to her in jubilation. "I showed him, didn't I? I showed him I'm the master!"

"You did. We'll let him be for a while." She regarded

Sam with pride. He'd be a trainer himself before long.

She heard her name and saw Rose waving at them from the gig. Daisy was seated in it. Lily stood nearby, talking with Violet. "Come with us, Louisa."

"Where are you going?"

"To Mr. Sinclair's castle. All of us except Violet. She needs her rest."

Louisa stared at her blankly. "Sinclair's castle?"

"Did you not hear us last night? We have promised to help him restore his ancestral home."

"I heard Sinclair say he had no intention of restoring the place."

"He won't have to do a thing." Rose frowned at her. "It was unlike you to miss breakfast."

Louisa ignored that. "Did Sinclair change his mind?" She could not imagine him agreeing to such a plan.

"He wasn't at breakfast, either. Like most men, Mr. Sinclair doesn't know what's good for him. But he needs us, dear. And even if he's not there, it couldn't hurt for us to see the place."

This was a disaster in the making, Louisa thought. It was on the tip of her tongue to say she had already seen Sinclair's estate. But she hadn't really — only that fallen statue of Apollo at the temple ruins. She hadn't inspected the castle or the house in which he lived as a child.

By now, Sinclair had probably sailed off to his island, so she'd be spared the ordeal of meeting him again. He'd had happy times in that house. Maybe seeing it would help her sort out the puzzle of Gabriel Sinclair and put to rest the foment he'd brought to her life.

"Give me a moment," Louisa called as she moved toward the paddock and Starfire.

She would have Sam put Midnight in his stall while they were away. She wouldn't risk the chance a storm would blow up while he was outside and unsettle him further.

A small voice in her head demanded to know what she thought to gain from going in search of Sinclair's past.

***

"Don't worry," Violet reassured Lily as she shifted baby Elizabeth to her other arm. "If I need you, I will send Sam. It is only a few miles."

Lily frowned. "Perhaps I should stay."

"David is here, if I need him."

"You must not exert yourself with the children," Lily warned. "Mrs. Hanford has promised to come this afternoon to help if the weather holds."

Violet eyed the darkening horizon as she stroked the baby's cheek. "It may not, but the children are no trouble. And they adore David. He does not let me lift a finger to help."

"There. You see?" Rose hustled Lily into the gig. "Violet will be fine."

Violet watched them leave, not as certain as Rose that Mr. Sinclair would welcome their intrusion. He had sounded quite firm on the subject last night — but then Violet's mind had been elsewhere.

As she watched David hitch up the dray horse, she knew exactly where her mind had wandered.

When he removed a barrel from the wagon to make room for the children, Violet had the distinct impression he could have lifted the entire cart. His broad back had the strength of ten men. And yet, he never put his strength on display. He was quiet and respectful; more than once Violet had heard him reprimand Sam for bragging about his uncle's brawn and might.

There was a sadness in David, though. Perhaps it stemmed from his time in prison during the war. Like those scars, the sadness seemed to be part of him. Still, his brown eyes radiated kindness. Whatever he had endured had not erased that.

His soft burr and rough accent stirred something within her. Perhaps if she had met him years ago instead of Will, her life might have been different.

Now, though, she was bloated and fat and ungainly. No man — even a kind one — would look at her twice. Violet wished she'd never told David about Will's beatings, for the story had caused him to look at her with pity and sorrow, and she did not want those things from him. Just once, she wished he would look at her as a man looks at a woman he desires.

But she was daydreaming. And daydreams were for foolish chits who weren't pregnant and penniless.

"Sam and I will take Mary and the twins with us while we see to the corn seedlings," David said, looking down at her from his great height.

Violet glanced at the sky again. Though she'd heard thunder earlier, now the storm clouds seemed farther off. David followed her gaze.

"A little rain won't hurt us," he said. "We'll be close enough to get back here quickly if a storm brews up. Try to rest."

Minutes later he had the children sitting on the cart, squealing delightedly as they drove off toward one of the lower fields. They would be gone into the afternoon, if the weather held and he decided to bed them down on the cart for their naps.

As they pulled away, Violet looked at the babe in her arms, "It's just you and me, Elizabeth. What shall we do with ourselves?"

Baby Elizabeth yawned. Her eyes closed. She would probably sleep for several hours.

An ineffable sadness filled Violet. Her gaze followed the wagon as it traveled along the lane in a cloud of dust that got smaller and smaller.

Between her and happiness lay a wide, wide gulf. She was a woman with broken dreams and foolish desires, as big as a cow, and about as desirable. No man would want her. Certainly not the man driving that speck of a wagon.

David probably had the children singing by now. He liked to entertain them with nonsensical songs that left them in giggles. It amazed Violet that such a quiet man had such silly songs in him. It was only to the children that he offered this side of himself. Perhaps their laughter swept aside the pain. With them he returned to a time when life was as simple and rewarding as a child's smile.

In a way, she and David were two of a kind.

Both of them understood that life could be mean. Both received solace from the pure delight of a child's love. But though Violet cared deeply for the children, she craved something else. Loving a child was easy. Loving an adult took courage — especially if love had betrayed you.

Though strong in so many ways, David didn't have heart or courage for love, Violet suspected. The pain in him was too palpable. Anyway, she had no business daydreaming when her thoughts should be on the babe growing under her heart.

Elizabeth made a soft, gurgling noise. As Violet stroked the baby's cheek, she prayed that somehow she could protect her own child against the travails of life that chipped away at strength. She prayed for David, prayed that wherever life led him, he would recover his courage. For a long moment she stood there, watching that speck on the horizon get smaller.

"The very picture of maternal bliss," a rough voice said.

Violet jumped, which made baby Elizabeth grumble in sleepy protest. She turned to see an unkempt rider atop an old, broken-down horse.

"Will!"

Her husband glanced around him, taking in Louisa's house and the grounds. "You've come up in the world, Bess girl. Shouldn't wonder if you're reluctant to come away with the likes of me."

"Come away with you?" Violet stared at him in horror.

He grinned, displaying a gap where his front teeth had once lodged. "What's the matter, sweets?" He swung himself off the nag. "My looks not the same as they used to be? Got your man to thank for that. And that spitfire of a woman that was with him."

"I have no man." Violet edged toward the house.

"No sense in running. Can't get far in your condition. Are you alone, then? Did they leave you in this big old house with no more company than a babe? Now that's a shame. Guess it's good that I'm here."

Violet opened her mouth and screamed.

Baby Elizabeth jerked awake, and began to wail. As the baby's cries joined with Violet's, Will put his hands to his ears in mock terror.

And then he laughed. A great booming laugh that sent shivers down Violet's spine.

***

His boat needed paint, and the cables were shot, but that would be someone else's problem; Gabriel intended to sell it after he was done with the submersible. He'd hoped to sail to the island today, but some minor repairs had been needed first — not a surprise, since he'd acquired the sloop for next to nothing from a castaway old salt in Woolwich. Still, it would take him to the island and back, which was all he needed. Drew's men had left the boat in the cove and vanished, which suited him fine. The less Gabriel saw of Drew's ilk, the better.

Gabriel had arranged to stable the gray with one of the village boys while he was away, but by the time he made the boat repairs, those dark clouds on the horizon had swept too close and he decided to put off the island trip until tomorrow.

Sleeping on the boat would be anything but restful in a

storm. With the mooring as secure as he could make it, there was nothing to do but fetch his horse, return to his dilapidated property, and hope the house would have him for the night.

He had inspected the place briefly this morning. The castle was a lost cause, just waiting to crumble into the sea. He hadn't gone into the manor house, though he could see through broken windowpanes that dust lay thick over the Holland covers. Outside, his mother's garden had been taken over by the tenacious wisteria she had always regretted planting. Weeds grew through the privy.

Shabby though it might be, the house would be shelter from the storm. Gabriel wasn't about to return to Louisa's house and give her reason to think he'd agreed to her rescue scheme.

His mood was as dark as those clouds above. He had taken no care with Louisa last night. That bone-rattling kiss she'd given him gutted his resolve, turned him into a weak-willed adolescent consumed in lust's flame. She probably had marks from when he crashed her against the wall and from the prickly straw on the floor. He had intended to show her the joys of the flesh. Instead, all he'd shown her was pain and his selfishness.

How cocky he'd been before. How humbled now. He had become a caricature of himself, a rogue without conscience or caring, living only for his own fulfillment. Image had become truth.

He hadn't even sought her out to say goodbye. The devil on his shoulder pointed out that he'd made her no promises, that he was who he was. That he couldn't, wouldn't, change.

All true.

But there was another, tantalizing truth: Louis had wanted him, at least for a moment or two — all he'd given her. Gabriel had felt something in her soften during that kiss. But he had left her passion unfulfilled, never even tried to erase the horror of her demon husband. She'd never know how it could be.

Too late now. He had set something in motion he couldn't change. Drew wouldn't hesitate to have Louisa and the rest of the Flowers arrested if he didn't live up to his end of things.

If all went well, Louisa would have no trouble from the law, provided she stopped breaking it. She could turn her hand to more profitable endeavors. That stallion would bring hefty stud fees. She could open a women's shelter, hire barristers for female defendants, publish radical pamphlets, even address unruly crowds from the speaker's corner in Hyde Park, if she wished.

But all that hinged on her not embarking on more illegal rescues, prison hulks being high on the list. Gabriel hadn't figured out how to put a stop to her illegal activities. She wouldn't be amenable to persuasion, logic, warnings, or threats. Louisa was not a woman who backed down, even for her own good.

So he supposed he would simply follow the philosophy by which he'd lived most of his adult life: When things get tricky, move on.

It was a great character-builder.

Riding toward his boyhood home, Gabriel fought a bittersweet smile as the castle ruins came into view. After he finished with the submersible, he'd sell the property. He didn't want a castle or a house full of memories. His own memories were sufficient.

Strangely, though, he could no longer summon his mother's face. Her portrait had once hung in his parents' bedchamber, but Aloysius had not taken it to the island. In fact, Gabriel had seen no likeness of her since the day he'd been packed off to Eton. If the painting still hung in their room, perhaps he would have a miniature made to take on his travels.

A man didn't need roots or a house. He didn't need a

castle, and certainly not a temple to an ancient god. A portrait would suffice, though it was probably faded and dark by now. Gabriel did not want to remember his mother as faded and dark. He wanted to remember her as she'd been, full of laughter — jollying his father when his inventions failed, rejoicing when they succeeded.

But alas, life held no permanence. Even madness was silenced by the grave, unless it was visited on succeeding generations, and then a man had to watch for it every step of the way.

Sometimes, he had recently discovered, madness took the form of soulful musings about a particular woman. The overwhelming desire to possess Louisa Peabody against all sound judgment was such a madness. This odd seed that the Flowers had planted in the barren soil of his soul — the possibility that his house could be habitable once more — was another.

Gabriel knew better. He would not rebuild his father's kingdom. In the end it would all vanish, like childish hopes and dreams and the image of his mother. Like the king in Shelley's poem, brought low by one great truth: Kings and castles, gods and temples, portraits and inventions, love and hate — all were destroyed by time.

Even angels were a notoriously unreliable lot. As best he could recall, they popped in and out of Scripture with a distressing lack of dependability. Not for the first time, Gabriel wondered why his mother had given him such a name. Had she counted on his working miracles?

The only miracle he hoped for now was reaching the old house without getting soaked. The wind had whipped itself into a fine fury by the time he settled the gray in the old stable. With a faint hope that the structure would hold against the storm, Gabriel trudged toward the house.

And halted in his tracks.

There, on what had once been his mother's neatly trimmed lawn, was a gig and two hobbled horses —

Mainstay and Starfire, if he did not miss his guess —
nibbling the overgrown wisteria.

The Flowers seemed to be an exception to the natural
law of impermanence. They were everywhere, blossoming
like bindweed, tenacious as his mother's wisteria. Girding
himself, Gabriel stepped through the front door of his
boyhood home for the first time in nearly two decades.

An army had invaded.

It had swept the floors, washed the walls, removed the
Holland covers. It was apparently reconnoitering in the
dining room, for a cacophony of fractious voices floated out
to him.

"Pink. It must be pink. With gold leaf trim."

"On the moldings? You are quite mad, dear. Nothing
but good stout oak will do. It is a man's house, after all."

"Just because he is a man, he needn't have the aesthetic
sense of a moose. No, it must be gold leaf. If Mr. Adam used
it, you can be sure it is acceptable."

"Did you notice the marble fireplace? Pink Italian, I'll
wager."

"All the more reason for gold leaf."

"No man wants pink and gold in his study."

"Since when did you become an expert on such
matters?"

"I have had three husbands, and if that doesn't qualify
me to judge what a man wants, I don't know what does.
Although all of them were pigs in their own way."

"My point exactly. We can't trust their tastes, can we?"

Gabriel stepped into the room. The Flowers were
seated around the old dining room table, poring over
sketches. They did not notice him.

Sitting alone in a tall chair, one foot drawn up under
her riding skirt, the other swinging aimlessly, was a glum-
looking Louisa.

Gabriel had thought he preferred her in breeches, but
that hitched-up skirt afforded him a riveting glimpse of her

bare knee, just above her boots. Rather than the usual high-buttoned riding jacket, Louisa wore a plain, loose-fitting shirt, perhaps one of her father's or Sam's. The laces in front all but begged to be undone.

She must have sensed his presence, for she looked up. Their gazes met.

He wanted her even more.

"Now that we know what must be done," Rose said, "we can return tomorrow to hire some workers from the village."

Lily shook her head. "Violet is near her time. We should not leave her again."

"Sam can fetch Mrs. Hanford in the morning," Rose said. "Those who can, will come back tomorrow. For now, it's time to return home."

"I am afraid you won't be going anywhere tonight, ladies," Gabriel said, feeling the heavy hand of fate. "Apollo has made a hasty journey across the sky, and Zeus has seen fit to send us a storm. Chaos, it seems, has come to rule."

Startled, the Flowers stared at him. As one, they broke into smiles.

"Mr. Sinclair!" Daisy exclaimed. "Come and look at our plans."

"What's this nonsense about a storm?" Rose demanded.

A great boom resounded from the heavens.

"Oh, dear," Lily said. "Violet will be worried."

"David will look after her and the children," Louisa said.

Rose grinned at him. "We have taken the liberty of conducting a thorough cleaning and inspection of the house — the downstairs, that is. We haven't made it to all of the upstairs rooms. Your house is in dreadful shape, I don't mind saying. But a few improvements will make it habitable. Would you care to hear my ideas?"

Gabriel opened his mouth to reply.

"You do not need to thank us," Daisy said, before he could speak. "We think of you as one of us. You may consider us your family."

A family. Sweet Jesus. Inadvertently, his gaze traveled to Louisa, just as a great clap of thunder boomed overhead. A bolt of lightning crackled close to the house.

Gabriel wondered whether the gods had at last decided to speak to him. And if so, why the devil they had to be so noisy about it.

Chapter Eighteen

Violet could smell the gathering storm. It mingled with the scent of fear — hers. The air was heavy and thick with foreboding.

Baby Elizabeth had cried herself to sleep. The tears had dried on her cheeks, leaving little trails of sorrow on her smooth, delicate skin. She slept on the daybed in Louisa's parlor, because Will had refused to let Violet take the child upstairs to the nursery.

"Did you think I would let you out of my sight again?" Will gave a rough laugh. "Not bloody likely, wife."

Wife. On Will's lips, the word was a curse. She had changed her name, her home, her friends, but nothing could change the fact that she was his wife. She had no right to dream about another man. She would always belong to this one.

"What about Helen?" Violet asked quietly.

He shrugged. "She is old. I tired of her."

Violet's gaze narrowed. "She is but two years older than me. I'd wager she found someone better. How easy that must have been. Any man is better than you."

Will reddened. The anger that was never far from the surface exploded. He jerked her to him, wrenching her arm. "Watch that tongue of yours, Bess," he snarled, "or I'll cut it out."

"My name," she said, "is Violet."

Will guffawed. "Violet! Now that's rich. Got yerself a fancy name, a fancy house, and a fancy man to go with 'em." He bent closer, and his foul breath nearly suffocated her. "Where is he? Where is the man who rode into town and stole you away from me?"

"No one stole me away." Violet tried to slow her breathing, to keep panic at bay. "You forfeited your claim to me the minute you took up with Helen."

His big, filthy hand closed over her breast. The stench of drink made her flinch. "I didn't forfeit anything," he growled. "You belong to me and you always will. We had something once, didn't we, Bess?"

"No." Violet closed her eyes, denying his words, hating his touch. Perhaps she had loved him once, but that was long ago. She'd been weaker then. Three months of living with Louisa and the others had shown her a woman's strength. And though the fear rising within threatened to shut out reason, Violet would not cower before this man. For the sake of Baby Elizabeth and her unborn child, she would keep her wits about her.

She shrugged off his hand. "How did you find me?" she asked, buying time, knowing he loved to boast about his cleverness.

Will laughed. "The stallion. Everyone who's ever seen him remembers that one. A tooth drawer at the Chatham fair had heard of a woman with yellow hair who kept a big black stud. It was easy to find him."

"Helen threw you out, didn't she?" Violet taunted. If she made him angry, all the better. Will never thought clearly in the throes of rage. "What happened, Will? Did you seduce one of her friends?"

He struck her full across her face.

Violet reeled with the force of the blow, tasted blood.

"Don't say I didn't warn you about that mouth of yours, Bess." Suddenly, a knife glinted in his hand. "Helen was a stupid woman. She told the constable I was the one poisoned her oaf of a husband, not you. I had to kill her. I'll kill you, too, Bess, if you don't come along nice like."

"Temper always was your worst feature," she said with forced calm, letting her gaze wander about the room, searching for anything to use as a weapon. But the fireplace tools were too far away, and she knew she couldn't lift the heavy vase on the side table.

Will took the decision out of her hands.

"Enough of this," he growled. He jerked her toward the door.

"I cannot leave Baby Elizabeth," Violet protested.

Will shook his head. "I don't need another mouth to feed."

"Then you don't want me," she retorted. "My babe is due soon. There'll be two of us then."

"It's none of mine."

Violet was incredulous. "The babe is yours. Don't you remember how you forced yourself on me? To put me in my place, you said."

"Force? Not bloody likely." He scoffed. "A husband has rights. As for that babe in you, it can be disposed of easy enough."

Violet stared at him. "How could I ever have loved you? You are a monster!"

Will laughed. "Because I knew how to kiss you without rushing my fences. Stirred you up, didn't I, Bess? You were ready for it."

Yes, she had been ready. For love, a husband, children. So ready that she had not opened her eyes to the truth about Will's character. He had been handsome, clever, brash. And yes, he had known how to kiss her, how to stir up a heat she had never dreamed existed. She'd gone to him breathless and full of that heat and longing, mistaking those for love. But he had taken her roughly, never fanning the flames of the fire he'd stirred within her. Then came the beatings, other women. Too late, Violet realized that he hadn't cared for her at all.

She hadn't loved Will, she realized now. She had loved the man she wanted him to be.

The man of her dreams.

Foolish woman. She'd been dreaming those same dreams about David, imagining herself in love with him, as she had once imagined herself in love with Will.

"Come, gel," Will barked. "Law's after me. This broken-down nag won't last as far as the next town. But I'm thinking that big stud will do just fine."

Of course. He had come for the horse, not her. But he would take her, too, as payment for the humiliation he'd suffered the day David and Louisa rescued her. Helen was dead; he needed a woman. Will always needed a woman.

Violet cast one last, worried look at the sleeping Elizabeth before Will pulled her out of the house. She scanned the horizon, searching for any sign of David and the children, though they wouldn't be back for hours.

Unless that bit of dust on the far side of the hill was the dray, which meant David had sensed the coming storm and decided to bring the children back early. He wouldn't expect to find a dangerous madman with a knife. He and the children would be easy targets.

How could she protect them? Her mind raced as they neared the stable. "Midnight is in the last stall."

"Horse like that don't belong in a stall," he growled.

"He's not easy to handle. Even Louisa sometimes has trouble with him."

"The day I can't handle a woman's mount is the day I have one foot in the grave."

Midnight snorted a greeting as they entered.

"See, Bess?" Will gloated. "A horse knows the measure of a man."

"My name," she said again, "is Violet."

Ignoring her, Will studied the stallion. "He's up to both of us, even with your extra weight."

Violet felt weak and eased herself down into the straw, praying that Will's skills were up to his boasting. He'd always claimed to have a touch with animals, but she had never seen him handle any horse as spirited as Midnight.

Moreover, he was not a patient man. The thought of riding the stallion with him frightened her. What if they were thrown and the babe was hurt?

Will opened the stall door. Midnight snorted but allowed himself to be led out. A metal bit hung on the wall. Will grabbed it. When he tried to put it on, Midnight tossed his head defiantly.

Violet thought of that speck of dust across the field growing larger and nearer. She thought of the children coming to find her as Sam and David unhitched the dray. She imagined them all, relaxed and unwary, running into the stable, and Will's knife.

"Please hurry," she pleaded.

"A moment ago you were too good for the likes of me," Will snarled as Midnight did a sideways dance away from him. He yanked the horse's mane, trying to force the stallion to the bit. Midnight's nostrils flared.

With a curse, Will struck the horse on the nose. Midnight bared his teeth and sank them into his hand.

"Damned cur!" he roared, but the horse didn't release him. With his free hand, Will fumbled for his knife, but the weapon slipped and fell to the floor.

Blood flowed from Will's hand as Midnight held on. Will strained for the whip on the wall. Finally his fingers closed around it. He brought the whip down hard on the horse.

With an enraged cry, the stallion reared. His powerful hooves lashed out. Will raised the whip again. Outside, thunder boomed. Midnight bolted from the stable.

His face pale, Will examined the mangled flesh of his hand. At last his murderous gaze settled on her.

Violet stared at the man who had given her this babe she carried and who now regarded her with such vicious rage. His only virtue was this one, unintended treasure, which she loved as much as she hated the man who had begotten it.

Will groped on the floor for his knife and came at her with a roar.

Violet rolled away from him, trying to protect her belly. She wished she had Midnight's strength. And that the heavens would strike her husband dead before he killed her only treasure.

***

Thunder exploded around them like cannon fire. The wind whipped up so fiercely that Louisa couldn't make herself heard over its insistent cry. An angry swirl of low, black clouds obliterated the horizon. Lightning knifed from the skies, infusing the air with its acrid heat.

The heavens hadn't loosed a deluge yet, but that was moments away. Mainstay and Starfire snorted uneasily as and she and Sinclair struggled to get them into the old stable before the storm unleashed its fury. Louisa was relieved she'd left Midnight at home in his stall. He would have been difficult to handle in these conditions.

An uneasy kinship surged between her and Sinclair, as if the race against the storm bound them together in some elemental way. They had not spoken of last night, of the intimacy they had shared, more unsettling than any storm. Indeed, the brooding intensity in Sinclair's eyes precluded words. The silence between them stood in stark contrast to the rumbling of the elements, but felt just as ominous.

Louisa did not want to look at him. She did not want to see how effortlessly he lifted the saddle from Starfire, how the wind ruffled his thick red hair into a tousled halo that was anything but angelic. She did not want to think of the sensual sparks that lurked within those green eyes, or of the wildness in him that made a mockery of her carefully ordered world. The man threatened everything she had become since Midnight sent Richard to his reward two years ago.

Her feelings for Sinclair had undergone a sea change

since that day he'd lain senseless at her feet in the carriage. How, she wondered, had her loathing transformed into this heavy awareness that suffused the air between them like the gathering storm?

Perhaps the change started with Alice's rescue; yet her feelings went beyond mere gratitude for saving their lives. Slowly, she had come to know the man he tried to hide: a man tormented by the deaths of his mother and brother and his father's irrationality, a man who worked to keep every feeling at bay so as to avoid further pain.

Last night, his control had slipped. Apparently, she'd been the cause, improbable as that seemed. But a man incapable of caring surely could control his passion. What did it mean that he had not?

It was useless to guess. Sinclair was as unreadable as the stars.

Louisa forced herself to concentrate on the horses. When at last they were settled in the stalls, she knew she could no longer avoid Sinclair.

She turned to him.

He had one foot propped on Starfire's saddle. His eyes held a dark, speculative gleam as he studied her.

"Shall we wait out the storm here or make a run for it?" His tone — low and lazy — asked a different question altogether, one that had to do with stables and straw and passion.

Only a fool would stay another minute here with Sinclair and the unstable current between them that owed nothing to the elements outside.

Louisa's heart sank as she recognized the futile hope, rising anew, that more than a moment could bind them. Sinclair was incapable of commitment; for her, commitment was all. There was no room in that yawning gap for hope. If he touched her now, that would only make it worse.

"Run," she said.

Without waiting for his reply, Louisa stepped outside, just as the keening wind whipped into a frenzy. The deluge was upon them, but the danger behind her was worse.

Mocking her cowardice, the wind lashed her hair into her face and caught at her cumbersome riding skirt until it was an impossible tangle of fabric. She stumbled, tried to regain her footing, and went sprawling.

Anger surged — at her clumsiness, at him. She'd been content before he came into her life, bringing chaos and odd longings. If only the storm would wash away this pull he had on her.

The only thing in danger of being washed away now was her, however. The dirt was fast turning to mud. Tears, mixed with rain, rolled down her face. The temptation to sit here and wallow in self-pity was strong. Looking up, she saw Sinclair standing over her, one hand extended.

Louisa batted it away, refusing to need him.

With a muttered oath, Sinclair yanked her out of the muck and threw her over his shoulder.

"You don't want rescuing, do you?" he growled as he carted her toward the house. "Well, I've no taste for playing rescuer. I'd sooner leave you in the mud."

"Why don't you?" Louisa retorted.

At that, he halted. For a moment, she thought he did intend to drop her in the mud. But he only shifted her into his arms so he could carry her across his chest.

"You'd like that, wouldn't you?" Sinclair looked down at her through lashes that caught the rain, framing his eyes with a lush, primeval magic. "That way you could tell yourself I was just another man using you ill. That I was not worth caring for."

"I *don't* care for you."

"You do. You care too damn much for everything."

Louisa tried not to notice how the water ran down his jawline and onto his shirt, how the wet fabric outlined the contours of his shoulders. Wanting to consign him to the devil, she huddled against his chest instead, knowing that neither of them would have gotten soaked if she'd had the courage to wait out the storm with him in the stable.

Rose was waiting at the door. "You look terrible! Best get out of those wet things."

"Trapped by the elements," Lily murmured happily behind her. "Forced into each other's arms by the wild thundering of true hearts."

Sinclair made an unintelligible sound as he carried her inside.

"I am afraid of storms," Daisy said suddenly.

"It's the tumult of the spirits," Rose said. "Storms can do strange things to people. My Billy drank himself silly one night and climbed out on a tree limb, thinking it was his horse. Lightning came down that limb and struck him. He was scared to death of horses ever after."

Daisy frowned. "Why not of the lightning?"

"Fools see what they want to see, dear," Rose replied. "And Billy was more foolish than most. I should know — I lived with the man for ten years." She paused. "Or was that James?"

Sinclair looked down at Louisa. Despite the anger and unsettling currents between them, despite the fact they were both wet to the bone, his mouth curved upward in a slow, lazy grin.

His crooked smile encompassed absurdities big and small, from Rose's hard-luck husbands and Daisy's fears to Lily's dreams and her own heart's foolish fancies. It was reckless and daring, that smile. It said this night was rare and precious and worth the storm. The force of that grin sent her pulse skittering.

Oh, my. Louisa's world shifted anew. She tried to return his smile, but couldn't.

How had she come to such a state that smiling was foreign to her? Sinclair's capricious humor might be his weapon against the world, but Louisa almost envied his gift.

Her inability to close her eyes to the world's countless injustices overwhelmed her at times. Apparently, it had also turned her into someone who couldn't smile.

"You can put me down," she said. "I can scarcely —"

"Get us any wetter? True enough." He set her on her feet, none too gently.

"Come, girls," Rose said. "You, too, Mr. Sinclair. We must find out if any of the chambers are acceptable for the night and look for bedding that might serve."

Candles in hand, the others set off, leaving Louisa and Sinclair standing stiffly next to each other, dripping in the foyer. He reached for the solitary candle they'd left behind and moved toward the parlor, giving Louisa no choice but to follow or be left in the dark.

Sinclair was inspecting a chest when she caught up to him in a little room off the parlor. He fished out a blanket and offered it to her. She shook her head. He merely arched one eloquent brow, a wordless commentary on her foolishness, and tucked the blanket under his arm.

In the end, Rose pronounced three downstairs beds serviceable.

"Daisy and Lily will share a bed," she announced. "I will have my own. Three decades of sharing a bed with husbands is enough sharing for one lifetime."

"That leaves the last one for Louisa," Daisy said, "and —"

"Mr. Sinclair." Lily put in, with a mischievous smile.

Louisa was about to say they were quite mad to think she would share a bed with Sinclair, but he simply put his hand under her elbow and steered her toward the stairs.

"Save your protests," he said. "A conspiracy is afoot. It wouldn't surprise me if they overlooked a decent bed or two. We'll see for ourselves."

"I wouldn't dream of sleeping alone," Lily called after them. "There isn't a window in the house that isn't broken. Think of the bats and other creatures that fly in."

When Louisa turned to protest, he nudged her forward. "They merely want your happiness."

"My happiness doesn't include sharing a bed with you."

"Farthest thing from my mind," Sinclair snapped, and started up the stairs.

Louisa thought about staying with the others, but curiosity won out and she chose to follow Sinclair deeper into his house — and his past.

At the top of the stairs, he turned down the dark hall they hadn't had time to clean today. In the flickering candlelight, Louisa could make out few details, other than paneled walls and sconces that at one time must have been cheerful and welcoming.

Now, though, the hall was dark and dank. A draft blew from somewhere, probably one of those broken windows. As Sinclair took them further down the hall, Louisa felt increasingly curious. He didn't stop at any of the rooms, even though they were supposed to be searching for beds.

Finally, he halted before a door. With a deep breath, he pushed it open. The hinges protested loudly as the door swung into the chamber. A large four-poster bed with heavy bed hangings anchored one wall.

His solitary candle didn't penetrate the deepest shadows, but as they drew nearer the bed, Louisa saw a coverlet that had been embroidered by a skilled hand. Shades of blue and amber spread from end to end. A froth of waves washed over the bow of a boat, with a spit of land in the distance. An island, perhaps.

Sinclair tossed the blanket over it. Then he held the candle aloft and turned slowly, studying each part of the room, as if trying to imprint every detail on his memory.

Louisa watched him in fascination. She had never seen him so silent and still — pensive, she might have said, if he'd been the reflective sort.

At last, he walked over to a portrait on the wall near

the bed. A young woman with reddish hair looked out from the frame. Even on the flat canvas, her smile radiated a lively warmth.

So he came by it naturally, then, that charm.

Gingerly, Sinclair touched the painting. His fingertips traced over the woman's face. "I had nearly forgotten," he said softly. Louisa read sorrow in the slant of his shoulders.

That is when she realized how selfish she'd been, how absorbed in her own world.

She'd fled that ramshackle stable fearing that if Sinclair touched her again he would breach all her boundaries, alter her life in some fundamental way, then sail away heedless of what he'd wrought.

But perhaps he hadn't been thinking of touching her. Perhaps the turbulence she had sensed in him was caused by his memories of this very room and the childhood he left behind.

Another irony struck her: She had vowed never to let another man turn her into a mere object — as Richard had when he made her the price for erasing her father's debts. But she'd done that to herself — and to Sinclair — by making her body the currency for purchasing his help with another rescue, by reducing him to a tool for her plan.

Last night, Sinclair had put her mercenary intentions to shame, simply by showing her his unbridled passion. He leveled her defenses by relinquishing his.

And though Louisa could never care for a man who cared for nothing, Sinclair was right: She did care for him a little. Maybe more.

Besides, Sinclair *was* capable of caring. Not about her, perhaps. But as he stood before his mother's portrait, she saw the softening about his eyes, the unsteadiness around his mouth. They were the marks of a man who cared deeply, but kept that fact deeply hidden.

"What was she like?" she asked.

He turned, as if he'd forgotten her presence. It took a

moment for his eyes to focus on her. He set the candle on a table.

"Strong," he said. "She kept the world around us sane, so my father could dream his dreams. I never understood why she married him. They were so very different."

"Perhaps she liked that he was a dreamer."

His mouth thinned. "Much good that did her."

"Perhaps he inspired her. That's what dreamers do, Sinclair. They don't accept the way things are. They inspire change. How would it be if there was no hope of change?"

"Ah." His gaze narrowed. "You want to make this about you."

Louisa knew she deserved that. She certainly wouldn't argue with him, not here. She moved closer to the painting. "There's a physical resemblance. Were you alike in other ways?"

Silence. Then: "She had a lively sense of humor. Made me feel as if laughter was the point."

"The point?"

"Of life. But it's not. Life's about figuring out what's real, then managing one's expectations accordingly."

"You've given up on dreams, then?"

"I accept what is," he said.

"Is that what she would say?" Louisa pointed to the portrait. "That mere acceptance is what we're here for?"

Sinclair scowled. "That's a low blow. Must you always push and push?"

Must she? Here, now, with this man deep in his grief?

Louisa took a deep breath. "You're right. I push too much."

He stared at her. "My hearing must be amiss. Did Louisa Peabody just admit to a fault? To trying to force the world to her singularly uncompromising view —"

"I don't know how else to be." Despair filled her. She turned toward the door, every instinct telling her to flee before he found another chink in her armor.

But he caught her arm. "You don't hand me a gift like that and walk away. Say it again."

His gaze was hard, unyielding. Louisa sighed. "Very well: I push too much."

"Why?"

"You know the answer." She looked down at the floor. "Because of Richard. I resolved to use his money to aid others, women who cannot help themselves. If I don't fight, who will?"

Sinclair touched her chin with his fingertip, tilted her face up so she had to look at him. "By all means, let us stipulate that the Richard Fiend was evil. Yet it is as if his assault happened only yesterday. You've erected a wall to protect yourself."

"Why is that wrong?"

"You're a prisoner inside that wall. You can't move beyond it." His gaze softened. "Don't you see, Louisa? You define yourself by the worst that has happened to you."

Louisa shook her head. "I cannot dispense with my wounds merely by wishing them gone."

"I begin to think you enjoy suffering."

"That is harsh."

"Perhaps it is also true."

It was a stiletto, deftly inserted into the heart of her darkness — the swirl of pain and emotion that at times nearly paralyzed her. She had found only one way to obliterate it — to fight to turn what Richard had done to her into a force for good. But always standing ready to fight came at a cost: Emotion swamped her, then fled in a rush, leaving her empty and exhausted, teetering between certainty that her cause was good and doubt that she could achieve her goal.

"It may be," Louisa conceded, "that I suffer from an excess of feeling."

Sinclair arched a brow. "What sort of feeling?"

"Outrage. Anger. Despair. Fear, if I am honest."

"Fear of what?"

"Failing. Losing my will before I can —"

"Save the world?" His gaze darkened. "You really must do something about this Joan-of-Arc conceit, madam. Last time I looked, fate had dealt you a comfortable lot in life. Setting aside the evil husband, of course."

Louisa glared at him. "Indeed. Let us simply set aside Richard and his cruelty, as if they hadn't existed. Let us set aside the plight of the women on that ship. Let us go on about our lives as if suffering didn't exist. Perhaps *you* can live with misery all around you, but I can't."

"Right. You're the wealthy widow who rides in to rescue the poor and downtrodden. Mucks about in their grim world, then retreats to her own well-cushioned one."

"Think what you will. I still believe I can change things."

"Ah, yes. Emotion overrules logic. That's been clear enough since the day I met you."

Louisa fought back tears. "Sometimes belief is all one has. I must follow my heart or die."

"And you *will* die, my lovely warrior queen," he growled, "if you are so unwise as to have another go at that prison ship. You will find yourself on the wrong end of a carbine, or worse."

She blinked. "Warrior queen?"

Sinclair cleared his throat. "My, er, term for certain beautiful but irrational women intent on fighting to the death. Boadicea, avenging herself on the Romans for some ill done to women —"

"Her lost freedom and the rape of her daughters."

"Ah. Since you know the story, you also know her revolt failed and she died —"

"By her own hand, to avoid capture."

"But she was indisputably and irreversibly dead," he pointed out. "Where's the victory in that?"

"I will not die," Louisa said crossly.

"Ever? Allow me to cite that as another instance of belief getting in the way of facts."

The wretched man tried to wear her down at every turn. "May we have done with this discussion?" she demanded. "I've owned that I push too much. Isn't that what you want?"

"As to the first question, by all means. If I never have another discussion like this until I am ninety-seven it will be too soon. As to the other..." A provocative light came into his eyes, and he seemed to shift almost imperceptibly into the man who had captured a thousand hearts with little more than the amber sparks in his velvet gaze.

Louisa knew it was past time to leave Sinclair and his practiced magic, which seemed always at the ready. But her feet would not move. That gleam held her captive.

The air between them thickened.

As if for emphasis, a flash of lightening illuminated the room. The sudden glow flashed over Sinclair's cheekbones, the curve of his mouth, the line of his jaw. It swept over his broad chest and chiseled his features into every sculptor's ideal of raw masculinity. Like the storm, Sinclair was a force to be reckoned with.

"Louisa." His voice was low, caressing. "So fierce and proud. Did I hurt you last night?"

She wouldn't pretend to misunderstand. "It was nothing of import."

"Nothing of import?" His gaze grew black. "I wanted to please you."

Louisa shrugged. "I found nothing amiss."

He gave a harsh laugh. "Nothing amiss. That is all?"

"Yes."

"It was not what I wanted."

Of course. She had disappointed him. How could it have been otherwise? She knew nothing of the womanly arts, least of all seduction. He must have found her efforts laughable. Louisa turned away so he wouldn't see her embarrassment.

Sinclair touched her arm. "You misunderstand," he said softly. "It is I who must apologize."

"There is no need." Louisa's gaze fixed on the portrait. His mother had been beautiful, self-assured, humorous, skilled with a needle. He'd grown up with the perfect woman. Nothing like her.

"There is every need. Look at me, Louisa."

Reluctantly, she met his gaze. Sinclair searched her face. "You're afraid."

"Not of you."

"It's passion, isn't it? You fear passion."

"I...fear what may come," Louisa acknowledged.

His brow cleared. "There are French sponges and the like that can prevent —"

"I am not afraid of conceiving a child. I would raise it on my own, as Lily and Daisy have done. As Violet will."

"What, then?"

Louisa sighed. "I don't want to be swept away, Sinclair. Nothing would be the same ever after. So, no, I don't want passion. Last night wasn't a watershed moment, if that's what you think. I gambled and lost. I do not regard it in the least."

The lie on her lips sent a chill through her. He saw.

"You're trembling." Sinclair took the blanket from the bed, held it out to her.

She ignored it.

"No woman has ever made me lose control like that," he said.

Her chin rose. "Am I due a medal, then?"

"I *have* hurt you."

"Don't pretend to care whether I am hurt or no."

"I won't pretend," he agreed. "One can't with you."

Something wild and dangerous spiraled through her. "But you *do*. You pretend that you are special. That I am." She shivered again.

This time, he wrapped the blanket around her, smoothed it over her shoulders. She caught the corners, and his hands covered hers.

"I want to please you, Louisa."

She wrenched herself away from his beguiling warmth. "The only way you can please me is to rescue those women. I'll have you on my own terms or not at all."

"That is not the only way."

But it was, she told herself. Nothing had changed.

Yet it had.

For with no more pressure than his hand at her elbow, Sinclair brought her back into the circle of his arms. And despite the fact that she wanted to loathe him for being exactly who he said he was, Louisa melted into him.

When he took her mouth in a kiss, it was as sweet and winsome as an angel's song.

***

David found her in the stable, curled up in a ball, her hands gripped protectively over her belly. His heart leapt to his throat. His chest constricted as he felt frantically for her pulse.

Strong and steady. He nearly died in relief.

He brushed the hair back from Violet's face. A bruise the size of a man's fist swallowed one eye. Her hands bore cuts from the struggle. But the bleeding had stopped, and he did not think the wounds were life-threatening.

As he lifted Violet into his arms and held her still form against his heart, the rain came down harder. Thunder boomed like the guns he had once dodged on the Peninsula. But the nightmare of battle was nothing like the terror he felt carrying Violet and her unborn child into the house.

Laying her on the bed in her room, he carefully pulled off her half-boots. She bore no other obvious injuries, but perhaps there were internal wounds. Her arms were cold and mottled purple, covered with goose bumps. Her wet clothes matted against her skin. He knew they should come off. Still, he hesitated.

"David?" Sam stood at the doorway of her room.

He nearly jumped. "How are the children?" he asked in a voice that sounded nothing like his.

"The twins and Mary went right to sleep. I gave Baby Elizabeth a bit of watered porridge. She's sleeping, too."

David stared at the motherless boy who suddenly looked so tall and manly. He had grown up almost overnight, it seemed. So many responsibilities rested on his young shoulders.

"Is Midnight settled in?"

"Went right into his stall, docile as you please. I guess he didn't have any more fight in him after stomping Violet's husband." Sam hesitated. "Should I go for the doctor?"

David shook his head. "I'll nae send you out in the storm, lad. Midnight's too dangerous to ride now, and the dray horse won't lift a foot in this weather." The man in the stable would either live or he wouldn't. In his condition, a doctor wouldn't make much difference.

He had known the moment he'd seen Midnight, foaming and breathing hard out in the yard, that something beyond the gathering storm had caused the stallion to flee the stable.

Inside, David had instantly recognized Violet's husband, or what was left of him. The man lay senseless in the straw, his features frozen in rage, the same expression he had worn that day in the village when they freed Violet. The knife clutched in his hand, and the imprint of Midnight's hooves on his back, told the terrible story.

Violet had lain a few yards away, her eyes closed in a deep, unnatural sleep. How and why Midnight had saved her life David couldn't begin to guess.

"Is Miss Violet all right?" The boy's question brought David back to the present.

"I think so. The cuts need cleaning." David didn't

voice his fears about internal injuries. Tomorrow, when the storm cleared and the ladies could return, Rose would examine her. David trusted Rose a damned sight more than any quack. For now, the storm held them all hostage.

Violet's fate was in his hands. And while he had tended men felled in battle, this was very different. This was Violet lying on that bed with her unborn babe, and he could not bear to think of failing her.

He met Sam's searching gaze. "Go to sleep, boy," he said. "I will call if I need ye."

Sam nodded. And then David was alone, with nothing to stand between him and fear.

***

There was something different about her, Gabriel decided, something soft and yielding that bespoke a crack in her iron resolve. Something vulnerable, he might have said, if she hadn't been the last person to display that. He saw it in her eyes, in the way her lips parted for his kiss.

There was a yearning in her. Perhaps it even matched the yearning in him.

When their lips met, hers told him more than words. She wanted him. Maybe not in the cold light of day, maybe not for all time, but here and now, with the storm raging a thunderous accompaniment to desire. Her clothes were damp, her temper was high, and she wanted him at least as much as she hated him.

Longing filled him.

Longing.

Her mouth was swollen from his kiss, ripe with a need she'd be loath to acknowledge but he could sense as if it were a great, sweeping wave washing over them. He wanted her flesh on his, her fierceness consuming him, her dauntless spirit killing him with need.

As his hands slid over her, Gabriel felt himself die with desire. Liquid fire flowed between them. This time, he wouldn't let it incinerate him.

But just then — because it would kill her to accept that two people as different as night and day could want each other without it being a battle to the death — Louisa pushed him away.

"I hate what you are doing. You are trying to make me want you. I won't."

Gabriel fought to salvage the shreds of his sanity. The scant distance she'd opened between them might as well have been an ocean — an Arctic one, judging by that determined ice in her eyes.

"You already do," he said.

"You rejected my terms," she insisted. "That should be the end of things between us."

Why did she always paint everything in black and white? Why didn't she see the delicious grays, the space where a man could escape his destiny, if only for a time? Why must she fight him at every turn, demanding some do-or-die bargain he wasn't about to embrace?

Suddenly, the defiance left her. Something very like bewilderment swept her features. "I don't understand why there is always this *more* between us. The truth is I don't want passion. I don't want to —" She broke off.

"Lose control?" he offered.

She didn't respond, but Gabriel saw her shudder, perhaps from the dampness, perhaps from something infinitely more interesting.

"Louisa." He fought to keep his voice steady. "I am standing here, in my parents' chamber, ready — nay, *burning* — to commit the unpardonable sin of making love to you before a portrait of my dear, deceased mother. Here's the only truth I know: Passion like this doesn't come along in an eon. You wouldn't know that, of course, nor trouble yourself to find out."

Her cheeks, so flushed a moment ago, paled.

"Christ," he growled. "I must be insane to want you."

The tiny birthmark above her lips wavered, betrayed by the slight trembling of her mouth. She was trying to keep her guard up.

Losing the battle.

And maybe he didn't know how to reach a woman who guarded herself so closely and whose despicable husband had ruined something priceless in her. But he would learn, if she let him.

"Louisa."

Her chin went out again — bravado to the end.

"Come here," he commanded.

Cajoling, beguiling, seducing — beyond him now. When she didn't move, Gabriel teetered on the edge of an abyss. He braced himself for defiance, rejection.

Instead, her eyes filled with a tremulous hope that shot right to his gut.

She walked into his arms.

Chapter Nineteen

It had been easier to stand at the altar with Richard than to take those few steps into Sinclair's arms.

Louisa buried her face in his chest. He stroked her hair. "It's all right."

But it wasn't.

No miracle would happen if I made love to you. I'd still be on my way in the morning, and you'd still be plotting to save womankind. Only you'd have one more man to hate.

What she felt for him wasn't hate, though. She had no name for it.

Sinclair kissed the top of her head. Louisa raised her face to look at him, searching for some reassurance she wasn't utterly lost. Instead, he simply brought their lips together in a kiss as soft as a sigh.

The space they shared, so intimately they breathed the same air, filled with longing.

Longing.

This wasn't surrender, Louisa told herself. This was just for tonight. She could still keep herself whole.

So she pressed into him, let his kiss take her where it willed. Her arms slid around his neck. When the pressure of his mouth increased, she met it with equal force, daring him to take his fill.

He made a rough, unintelligible sound. His mouth bruised hers, claiming her — for now. Tomorrow, she knew the storm that raged between them would be gone, and so would he. Even so, Louisa could not spare herself this fierce fire. She would not think about his wanderlust, only the need he kindled within her.

The blanket fell to the floor, pooling around her feet. Sinclair's arms imprisoned her, but that wasn't what kept her here, rooted to the spot. It was his heat, his raw, unfettered desire. It curled in and around her, pulled her into the fire. As if it was her destiny.

Impossible to escape.

His violent kisses banished all illusion that she could protect herself. They owned her, as if for all time — even though nothing was for all time, least of all a kiss.

Regret tried to get its hooks in her. But Sinclair simply locked his arms around her waist and lifted her off her feet.

At her gasp of surprise, a bit of mischief crept into his eyes and his mouth curved into a sensual smile. Regret, helpless against that masculine charm, slipped away.

With nothing but a spit of air below her feet, Louisa had only the amber fire in his eyes to ground her.

Strangely, it did.

Her face was mere inches above his. Louisa looked down at him in dazed wonder as Sinclair held her aloft and began to move them in a slow turn around the room.

Around and around they went, unhurried at first, then faster — so fast Louisa could scarcely catch her breath. It was as if they were dancing to some wicked waltz, with her floating above the dance floor, secure in his arms. The portrait, the candle, the bed, the windows — a kaleidoscope of objects whirled through the periphery of her vision. In the center, that amber fire was a beacon, summoning her into its core.

Louisa put her hands on the top of his shoulders to steady herself, but it was a lost cause — Sinclair set the pace. He alone determined whether she would fly or fall. She had never felt so vulnerable, so uncertain of her fate.

A raw, unfamiliar thrill — feral and terrifying — rose in her. It flung her into the vast unknown, with no assurance of survival. For that, she had to trust in the magic in his eyes.

And it *was* magic, Louisa realized, as he spun them

even faster, past the painting again, the sconces, the shadows wrought by the flickering candle. The more he flew them, the more it felt as if Pegasus himself was carrying her to Mount Olympus.

The magic in him set her free.

Louisa forgot about holding on. She lifted her arms toward the ceiling, embraced her flight. She heard laughter — *her own* — and marveled at it. She saw the answering amusement in Sinclair's eyes as they bound her in his spell. He swept her away, and she surrendered all hope of resistance.

Around and around he whirled her, as a wild spirit surged and she gave herself over to that reckless joy. On and on they went, moving as one, twirling through the universe. Louisa lost all awareness of where she left off and Sinclair began. She wished the dance would never end.

Alas, it did.

Slowly, Sinclair brought them to a stop. He eased her down the long, muscled length of his body. Even after her feet found the floor, Louisa held fast to him, trying to regain her equilibrium, unwilling to abandon his strength just yet.

At last she looked up at him with a giddy smile. "How wondrous! I wanted it to never end."

Amusement vanished from his eyes. His expression grew wary.

"I didn't mean never," she said quickly.

"Ah. What, then?"

"I don't know. You have chased every coherent thought from my head."

That seemed to please him. The gleam in his gaze returned, though his lids descended slightly, giving her only a sliver of it.

Louisa eyed him uncertainly. Whirling around the room in his arms had been pure joy, yet he was regarding her with almost palpable reserve. "What is wrong?"

"Never mind." His gaze softened. "Tell me what you

want."

"I-I don't want anything." But that wasn't true. That wicked dance had created something unsettling that would not let her go: a wanting beyond all wanting.

As if he'd read her mind, Sinclair's lips brushed hers — lightly, teasingly — then retreated, leaving her desperate for something that wasn't teasing or fleeting, something that would *last*.

"What about that, Louisa?" he murmured. "Is that what you want?"

"Stop," she said.

"Certainly." He stepped away from her.

"No." Louisa caught his arm. "I only meant for you to stop tormenting me."

Sinclair arched a brow. "Torment, my dear, is precisely the point."

His arms slid around her, and he bent to kiss her earlobe. His breath warmed her skin. "Does this make you dizzy?"

Butterflies gathered in her stomach, clawed at the edges of her rationality, left her brain as thick as cotton wool. For all that, it was not an unpleasant sensation. Mutely, she shook her head.

"Progress at last. Let's try another test. May I touch your breasts?"

Louisa blinked.

"Too crass? Never mind — those lovely blue eyes of yours tell me plainly that it is."

"What are you doing, Sinclair?"

"Provoking you." His lips brushed her cheek.

She pushed at him. "This is all a great joke to you, isn't it? You know that I want you —"

"Do you?" An arrested expression swept his features. "Why did you not say so? A cowardly omission, that."

The man was infuriating. "I'm no coward," she declared.

"We're all cowards at something," he said. "Right now, for instance, I am scared out of my wits."

That startled her. Sinclair looked anything but frightened. His hair had dried into an undisciplined red mane, giving him a more rakish appearance than usual. He towered over her, radiating pure masculine power. There was no denying the strength in those arms that had held her aloft. And yet, there did seem to be something vulnerable in his gaze.

"It's true," he said softly. "I'm scared you'll run out that door before I have a chance to make love to you properly. That you won't like it when I touch you. That I'll like it too much. That I'll not be able to forget you."

Louisa saw the truth in his eyes. It demanded truth in return. "I-I have similar fears," she confessed.

"Something real from you at last. It's a start."

"You make my head spin, Sinclair. I never know if there is anything real in what you say."

His lips brushed her forehead. "This is real." He kissed the tip of her nose, the corner of her mouth. "This, too. Real."

Sinclair's hands slid down her spine as his mouth slanted over hers, drawing her into his heat. Her body molded to his, as if it belonged there. His hands trailed upward, along her sides. Louisa wrapped her arms around his torso, wanting him closer.

But he pulled back to look at her. As their gazes met, the back of his knuckles lightly skimmed her breasts.

She swallowed hard. "I-I thought you intended to ask permission."

"You misunderstood." Slowly his fingers began to work the laces of her shirt. He slipped the fabric aside. His fingertips grazed her bare breast.

Her skin tingled where he touched her. Then it burned white hot. Surely, he did not know the effect he had on her.

But he was Sinclair. He did know.

"Don't —" Louisa broke off. Her knees felt weak.

"What, Louisa?" His gaze held hers. "What is it I am not to do?"

Perhaps she was a coward, after all, for she lowered her gaze. "Don't stop," she whispered.

"Farthest thing from my mind."

Sinclair slipped the bodice off her shoulders, revealing her. He drew in a long, shuddering breath, and simply regarded her for a long moment. Louisa felt far more exposed than when she'd stood fully naked before him in the stable yard. She brought her hand up to cover herself, but Sinclair caught it and brought it to his lips.

"You are beautiful." He placed her palm on his chest.

She felt his racing heartbeat. Her startled gaze met his.

"Yes, you are killing me," he murmured. "But it's such sweet torment."

Then every thought in her head vanished as he covered her mouth with his. His hands explored her, and Louisa leaned into his caresses, marveling at her wantonness. When he bent down and kissed her nipple, she shivered in wicked pleasure. "What are you doing to me, Sinclair?"

"Kissing you," he said. "Only that."

Louisa felt his arousal press against her. She reached for him, as she had last night.

Instantly, he covered her hand. "No."

"But I want —"

"You don't know what you want. Not yet." He released her and picked up the blanket from the floor. Moving to the bed, he laid the blanket over the coverlet. "Come over to the bed, Louisa."

"Don't give me orders, Sinclair."

"I wouldn't dream of it." His voice had roughened. "Come here."

Louisa's feet wouldn't move. "I-I can't."

The shadows hid his expression. "Why not?"

"I am no good at this," she said. "I don't know who I

am with you. All I know is that —" She broke off.

"What, Louisa? What is it that you know?"

"That I-I cannot do without you just now." She shook her head in dismay. "Dear Lord. I cannot believe I said those words to the most arrogant man in all England."

With a low laugh, Sinclair closed the distance between them. He lifted her off her feet and into his arms. In the next moment she was lying on the bed, looking up at him with helpless longing.

Longing.

She had tried to protect herself against this raging need. But there on the blanket in that four-poster bed, Louisa ceded the futility of control, abandoned the fight against that which now consumed her. She gave herself over to the maddening man who looked down at her with such fire in his eyes. And though she had vowed to surrender to no man, she surrendered to Sinclair.

He saw.

But instead of claiming her with the ferocity he'd shown last night, instead of gloating, instead of any of a hundred arrogant things he might have done, Sinclair simply kissed her forehead as if she were a child — gently, patiently, as if he understood the cost. He kissed her cheek, her chin, the base of her throat, with excruciating kindness.

His mouth brushed her breasts in a fleeting caress. Too fleeting — she wanted more. He saw that, too. He kissed her nipple, his tongue drawing the tip into a taut bud. But it seemed he was in no hurry to claim what she had already surrendered. He filled his hands with her fullness, abraded her nipples with his thumbs, kissed them anew.

All this she wanted, and more.

"Sinclair."

He raised his head to look at her. Louisa expected the passion she saw in his eyes. But they held something else she could not identify. For a moment it was as if she were seeing into the wild heart of him. But that couldn't be.

Sinclair would never show his heart, if he had one. She mustn't allow herself to believe in what could not be.

What, Louisa wondered, did he see in her eyes? She had no skill at obfuscation. Every incoherent emotion knifing through her was as plain as day.

"Don't look at me," she pleaded.

But he *did* look — because he was Sinclair, who respected no boundaries. Louisa could not turn away from the hunger in his gaze. She felt that same hunger spiraling within her. It shattered her, left her without defenses.

He saw that, too. But when he might have shown triumph, he simply enfolded her in his arms, allowed her to feel the warmth of his chest, shored up her weakness with his strength.

"It is all right," he murmured. "I have you."

There was everything — and nothing — in his words, but it was enough that he had said them.

Suddenly, Sinclair gifted her with a reckless grin. It called forth Louisa's yearning, bade it come out of the shadows. His grin said that while it was foolish to expect more than this moment, this moment was all.

All. Yes, she would have that.

Louisa grabbed a fistful of his hair. "Make love to me, Sinclair," she commanded. "Do it properly, so I won't forget."

For a moment he looked stunned. Her arms locked around his torso, pulled him down to her.

Sinclair's muscles tightened under her touch. He moved his body over hers, and she gloried in the weight of him, in the passion that owned her. As his hands slid under her, Louisa arched into him, wanting their bodies touching *there*.

He groaned — a sound so primal and masculine Louisa nearly laughed in wonder that she had drawn that from him. She opened her mouth to his, teased him with her tongue, drew him into her warmth. Drowning in the scent and feel of him, she felt wholly, splendidly alive.

Suddenly, he muttered a curse as his hands became lost in the heavy folds of her riding skirt. "Why do women wear such things?" he growled.

"Stop talking, Sinclair."

Another curse. Then Louisa felt his hand on her bare calf just above her boot. *Her boots.* Dear Lord, she still wore her riding boots!

Their gazes met. Sinclair's held naked masculine satisfaction. Doubtless he saw she was too overwhelmed by desire to bother with them.

"Boots on, then." His hand slid upward.

As he caressed her, Louisa discovered that last night had given her no true sense of his art. No man had touched her like this, nor awakened in her such need.

Closing her eyes, she moved her hands over his back, savoring the taut muscles there. She arched upward, wanting — demanding — him.

Sinclair needed no urging. His kisses claimed her, seared her flesh. When his knee nudged between hers, Louisa opened to him like a flower unfurling in sunshine after a long winter.

When his hand found the soft curls between her legs, she gasped.

That.

He explored her intimately, discovering delicious places — places that led into other places. The heat built within her, as if a thunder cloud was ready to burst. Louisa moved into his touch, and when his hand withdrew, she nearly cried out in protest.

But then — *dear Lord* — his mouth followed the same path, kissing her bare thigh, trailing upward to the very place that burned for him.

"Sinclair," she pleaded. "What are you doing to me?"

He lifted his head, shot her a wicked gaze. "Kissing you. Only that. Should I stop?"

Louisa shook her head, that mute denial her last coherent act as the ache deep inside her merged with the fire he stoked. And she knew, then, that he was right — that the other side of fear was desire, and she had no choice but surrender to it.

She felt something in her dissolve and flow out to him, seeking the heart of that flame. She burned and burned, until at last she heard herself cry a wild, keening sound.

As waves of pleasure rocked her, the savage roll of thunder sounded overhead and a jagged streak of lightning lit up the room like the devil's own torch.

And the pleasure he brought her was joined by the acrid scent of fire.

***

David's hands trembled as he eased Violet onto her side to get to the buttons on the back of her frock. Her dress was soaked through; it would have to come off. He wished to hell there was another woman in the house.

His large fingers were not suited to the tiny buttons that ran from her neck down to her hips. As he fumbled with them, David prayed that Violet would not awaken just yet. He didn't think he could make her understand that his intentions were honorable, that even strong men weakened by combat had been known to die of exposure as wet and cold seeped through their clothes.

Already, goose bumps dotted her skin. He saw them as soon as he slipped off one shoulder of her dress, then the sleeve. Sam had built a fire in the hearth, but its cheerful blaze would not banish this kind of chill. Her arms were mottled and purple.

With renewed determination, David eased the dress off her other shoulder. His heart leapt to his throat as he realized she was wearing nothing underneath. He didn't know what he had expected — a chemise, perhaps — but Violet wore only this sodden frock. Perhaps women nearing confinement were not comfortable in layers of clothing.

David couldn't help but stare at her breasts. They were full and lovely, ready for the babe that would soon claim them. He swallowed hard as he eased the dress over her abdomen. Her belly was smooth and firm, filled with new life. The man who begat the babe was a monster, but the child would be innocent of that stain. David had seen the sorrow in Violet and knew her husband had caused it. He prayed she could set it aside once the babe came.

Some sorrows, he knew, never went away. Their pain could suck the joy out of life, deny the soul its nourishment. It had happened to him, and to Louisa — and though he hoped Sinclair could heal her, David knew better than to bet on the future. The present was all a man had.

As he slid the fabric over Violet's hips, David saw the scars. They ran the length of her back, and although months had passed since Violet had stood in that village square, the scars were still visible. David would gladly have killed the man who had given her those marks, but Midnight, it seemed, had beaten him to it.

He tossed the dress on the floor and placed a blanket over her, tucking it under her chin as one might tuck in a child. Violet lay on her side, her hands pillowed under her head, her knees bent. Her face was pale but unlined, as if in sleep she had finally found peace.

She still looked cold. Her lips had a bluish tint. David sat on the bed and rubbed her arm, willing her blood to rise and warm her. His hands moved to her shoulders, then her back as they massaged her briskly through the blanket. And though he tried not to think about the fact that she was naked underneath, every place his hands touched, he found himself imagining it was her skin, not the soft wool of the blanket.

Touching her, even over the blanket, made him feel strong in a way that had nothing to do with his physical might. It was as if she was giving him strength, rather than the other way around. He had a sudden, vivid image of Violet in his cottage, nursing her babe while he massaged her feet.

David's shoulders slumped. He knew better than to put faith in dreams. Who was he to think Violet could come to care for the likes of him? He wasn't even a man, not in the way a woman had a right to expect. He had the strength to slay dragons, but he couldn't begin to measure up.

"Don't stop."

He nearly leapt off the bed, so startled was he to hear Violet's soft voice. "Ye are awake," he stammered.

Her gaze clouded, and he could almost see the memories of her ordeal come flooding back. She touched her abdomen, as if to reassure herself the babe was still there. Then her fingers went to the wound on face. She winced.

"Where is Will?"

"In the stable. He'll nae trouble you again." He wished her thoughts had not instantly gone to her husband. Despite the man's cruelty, she must have kept a place for him in her heart.

Violet regarded him with solemn brown eyes. "I remember Midnight," she said slowly. "Lightning was flashing. He raced out into the storm, then galloped back into the stable and —" Her eyes widened. "Is he dead?"

"The horse is unharmed," David said gruffly. "He pummeled your husband to a fare-thee-well. If the knave is nae dead by now, he deserves to be." He searched her gaze, wondering how she would take the news.

Violet said nothing.

"How do ye feel, lass?"

"Cold." She gave him a rueful smile. "And fat. Enormously fat."

"Ye are beautiful." The moment he said the words, David wanted to call them back.

Violet stared at him.

"I only meant —" He eyed her helplessly. She adjusted the blanket, and he saw the instant she realized she was naked under the covers.

"Where are my clothes?"

He sprang to his feet. "On the floor. The dress was wet through, and I —"

"You took my clothes off."

David could not meet her gaze. "I did nae want you to get a fever. I tried not to look, if that means anything."

"You were repulsed." She sighed. "It's all right, David. I know I look like a cow."

"No. Ye and the child — 'tis beautiful. I wanted to touch the babe, but —" He broke off, horrified that he had confessed so much.

Violet reached out and captured his hand, pulled it down to her. That left him no choice but to lower himself awkwardly to the edge of the bed, trying to look anywhere but at her and the feminine hand that gripped his. He stared hard at the intricately carved mantelpiece over the fire.

"Touch the babe, David."

He froze.

"Please," she said softly.

He could not move.

She lifted the blanket and placed his hand on her bare abdomen, drawing him closer. Then she pulled the blanket over his hand, patting it through the cloth as she met his terrified gaze. "It is all right, David."

Under his callused palm, her skin felt smooth, like satin. He had no right to such an intimacy, but she had granted it, and so he sat awestruck with his hand on her under the covers, wondering what he was supposed to do next.

To his dismay, her eyes filled with tears.

"Violet," he rasped, shamed. "I'm sorry about looking at ye, lass. I did nae mean to —"

"I'm cold, so very cold. Lie with me, David."

His breathing halted. Panic filled him.

"Just for a little while," she whispered. There was a world of sorrow in her tone, and he knew he would do anything to make it go away.

David eased himself down next to her. He tried to keep a respectable distance, but she turned on her side away from him, still holding his hand on her abdomen. He had to nestle against her backside, the curve of his body mirroring hers. He had never felt so awkward and large.

"Thank you," she said.

It broke his heart to hear the gratitude in her voice. Warming her with his body was such a little thing. He didn't want to be thanked for it. Beneath his hand, he felt a sudden twitch. "What was that?"

"The babe."

"Does it do that often?" he ventured.

"More and more these days." Though she faced away from him, he heard the smile in her voice. "He is eager to meet us."

Us. David swallowed hard. He steeled himself against that image of Violet and her babe in his cottage. He wouldn't take her words to heart. She couldn't have known that he dreamed of this.

"David?"

"What?" His voice was ragged; he didn't recognize it as his.

"I have wanted you for so long."

David stared at the back of Violet's head and wondered whether his hearing had failed him.

She turned toward him, and he saw tears on her cheeks. "You don't need to say it. I know you can't possibly care for someone so huge and unattractive. I've been lonely, that's all."

"Damnation, Violet. Stop saying that. Ye are beautiful."

She tried to smile. "I know the truth. I'm afraid I've

been feeling sorry for myself again. I seem to be all mixed up these days. Please forget I spoke."

And pigs would fly. "Did ye mean it?" he croaked. "About...wanting me?"

Her brown eyes searched his. What he saw there made his heart ache. Slowly, she nodded.

"I'll always stand as yer friend, lass," he said carefully.

She shook her head. "That is not what I meant."

David took a deep breath. "Ye want us to be —?"

"Lovers," she said.

Everything a man could want was contained in that word, but David knew she didn't mean it. Pregnant women were said to have strange yearnings. This had to be one of them.

"I can nae," he said gently.

Her expression crumbled. She turned away.

"Violet." He hated himself for hurting her. "It's not that I do nae want...It's that the war left me..." He took a deep breath. "I haven't had a woman in years. I can nae."

Her startled gaze found his once more. "Were you injured?"

"Not in that way." David could scarcely believe he was telling her this. "They did things to us in prison, Violet. I can nae get beyond it. And even if I could —" He broke off.

She waited. He plunged on. "The babe is nearly ready to be born. Ye can nae wish to —"

"Make love with you? Yes, David, I do." She closed her eyes, as if in pain. David cursed his awkward tongue. He had to make her understand.

"I would nae know what to do. Even if a miracle occurred, and I could manage to...I'd be afraid of hurting ye and the baby. Ye are a pregnant woman —"

"I'm still a woman. With a woman's wants and needs." She paused. "I do not think the baby would mind."

David eyed her helplessly. She had no idea what she was asking. "I'd give my right arm to please ye, Violet."

"I'll take it." She reached under the covers and patted his hand — his right hand, as it happened — resting on her abdomen. She turned on her side again, away from him, and locked their fingers together. "If that is all I can have, that's enough. For now."

She fell silent. For a long time David stared at the curve of her shoulder, wondering whether he should say something else, wondering what that might be. But she did not seem to expect it, and when she stretched out like a lazy cat and yawned, he began to relax.

Eventually he heard her steady, even breathing and knew she had fallen asleep. He nestled against her backside, warming her with his body all night long, his hand still on the place where the babe grew. And every time the baby kicked, he smiled in silent wonder.

He had no nightmares that night.

Chapter Twenty

From the shelter of the stable, Gabriel watched his boyhood home burn. Not the stone walls, of course, but everything inside, judging by the flames that licked up from the windows, menacing the roof timbers and frame.

The downpour kept the fire from spreading to the outbuildings; finally, about dawn, the blaze burned itself out. Nothing remained except the stone. The rest was a charred mess, doubtless including his mother's portrait, Rose's drawings, and the musty bed in which he had brought Louisa pleasure.

At first, Gabriel hadn't noticed the scent of fire. He'd been consumed with Louisa — nearly unhinged from wanting her. The sudden explosion that reverberated above the noise of the storm might as well have been miles away.

The Flowers' screams had finally penetrated the fog of desire. Gabriel and Louisa had stumbled out with the others to huddle under a blanket in the stables and watch the conflagration wrought by a vengeful bolt of lightning that had hit the roof.

"Such a shame." Daisy dabbed at her eyes with a handkerchief.

"A pity." Lily nodded.

"A disaster." Rose gave a heartfelt sigh.

Gabriel shrugged. "For the best."

They gazed at him in disapproval — not that he cared. The house meant nothing to him now. In a way, he was glad to be free of it. In his mind's eye, he saw Sinclair Isle as vividly as he did that stone shell of a house. He'd soon be free of it, too. He would sail there this morning and start work on the cursed thing in the cave. When he was done, he'd catch one of the trade ships to the far corners of the world. England — and the past — would soon be behind him.

So seductive, that pile of stones. It suggested the possibility of permanence. But that was illusion, no more than a trick of the mind. None of it was permanent — not the portrait or the bed or even Louisa. How fitting that her cries of fulfillment were overrun by the fire. How swift was revenge on fools who tried to shape the flames of desire into something lasting.

I wanted it to never end. She'd meant the dance, but her words conjured something he knew better than to believe in.

Gabriel had not looked at Louisa in an hour or more, though it seemed longer. He had stood here much of the night, his gaze fixed on the flames, watching the past shoot heavenward in plumes of smoke as if it had never existed. Making love to Louisa in his parents' bed was part of that past. That, too, was gone.

"Stop." Her voice was low and fierce at his side.

Gabriel turned. "I beg your pardon," he said stiffly, as if she was a stranger, not the woman he'd held in his arms only hours ago. The woman who had made him almost believe in what he saw in her eyes.

"Stop telling yourself that it doesn't matter. You know it does."

Of course. She meant to make him face it. The crusader in her wouldn't let him be. "Leave it alone, Louisa. I'm not one of your desperate causes."

"Your family is dead. Everything they touched — the beds they slept in, the table they ate upon — has just gone up in smoke. All of it, gone."

"Stop trying to cheer me up."

She stared at him, appalled.

"It was just a house," he said. "The past is over and

dead. I buried it a long time ago."

"No," she insisted. "That is the problem, isn't it? You've never buried it. You've carried it around with you like a stone. You've run to the ends of the earth to rid yourself of its weight. Now you're pretending it doesn't matter, just as you pretend not to care about anything."

Behind them, the Flowers had fallen silent.

"Be quiet," he growled.

Her brilliant blue eyes glinted angrily. "Tell me, Sinclair" — she bit off each word — "are you also pretending that you didn't make love to me last night? If so, I'm going to hate you for a long, long time."

He heard a collective gasp behind them.

"Louisa," he warned.

"Don't," she snapped. "Don't remind me that you didn't make promises, that you must be on your way, that what happened between us doesn't change things. I know that. I also know that you're so dead inside you wouldn't recognize a scintilla of real feeling if it struck you like that lightning bolt."

"Oh, dear," murmured Daisy.

Louisa stood there like a hellion, eyes flashing, daring him to fight her. But the fight had gone out of him. Gabriel was tired of crossing swords with a woman who wouldn't let anything rest. Anyway, the rain had finally stopped.

He turned to the Flowers. "Goodbye, ladies. This is where we part. Allow me to say that I appreciate your kindnesses, individual and collective. I regret the inconvenience this night has brought. I will hitch up your horse and see you on your way. If we never meet again, I will count it as my loss."

Daisy sniffed loudly. Lily looked as if she would turn into a watering pot as well. Only Rose gazed at him with clear, assessing eyes. And Louisa, of course. Always Louisa.

The horses were uneasy after such a night, so it took

Gabriel a while to harness Mainstay to the gig. He was about to saddle Starfire for Louisa when she marched over and, without a word, took over the task. Gabriel turned his attention to the gray.

Silently, the Flowers climbed into the gig. Daisy dabbed at her eyes. Lily managed a watery smile. Rose merely shook her head. Gabriel turned to help Louisa onto Starfire, but she was already mounted.

He swung himself onto the gray. He'd always detested sentiment, but an unfamiliar lump in his throat made him stumble over the final round of goodbyes. Perhaps they were a family, after all. Thank God, he would never see them again.

Rose maneuvered the gig toward the road. Courtesy dictated that he remain until they had departed, but Louisa was, as usual, making things difficult. Atop Starfire, she was silent and still.

Gabriel forced himself to look at her. This was farewell, after all. The storm had turned her hair into an impossible mass of golden tangles. Her clothes were no longer wet, but the fabric of her riding skirt was limp, formless.

He waited for her to leave.

She didn't.

"Now what?" he demanded.

Her gaze held his. "Is it always like that? Lovemaking?"

"Like what?" Gabriel prayed that she would not explain, but they both knew she would.

"Conquering the tallest mountain. Flying above the clouds. Touching a piece of heaven." She studied him for a long moment. "Finding a kindred soul who sees into the very heart of you."

Well, at least he had pleased her. He'd wanted to. Yearned to, in fact. *Burned* to.

"Always." Gabriel hoped he sounded suitably

nonchalant.

"Liar."

He looked away from that intense blue gaze. "It's only that you have no experience —"

"You wish me to believe it was nothing out of the ordinary. You're a fraud, Sinclair."

Out of the corner of his eye, Gabriel saw that Rose had slowed the gig, doubtless to eavesdrop.

"I am coming with you," Louisa said.

"No." For good measure, he said it again: "*No.*" When she didn't react, he turned the gray toward the cove, away from Louisa and her cursed poetic insight.

But instead of the angry defiance he expected, Gabriel heard her low laugh. Since Louisa was not given to odd moments of humor, he felt compelled to turn and look at her.

A mistake.

Her provocative half-smile instantly pulled him back into those moments before the fire turned everything to ashes. To when she surrendered, when his hands memorized her, probably for all time. Gabriel couldn't blink the images away.

"Take me to Sinclair Isle," she commanded.

Make love to me, Sinclair. Do it properly, so I won't forget.

"Show me your kingdom, Sinclair." Her voice was low, sultry. "Mayhap I shall pretend to be your queen. We will make love in the sand, and you can show me how little you care."

She was mad, Gabriel decided — and he was something of an expert on the subject. "This isn't a fairytale," he said roughly. "There's no happily ever after."

"No," she agreed.

"It's the same with all your causes," he snarled, desperate to flee her relentless do-or-die-ness. "You refuse to see what's before your eyes. You create your own distorted truth, convince yourself that you can fix things, even if they're hopeless."

She tilted her head, measuring him with a look. "Hopeless causes are my specialty."

"Leave me be," he growled. "I'm in no need of rescue."

He spurred the gray, but she brought Starfire alongside.

"Did you like touching me, Sinclair?" she taunted. "Did you like it too much? I'm sorry for you, then. You were right to be scared. But I was scared, too. And now I'm not. Because I learned something last night."

"Always glad to oblige," he muttered darkly.

"It's this: We fit together. You and your refusal to care about anything, and me caring too much. We are two sides of the same coin."

Gabriel stared at a fixed point on the horizon, where his boat and hopeless future awaited.

She reached across the space between their horses and touched his arm. "No one has ever made me feel as you did last night."

"Allow me to point out the obvious, which is that your only standard of comparison is a rapist."

"Go ahead and joke about it. But —"

"Don't say it," he snapped, desperately afraid she would. "Don't confuse pleasure with love."

"Why would I?"

Gabriel eyed her suspiciously. "I have nothing to offer you. The last thing I want is —"

"Anything that smacks of permanence. Yes, I know. Who's the coward now?"

"For God's sake, woman, leave me be."

"Too easy."

Further argument would be futile, he knew. So Gabriel pointed his horse toward the cove and did his best to ignore her. He knew better than to think she would give up.

Louisa said nothing more, but kept pace with him. When he stepped onto the deck of his boat, she was at his side.

Gabriel shot a quick prayer heavenward, though he doubted anyone up there was paying attention. He prayed that this trip would be mercifully short. And he prayed, but not quite as fervently, that he would never have to make love to Louisa again.

***

The wind ruffled her hair. The sun bathed her in its warming light. The sea spray kicked up; the salt tingled her senses. Louisa found she liked the peacefulness of staring out at the wide expanse of sea, being rocked by the waves toward a pinpoint of land.

She studied Sinclair. On deck, he walked like a cat, his weight perfectly balanced on the balls of his feet. He did not lurch as she had when a powerful swell splashed them or when a gust of wind caused the boat to lean precariously. He handled the little craft as if he had been born to test his mettle against life's unpredictable seas.

What he resolutely did not do was look at her.

The journey to his island took little more than an hour, during which Louisa offered to help with the mysterious maneuvers he did with the sail — pulling it in, letting it out, adjusting its tension and direction — tasks she knew nothing about. All she got were black looks.

And silence.

Sinclair was perfectly at home on the water; perhaps it was the only place where that was true. Endless and churning, never the same from one day to the next, the sea reflected his mercurial nature, offering a vast canvas upon which to write — and rewrite — each day's truth.

But he was wrong in thinking she couldn't face truth. There was one deeply disturbing truth she had discovered: Somehow, Sinclair had ensnared her heart.

That a man with such an empty soul had done so with no effort at all mystified her. How could she care for someone whose moral compass was so askew, who asked only to be left alone so that he could partake of pleasure without cost to himself? Who held no cause dearer than himself?

Perhaps because he was not really that man.

Sinclair kept the world at bay by design. He had dedicated himself to avoiding the pain of caring too much. Only a man who had known such pain would so purposefully seek to avoid it.

But was she simply rewriting the truth, as he so often contended, bending it to her will, making him the person she wanted him to be? Sinclair had tried to tell her who he was, and she would not listen. Why did she think she knew him better than he knew himself? Was it because he had swept her beyond her wildest dreams?

Louisa had never thought she could respond to any man's touch. But Sinclair was not any man. In him lurked a fire so wild and elemental that her heart thrilled to it.

She wouldn't have responded to a man who was unkind or selfish, who cared for no one but himself. Yet this man who professed to care for nothing had awakened something new and fragile within her — something as sweet and fierce as any love.

Don't confuse pleasure with love. She didn't want to. But she didn't know the name for this strange yearning she felt for him.

Still, it was not the yearning in her that had brought her here to his side, but the yearning in him. The longing in his eyes, the vulnerability he couldn't completely hide. She wondered if beneath the sardonic facade was a man who wanted to love but did not know how.

What had he said? *No miracle would happen if I made love to you.*

Ah, but one had. He just didn't know it yet.

Louisa stared at that spit of land, growing larger on the horizon. The key to Gabriel Sinclair was there, on that island. It was why she had come — to discover who he truly was and why he had stolen her heart.

She was a fool to believe in miracles. But more a fool not to.

***

Gabriel brought the boat into the island cove he knew so well. The empty beach fanned out in a half-circle. Exotic shells dotted the fine, white sand. The original quay had long since disintegrated into rotting timbers half submerged by the sand. He had been prepared to wade ashore, but someone had recently built a pier, a smaller version of those new landing stages the ferries used in town. It was raised on pillars and extended out into the water — suitable for a boat considerably larger than the one he was on.

Drew's men had been busy.

Just off the cove was the boathouse, its foundation mostly washed away. It was falling in on itself, an eyesore on the otherwise picturesque beach. Drew hadn't bothered with it.

Gabriel's father had chosen the island because it was a perfect vantage point from which to see an invader approaching from the east and south. Here, a man could see for miles in any direction. A boy could point his spyglass at that fierce, lonely sea and wonder whether the world out there was as desperate and empty as this island paradise.

"It's lovely."

Gabriel didn't look at Louisa. He didn't want her to see the desolation in his eyes.

"I want to see everything," she said.

He scowled. "Let me be clear: I'd prefer to be anywhere else. Failing that, I'd rather be here alone. Do not expect me to show you the sights."

Her mouth tightened, and Gabriel waited for her biting retort. She had been strangely silent during the trip. He preferred the sharp-tongued revolutionary to the woman who looked at him from eyes as calm as the lapping waves that masked a treacherous riptide.

"No," she said. "I don't expect that."

He eyed her suspiciously. "Meekness does not suit you."

She didn't reply, which unsettled him further.

Fit together, did they? An alarming notion — they could not be more different. She was a meddler who must bend the world to her view or die trying; he would never tilt at windmills or chase the impossible. She didn't know when to give up; he walked away when he was dealt a bad hand. She let emotion rule; he survived by his wits.

Easy as it was to enumerate the many ways they diverged, doing so gave Gabriel no comfort. The meddling was in her bones; she would try to rescue those women on the prison hulk whether he helped her or not. That meant she *would* die — or be trapped in the ship's depravity. Even if she somehow survived, he wouldn't be around to protect her from future foolish schemes. He had to make himself accept that fact. You let go of things you couldn't change, or went mad fighting fate.

Feeling like a man about to be sucked into deadly waters, Gabriel trudged up the path from the cove. He didn't bother to see whether Louisa followed, knowing that she would. They hiked a half mile through sawgrass that clung to their clothes, batted away dragonflies that darted about with reckless abandon. Noisy gulls flew overhead, and now and then an osprey rode a downdraft to see what they were about. The sea breeze blew steadily, pulling him inexorably into the past.

The grave was there, just as he had envisioned it every day for ten years. Aloysius's resting place lay atop the island's highest hill, where east wind met west and where a ghost could spend eternity staring at the far horizon and plotting his revenge. This beautiful spot, Gabriel's favorite perch as a boy, had been his final gift to his father and perhaps the only lasting one.

He had carved the stone himself. It bore only Aloysius's name and the dates of birth and death. His father had made him promise to carve a likeness of the bayberry crown he'd worn until the day he died, but Gabriel had not.

A betrayal, to be sure. The last wishes of the dying must be honored. But Gabriel had not been able to bring himself to inscribe that crown on his father's tombstone. If it meant that he would be haunted by a vengeful ghost for the rest of his days, so be it.

Looking at that stark, spare stone, Gabriel expected to feel grief or regret or anger. Instead, he simply felt numb.

He lifted his gaze to the horizon. The sea that had beckoned him when he was a virtual prisoner on this island looked the same. White frothy sea caps frolicked under that wide expanse of sky as if they possessed some profound secret to happiness. Gloating gulls swooped down to pluck a meal from the churning waters.

The sea teemed with life, with vibrancy. It was the same — and yet not, for the man who looked out upon it now was not the same as the boy.

"It must have been lonely here for you, with only your father," Louisa said.

He didn't respond.

"What did you do after he died?"

"The Royal Navy. Let it be, Louisa." He had no wish to delve into more of his past than he had to.

Gabriel turned away from the gravesite and started toward the small cabin that lay just through the copse of elder and willow. He'd forgotten that orchids grew wild in these woods — the purple ones that attracted the warblers. They were in full bloom now, heralding the prodigal's return. He swallowed a bitter laugh.

Doubtless Drew had spruced up the old place. When Andrew Maitland determined on a course of action, no obstacle was permitted to stand in the way. The rotted boards had likely been replaced, the wood freshly painted.

As Gabriel walked deeper into the past, it seemed to rise up and hit him all at once. A wave of emotion swept him; he desperately wanted it gone. But like any wave, it set its own pace; this one, it seemed, wouldn't be hurried.

He exhaled a shaky breath, scarcely able to believe that he had returned to this place of ghosts. He hadn't expected the island to feel so empty and menacing. For one bleak moment he wanted to sink to his knees in despair.

Louisa's hand pressed his, offering silent comfort. It was futile. The only true comfort would come when he was gone from this place.

Suddenly, Gabriel knew that the worst of this day wasn't over. After his father's grave, after that cabin, after the inevitable confrontation with the thing in the cave — after this empty pilgrimage was said and done, he would still have to reckon with Louisa.

God save him from a woman who cared.

Chapter Twenty-One

"**W**hat is this?" Louisa stared at the round-bodied object the size of a small whale. Since their arrival this morning, she had followed Sinclair all over the island. Now he'd brought her to this cave, which opened onto the far end of the cove and ran deep into the rocky hills. Though they were only a hundred yards or so from where Sinclair's boat bobbed serenely, the watery cavern was hidden from the view of anyone who didn't know it was there.

"My father's last invention."

The underwater boat — the thing Sinclair hated for stealing his father away.

Louisa had never seen anything like it. The oval-shaped exterior was made of copper and banded with iron stays. One end tapered to a snub nose; the other held a propeller. A large support frame that nearly spanned the cave's width kept the craft above the water's reach. On the domed top was a small door with a tiny glass window.

The iron looked rusty, the copper tarnished, the propeller blades dented, but the submersible itself was splendid. Seemingly frozen in time, it presided over the shadows of the cave like a creature from another world.

"It is magnificent," she said softly. "How does it work?"

The remoteness in his gaze chilled her. "The details would bore you."

"I want to know," she insisted.

"Of course you do." He sighed. "It has a retractable mast and sails like an ordinary boat on the water. To descend, the mast is pulled inside, the sail collapsed, and the ballast tanks — those cylinders you see on either side — are flooded. The propeller moves the ship forward. There are two rudders — horizontal controls depth and angle of descent; vertical controls direction."

"How does one breathe?"

"There's sufficient air for a short trip, tanks of compressed air for a longer one. It can support a crew of three for about three hours, depending on how many candles are lit."

"Candles?"

"The small window on top picks up light from above, but the deeper one descends, the darker it is inside. The steering controls aren't visible without a candle."

She eyed him curiously. "You have sailed it?"

"Yes."

The boat certainly looked unwieldy. "How do you get it into the water?"

"Pulleys raise and lower the frame."

For the first time she noticed the spike on the top. Sinclair followed her gaze. "That's meant to hold the submersible under the enemy's hull long enough to deliver an explosive charge. My father called it a torpedo."

Louisa was awed. "Your father was a genius."

Sinclair made a dismissive gesture. "Every inventor had a submersible. Fulton, Johnstone — no one was able to get one to work as they envisioned. My father certainly didn't."

"Why do you hate it so?"

He was silent for a long moment. "After my mother and brother died, the submersible consumed him. Selfishness consumed him."

"But he was trying to help win the war," Louisa pointed out. "He would have destroyed that underwater channel if Napoleon had tried to build it."

Sinclair scowled. "Don't paint him in hero's colors, Louisa. He wasn't some noble patriot. He was a sad, embittered man who let grief rob him of whatever rational mind he had."

"As you've let anger destroy your love for him."

A muscle clenched in his jaw, visible even in the shadows. "I don't wish to discuss it."

"Yes, I can see you don't want to face any of this. It hurts too much."

His hands went around her upper arms. It was the first time he had touched her since the storm, but this touch wasn't gentle.

"Don't pretend to understand me," he growled. "You don't."

"You're right," she flung at him. "I don't understand a man who can make love to me one moment and pretend I'm a stranger the next."

"Ah. This is about last night. You're just like all the other women I've known. You want to dress it up and call it something more, when it was only lust." He released her, his expression hard. "Don't try to make it mean something. It didn't."

Louisa balled her hand into a fist. And though he must have seen it coming, and could have stopped her in time, she slammed it into his gut.

Stunned, he stared at her.

"Richard showed me lust," she said. "It was violent and cruel. Nothing like last night."

"Louisa —"

"Shut up, Sinclair. You don't get to talk. You only get to listen."

Her hands went to his chest, and she shoved him, hard. "I know about selfish fathers, too. Mine traded me to Richard to satisfy his gaming debts. I wanted to hate him for making me no better than a whore. I did hate him some. But I loved him, too. Children do, you know."

She exhaled a ragged breath. "Love hurts, Sinclair, but you can't let the pain make you turn your back on the world." She twisted away from him and ran toward the cave entrance. Tears stung her eyes as she stepped into the late afternoon sun.

"I am not like the other women you've known," she shouted back at him. Her voice echoed deep into the cave. "Not by a long shot."

With that, she fled blindly toward the sun, away from the shadows of Sinclair's bitterness.

***

Gabriel found her near the shell of the boathouse. She sat on the beach, staring at the horizon, arms wrapped around her knees, not bothering to hide the tears that streaked her cheeks. The sinking sun bathed the sand in forgiving shades of amber. Its light glinted off her hair, turning it into warm gold.

He tried to freeze the image: Louisa. Sunlight. Gold. He wanted to commit it to memory so he could summon it later, when she was gone. Ah, but the sheer power of her presence — her fierce beauty, her fiercer ideals — no memory could replicate that. It would be like trying to recall a priceless work of art that could only be fully appreciated if you were standing before it.

She didn't stir when Gabriel sat beside her.

"You're right," he said. "You're not like other women. Damn it all, Louisa, you're worse."

She looked at him, her blue eyes deeper than the sea as she searched his face. Gabriel did not flinch from her scrutiny, though he knew it was bound to leave her unsatisfied.

"I can't change," he said quietly. "If my father's life taught me anything, it's the folly of flailing away at futile causes. I'm no hero. I'm not the man you deserve."

She shook her head. "You're wrong."

"No." Gabriel felt bereft, as if acknowledging that simple truth marked the death of something precious between them. "Your head is full of illusions. About me, anyway."

"Touch me, Sinclair. Then tell me what is illusion."

He looked away from the sensual challenge in her eyes. "Face the truth, Louisa."

"The truth is I care for you. If that scares you, more's the pity."

Gabriel wanted to pretend he hadn't heard, but she touched his shoulder and gave it a rough shake so he had to turn and look at her.

"Last night you showed me a woman's pleasure," she said. "You forgot about your own."

"I didn't forget," he growled. "The damned house burned down around us. See what I mean? You twist the facts."

Her low laughter shot past his futile exasperation and connected with something deep in his gut. Staring at her, Gabriel felt the foundation of his own reality slip away like that sun disappearing on the far horizon.

What came to him next was a sudden thought — possibly even a deep conviction, though he'd had so few of those in his life as to make recognizing one a challenge — that he had never wanted any woman as much as he wanted Louisa Peabody.

It was a strange, unfamiliar kind of wanting. Not the have-and-done sort of wanting, not the right-this moment-or-die wanting, not the are-you-insane-don't-do-it wanting. Those were recognizable, even manageable.

No, this was a never-get-one's-fill wanting. A wretched, bottomless pit of wanting that conjured the wild, irrational thought that he'd gladly go back to that gallows tomorrow if he could only spend the next few hours in her arms. Well, not gladly. But he would go, and his last words would be for her alone, and they would be something like —

"Make love to me," she commanded.

Louisa's hands cupped his face, and she brought her lips to his. Her mouth was salty and sweet, bold and brash. It made his pulse thunder and his feeble heart seek desperately to flee.

But since it was *that* type of wanting, Gabriel reached for her as if she was his lifeline in storm-tossed seas. His arms wrapped around her as she kissed him with all of her Louisa-fierceness. He kissed her as if he'd suddenly been given his last, best wish.

Wrong, wrong, wrong, an inner voice said. He could offer her nothing. Wouldn't be around for the consequences. Unfair to her.

All of that.

But her tongue invaded his mouth, seared him with its low-minded intentions. Her arms snaked around his neck, dared him to try to free himself from her bondage.

She moved onto his lap and straddled him, pressing her body into his, as if — *as if* — their bodies were joined in all the best places.

Guilt retreated. Misgiving fled. Conscience — never overworked to begin with — went on holiday.

His senses exploding in a great, galloping rush, Gabriel pulled her down with him to the sand. She fit nicely atop him, her breasts pressed against his chest and the most feminine part of her within a hair's breadth of its masculine counterpart. He ran his hands down her spine and over her bottom and under the thigh of the leg she audaciously inserted between his.

And still she kissed him, ever more urgent and insistent. Her palms flattened in the sand on either side of him. Her body undulated over his like the wicked woman he had taught her to be.

Gabriel looked up into her face, into those fierce blue eyes, into the savage warrior who wouldn't be denied, and thought — with the tiny piece of his brain still capable of thought — that he could follow this woman to the grave.

With a low growl, he hooked a leg over hers and rolled them over as one. Now he was on top — not that he minded the other, but he thought it best to be in charge if he was sailing to his doom. As in-charge as she would permit, anyway; with Louisa one never knew.

As he rose over her, he met her clear, blue gaze and saw the wanting there. It, too, looked like the never-get-one's-fill kind of wanting.

Hell.

Gabriel's heart — feeble though it might be — caught in his throat. He instantly flung it elsewhere and plunged into the sensual haze thickening around him. He ground his body into hers as if they were already one — which they *would* be if he could but find her under that cumbersome skirt and the sand that was everywhere.

Louisa made an impatient sound low in her throat. She tore at the laces of her bodice, caught his hand, placed it on one bare breast. Her satin roundness was made for his touch — only his. The nipple stood at attention for his kisses — *only* his.

But she gave him no time to linger there. Instead, she arched upward, lifting her hips, straining for him. Her hands glided over his back, pressed him closer. She slid one hand between their bodies to touch him intimately.

Done for.

Her boldness swept him to a place from which there was no earthly escape. Just to be sure, Gabriel crushed their bodies together so there was no space between them, no place where desire could not chase away doubt.

The wanting was all, and it consumed him.

Humbled him.

She murmured his name — *Gabriel.*

Hers was on his lips and in his heart when he joined their bodies and filled her with his desperate need.

For the first time in his adult life, he held nothing back.

***

"There is a man here for you." Lily peered into the kitchen, where Daisy was showing Mary how to wash dandelion leaves. "Tall, strong-looking. Says you wrote to him. Called you by a different name, but I knew it was you from his description."

Henry.

Daisy stilled. "Will you take Mary?"

Lily's eyes widened. "Should I have said you weren't here?"

"No. I-I did write to him. But I hadn't expected him to come — not so soon, not ever, really." Writing to Henry had been a wild thought rattling around in her head since that conversation in the kitchen with Mr. Sinclair. Impulse led her to write that letter and give it to him to post in the village on his way to London. She never imagined Henry would respond.

Panic filled Daisy as she walked toward the front door and opened it.

Henry stood on the drive. *Her* Henry.

Was he still? Surely no man betrayed as he'd been would wish to see her again.

Yet, there he was. Looking toward the stable and fields beyond, squinting against the sun. Perhaps he was seeing the land with his farmer's eye, figuring its production worth, the crops it would sustain. His hands clutched a threadbare gray cap.

Daisy had forgotten how tall he was, how strong. He could carry a barrow's full of wood or feed or stone as if it were straw.

He turned and saw her.

"Catherine!" He moved toward her, then halted, his expression wary. "Is Mary here?"

His face was more lined than she remembered. His eyes were the same — hazel, flecked with brown — but something new lived in them now. Pain, perhaps. Caution, certainly.

The spark that had existed for her alone was gone. Henry was usually preoccupied with work; his eyes often held a distracted air. But sometimes, they would shift to her, and the light there warmed her. He was not one for words, but Daisy could gauge his feelings by his eyes.

Today they were guarded.

The months had not diminished the sun-burnished planes of his face, the disheveled sand-colored hair that fell over his forehead, or the appealing indentation in his chin.

Anguish swept those features now. "I didn't know where you were, whether you were safe." His voice was thick with emotion. "Have you any notion what you've put me through?"

"But…you cast us out," Daisy said.

"Not Mary," he growled. "You took her."

Across the way, Sam looked up from his chores in the stable yard.

"Because I would never abandon my daughter, especially not to a man who found me abhorrent," Daisy said stiffly.

"I did not find you abhor —" He broke off.

They stared at one another for a long, silent moment, anger suffusing the space between them. And though that distance was no more than a few feet, it seemed much greater.

Finally, Henry took a deep breath. "I would have raised her on my own, if need be."

"Pray, how would you have done that?" Daisy demanded. "Could you teach her to cook and sew so that she might have a woman's skills when she is older?"

"I would learn to do those things." Determination was etched in the lines of his face, and Daisy had no doubt he would have. Henry did not lack for grit.

"And compassion — could you learn that?" she challenged. "Could you teach her compassion for those who are different? You, who so roundly condemned me, and all womankind?"

"I did not condemn women," he protested, "only the unnatural kind."

"Who are you to decide what is natural?"

His answering scowl brought back that ugly scene months ago, when she'd finally told him about Sarah. Some men would have resorted to violence, but that was not Henry's way. In the end, he had simply told her he wanted her gone.

Suddenly, the anger seemed to leave him. He stared down at the dirt.

"Henry?" Guilt filled her, along with deep sorrow at the mess she'd made of things.

He looked up, his gaze softer. "I want you back, Catherine. You and Mary. I have missed you. I'll not pretend otherwise. I wish to return to the way we were."

Tears sprang to her eyes. "The way we were was a lie."

His gaze filled with confusion and hurt. "I thought you loved me."

Daisy turned away, but he touched her shoulder. "A heart doesn't forget, Catherine."

Out of the corner of her eye, Daisy saw that David now stood next to Sam, watching them. That gave her courage — not because she feared Henry, but because she needed to tell him the truth. She faced him squarely. "I have taken a new name. It is Daisy — like the flower."

He looked bewildered. "What was wrong with the old name?"

"Daisy suits me. It is happier, somehow. Freer."

Henry ran his hand through his hair, making it more disheveled. "I don't understand any of this — why you turned to someone else, a woman, at that. Did I neglect you? I know women like to talk more than men. I'm not good at it — comes of spending so much time in the fields in my own company."

She shook her head. "It wasn't that."

"I shouldn't have turned you out. But you betrayed me. Did you expect I'd accept that?"

"No. I ought to have told you about Sarah earlier. I didn't have the words."

"I don't know that there are words for such as that."

Daisy sighed. "I was searching for something, Henry. Something…more."

His jaw hardened. "More than me."

"More than *me*," Daisy corrected. "With her I became someone else, at least for a time."

Henry looked baffled. She couldn't blame him, for she struggled to understand it herself. He looked down at her in that earnest way of his. "You cared for her as a woman cares for a man?"

She nodded. "It did not feel wrong or unnatural to do so. But our relationship was only a lark to her. It amused her to teach me…things."

"Things," he repeated.

"I thought she understood my heart," Daisy said. "But she…she didn't. She didn't love me."

Henry regarded her for a long moment. "I do."

His honest, open gaze went straight to her heart. Daisy eyed him in wonder. "Even…now?"

He pulled a handkerchief from his pocket and wiped his brow. "I have had months to think on it. All of planting season, and then some. I looked for you everywhere. I'd almost given up hope. Then your letter came." His hopeful smile nearly broke her heart. "Will you return with me? So that we may be a family as before?"

"I have a family here. We are a company of women."

Henry glanced toward David, who was still watching them. "And who the devil is that?"

"David lives in his own cottage."

He returned his attention to her. "I want you back. I don't care who you have been with."

His honesty seared her. He deserved nothing less in return. Daisy took a deep breath. "Sarah…knew how to please a woman."

Henry stared at her blankly. Then comprehension dawned. "Did you not like it when I touched you?"

Daisy flushed. "I wanted you, Henry. So very much. But —" She broke off.

"But what?" he demanded. "For God's sake, what?"

She gently touched his arm. "You never showed me such."

It took a moment for that to sink in. "I…did not satisfy you," he said slowly. "My God, Catherine. Is that what you are saying?"

Daisy looked around, embarrassed. "Keep your voice down. I do not want others to hear —"

"Damnation, woman! Do you think *I* wish anyone to hear?"

David took a step toward them, but Henry took no notice. Instead, he turned away from her, stricken. Daisy felt wretched. But the words would not be unspoken, and she did not wish them to be. Just as her new name made her feel freer, so did speaking the truth.

Still, her heart filled with sorrow. Nothing could have prepared him for this. They had known one another since childhood, and yet perhaps they had not known enough.

"I was so very glad to marry you, Henry," she said. "It felt as if we belonged together, as if my heart had a home. But I got swallowed up by our lives — the baby, the chores, the cooking. You were always out in the field. I was managing the rest, but I wasn't very good at it. I suppose I lost sight of us, of myself. Sarah made everything feel new again. Exciting."

He turned. "Planting, cleaning, cooking, raising children — it's what we're meant to do. It's how we fill our time. It's *living*, for God's sake. Excitement doesn't last. It's not worth throwing away the rest for."

Daisy considered that. "There is truth in what you say. But surely there is room in everyday life for excitement. Not all the time, of course. But maybe it can exist in the background — something to take out and appreciate now and then to make the rest worthwhile."

He frowned. "Keep it in a closet, you mean, but still at hand?"

She gave him a wobbly smile. "Yes."

Henry's mouth quirked upward. Something tantalizing bloomed in those hazel eyes. "Will you show me how to please you?"

Daisy blinked. "I-I did not think men wished women to be so frank. It is embarrassing to think of describing..." She trailed off.

His gaze darkened. "You had relations with another woman. You took our child and left your home. I do not see how a woman with the courage to do those things can cavil at plain talk with her husband." His eyes searched hers. "Unless you don't even wish to try. Do you?"

Daisy stared at him. "I-I don't know what to say."

"It's either yes or no, I'm thinking."

She swallowed hard. "I wonder...could you stay here for a time, to see if we can sort things out?"

"Stay here?" He frowned. "With a group of women and...whoever that fellow is?"

"With Mary and me," Daisy said. "I have not known what to tell her about our parting."

"I cannot leave the farm."

Tears threatened, but she willed them away. "Of course. I have come to think of this as my home, but yours is elsewhere."

He absorbed that in silence.

"I was afraid to let you know where we were," she confessed.

Henry stared at her in disbelief. "I'm your husband. Mary's father. What did you think I would do?"

Her gaze clouded. "Not all of us here have been well-treated by men."

"By my oath, I would never harm either of you. You must know that."

Daisy nodded. "I know it in my heart. I was just so…confused."

"I'll grant that I was angry. You shook the foundations of my life." He looked off at the horizon. "So I guess it *was* all a lie, what we had."

"And yet," she said softly, "you looked for me."

"When I could get a neighbor to see to the farm. I went to villages on market days. Week after week, there was nothing. But just last week —"

"Last week? You were still looking for me as recently as that?" Daisy felt something in her soften, like a barren field that someone — *a farmer* — had begun to tend after a long winter.

Henry nodded. "I was in Newton. People there talked about a big stallion. They spoke about the woman who owned him — a widow, who lived in a big house with a group of women and children. I wondered — I hoped — you might be here."

Shyly, Daisy tucked her hand into the crook of his elbow. "That was smart of you, Henry."

"I was trying to assemble my thoughts, what I'd say to you, when your letter came. I took that as a sign."

"I-I thought you would throw it away."

His gaze locked with hers. "Never."

Daisy looked into those honest hazel eyes and felt the seed of something take root. "I am not entirely certain who I am, Henry. I am sorry I hurt you. You are good and kind and faithful."

His brows drew together. "Like an old sheepdog."

"What I meant is that you deserve better than me."

He weighed her words, his expression grave. Was there anything between them to be salvaged? Daisy wondered. If so, it rested on the broad shoulders of this man she had wronged. He understood now that she couldn't go back to the way things were. Could he forgive her? Could there be a future for them?

"If I can arrange things so I can stay here for a time," he said at last, "will you discover whether being with me is who you are?"

Daisy hadn't expected that. Stunned, she stared at him. "I-I hope so."

That drew from him a lazy smile. "Perhaps you will find that your heart still belongs to me."

That familiar light came into Henry's eyes, and Daisy remembered why she had loved him.

***

"What will you do with the submersible?"

Sinclair was scraping rust off one of the iron bands encircling the craft. "Try to make the blasted thing seaworthy."

Louisa eyed him in surprise. "You wish to put it into operation? I thought you loathed it."

He did not look up. "The War Office believes it can be useful against the French. I suspect it merely wants to keep an eye on potential weapons that could be used against our fleet. I suppose it's possible the submersible might be dangerous in the wrong hands, but I doubt anyone besides me knows how to work the thing."

"Then…you are helping England as your father did."

"Not by choice. I was persuaded to do so by an old acquaintance."

"A friend?"

Sinclair shrugged. "We served together in the Royal Navy. We were on separate ships ambushed by the French in the West Indies."

He lapsed into silence. Clearly, she wasn't going to get the tale from him without effort.

Louisa sighed. Their lovemaking on the beach yesterday had only made Sinclair more withdrawn and withholding. In the cabin last night, he'd given her the only usable bed, while he slept on a pallet and hadn't come near her. Today, he'd been taciturn and remote.

"I'd like to hear the story," she said. "Unless you'd rather I made love to you. I believe I have learned enough to do it properly by now."

His scraper clattered to the floor. Sinclair shot her a dark look. "It was in '09. I was a junior officer on the *Junon*. We were near Guadeloupe enforcing the blockade against the French."

"And your friend?"

"Andrew Maitland served on our escort sloop, the *Observateur*."

Silence. Louisa reached out and touched his shoulder, trailed her finger down the length of his arm.

He pulled away.

"We'd sighted a group of ships," he said. "They ran up Spanish flags to make us think they were allies. The captain of Drew's sloop was green, and an idiot besides. He signaled it was safe for us to approach. But when we pulled alongside, they raised the French colors and opened fire. Drew's ship abandoned us. Many on the *Junon* died. I was among those taken prisoner."

Prisoner. The man was full of secrets. "How long were you held?"

"Long enough to get a good look at how desperate the French stood in the Caribbean before I escaped. The War Office found my information useful. It sends people around now and then to remind me of my obligations to my country."

"How did you escape?"

"Child's play. The French aren't sailors. The ship on which I was held ran aground."

"Is restoring the submersible one of those obligations

the War Office has reminded you of?"

He didn't respond.

"Hasn't your debt to your country long since been paid?" she persisted. "Why do this, especially since you are loath to recognize any authority other than your own?"

"I'd say she has you pegged, Gabe."

Startled, Louisa turned toward the voice. A tall figure stood at the cave entrance, silhouetted against the sunlight — indeed, blocking much of it. Sinclair hadn't said anything about expecting a visitor. But then he'd said very little at all today.

"Do come in, Drew." He didn't look up from his work.

As the man moved toward them, agile as a cat despite the shadows and uneven footing, his dark gaze shifted to her. "I have heard of your accomplishments, Miss Peabody. They are, if I may say, quite estimable." He bowed politely. "I am Andrew Maitland, and it is my very great honor to meet you at last."

"Very smooth, Maitland," Sinclair growled. "I wonder that she does not swoon in the face of your very excellent — not to say reptilian — manners."

So this was the man who had persuaded Sinclair to restore the submersible. Despite Maitland's cordial words, the atmosphere between them was more combative than friendly. Perhaps the West Indies incident was to blame.

Louisa hoped Mr. Maitland's intentions were benign, for he looked to be a formidable opponent, if it came to that. As tall as Sinclair, he was dressed more formally, in buff pantaloons and dark jacket.

As she studied him more closely, Louisa realized that while his clothes were cut with classic elegance, they were also unremarkable; his neck cloth was tied in a simple, straightforward manner, without the excess or architectural daring she'd seen in newspaper illustrations of fashionable gentlemen.

His posture seemed both alert and relaxed. Perhaps

that was typical of former naval officers accustomed to rolling seas.

What had he meant that her actions were known to him? Surely there was nothing about her to attract attention beyond their little village. Unless he referred to her rescues. The thought chilled her. How could he know of those?

He bore her scrutiny with a polite expression that did not alter when she failed to return his greeting. Instead, he simply turned to the submersible. "It's an ugly-looking thing, isn't it?"

Sinclair looked up. "Not at all. It's a thing of beauty, a perfectly balanced sphere — classic yet modern, graceful yet functional. Its shape allows it to glide through water with very little resistance."

Mr. Maitland arched a brow. "I am riveted. Pray, continue."

Sinclair pointed to the two metal protrusions. "Those are the rudders. Horizontal and vertical. The controls are worked inside the craft."

Mr. Maitland peered into the small door. "How many men does it hold? How do they breathe?"

"It can take up to three men in close quarters," Sinclair said. "Compressed air in these copper bottles" — he pointed to the cylinders — "is sufficient for a few hours. But the air in the bottles is the same air that must be pumped into the ballasts so that the craft can surface."

"I see." Mr. Maitland stroked his chin thoughtfully. "Choices must be made."

"Yes." Sinclair's tone was brittle. "If the crew uses all of the air, they won't be able to surface."

The atmosphere in the cave, already colored by Sinclair's dark mood, took a more menacing turn.

Mr. Maitland seemed not to notice. He walked around the craft, studying it. "What is the purpose of the window in the dome?"

"It affords some light from above when the craft is

submerged. That helps the crew see to work the controls. The lower the craft descends, the less light comes in."

The other man frowned. "So it can only be used during daylight, and close to the surface?"

"Actually, daylight is its chief drawback."

Mr. Maitland's gaze narrowed. "Perhaps you might simply explain things fully instead of this cat-and-mouse nonsense."

Sinclair smiled thinly, but Louisa did not miss the hard gleam in his eyes. "In daylight, if you steer the craft too close to the surface, it can be seen from above. A ship's lookout might take it for a large fish or whale at first, but he has only to wield a spyglass to see it's no fish."

"It's useless as a weapon of surprise, then."

"Not quite," Sinclair said. "At nighttime, it would be formidable."

"You said the crew needs light to steer."

"But not necessarily daylight," Sinclair said. "A full moon, for instance, would provide significant light through the dome. And, since darkness renders the water opaque, it's unlikely anyone could discern the submersible from above, even if it's just below the surface."

Mr. Maitland peered into the craft at the instrument levers. "What if the moon is not full? Will there be enough light for the crew to see the controls?"

"No. Even with the moon they'd need a candle inside, maybe two."

"Won't the candlelight be seen from above?"

Sinclair shook his head. "Too faint. In any case, candlelight would be subsumed in the moonlight reflected on the water."

"Which means the craft would be undetectable at night. I say, Gabe, that's quite extraordinary." When Sinclair did not respond, Mr. Maitland sighed. "I sense there is a 'but' you are dying to tell me."

"More than one," Sinclair said.

The other man looked pained. "Continue."

"There is a limit to how long the crew can stay submerged," Sinclair said. "Candles consume air. The hand crank inside must be turned constantly to move the blades propelling the craft. The exertion causes the crew to breathe air faster."

Mr. Maitland considered that. "Which means the craft cannot travel far underwater. How far?"

"If a crewman constantly turns the crank, it could make six miles over the available three hours of air." Sinclair paused. "That exposes another limitation, not to mention an ethical dilemma."

Leave it to Sinclair, Louisa thought, to find the fault line between principle and practicality.

"For instance," he said, "if you send the submersible to blow up a French ship in the Channel — submerged, as it must be to avoid detection — the target can be no farther than three miles out from our shores. In plain sight of England, in other words. I believe we can stipulate that French warships do not venture quite as close as that."

Louisa saw where he was going. Judging by Mr. Maitland's expression, he did, too.

"If you send the submersible farther out than three miles," Sinclair continued, "it's a suicide mission for the crew, as they'd be left without sufficient air to return submerged. If they surface to save themselves, they are visible to enemy ships." He eyed the other man. "And we both know the War Office does not send crews out on a mission only to abandon them when they are in distress."

Mr. Maitland scowled. "Damnation, Gabe, it was not my decision to leave the *Junon* —"

"Defenseless amid a barrage of 18-pounders as you sailed away unscathed?"

"Let it go, will you?"

"Certainly." Sinclair's gaze slid to Louisa. "In the spirit of our agreement."

She frowned. There was something he did not wish her to know. It was one of Sinclair's more maddening traits that he revealed himself only piecemeal — and rarely voluntarily. Only today had she learned that he'd narrowly escaped a fiery death at sea, been imprisoned on a French ship, and escaped when it ran aground.

Would the man never give freely of himself?

He would not. Knowing that, she had nevertheless followed him to this island to try to discover who he was. Once more, she had allowed herself to be carried away by rash emotion and false hope.

"You haven't told me how deep she can go," Mr. Maitland said.

"No more than twenty-five feet. Even that's a risk," Sinclair said. "The deeper she goes, the greater the water pressure. Too much, and the craft could collapse in on itself. Copper's too soft for submersion at greater depths. The iron bands reinforce it, but a reef or rock could tear the thing open."

"Twenty-five feet?" Mr. Maitland frowned. "But that's no deeper than —"

"The Thames. At high tide."

"So it's not seaworthy?"

"I didn't say that."

"God's teeth." Mr. Maitland made an impatient sound. "What the devil do you mean?"

Sinclair seemed to be enjoying himself. Louisa guessed that few people could draw Mr. Maitland into any display of emotion. The man looked to be as full of secrets as Sinclair.

Sinclair pointed to the tanks on either side of the craft. "By regulating the buoyancy of the ballast tanks — that's done by pumping air in and out, you'll recall — and keeping a tight hand on the horizontal stabilizer, one can pilot the craft in full seas, provided it doesn't descend lower than twenty-five feet. In theory."

"In theory?"

"As with all inventions, one doesn't really know they will work until they do," Sinclair said.

"The French managed it. They experimented with submersibles."

"Ah, yes. Fulton's *Nautilus*. If only it hadn't leaked."

"But it destroyed a 40-foot sloop," Mr. Maitland said. "Why the French abandoned the project is a mystery."

"The bigger mystery is why, after Fulton brought his proposal here, you let the man take himself off to America instead of building a new submersible."

The other man sighed. "You know the answer."

"You made the mistake of believing that Trafalgar settled things."

"Ancient history," Mr. Maitland said dismissively. "Can the thing be made to work or no?"

Sinclair shrugged. "I've studied my father's drawings. It looks sound on paper. I sailed it with him on the surface and below more times than I can count."

"And?"

"Some of the limitations can be got around — for instance, sailing on the surface as much as possible so as not to compromise the interior air supply. But that renders the craft visible, which removes hope of surprise. Then there is the fact that the air the crew breathes is also needed for surfacing. In short, I would caution against high expectations."

"I felt sure you would. When can we see it in action?"

Sinclair looked thoughtful. "I assume you wish to see it at night, to assess its prospects as a weapon of stealth?"

"Yes. You will notify me when it is ready to test?"

"The very instant." Sinclair's gaze shifted to Louisa. "Give us a moment, Drew."

Mr. Maitland betrayed by not so much as an eyelash whether he thought this an odd request. Instead, he moved away from them, toward the cave opening.

Sinclair turned to her. "I mean for you to go with Drew to the mainland. He will see that you get home safely."

Louisa stared at him. "I have no wish to leave."

"What I am about is dangerous," he said. "I do not want you involved."

Her chin rose. "I am already involved, since I heard every word. Isn't the truth that you don't want *me?*"

Sinclair's gaze grew bleak. "You cannot think that. Not after yesterday."

No, she hadn't doubted his desire during that interlude in the sand. But why had he spent today pushing her away? "What is wrong, then?"

"You demand too much — more than I can give."

"You don't know what you are capable of giving."

"Stop deluding yourself, Louisa. For once, see things as they are, not how you'd like them to be. After I finish here, I will leave England. The longer you stay, the harder parting will be."

"Harder for me or for you?"

"Don't you see? I am trying to be noble." He gave a bitter laugh.

"Noble doesn't suit you, Sinclair. You're too selfish."

"I won't deny that," he growled. "But unlike you, I can see the truth. And the truth is that I'm just another of your hopeless causes you've persuaded yourself you can fix."

Louisa shook her head in mute denial.

"I'm sorry if you care for me." His gaze was hard. "I'd never meet your expectations. In fact, I'd destroy every one of them. There is no permanence in me, no hunger for love or family. I'm not the man for you."

Shattered, she could only stare at him.

"We are not two sides of the same coin," he added ruthlessly. "We don't complete each other. I would only disappoint you and you would —" he broke off.

"What?" Her voice was a ragged whisper. "What would I do?"

"You would consume me. You'd have me constantly striving to be better than I am. I can't. I won't. Why won't you accept that?"

Louisa turned away so he would not see her despair. She felt as empty and desolate as that sliver of beach visible through the cave opening. "Perhaps for the same reason you can't accept who I am. You want me to give up. But that isn't me."

His hand touched her shoulder. "Louisa — "

She shook it off, and he sighed. Perhaps it was a sigh of relief that she'd be leaving, perhaps only an empty sigh — as empty as she felt now, with his rejection knifing through her.

Tears rolled down her cheeks. Before she could disgrace herself further, Louisa fled toward the cave entrance, toward the mysterious Andrew Maitland, who stood on the beach calmly regarding the horizon as if he had all the time in the world.

***

Gabriel watched her flee toward the light, away from the darkness he caused. He couldn't allow her feelings for him to deepen. The wounds from caring too much didn't heal, as he well knew. She deserved a man fool enough to give her all that was in him. He wasn't that man.

"Lovely creature," Drew observed. He had returned to the cave, while Louisa waited for him outside. At least Gabriel assumed she did. He couldn't bring himself to look.

"Rather fierce, isn't she?" Drew said. "I can almost imagine her riding into battle, leading the troops to victory. Athena, perhaps."

Gabriel fixed his gaze on the iron bands. "Boadicea."

"I see. A fighter indeed."

And that was the problem, wasn't it? Louisa didn't know how *not* to fight. Sending her away might protect her from developing deeper feelings for him, but it wouldn't stop her from trying to free those women — or attempting other dangerous missions.

That knowledge sent a shaft of terror through him.

Last night, he'd lain awake for hours as the threads of an idea came to him, but they had floated just out of reach. He'd been too consumed with worry to think clearly as he imagined her leading the Flowers to the prison hulk.

Gabriel told himself that her future was out of his hands, that he wasn't up to the task of loving her — or anyone, if it came to that. Loving his family hadn't kept them alive or sane. His dreams had been crushed, his affection wasted, his soul ripped into pieces.

As for the romantic kind of love — that was a bit of nonsense aimed at shackling a man for life, obligating him to doing a woman's bidding, accepting her mad schemes, pledging a faithfulness no mortal could manage.

Wasn't it?

Unbidden, his mother's face appeared in his mind's eye, as she had looked in that portrait, and in life. Gabriel never doubted that she loved Aloysius with all her heart. Her children, too. Likely she'd have been disappointed that Gabriel had never learned how to love.

One more failing to add to the growing list.

But he'd seen no way around their impasse: Louisa wouldn't compromise, and neither would he — otherwise, his heart would be at her mercy, constantly teetering on the edge of a great, dark abyss.

Like now.

Gabriel could feel Drew studying him in that unnerving way. It was a skill at which he excelled — seeing whatever lay beneath the surface of a man so he could manipulate the poor devil to a fare-thee-well. But Drew's suspicions didn't concern him. The man needed him, had no choice but to continue down the path they had agreed on.

"Do you remember the *Defiance*?" Gabriel asked.

Drew looked thoughtful. "Durham had her command,

did he not? Rammed a French ship at Trafalgar. Tore off most her bow, if memory serves."

"She's a prison hulk now. In the Thames."

The other man's gaze narrowed.

"Several female inmates are being held there," Gabriel said. "In deplorable circumstances, I understand."

"Wherever you are going with this, think again," Drew warned. "The War Office does not concern itself with domestic criminals."

"No?"

"Parliament has its hands full trying to get the Millbank prison built," Drew said. "The Reformers, Quakers, scholars — everyone has proposals on improving prisons and punishment. Romilly even got hanging, drawing, and quartering abolished."

"Not hanging by itself, I am obliged to point out, having some experience with the state myself."

"My point, Gabe, is that the politics around this issue are noisy and extreme. The War Office cannot be involved in any way with prisons or prison hulks."

Gabriel shrugged, as if such a thought had never entered his brain. Those threads of an idea, however, continued wrapping themselves around each other, wanting to become something.

Drew's expression darkened. "We agreed not to arrest Miss Peabody. That's as far as our arrangement goes. I won't protect her if she continues to attempt these unlawful rescues."

"The submersible will be ready for testing within a few days," Gabriel said.

Drew accepted the change of subject. "Perhaps the test should be in open waters, since that is where we will ultimately wish to use it."

"It would be the devil to fish out of deep water if something went wrong. We'd lose it."

"I see." Drew was silent for a moment. "Shallow

waters, then. Where?"

"River's the right depth," Gabriel said. "Convenient for you and anyone else in the War Office who wishes to watch the test."

Drew regarded him closely. "Sensible notion, I suppose."

"A full moon will provide the best light for your viewing party and for steering the submersible," Gabriel said. "High tide will produce a heavy chop to simulate open seas."

Another silence followed, during which Gabriel could almost hear Drew's brain working — dangerous for anyone seeking to play him for a fool.

"I do not suppose you know when the next full moon is?" Drew gave a rough laugh. "Never mind — of course you do."

"Four days hence. I'll have the submersible ready by then."

"I'll hold you to that. And now, if I don't miss my guess, you wish me to escort Boadicea to the mainland."

Gabriel's gaze shifted to the beach, where Louisa stood in silhouette, still as a stone.

"Yes," he said.

***

Dry-eyed, Louisa sat atop Starfire. How had she become so lost in the walking maze of contradictions that was Gabriel Sinclair? The shock of his rejection settled over her like a dead weight. She felt empty, dazed.

Her heart had been stolen by a man incapable of keeping it. Against all evidence, she had nurtured a fragile hope that Sinclair would return her love.

Love. For the first time Louisa dared to think the word. It settled over the morass of her complicated feelings for him, insisted on making a home there above all others.

Every instinct had told her to follow Sinclair to his

island, though she'd known that there would be a cost, that she could lose herself in him. And she had. The only question now was how to pick up the pieces of her life.

Mr. Maitland had escorted her to the stable near the cove where Sinclair had left their horses with a village lad. His new gray remained there still. The mare was a fine horse. She would take Sinclair to whatever far horizons called him.

Louisa would never see him again.

Every fiber of her being rebelled at that bleak prospect. Love had somehow taken root in her heart. Sinclair had banished the poison Richard put there. Surely, within Sinclair lay a soul capable of love. If only he could see what she saw, if only he would try —

"And beggars would ride," Louisa muttered as she slid off the horse. Sinclair was right: Once again, she was seeing things as she wished them to be, not as they were.

Midnight was in his stall munching on the carrots Sam had placed on the saddle. The stallion would soon be ready to take the saddle. If a fearsome stallion could change, why not Sinclair?

But there was no use in asking such questions. Louisa made herself focus on the future. Her life would continue, and it would be a useful life. Those women on the hulk had no one else.

Minutes later, she knocked on the door to David's cottage. When it opened, David's massive body filled the frame, blocking her view of inside. Behind him she saw a movement.

"Louisa!" Violet nudged David aside. "I have been worried about you! Rose and the others told me about the fire. Is Mr. Sinclair with you?"

What was Violet was doing in David's cabin?

"No. He has gone."

Violet walked to the hearth and reached for the tea kettle. When she turned, Louisa saw the bruise over one eye.

"I hope he will return," Violet said. "Rose has begun work on new plans."

"Plans?"

"To rebuild Mr. Sinclair's house. Rose is not a woman to admit defeat. Oh, and Daisy's husband Henry is here. He seems quite nice. Nothing like Will."

Louisa eyed them in confusion. "Forgive me, Violet, but have you — that is, did you…?" She looked from Violet to David and back again.

"Move into David's cottage?" Violet nodded. "I hope that does not distress you. Sam is in sore need of a mother, and I believe he is happy I am here." She touched David's hand. "David and I have become close since Will's unfortunate visit —"

"He was here?" Now the bruises made sense. "He hurt you!"

"Only a little." A shadow swept Violet's features. "Midnight trampled him after Will came at him with the whip. He was…killed." She put her hand on Louisa's arm. "I do not rejoice in his death, but I cannot pretend I am unhappy that David and I are free to marry."

Louisa blinked in astonishment.

"Not yet, of course," Violet said. "It is too soon. It would be unseemly."

"That is nae the only reason," David said darkly.

"There is another inconvenience." Violet slipped her hand in his. "But with time, all will be well."

David stared at Violet with such longing that Louisa felt she was intruding. "I am glad for you both. I wanted to talk to David about plans for the rescue of the other women on the hulk, but I can see this is not the time."

Concern filled Violet's eyes. "You intend to rescue those women Alice spoke of?"

"Yes. Sinclair refused to help. It is up to David and me."

David tore his gaze from Violet. "I can nae help ye,

lass. Not this time."

"David!" Violet looked dismayed. "Think of what those women endure. Think of what Louisa has done for all of us. You must."

He shook his head. "I have too much to lose now. I mean to take care of ye for the rest of our days."

"And you will," Violet said gently, "but first we will help them."

"We?" He glowered. "I will nae hear of ye lifting a finger — "

"My mind is made up," Violet said firmly. "We owe Louisa a great debt. It must be paid."

"Nay. Think of the babe," he protested.

"I do think of her or him every day. I shall not jeopardize this precious life growing inside me, but one must follow one's conscience. It will be all right, David."

"Violet," he growled. "I won't allow it."

Neither of them noticed when Louisa slipped out of the cottage and closed the door.

Chapter Twenty-Two

Gabriel had scrupulously followed his father's notes, taken care with each detail, even piloted the submersible around the island using its ungainly junk sail. What he had not done was take it more than a few feet below the surface. He knew the submersible worked, up to a point. He didn't know what that point was — the breaking point.

He had certainly found his own. It had been here, in the cave with Louisa, the day Drew came to check on his investment.

There is no permanence in me, Louisa, no hunger for love or family. I'm not the man for you. Genius, that was. Positively brilliant. He'd sent packing the only woman who had ever come close to…to what?

He had no words for it. All he knew was that her leaving had left a hole in him as deep as the ocean. He was trying to navigate it by the markers he'd always used — no strings, no ties, nothing to hold him. Those were the pillars of his independence. They had served him well.

Hadn't they?

What, exactly, did he have to show for his artful dodging of all commitment?

Freedom, to be sure. Nothing would stop him from wrapping up his business with Drew and sailing away in search of new adventures and new women. Life would continue in the usual way, the way he wanted it. He alone would set his course, determine his future.

He alone.

Alone.

Without Louisa.

Ever again.

Idiot.

He didn't know how to be other than an island, a spit of rock surrounded by a sea of turbulence, waves buffeting him all around but not affecting him because he was, after all, an island.

Without Louisa.

Yes, he had sailed himself right into an ocean of meaninglessness, hadn't he? Everywhere he looked, whether the far horizon or the near shore, was barren and empty.

Without Louisa.

He wouldn't change for her. His life was perfect as it was.

Perfectly awful. Without Louisa.

She had to accept him as he was, or not at all. But that's where he was now, wasn't it? The not-at-all part: him, here, alone.

Without Louisa.

Gabriel kicked out at the submersible and winced as his foot hit the iron banding. He uttered a string of curses to make a nun blush, not that he was likely to run into one of those.

A nun.

He stilled.

Slowly, those chaotic threads of an idea began to drift toward him once more. They curled around each other, knitting themselves into larger pieces, perhaps even a cohesive whole.

For the first time since he'd sent Louisa away, Gabriel felt the beginnings of a smile.

***

"What plan?" Rose demanded.

Sam felt awkward speaking to the ladies and Mr. Henry, but he had known the minute he heard Violet and

David arguing that he needed to tell someone. He didn't know what had caused Violet to move into their cottage to take care of them, but he wasn't about to lose her.

"To save those women on the prison ship," he said. "David doesn't want to, but Violet says they owe it to Louisa."

Rose frowned. "So that is why Louisa is being so closed-mouthed. Here I thought she was moping over Mr. Sinclair, when it was only another rescue."

Henry frowned. "What prison ship?"

"In the Thames," Daisy said. "The women there are horribly mistreated. They do not deserve such a fate."

"Aren't they criminals?"

"There's a difference between paying for one's crime and being forced into slavery," Daisy said.

Rose looked around the table. "It is time to stop letting Louisa do all the work."

"Then you'll do something?" Sam ventured. "Violet doesn't have to risk her life?"

"Nobody will risk anything," Rose said. She returned her attention to the food, then looked up, this time at Daisy. "This stew is an improvement."

Lily nodded. "Is there some new ingredient?"

"Henry discovered a cellar pit," Daisy said. At their blank looks, she added: "A hole dug in the ground for preserving root crops. The vegetables were still good so I used some for the stew."

"Looks to have been there for a few years," Henry said. "Probably dug by a previous owner. Parsnips, carrots, turnips — they last through the frosts if you don't cut off the tops. But it's the devil to construct one of those pits. First, you must pick an elevated spot for drainage. Then dig the hole deep, flare out the sides so water doesn't come in. Line the hole with straw, cover it with a lid — wood works best — then cover that over with soil."

"Yes, well," Rose said.

"The dirt and leaves built up over the years, which is why this one looked like any other hill," he added. "I haven't seen a root pit in years. They've been around for centuries, though. Primitive, but —"

"Henry," Rose said loudly.

He reddened. "Sorry. I tend to go on about farming subjects. Truth is, only another farmer would have recognized the signs. The reason I saw it —"

"The stew is delicious," Lily interjected. "Daisy, you must show me how to prepare it."

Daisy beamed. "It was Henry who showed me."

Rose regarded him with a frown. "We are not much inclined to husbands in this house."

The room fell silent.

"It's up to Louisa whether you stay," Rose said. "I haven't put it to her because she's kept to her room. Maybe it is Sinclair who's bedeviled her after all. He practically lived here for a time."

"So you are not averse to all men — only husbands?" Henry asked.

"*Especially* husbands," Rose said. "To be frank, Henry, you've upset the balance. Daisy hasn't said how long you mean to stay, or whether she means to leave with you, or even where we are to put you. You have Sinclair's room for now, but surely you and Daisy —"

"Where people sleep is not your concern, Rose," Daisy said stiffly.

"As I say," Rose continued, unruffled, "though we are averse to husbands, I am willing to acknowledge that some men can be useful. You may be such a one. With Daisy and Lily taking turns cooking, half the dinners are passable but the others are awf —"

"What Rose means to say," Lily said, "is that inspiration is always welcome in the kitchen."

Henry smiled. "I shall try to provide inspiration in whatever area I can be useful."

His gaze settled on Daisy, and remained there.

***

Time had dimmed Gabriel's memory of Mother Dolores's red nightcap. The woman slept the sleep of the dead, emitting moose-like snores. The covers were pulled up to her bulbous nose. He caught a whiff of spirits.

He couldn't take the chance that her well-lubricated voice would summon that army of virgins, so he covered her mouth with a cloth. She came awake slowly. Her red-rimmed eyes blinked as she tried to discern what demon had invaded her sanctuary. Recognition set in as he pressed the cloth firmly to silence her.

"I am prepared," he said politely, "to donate a generous sum of money to your convent."

Gabriel could almost see her brain struggling through the layers of sleep and whiskey to make sense of it all. "Yes, I know that's a bit queer, but I am afraid you have been mistaken about my character."

Her gaze shot to the closed door to the next room.

"No help there, alas," he said. "Everyone is abed but us." Gabriel might have felt sorry for the woman but for the memory of her testimony at his trial.

"You embellished, you know," he said reproachfully. "I never touched your girls. I only wanted a lock of hair. It was a bet, you see. A drunken one — most unwise, but perhaps you understand what spirits can do to a desperate soul."

She looked away, and Gabriel knew he had correctly surmised her secret weakness. "And now, I'd like to tell you a tale, a sad one. I warn you, it gets ugly in spots, but life outside the convent is like that. My story is about some women. Four, to be precise, who have been given over to a bunch of vile criminals for their base amusement."

Her startled gaze met his.

"I see that I have your attention. What I wish you to

understand is that while my crimes exist primarily in your fertile imagination, there are real crimes against humanity toward which you could better direct your efforts."

Gabriel paused to allow that to sink in. "How long has it been, Mother Dolores, since you re-evaluated your mission on this earth?"

She frowned.

"Oh, I am no proselytizer," he added. "I merely suggest that you could do much good in this world. Will you hear me out?"

Slowly, she nodded.

"Now, as to the specifics: I shall require that you go to the Old Bailey — tomorrow, if you don't mind — and swear an oath as to grievous errors contained in your account of the night I so unwisely made your acquaintance. When this statement is entered into the court records, a copy of which is to be sent to the Honorable Andrew Maitland with this note from me explaining our arrangement, the balance of a thousand pounds will be delivered to Our Lady of Mercy convent. This you may use in any way you choose, but I imagine it will be no great sin if you decide to use a shilling or two to purchase a new nightcap."

Gabriel pulled an envelope from his pocket. "You will wonder at my sincerity. As our previous encounter was not the sort upon which trust is built, I am providing five hundred pounds in advance. I hope it may begin to alter your opinion of me."

Mother Dolores stared at the bank notes.

"Words fail you, do they?" Gabriel said. "I quite understand. Now I will remove the cloth so we can discuss the upcoming events. There are one or two items I have neglected to mention."

***

"This seems unwise." Henry peered out from the carriage after Rose pulled it to a stop in the shadows of the docks. "Why was there a need to act tonight?"

"Because tonight is the full moon," said Daisy. "Louisa said —"

"Let us hear no more about what Louisa said," Rose groused as she peered into the carriage window. "My plan was superior."

"You wanted to storm the hulk," Daisy protested. "That might have gotten us killed."

"And this won't?" Henry demanded. "Daisy, this is madness. I do not like that wild look in Rose's eye. Any woman who did away with three husbands —"

"Is the woman you want on your side at a moment like this," Rose snapped. "Quiet. The ship is just ahead."

Leaving them alone, Rose took Midnight's reins from Louisa, who had ridden the stallion so as to save space in the carriage for the rescued women. David and Violet were a hundred yards behind in the landau and would remain there unless they were needed. Lily had stayed behind to care for the children. And though Sam had begged to be included tonight, Louisa had refused.

"I do not like this," Henry said.

Daisy glared at him. "Why are you here, then?"

"Because you are."

Her expression softened. She touched his hand. "I do not think we will be killed. Indeed, I believe that whatever happens this night will inspire us for all the years to come."

He regarded her thoughtfully. "All the years to come. Years together, you mean?"

That spark had come into his eyes, the one for her alone. "Henry," she began, "you are —"

"Just an ordinary man," he said. "One who would count it as the greatest privilege to be your husband for all the years to come. Do you know your heart now?"

Daisy hesitated. "I should not have asked you to stay on at Louisa's. We have no privacy, and it's another barrier between us. I wish to be where we can discover what we have together."

"And where is that? Say it straight out, Daisy. Will you come home?"

She nodded. "After this. Louisa has given me a chance to help tonight, and I mean to see it through. Then I'll come with you."

"And there'll be only truth between us?" Henry persisted. "Even — *especially* — with respect to those matters that embarrass you to speak of — by which I mean the pleasuring?"

Daisy's face flamed. "What…if what I say repulses you?"

"It won't. Anyway, we'll make room in the closet."

"Make room?" She eyed him in confusion.

"For excitement. See what fits, what doesn't." He tucked her arm in his, his expression thoughtful. "I'm thinking I already know."

***

"Wish I was back at Coldbath Fields." Captain Josiah Selby gave a bored yawn and took a swig of rum. He hated the hulk, hated the river's damp, hated that he spent his days and nights in charge of the dregs of humanity and a group of sodden guards vastly beneath him in every way. Sometimes he relieved his boredom by taking his pleasure with the female inmates — a whining lot — though it lowered him to the level of the other guards, some of whom possessed notoriously unsavory tastes.

"That hellhole?" A guard, Bill, spat on the floor. "Wretched place. Lost my arm in the aught-hundred riot."

Tom, the other guard, nodded. "Prison's no place for politics. Reformers nearly turned Newgate into a church. I hear some duke even makes a show of praying in the chapel on Sundays."

The three men turned their attention to the cards.

"We're due a dozen more prisoners by the end of the

week," Selby said.

"Hope there's more women," said Tom. "None here can hold a candle to Alice."

Bill raised his glass. "A woman who understood her proper place."

"Deserves to be whipped for running off," groused Tom, whose well-known taste for punishment made him the only one among them truly happy with his assignment.

A respectful silence followed, during which each man indulged in fond and considerably varied memories of the departed Alice. Just as Selby returned his attention to his cards, another guard entered the cabin, pushing two women ahead of him.

"Found these two on the gangway, Captain." His mouth curled. "Claim to need our help."

Selby frowned. One of the women particularly drew his eye — and, he suspected, that of every man in the room. She wore breeches that outlined a pair of lissome legs. Her golden hair was tied back, although some loose strands curled appealingly around her face. Her blue eyes radiated authority, and it was to her that he spoke. "What is the trouble, er, ladies?"

"Our carriage struck a rock, and the wheel is damaged," she said. "We are in grave need of assistance. My sister is very near her time."

Selby had never seen a woman in breeches and rather liked the view. The other woman wore bulky clothes and a shawl; she might have been increasing, as the other woman suggested, or not.

"And remiss we would be," he said gallantly, "if we failed to rise to the occasion. How can we assist your poor sister who was so unwise as to leave her confinement?"

"Ought to whip her," Tom said pleasantly.

The woman eyed Selby anxiously. "Would it trouble you to examine our carriage?"

His gaze narrowed. "I do not allow my guards off the

ship at night. Every man is needed, for we harbor heinous criminals."

The woman looked startled. "Criminals? I had not realized —"

"You need not worry," Selby assured her. "They are under lock and key." He gestured to the wall, which held a large ring of keys.

The other woman moaned. The one in breeches eyed him in alarm. "I beg you to send someone for a doctor or midwife," she pleaded.

Something was not right, Selby decided. Perhaps they were whores trying to make up for an unprofitable evening. Or gypsies, notorious for haunting the docks. Suddenly, the night looked much more interesting.

As he was mulling the possibilities, Selby heard loud scuffling sounds out on the deck.

"Step aside!" growled a male voice.

The two women exchanged puzzled looks. A tall, angular man burst into the cabin.

"Henry!" cried the woman in the shawl.

Selby reached for his carbine. "Who the devil are you?"

The man drew himself up to his full, and considerable, height. "A farmer."

Selby frowned.

"This woman is my wife. I have come to take her home." The farmer turned to her. "The sooner the better, I'm thinking."

Suddenly, there came a great clamoring out on the deck. Selby moved toward the noise, weapon raised. The other guards followed — only to pull up short at the strange apparition.

More than two dozen women in flowing white robes stood in formation behind a larger, similarly attired woman with an imposing headdress.

"Sweet Jesus," Tom muttered. "It's a bunch of angels."

"Not angels, you idiot," Selby corrected. "Nuns."

The woman in front regarded Tom with cold fury. "You, sir, ought to be whipped for taking the Lord's name in vain."

When Tom gave a happy sigh, Selby knew it was time to take control. "What is this about?"

She regarded him over the tip of her reddish nose. "We have heard about the foul sins you foster and permit upon this vessel."

"Aw, hell." Bill rolled his eyes. "It's Reformers."

The woman eyed him contemptuously. "Now is your chance to redeem yourselves, turn your backs on sin and release the martyred women upon whom you have visited vile deeds."

"Take your flock and get off my ship," Selby ordered. "I have other business tonight."

She did not move, nor did the women behind her.

"If you do not leave, Sister —"

"Mother," she corrected.

"— I shall shoot you." Selby waved his carbine at them. He wouldn't, of course — the politicians would have a field day with that. But the sooner they were gone, the sooner he could return his attention to the women back in his cabin. First he'd kill the idiot farmer, then have the flaxen-haired one. He liked gumption in a woman.

Before he could finish the thought, he heard the head nun issue a strange command.

"Sit on them, girls!"

***

It was dark down here.

The glass scuttle in the dome picked up the moonlight, but Gabriel could barely see to steer. He had sailed the craft from Sinclair Isle to Woolwich before submerging. The river chop was up — courtesy of moon tide — but the eastward current fought him the entire way. He'd been an hour underwater, most of it spent working the crank, using precious air.

Yes, he was piloting his father's obsession up the Thames in the service of his country and four females he'd never met. Somehow, he had become involved in Things That Mattered.

Oddly, gliding under the water with only the moon and a single candle to steer by filled him with a heady sense of adventure.

Disaster might yet wait. Perhaps someone who'd seen him before he submerged was even now sounding the alarm that England was being invaded by a madman riding a whale. Perhaps Mother Dolores's black heart had betrayed him. Perhaps Drew, as slippery a character as he'd known, wouldn't hold up his end. Perhaps the craft would turn on him, repaying his years of neglect and scorn.

Even as he formed the thought, the submersible lurched. The spike came up against something hard and hung there like a pesky fly on a cow's underbelly. He looked at his compass. If his calculations were correct, this was his target. All that remained was to shoot a test charge from the cylinder to show he could deliver it to an enemy ship.

Tonight, that enemy ship was the prison hulk.

Chapter Twenty-Three

"There is an odd group of women on the hulk." Violet peered out the window of the landau. "I do believe they are some sort of religious order. Look, David!"

He frowned. The landau waited some distance from the ship. All he could make out were dozens of white figures bobbing about on the deck. "Must be about thirty or so. Nuns, maybe."

"Do you see Louisa or Daisy?"

"Nay."

Violet reached for the door. "I will just stretch my legs a bit."

David's hand clamped down on hers. "You agreed to remain in the carriage. I do not know why those nuns are there, but it's a fine distraction. Naught for us to do but wait." He shook his head. "I should nae have allowed ye to come tonight."

"I am my own person, David Ferguson," she said stiffly. "It was my decision."

He eyed her darkly. "What am I going to do with ye, lass?"

Impulsively, Violet reached up and stroked his cheek. She loved the feel of those coarse whiskers that defied even the sharpest razor. "As to that, I've a few ideas."

David looked away. "I'm content with what we have. Holding you at night —"

"Is a start," she agreed. "And if it is all we ever have, it's more kindness than I've known in a lifetime. But there is more for us in store, David. Much more."

"Nay, lass. Do not tempt the heavens by asking more

than we've a right to claim."

Violet ran her fingertip along the long, jagged scar that disappeared into his shirt. "It is no sin to wish to share the pleasures of the flesh with a loved one."

"Wishing is one thing —"

"And doing is another. Yes, I know." Violet toyed with the edges of his shirt. "May I touch you, David, the way I have wanted to touch you all these nights?"

The longing in his eyes almost broke her heart. "'Tis no use, Violet. I am only half a man."

Violet took his hand and placed it over the fullest part of her belly.

"'Tis a privilege to feel that life within you." Emotion filled him as he stared at his hand, and then sorrowfully removed it from her swollen abdomen.

"Don't pull away," she pleaded. "You have good, strong hands. Made for a woman's body. It is not your fault that you survived that horrible prison while other men were maimed. You must shed this guilt. It is robbing you of every pleasure."

David's tormented gaze held hers. "When my strength was most needed, I was helpless as a lamb. Every night I'd hear the screams, and stare at those bars on my cell, and know that I could have stopped them if I'd been man enough."

"Even you can't rip apart iron bars."

He shook his head in defeat.

"Damnation, David," Violet said crossly. "You might as well have stayed in prison."

His eyes widened in shock.

"I'll never forget what Will did to me," she said. "But I won't give in to the evil that happened. *We* won't. Hope doesn't die. I won't let it."

"I wish I had your faith," he said bleakly.

Violet began to unlace her bodice. "Look at me, David."

David closed his eyes in pain. "Do nae do this. It only makes me yearn for what can nae be."

She caught his hands, brought them to her breasts. "I'm told that after one stops nursing, they shrink and shrivel. Will you still care to touch them when they are small?"

David stared at his trembling hands, which, seemingly of their own accord, caressed her. His thumbs brushed her nipples, teasing them until they were erect and weeping with pleasure.

"Aye," he said roughly. "We must stop this, Violet."

"Not yet. Maybe never." She brought one of his hands to her lips and kissed his fingertips. Her tongue lingered over the rough, callused flesh.

David groaned. "Violet."

"Are...are the nuns still there?"

David ripped his gaze from her and looked out the window. "Aye. Looks like they've taken over the damned ship."

"Heaven-sent," Violet murmured. She slipped his hand under her frock, placed it on her bare thigh.

His eyes closed in tortured pleasure. "You are soft and smooth, like nothing I've touched before. You are...perfection."

"That is how you feel to me," she said. "You are rough in the places I am smooth. I love that roughness and the tenderness underneath. I love you, David. Forever and always."

Slowly, she guided his hand upward.

"Violet." He whispered her name like a prayer.

"I am yours, David," she said softly. "I shall die if you do not touch me."

He held her gaze and dared to hope.

When at last his hand moved of its own accord to the place that burned for him, it did not surprise her to discover that he knew precisely what he was doing.

And when she reached for that most masculine part of

him, Violet found that it, too, was swollen with precious new life.

***

Clutching the ring of keys she had plucked from the guard cabin, Louisa crept toward the hatch to the lower decks. She was alone. Henry had spirited Daisy away when the guards ran toward the commotion.

There were certain to be other guards on the ship, however; she'd have to be quick. She opened the hatch and climbed down the ladder.

The deck below was dark and forbidding. A few lanterns hung on pegs, but they didn't banish the shadows or the oppressive air of gloom and decay. As her eyes adjusted to the dark, Louisa noticed a square outline in the body of the ship — an opening that had been covered over.

Square. The holes are square.

These must be the gun ports, and this the gun deck — where Sinclair had said the women would be kept so as to be "accessible" to the guards.

How little Louisa had known him then. A rootless renegade, she'd thought, and time had proven that so. Yes, much had changed between them, but he had been right when he said he wasn't the man for her. She couldn't abandon every principle she held dear just because Sinclair made her heart sing in a way she had never dreamed possible.

Quite the lofty one, aren't you? Shouldn't wonder if the weight of all that self-righteousness is too much to bear. That sudden, insistent inner voice bore Sinclair's insolent irony.

Sinclair. The full moon!

In all her planning for this rescue, Louisa had forgotten that tonight was also to be the submersible's test. It was the last thing he intended to do before leaving England for good.

But she couldn't think about that, not now. Louisa forced herself to focus on her surroundings. Keys at the ready, she moved into the forbidding darkness.

***

Gabriel perched on the top of the submersible, which now floated serenely on the water. He'd been able to affix the spike to the ship's hull, fire the test charge, and disengage the craft. The submersible performed flawlessly.

Aloysius had been onto something. The realization humbled him. But he couldn't dwell on it now. It was time to see whether Mother Dolores had done her part.

Gabriel tied the submersible to the hulk's anchor cable using the thick rope he'd brought. His knife and scraper were secured at his waist. With the vague thought that he was getting too old for these sorts of antics, he began to climb the cable.

When he reached the gun port, he saw that someone had made a half-hearted effort to nail the cover closed — perhaps as a result of his previous visit. But it was a sloppy job. He'd have no problem wedging it open.

Balancing on the port flange, Gabriel stopped to listen for anything unusual. All he heard was the thundering of his own heart. His brain demanded to know why the devil he was here, perched on a tiny spit of wood, breaking into a fetid, godforsaken prison ship.

No mystery there. All of the questions and all of the answers came down to Louisa. He had to preempt her mad scheme before she tried to carry it out herself. Yet even if his plan worked, it would only forestall the inevitable: She'd continue her rescues until her luck ran out. By then, of course, he'd be sailing on other seas, basking in new adventures, avoiding anything lasting or worthy.

Yes, he yearned to be better than that, to live not solely for himself, but for a woman with golden hair and merciless blue eyes.

But if that were his compass, there'd be no end to torment. He'd be constantly bargaining with the devil, selling his soul to keep her safe — and failing, because she would not be dissuaded from her mad causes.

He couldn't live that way.

He would have to live without her.

Yet already, her loss burned and festered, made it impossible to take a single breath without wanting her. Was this constant yearning to be his fate for all time?

Suddenly, his feet slipped. Gabriel lunched for the flange above, hung there for a precarious moment as his feet tried to stake a claim on the slender port lip. Below him, the river yawned, malevolent and dark.

When at last he regained his balance, he willed away the pointless contemplation of life without Louisa that had shattered his concentration — a perfect metaphor for how she threatened his very survival.

Slowly, he ran his hands over the port cover, found the expected gaps. He wedged the cover loose with his scraper, slipped inside, and propped the cover against the inside of the hull.

Exhilaration filled him. It was instantly replaced by a sudden, undeniable truth.

For rejecting Louisa's precious gift of caring, he deserved to sail on meaningless, empty seas for the rest of his hopelessly untethered life.

He didn't want that. He wanted Louisa Peabody.

That meant his future was as muddled and unfocused as the yawning darkness surrounding him now. Impossible to see the way forward.

But perhaps all one needed was the right compass.

With that, his world reordered itself. Gabriel took a deep breath and moved into the hulk's relentless gloom.

And saw Louisa, running for her life.

Two guards and a throng of prisoners were chasing her and several women toward the open hatch to the upper deck.

As each woman gained the ladder, white-draped arms reached down and helped them up to safety. *Bless you, Mother Dolores.*

But just as Louisa reached the ladder, a guard raised his carbine and drew a bead on her.

Gabriel grabbed his knife, threw it straight and true. It found the guard's arm. The carbine clattered harmlessly to the floor.

But the hatch slammed shut, cutting off Louisa's escape. She clung to the ladder's bottom rung, her eyes wide with fear as the mob closed around her.

Then she looked up, saw him. Her eyes filled with disbelief.

The injured guard was shouting, drawing the prisoners' attention. The other guard moved to help him. For a moment, no one noticed the breeches-clad woman who suddenly plunged into their midst.

Gabriel fought through the sea of bodies toward her. Finally, he was close enough to grab her arm. He yanked her against his chest.

"Oh, Gabriel!" she cried. "I dropped the keys. The other prisoners escaped!"

It was almost too late for their escape. The mob surged toward them.

Gabriel shoved Louisa behind him and edged them backward. But they quickly came up against the ship's hull and the port cover he'd propped there.

Trapped. Only one way out.

He pushed her through the gun port, out into the darkness and the water below. Then he leapt after her.

A rush of air, a blast of river water, and they were free of the teeming hulk.

Gabriel fought his way to the surface and looked up. None of their pursuers or guards had been crazy enough to follow them into the river. Euphoria filled him.

Then he remembered: Louisa did not swim. And the

dark depths of the Thames were notoriously unfriendly at moon tide.

***

Louisa let herself go limp and tried not to flail. But the water was cold and so very, very dark. She could not hold her breath much longer. The river's icy fingers sucked her down.

He came through for you, didn't he? That inner voice, ironic and taunting. *You ought to have had faith. Not to mention a few swimming lessons.*

Louisa's heart filled with love for Sinclair. She yearned to tell him so. Since that was to be denied her, she prayed that somehow he would know that her last thoughts were of him.

Coming it a bit too brown, dear. Get those feet and arms moving before you turn into a bloated piece of flotsam. That inner voice — *his* voice — would not let her go. Slowly, sluggishly, she tried to move her limbs. But she was so very tired.

She broke the surface just as her strength ran out and took a gulp of air before the water closed over her again. Loud sounds — gunfire? — exploded above. Bullets plinked into the water around her. Too weak to fight, she gave herself over to the water's downward pull.

This time she didn't sink. Strong arms gathered her in. Suddenly, she was plummeting head-first into the mouth of something hard.

The submersible.

Louisa heard a clanking sound, felt the craft lurch into motion. Coughing and sputtering, she rubbed her eyes, trying to focus. She could just make out Sinclair's form.

He was staring savagely at something, a lever, perhaps. "The horizontal rudder is broken," he growled. "We're sinking."

Her brain was as soggy as the rest of her. "I-isn't that

what the ship is designed to do?"

"Not below twenty-five feet. The current will take us to the mouth of the river, where we'll be in water four times that. The submersible will implode."

"Can't we escape before then?"

"The water pressure outside is too great. The hatch can't open."

As if to underscore their dire prospects, the submersible began to shake violently.

Chapter Twenty-Four

$\mathbf{A}$ man couldn't count on anything in this world. They had escaped the mob, the hulk, and the gunfire, but now they were sinking and the ship was trying to come apart. Yet another reminder that fate could make a mockery of his best efforts — and destroy the people he cared about.

How was he supposed to accept that truth? Wasn't it reason enough for a man to turn his back on the world, to flee to the ends of the earth to avoid loss?

"Gabriel." Louisa's voice drew him from the abyss. The moonlight had been lost as they descended through the river's black depths, but he felt for her in the dark, pulled her into his arms.

"Can nothing be done?" she asked.

"Probably not."

"Kiss me, then. I don't care about the rest."

Gabriel locked his arms around her, as if they could keep her safe. As if what was between them would last for all time — all time they had, anyway, which was all the time that mattered.

Got a bit of your own back, didn't you?

He stilled.

Thought you could slip by without paying the piper, but no one does that. Thought you could make it through without caring, but no one does that either.

"Quiet," he muttered.

"What?"

He forced a smile, not that she could see. "Voices in my head. Maybe I inherited my father's madness after all."

Louisa's hand pressed his. "Do you believe in second

chances?"

That gallows scene came hurtling at him across the days and nights that had passed since.

Might have made something of my life… Wouldn't have minded one last chance.

Louisa had given him that chance when she rescued him, but he squandered it. Sent her away, like an idiot who didn't know how to treasure something precious.

"I do." Her voice was fainter. "I believe in grace."

"Grace?"

"A reprieve. A roll of the dice — maybe luck, maybe something bigger. That day on the scaffold, what made them put your execution ahead of Alice's? Maybe it's because we're meant to be together."

What did it matter? he thought grimly. They were sinking to their doom. What kind of grace was that?

"I love you, Gabriel."

Ah. *That* was his answer: It did matter. Everything mattered, because Louisa Peabody loved him. Somehow, a miracle had occurred.

Might there be another?

Gabriel reached for the vertical rudder, wondering why he hadn't thought of it sooner. He couldn't control their descent, but if the vertical rudder still worked, he could control their direction.

"If I can steer us close to one of those new landing stages, we might clip it on the way down," he said. "A collision could open a hole. Water would come in, eventually equalize the pressure."

"The water comes in?"

He heard fear in her voice. "The water would have to fill most of the cabin before the hatch would open. But we're out of options, Louisa."

Silence. Then: "We have nothing to lose, do we?"

"No."

"Then roll the dice, Sinclair."

Gabriel's entire world was contained in that do-or-die command. Even if he got them killed — and a betting man would have to lay odds on that — it was worth his life to have Louisa Peabody send him forth into the darkest night with her fate and her love in his hands.

He worked the vertical rudder, rode the currents, reached for a miracle. In the unremitting blackness, he might as well be steering from inside a coffin. But he pressed on because she had commanded his spirit, seized his soul, and — somehow — come to love him.

For a while, he managed it. The eastward current was taking them downriver, where he didn't want to go, so he used the vertical rudder to tack back and forth, trying to slow their progress toward deeper water, hoping he'd find something in their path to stop it altogether.

He had no idea where they would end up. At the bottom of the river, most likely. For that, he definitely owed her an apology.

"Louisa —"

The sudden jolt cut him off, slammed them against the cabin. Then came the sickening sound of tearing metal. An angry torrent of water rushed in.

Gabriel held onto Louisa, protecting her from the surge. But he was no stranger to sinking ships and knew what would come next.

"We hit something, which is what we wanted," he said, trying to reassure her. "A little longer, and I'll have you safe." Which was perhaps the biggest lie he'd ever told.

Gabriel put his free hand on the hatch lever.

It didn't budge.

"Pressure's not equalized yet. Another minute." More than they had, apparently, for the water had come in too fast and hard. The hole in the craft must be enormous.

Within moments the last air pocket had shrunk to mere inches around their heads.

Fear dug its icy tentacles into him, for he knew he'd

have to release his hold on Louisa to apply his full strength to the hatch.

Suddenly, the submersible began to roll. Now the odds didn't matter. They were out of time.

"Take a deep breath," he told her. "Hold onto me."

Her arms went around him, but her grip wasn't strong. With a silent prayer, Gabriel pushed the hatch lever with all his might.

It groaned.

Shot open.

Gabriel pushed Louisa ahead of him, out through the opening. But even as the submersible released them into the river's embrace, she slipped away.

He lunged for her, caught her hand. With one arm locked around her, he began to swim them upward.

In the inky depths there was no way to judge how far they were from the surface. Gabriel's lungs were burning; he prayed she had sufficient air in hers.

The river's deadly currents menaced them, and the river itself was filled with debris. He'd fought worse, never with such precious cargo.

Louisa loved him.

He hadn't even acknowledged her words. For that alone, he didn't deserve her. But if he didn't have her, he would die. And if he did die in this putrid river, at least it would be death in her arms.

But the heavens, it seemed, were merciful. Gabriel saw a faint, shimmery glow reflecting down through the water.

Moonlight.

They had the river beat.

With a mighty stroke, Gabriel surfaced them.

They swallowed air in great, hungry gulps. Louisa was trembling and gasping. He held onto her, but he knew she wouldn't last long in this. They needed to get out of the river. Gabriel forced his burning eyes to focus on their surroundings.

The moon gave him a vague outline of land not too far away and a structure, perhaps one of the quay warehouses. If so, they were closer to the river bank than he'd thought. Even with the strong eastward current, they hadn't traveled more than a few hundred yards from the hulk.

Gabriel shot Louisa a crooked smile. "Best odds we've had all night."

He eased her onto his back, looped her arms around his neck, prayed she had strength to hold on.

Like a true warrior, she summoned it.

As Gabriel swam them toward that dark silhouette, calm enveloped him. They'd been given another chance.

Grace? A miracle? He'd ponder that another day. For now, he simply gave thanks for the river silt he felt under his feet at last.

Shifting Louisa into his arms, Gabriel cradled her across his chest. She curled into him and gave a deep, shuddering breath. She was spent.

Even so, a faint smile played around her lips. His warrior queen.

Gabriel staggered through the muck carrying his precious burden. And when he gained the river bank, he found another surprise.

"Hello, Gabe."

There, his dark gaze unreadable, stood Andrew Maitland. He was by no means alone. There were, in fact, a multitude of spectators: A half-dozen blank-faced men, probably Drew's. The Flowers. Some fellow making calf eyes at Daisy. Mother Dolores. The homicidal stallion.

Slowly, Gabriel grinned.

***

"I've never made love to you properly." Bleary-eyed and exhausted, Gabriel was lying in the most comfortable feather bed he'd known in years. Louisa sat on the edge, although his eyes could make out only her blurred outline.

"You've never made love to me at all," she said.

Gabriel frowned. "I'll grant that time in the stable, when I was not, er, in full command, was less than it should have been."

"Yes," she agreed — far too readily, he thought.

"And the house burning down was a nuisance, as was the sand on the beach — but surely the main event was not so forgettable as that." He paused. "Was it?"

"You said that was merely lust. Making love is different, is it not?"

Gabriel felt his eyelids growing heavier and heavier.

"How is it different, Sinclair?" she prodded, easing herself down to lie next to him.

His eyes opened to slits. "A subject that certainly bears exploring, if I could only stay awake."

"It has been a long evening, what with the rescues," Louisa conceded. "And Violet's baby."

"And the drowning. Don't forget that."

"*Near*-drowning."

"It felt real enough," he groused.

She nestled against him. "It was very fine of Mr. Maitland to bring us all here and spare us the journey home tonight."

"Drew likes his comforts." The townhouse he had turned over to them was the finest Mayfair had to offer. The bed in this room alone was worthy of a king. It felt all the sweeter for the fact that Gabriel had finally bested his friend. Or enemy. With Drew, one never knew.

In the island cave that day, Drew had flatly refused to involve himself in the prison hulk scheme. They had, however, come to an accommodation: If, in the course of observing the submersible test, Drew encountered women newly rescued from the hulk, he would see to their safety.

At the time, Gabriel hadn't yet thought of the nuns. Later, he realized their presence would seal Drew's help. The man couldn't allow them to come to harm in his presence, nor permit any incident involving nuns, prison escapees, and the War Office to draw public notice.

The ship's guards, as Gabriel had figured, posed no real difficulty. Their captain had no wish to end his career fending off a bevy of nuns or presiding over a riot below deck. The man had cut his losses, handed the women to Mother Dolores, and seen to the security of his ship.

Gabriel had figured on everything, in fact, except Louisa. Seeing her fleeing for her life had been the realization of his worst fears. "Why the devil did you have to choose tonight?" he growled.

"The full moon," she said. "You taught me its usefulness during Alice's escape. I knew we wouldn't need torches but could still see to board the ship." She hesitated. "There was much I didn't foresee, however. I fear my plan was not very good."

"Perfectly horrid."

"I know nothing of ships," she acknowledged.

"Worse than nothing."

"It was all I could do to find the women. When the other inmates escaped and the hatch closed, I thought I was lost." She smiled. "But you saved me."

"And almost drowned us."

"You *saved* us," she corrected. "You and your father's submersible."

His eyes were closing again. Through narrowed slits, Gabriel made out the curve of her dusky lips, the sparkle in her blue eyes, the radiant gold of her hair — and marveled anew.

Somehow, they had come about. All of them, safe.

Violet had given birth in the carriage while he and Louisa were swimming for their lives. Mother and child were healthy — although Ferguson looked as stricken and guilty as Gabriel had seen, and Ferguson was a man who did not take guilt lightly. The new babe slept peacefully in the room next to them with Violet and, Gabriel presumed, the ever-attentive Ferguson.

Drew's men had taken the rescued women to a hospital; Mother Dolores and her flock had insisted on being conveyed there to see they were treated properly. Though events had tried Drew's normally unflappable demeanor, he was pleased the submersible succeeded in docking at a target and firing a test charge. Tomorrow they'd go down to the river and try to salvage the thing.

Best of all, Louisa was here. With him.

A hundred times over Gabriel had feared she was lost — on the hulk, in the submersible, in the river.

Each time, she rallied. It was that do-or-die spirit that ran deep in her bones. Turned out, he had a bit of that, too. Because of what he felt for her: that never-get-one's-fill wanting.

Still, a sickening doubt plagued him. One day, she would not come about, for that was the fate of fighters who ignored their limitations. One day, her schemes would bring defeat or death. She had only survived this long because of luck and her conviction that right was on her side.

Conviction was a word he was coming to terms with.

Louisa's arm slid over his chest, and Gabriel shunted doubt to a small corner of his brain. Instead, he allowed himself to savor this blessed moment of pure contentment.

Her lips brushed his. "Show me how making love is different."

"It is probably the same as the other."

"Isn't the King of Hearts an expert in such matters?"

Gabriel groaned. "Will I never live that down?"

"Never." Her voice was low, sensual.

He forced his eyelids open. "The truth is I've no experience at that sort of love —"

She stopped his words with a kiss sweeter than any kiss had a right to be. And when he gazed into her clear blue eyes, Gabriel knew his heart was home.

His eyelids fluttered shut.

***

Louisa studied Sinclair as he slept, marveling how he had hidden his exquisite strength all this time, leaving her to learn for herself the dint of his will and stamina. That biting wit, that careless air, that effortless charm — they had hidden a man of courage and grit.

Even when he had shown her the worst of himself, she had fallen in love with him. Now she could only stare at him in awe. He had saved her life again and again, but that was the least of what Gabriel Sinclair had accomplished.

With breathtaking daring, he had given himself completely — to her cause, to the possibility of death, even. In doing so, he had breached the walls he had so diligently erected around his heart. She wondered if he felt this new peace and wholeness.

Love. Would he recognize it?

Through the windows in their borrowed room, Louisa watched dawn spread across the sky. She'd never felt more alive. When she turned to him again, his eyes were open.

Troubled.

"About the meddling." His voice was rough. "You must stop. It's all I'll ever ask of you, but I will ask it."

Her heart lurched. Would he have asked such a thing if he did not love her?

"And what will you give me in return?" She knew it was a risk to press him. This was Sinclair, after all — a man who shunned all commitment.

"Devotion. Loyalty." His eyes glinted with a sly bit of mischief, that wild and unpredictable thing that owned her.

"I want more," she said.

"Of course you do." He sighed. "Love. *My* love. There — I knew you'd drag it from me."

"And give it back to you in return," she said softly.

He shook his head in wonder. "Love, devotion — things I never dreamed I'd have, or give. I've never allowed myself to want them."

Louisa slid her arms around his torso. "What else do you want, Sinclair?"

He hesitated. "Mayhap a family, though I don't know what kind of father I'd —"

"A wonderful one."

His eyes searched hers. "You'll marry me won't you?"

She hesitated. "I've always been a meddler. I do not think I can stop."

"You can meddle in a different way. I'll take up my seat in Parliament."

"You have a seat in Parliament?"

"My father's lands are vast. There's a seat if I wish it. Sinclairs have always been land-rich, cash-poor. I'd thought to sell it all, but perhaps with Richard Fiend's money we can keep it up."

He touched her chin. "I mean what I say, Louisa. I will tolerate anything save the meddling. I'm too selfish. I can't take the risk you'll be harmed."

Their gazes held. "You ask much, Sinclair."

"Will you marry me anyway?"

"Yes."

He pulled her into his arms. For a long while they did not speak.

"Righting wrongs doesn't have to mean dodging bullets or a watery grave," he said at last. "We could work in political gatherings."

"You would turn yourself into a Reformer?" Louisa eyed him skeptically.

"No." He nuzzled her ear. "But *you* might turn me into one. I'd follow you anywhere."

A wave of contentment swept her. "Then follow me, home, Sinclair."

He planted a kiss in the hollow of her neck. "Let's tarry a while. I want to make love to you now that I am not half-dead. I want to celebrate everything we came close to losing. Then I'll take you to Peabody Manor."

"No. Take me *home*. To Sinclair Castle."

"It's a pile of stones," he protested.

"It's a pile of dreams," she corrected.

He exhaled. "I had to fall in love with a dreamer."

"The submersible was your father's dream. It saved our lives."

"It's flawed. My father always wondered how to manage the increased water pressure at greater depths. Perhaps I'll rebuild it, make some improvements."

Louisa hesitated. "The house — would you want to rebuild that, too?"

"I don't want to recreate the past, Louisa, only come to terms with it."

"I think you already have." Her mouth brushed his. "Give me your love, Sinclair. Give me your devotion. Give me a strange ship that sails under the water and a cave to put it in. And your dreams — I want those too. A home. A family. That most of all."

"You want the world." He pulled her onto his chest.

Looking down into that amber fire, Louisa grinned. "Stop talking, Sinclair."

"I like it when you give me orders." His hand slid around the nape of her neck, drew her face down to his. "My warrior queen —"

"No, just a woman with fire in her heart. For you."

As they kissed, Louisa felt something magical curl around them like a benediction, filling her heart with its song. It might have been only the cry of a seagull, heralding the new day.

Or the angels, rejoicing.

Epilogue

Perhaps not surprisingly, the name Sinclair became synonymous with meddling. Gabriel took up his seat in Parliament and worked to improve prison conditions. Louisa founded a ladies' society devoted to helping downtrodden women. The War Office purchased Sinclair Isle to use for development of various secret weapons; the money allowed Gabriel to restore the family estate in Kent, except for the temple, which he rebuilt as a playhouse for their children. Before he put hammer to nail, however, he insisted on teaching Louisa to swim.

Violet and David adopted Baby Elizabeth and built a new house to accommodate their growing family. Midnight came to sire a sizable brood himself, his stud services being much in demand. Though the stallion did eventually take the saddle, the only two people he permitted to ride him were Louisa and Sam, his trainer.

Louisa deeded Peabody Manor over to Rose and Lily, who turned it into a refuge for women. Two women from the hulk joined the Flowers, taking the names Camellia and Marigold. A third chose to join Mother Dolores and her band of novitiates, who were frequently seen at the Old Bailey testifying as to the character of female defendants, or at Our Lady of Mercy School, which Mother Dolores founded to educate poor young women.

Alice was eventually transported to Botany Bay, as was the fourth woman from the hulk (whose name, unfortunately, escapes this record), in lieu of being hanged for yet another crime. Lord Upton died of a malady acquired during too-frequent congress with the Covent Garden set.

Daisy overcame the hurdles of showing Henry how to please her. He proved a dedicated student, and Mary was not long without siblings. Daisy never learned to cook, but Henry became quite skilled at it. When mocked by other farmers who considered cooking women's work, Henry only smiled and said it pleased his wife, which was all any real man wished for.

Andrew Maitland dropped by now and then to further the War Office mission, with some success: Two years after the restoration of Sinclair Manor, Gabriel completed work on a twenty-seven-foot-long submersible that could descend to a depth of eighty feet. He called it the Aloysius Sinclair Submersible Marine Vessel, later known simply as Sinclair's Sub-Marine.

After his family, it was his pride and joy.

Author's Note

We think of the submarine as a modern invention, but it was hundreds of years in the making. The concept of a diving bell dates to the late fifteenth century, but it is to a sixteenth-century Englishman, William Bourne, that we owe the notion of a vessel that can submerge to evade or fight an enemy. Cornelius Drebbel, a Dutchman, made the first submersible to Bourne's design. It looked like two conventional boats, one inverted on top of the other, with holes cut out for oars and glass windows for the oarsmen. In 1620, Drebbel staged a public demonstration of the boat in the Thames. Some accounts claim that Drebbel's patron, King James I, took a trial run in the craft, but that is probably a tale grown taller with the telling.

In the 1770s, American David Bushnell invented a tiny egg-shaped ship, the *Turtle*, propelled by hand-operated screws. In 1776, the *Turtle* tried but failed to blow up a British ship in New York Harbor.

Robert Fulton, another American, brought the submarine nearer to something the modem world might recognize. His *Nautilus*, completed in 1801, used a folding mast and collapsible sail for propulsion on the surface and a hand-cranked propeller under water. A vertical spike held the submersible in place under an enemy ship long enough to deliver an explosive charge. In 1810 Fulton persuaded the U.S. Congress to put up $5,000 for a steam-powered submarine. He died before technical difficulties with the craft could be resolved.

Privateers, spies, and adventurers flirted with

variations on the submarine — often with disastrous results. One crew, on a bet, descended to a depth of twenty-two fathoms (132 feet) and was crushed by the pressure. It was left to Wilhelm Bauer, a Bavarian, to discover how to escape from a sunken submarine in 1851. When he hit bottom at sixty feet, his craft sprang a leak. He forced his crew to wait for six hours as water seeped in until the pressure inside the craft matched the external water pressure — whereupon the hatches could be opened.

Robert Whitehead, an Englishman, developed the modem torpedo. In 1870, the British purchased the rights to manufacture Whitehead's designs, which were tested, as it happens, off the coast of Sheerness in Kent.

League of Rogues series

King of Hearts is the first book in the League of Rogues series, about Andrew Maitland's extraordinary group of daring rogues who worked clandestinely for England during the Napoleonic Wars.

Heart of a Duke features Sebastian Traherne, Duke of Claremont, an erstwhile diplomat who has no wish to take up his ducal responsibilities in the wilds of Cheshire, where absolutely no one knows how to dress.

He soon tangles with Gwynna Owen, a determined Welsh miss who claims his name and his protection. She wields her antique dagger with reckless imprecision, speaks in an odd language with few vowels, and thinks cutting her hair is all that's needed for her to pass as a boy.

Forced to make her his ward, Sebastian is drawn to her tale of an island swathed in mystery and legend — a place that also intrigues Andrew Maitland.

It's bad enough that Sebastian is pressed into Drew's service again. Far worse is Gwynna's disturbing habit of making Sebastian forget that his heart will never be free.

Read on for an excerpt:

Heart of a Duke

Spring, 1816

Eerie figures marched in the night, silhouetted against the inky horizon by a thin sliver of moon. Flickering torches animated their ghostly forms. The moor's scrub grasses muffled the sound of boots, but Gwynna could hear their grunts from her position on the rise above them.

It was the cusp of summer, but she shivered with cold. Perhaps it was just the strange spectacle below that made her tremble, for she had always loved the night. At home, she always found peace and solitude in the twilight as she stood on the beach, inhaled the salt spray, and pondered the great snowcapped mountains disappearing in darkness beyond the serpentine strait.

But here, in this land beyond the mountains, the night was a sinister place where strange men drilled in secret on forbidding moors, preparing for unknown battles to come.

Her companion giggled nervously.

"Be quiet, Anne," Gwynna whispered, "or they shall find us out!"

The brown-haired young woman at her side looked fearful. "Papa would be furious if he knew I was here. He says it is dangerous even to speak of the Society. What would he do if he knew we were spying on them?"

"No one will know if you keep quiet. But I wish you had not worn that white frock. It stands out."

Anne shrank against the hillside, wriggling farther

behind the small bush that served as their cover. She glanced at Gwynna's dark cap, breeches, and brown shirt. "Perhaps I should have dressed as a boy, too."

Gwynna tried to imagine the buxom baronet's daughter in breeches and a rough-woven shirt. "I do not think that will suit you. But I have discovered in my travels that it is very freeing to be thought a male."

Anne regarded her sadly. "I wish you would let me tell Papa about you. I cannot bear to think of you sleeping in that old shack night after night. I'm sure he could help you." She hesitated. "Not that he knows the duke. No one does. He is said to be positively ancient. I have heard rumors that he is sick. But no one sees him. He has been shut up in that drafty castle of his for years."

Gwynna's eyes returned to the marchers. "It was a stroke of luck that you, and not your father, found me. The food you smuggle out to me has saved my life. But I must leave. I have to see the duke."

"You will not tell me why?"

"It's a private matter. I am sorry."

Anne stared at the resolute figure. It had been a week since she'd found Gwynna Owen hiding at the edge of her father's property in an old cottage fit only for the snakes and errant chickens. She claimed to have traveled, mostly at night, from a western island jutting into the Irish Sea.

Gwynna could scarcely be much older than twenty, but she had a world-weary air. She had resisted Anne's efforts to pry from her the reason for her journey, but she seemed troubled. Why was she intent on seeing the duke?

Whatever the reason, Anne prayed that Gwynna had the sense to give up her disguise before long. Darkness and Gwynna's slender figure had doubtless helped her pass as a boy at night, but her high, delicate cheekbones and brilliant sapphire eyes would give her away by day. Her thick, close-cropped red hair must have been magnificent unshorn. Anne sighed and pulled her cloak more tightly around her.

"We should leave. Papa will be looking for me soon."

"Another minute." Gwynna closed her fist around the hilt of her dagger. Here in Cheshire, the people weren't accepting the food shortages without a fight. "What do you know of these men?"

Anne eyed her nervously. "It is said that what they are doing is treasonous. Papa called it sedition."

"Your papa is a rich man. He has nothing to gain by siding with these folk. It is not in his interest to encourage freedom of association among disgruntled lower orders."

Anne was silent.

"I meant no insult," Gwynna added. "But the forces that rule are not always good. Sometimes it is necessary to rebel."

"The way you talk is so strange. It makes me afraid."

Gwynna laughed. "The Welsh have a saying: What is said of old will always stand, too long a tongue, too short a hand; but he that had no tongue lost his land.' It's from the Druids. They lived on our island long ago. They knew one must speak up to redress a grievance."

"This island of yours sounds very unusual."

"It is a lovely place. Sometimes I think it is paradise, but evil is there as well."

"Evil?"

Footsteps crunched behind them.

"Eh, Billy!" came a rough voice. "What have we here? A pair of young lovers?"

Anne and Gwynna looked up into a leering face darkened with coal dust. One of the marchers.

"Stifle it, man, else ye'll have the dragoons down on us. Let's have a look." Another face, also blackened, peered from behind the first. A slow smile exposed a coarse set of rotting teeth. "Just a scrawny lad and his wench. Pretty thing, too. What yer doing out here, missy?"

Anne shrank against the scrawny shrub.

"We are but taking the night air like yourself, sir,"

Gwynna said in a gruff voice. "We have no more desire to bring attention to ourselves than you do."

This last comment brought guffaws. "Lad's trying to scare us, Bill. Oughtn't to stand for that."

"Watch out, Davey," the second man said with a smirk. "The lad has spunk."

The first man growled at Gwynna. "Mind your tongue, unless you want Miss Pretty to come to grief."

With that, Anne burst into tears, which only provoked more laughter from the pair.

The men were so close that Gwynna could smell the sweat and thistledown on their clothing. She looked past them to the moor below. None of the other marchers seemed to have noticed that these two were missing. Besides, it was pointless to hope for rescue from that comer. No one with good intentions traveled these moors at night.

One of the men waved a length of rope. "If yer nice, laddie, you'll save yer neck and yer lady friend's, too. Maybe we'll even let you watch us with the wench here."

Gwynna pulled out her dagger. The men stared at the ancient weapon, then laughed.

"Look at that old piece of tin, Bill. And the lad's face! Ready to die for his wench's honor."

"Let me know when ye finish with this upstart," his friend said. "I'll just have me a bit of sport over here." He crushed Anne against him. She screamed.

Gwynna lashed out with her knife. But the other man grabbed her wrist and twisted it, and the dagger sliced harmlessly through air. Then he kicked her to the ground.

She stifled a groan of pain as she glared up at them. "Two fine manly specimens you are," she taunted, "hiding your faces and bullying people half your size. I give your revolution precious little chance if the rest are like you."

Her assailant's eyes were menacing. "And just what do ye know of any revolution, laddie? Don't remember mentioning it myself." He reached for his rope and snapped it taut.

Gwynna could almost feel the rough cord around her neck.

"Aye, this'll make short work of that scrawny neck of yers," he said, reaching for her. "Then there'll be no more talk about revolution."

"An utterly boring topic, in any case," drawled a voice.

Gwynna stared at lone figure on horseback regarding them with an air of extreme ennui. Under arched brows, his eyes evinced only idle curiosity at their plight. The wind ruffled his tousled sandy hair, giving him a rakish appearance at odds with his aristocratic demeanor.

His horse was a magnificent roan with an elegantly appointed saddle of highly polished leather. Its silver trim gleamed in the moonlight, imparting a princely air.

The rider held his body in such a relaxed pose that he appeared barely focused on them. He wore a dark blue coat with gleaming brass buttons, tan breeches, boots with a turnover top, and a stiff cravat tied in an extraordinarily intricate style.

Gwynna had never seen a London dandy, but she supposed he was the epitome of the breed. He cut a strange figure out here on the moors, but he eyed them as if they, not he, were the strange sight.

"Alas, it is as I suspected," he murmured, almost to himself. "No one around here has the slightest idea how to dress."

The two ruffians stared at the apparition. "Must be a madman," one muttered.

The horseman favored them with a smile. Then, as if noticing their particular circumstances for the first time, he tilted his head in apparent puzzlement. "Pray, is there some trouble here?" he asked in his richly cultured baritone. "I should not like to ruin my best travel clothes by embroiling myself in any local dispute."

Gwynna eyed him with open contempt. This man was

no rescuer, but a pretentious fop.

The two men exchanged glances. The man called Bill scowled. "No trouble at all, yer lordship," he said with a smirk. "Jest having a little fun."

The horseman's features cleared. "Some eccentric game, I expect, that requires grown men to gad about with coal dust on their faces and tussle with two young persons in this desolate wilderness. It shall take me a while, I'm afraid, to learn how to go on here."

The men touched their faces, as if suddenly recalling their disguises. They shifted uneasily. "We keep to our own business in these parts, mister," one man growled.

The horseman nodded. "So I've heard. Unfortunately, the denizens do have the reputation of being exceedingly unfriendly. That is why," he added almost apologetically, "I take precautions against inhospitable dispositions."

Gwynna could not have said how the gleaming silver pistol came to be in the horseman's hand. One minute it was not; the next it was. His composed, polite demeanor remained unchanged. He merely sat atop his great horse, gazing at them benignly, the pistol pointed at the two men. Something about the way he held the weapon suggested he was an excellent shot.

Their assailants elected not to stay for further conversation, but turned and raced off into the night. The horseman eyed their fleeing forms, then shook his head.

"Such manners." He rubbed the pistol barrel with the tip of one elegantly gloved finger.

Anne nearly collapsed in relief. Gwynna put an arm around her. "All is well, Anne. They are gone. And I do not think we have anything to fear from this one."

The horseman arched his brows. "I am honored at your high opinion of me, boy. Nevertheless, it seems that, however unfitting, I have been cast in the role of knight-errant. Your mistress appears to be a trifle indisposed. I suppose I must help you get her to her home." His brows knitted together. "She does have a home, I trust?"

Gwynna eyed him disdainfully. "You need not trouble yourself about us. We shall manage."

"What if those horrible men come back?" Anne asked.

"My sentiments precisely," the horseman said, dismounting. "Come, boy. Let us help your mistress up. She can ride with me. You can walk."

In short order, Anne was tossed onto the roan. The horseman swung himself up behind her and flicked the reins. Gwynna walked beside them, relieved that he had not seen through her disguise.

Following Anne's direction, he soon deposited her about twenty yards from her father's large manor house.

Anne gave Gwynna a hug and a tremulous smile. "With any luck, I shall slip in the side door, and Father will not notice my absence."

The horseman said nothing until Anne was safely inside. Then he turned to Gwynna.

"What sort of groom lets his mistress wander off across the moor in the dark of night?" His tone was haughty with disapproval. "Had it not been for the risk to the young lady's reputation, I would have insisted on informing her father of your lapse. A groom of mine who behaved as you have would have been turned off in an instant."

Gwynna lifted her chin defiantly. "I am not her groom. And it's none of your concern."

The horseman sighed heavily. "Unfortunately, I have only recently learned that everything in this area appears to be my concern."

"How so?"

"Regrettably," he replied in a bored voice, "I have lately gained the onerous title of Duke of Claremont."

Gwynna stared at him. "That is impossible."

He frowned. "I assure you, young man, it is true. Though why it should affect you, I am at a loss to guess."

Stunned, Gwynna sank to the ground. Her world was

suddenly in shambles. She clutched the hilt of her dagger, trying to draw from its strength. "You are t-too young."

"Too young for what?"

"Too young to be my father."

The expression of idle boredom abruptly fled from Sebastian Traherne's face.

Heart of a Duke, Book 2 in the League of Rogues series, will be available in 2018. For more information, see www.eileenputman.com

Books by Eileen Putman

Historical Romances:

League of Rogues series: Daring English lords who risk all for their country. Hardened and deadly, they have no use for love—until it ensnares them…

King of Hearts
Heart of a Duke

Regency Romances:

Love in Disguise series: A street wench masquerades as a debutante to fulfill a rake's wager; an actress pretends to be a lord's mistress to catch a killer. A war hero disguises himself as a much older man to woo an on-the-shelf spinster. An independent widow forces her disapproving business partner to pretend to be her fiancé. All are daring masquerades, with love as the prize:

The Perfect Bride
The Dastardly Duke
A Passionate Performance
Reforming Harriet

Also:
Never Kiss a Duke
Garden of Secrets
Noble Deception
Words of Love
A Worthy Engagement

www.eileenputman.com